Uncertain Weights and Measures

UNCERTAIN
WEIGHTS & MEASURES

JOCELYN PARR

Edited by Bethany Gibson.
Cover design by Ingrid Paulson.
Cover image (brain): © BlackJack3D/iStock.com.
Page design by Julie Scriver.
Printed in Canada.
10 9 8 7 6 5 4 3 2

Library and Archives Canada Cataloguing in Publication

Parr, Jocelyn, 1977-, author
   Uncertain weights and measures / Jocelyn Parr.

Issued in print and electronic formats.
ISBN 978-0-86492-982-2 (softcover).--ISBN 978-0-86492-983-9 (EPUB).--
ISBN 978-0-86492-984-6 (MOBI)

I. Title.

PS8631.A7665U56 2017   C813'.6   C2017-902819-7
                                            C2017-902820-0

We acknowledge the generous support of the Government of Canada,
the Canada Council for the Arts, and the Government of New Brunswick.

Goose Lane Editions
500 Beaverbrook Court, Suite 330
Fredericton, New Brunswick
CANADA E3B 5X4
www.gooselane.com

To my friends

It is possible, if we try, to lie our way to truth.

— Dostoyevsky, *Crime and Punishment*

1921

B efore Lenin was dead and before my life had properly begun, I used to spend all my time in a bookstore down on Nikitskaya. I was barely a person then, just a girl, and then just a girl staring down the women I'd meet, wondering if their fate had to be mine. The bookstore had no sign. Either you knew where it was or you didn't. The entrance was several steps below street level. To find it, you looked for the tobacco place next door because it had a glowing green lamp in its window. When the snow shrouded the entrance on winter afternoons, that blur of green was the only indication that you'd arrived. If you knew to look.

The owners, Rachel and Mikhaíl Osorgin, lived in the back room. The place smelled like potatoes most of the time but did not smell of dust. Nothing settled in there; everything and everyone just passed through. The men who ran it were academicians: specialists in Schopenhauer and Dostoyevsky and the history of carnival and the grotesque. If they specialized in other fields, I either didn't know it at the time or have forgotten it since. This is how memory works. We say memory is about the past, but it isn't, and secretly we all know it. I remember them as specialists in Dostoyevsky and Schopenhauer because *I* loved the grotesque, because *I* wanted to ask the beautiful terrible questions.

None of them knew a thing about budgets or inventories, but they didn't need to. They had no real expenses and no real income either. They called it a bookstore because they didn't want to call it a publishing house, or couldn't call it a publishing house, since that couldn't capture their mandate, which was this: keep everything in motion, make all knowledge available. If a book showed up with no binding or missing pages they didn't care, they'd bind it with rubber bands or staple together whatever pages they had, and then they'd put it on the shelves, ready for whoever wanted to spirit it away. I went there because I wanted access to everything they had; others went there because it was the only place you could find mystical and religious texts in those days. Obviously, their time was limited; dilapidated as it was, that place was a luxury. The era of thinking about the beautiful and the terrible as *abstractions* was coming to an end. Instead of abstractions, the beautiful and the terrible would become palpable: death would become fact, not figure. But in the era of abstractions, we weighed our riches in books and ideas, we had so many. Every book that lined the shelves or was left open on the table had either been stolen or donated, and every book was given away just as easily. Sometimes the books arrived in wheelbarrows. Sometimes on sleighs. An apartment would be subdivided somewhere in the city, and the books would be thrown out along with the bourgeois residents.

Mrs. Osorgin was always in the back room preparing one thing or another. The potato smell got into the wool of our coats. Everyone who went there left smelling the same. I sometimes fantasized that I could meet someone in an entirely other part of the city and know them as one of my own, because they'd smell like the shop and I'd know they'd been there. But the truth of the matter was most Muscovites smelled like potatoes then, since it was all anyone ate in those days, whereas very few had ever been to Osorgin's. Sometimes we ate dinner in the back room. Then Mrs. Osorgin—I never called her Rachel—added special things to the meal: nuts, butter, chopped onions.

As for Mr. Osorgin, when I think of him now, I cannot see his face. It is the hunch of his back that I remember, the way it told of a lifetime of loving books, though perhaps it also spoke of fear or shame; I have no way of knowing which. His voice resonated, sonorous and slow, as if it came from inside a much bigger body, as if no matter what he said, all you would remember would be the beautiful, solemn sound. He can't have been more than forty then, but I was so young he seemed older than that. Maybe if I'd paid closer attention to what he'd been saying, rather than how he'd said it, I'd have understood why everything happened the way it did.

When we wanted new books, we stole them from the stores on Tverskaya. If we wanted to understand the new books, we'd bring them to Osorgin's. (I say *we* but even if I envied the students who *would* steal from the stores, I couldn't manage it myself. I sometimes went into the stores on Tverskaya with a new volume in mind, but as soon as I found it, I'd feel as if everyone were watching me and then I'd look around the store until I found someone who was.) At Osorgin's, every wall but one was lined with shelves that sank in the middle with the weight of books. On the remaining bare wall hung a chalkboard, and every week some new idea would appear there. One week it might be a citation from Freud. Another, it might be Bertrand Russell: *Is there any knowledge in the world which is so certain that no reasonable man could doubt it?* Sometimes one citation would relate to another, but just as often there was no obvious link. Sometimes the citations were tributes and sometimes they made fun. Which was it when drawings from Tsiolkovsky's "An Airplane or a Birdlike Flying Machine" appeared? Subtly, these ideas rippled out from Osorgin's and into bars and late-night conversations throughout the city.

The students, the professors, the activists, the fighters —whoever went there, worked there, or sold books there— were my kind of people. I automatically trusted them. It was that kind of place.

On the day I met Sasha, the store was mostly empty. Sasha, Jack, and I were the only customers, but I didn't know them yet. My impression when I first met them was that Jack was studious and Sasha was wild. A simple conclusion based on nothing, really. Jack had arrived at the bookstore first and I'd not even noticed him bent over his book in the corner by the blackboard. Sasha, on the other hand, came in clamouring. He was slight but moved with confidence: strong, powerful. His straight black hair stuck up everywhere when he pulled off his hat. When he went to stand in front of the stove, I thought, I'm cold, too. Then, standing there, next to him, I was suddenly so hot.

It seemed as if we stood there for a while, but that can't have been the case, because when the explosion happened and the windows shattered and the shelves collapsed, so that the whole room was instantaneously a torrent of books and broken glass, that was precisely when I felt someone grab my hand. From the jolt in my shoulder I knew I was being pulled by someone strong; that someone was Sasha, and I remember distinctly that his hand was still cold.

Behind us, I heard Osorgin yell something about water. In the alley behind the store, Jack was already ahead of us, running without looking back. The sound of our footfalls ricocheted wet against the alley's walls. Jack disappeared around a corner. We ran after him, past crumpled-up buildings that had fallen to ruin a long time ago. Jack kept too far ahead for us to see him, until finally we rounded a corner and found him, doubled over, trying to catch his breath. I heard my own breath then, felt it cold and rough against my throat. I heard voices yelling out, heard the crackle of wood catching fire, or collapsing, I couldn't tell which.

Jack and Sasha were strangers to me, but already I felt as though I knew something about the one who'd held my hand and the one who'd run away. The one who'd grabbed my hand held on tight, and the way he did told me that he was good. That he was strong and wouldn't let go until it was okay. The one who'd run away had fled on his own, and it told me that he was an individualist and a coward, though it would take years for me to articulate it that way. The three of us walked the rest of the way down the alley until we made it back to Nikitskaya, ending up down the street from the front entrance to the bookshop. A figure ran past us, heading to the shop. I watched him go and was about to follow, when Jack barked at me, You can't go back.

Maybe it was the way he said it, with such conviction, or maybe it was because it was the first thing he'd ever said to me that made me listen. Somewhere in my stomach was a thought of the Osorgins, or a feeling, the feeling that I ought to do something, but what? We stood there dumbly, our sweat turning to ice.

I'm Alexandr, said the one who had held my hand, the dark-haired one who was loud and got cold in bookstores.

Sasha, I thought, what a soft name.

He's Jack, said Sasha, at which Jack stood taller. They stood side by side then and I saw that they had been friends for a long time. Standing there, still a little out of breath, Jack seemed taut and quivering, like a bow before its release; Sasha seemed like a man who could be still for a long time.

I'm Tatiana L—, I said, too formally, I thought.

Let's get a drink, said Sasha.

Everything's closed, I said.

I know a place, he said.

I can't, said Jack, and he slouched away, leaving Sasha and me like that, facing each other, on a winter's night in 1921.

—⧸—

In the fall, just a few months before meeting Sasha, I had met Dr. Vladimir Bekhterev, a man who very quickly felt like a father to me. Earlier that same year, I'd lost my own father in a manner that was all too common at the time.

Then, as now, the single most important factor determining one's access to everything, from a job to an apartment to a good man to work on your teeth, was connections. In the early years of Lenin's rule a temporary but insidious capitalism was reintroduced (small shops and tiny plots of land for individualized farming were permitted again, a good thing I suppose, but it made some people *very* rich). Those were the NEP years, after the innocuously named New Economic Policy, and we called the newly rich class it created the NEP men and NEP women. In those years two incompatible systems further complicated the power of "knowing a guy." Under NEP, the first system concerned one's identification as a member of the proletariat; the second concerned one's ability to contribute to the revolutionary effort. For this reason, a soil scientist from the upper classes could still, in the early to mid-twenties, be considered useful to society, despite a bourgeois background.

By the time Lenin died, it was clear the era of bourgeois experts was coming to an end. Anyone with a damning background had taken whatever measures possible to rewrite family histories. Faces were scratched out of family portraits. Loving couples divorced. Children denounced parents. People moved from country to city or city to country and, in the process, changed names.

So, a soil scientist could work in the office of the People's Commissar for Agriculture, could even have worked at the same desk in the same office for so long that he remembered the days under the Tzar when it was called the Ministry of Agriculture, and then one day, he might decide he ought to change his name and move far, far away.

My father was that kind of soil scientist.

One day he stopped being my father. He told me about it in a letter, which I read, and then, following his instructions, lit on fire. I was eighteen years old. Whether he'd decided to leave or had been forced to, I don't know. Apart from the salutation, which read *Dearest Daughter*, the letter barely mentioned me at all. In as few words as possible, he explained that his situation at work had changed and that if he stayed, his future (and mine) would be compromised, which was something he couldn't bear. The letter was written with such concision that I could hear the anguish behind every word. In life, my father had used all the words, all the stories, all the time. Never in my life had he been so cold, never so reasonable. It was as if he were already gone when he wrote that letter. I cried in angry confusion as it burned but shared my feelings with no one, this also according to his instructions. The only thing he left behind was his pocket watch and something less tangible: a belief in hard work. Amazing how lucky you get, he always said, when you work really hard.

When he was my father, he helped me with my studies and said that, of the sciences, it was the only field of study that would not be corrupted by politics.

In his letter, he admitted that he had been wrong.

$\longmapsto$

It was his friend, then, a man I'd met only once, who got me into university on the strength of Communist connections I did not have and, as such, into one of the only classes Dr. Bekhterev ever taught in Moscow. I called this man my uncle, but we were not related. Connections were different than beliefs. I believed in the Revolution and I believed we could sacrifice our way to progress, but I never joined the Party, so I had no real connections. I couldn't have. In those years, getting into the Party was harder than becoming an academician. I'd attended the Communist youth meetings before the loyalty tests became a standard rite of passage, which was a good thing, because if they'd asked after my loyalties I would have said I believed in what my father had believed: science, and science was separate from politics. Like him, I would also come to realize that I was wrong. Unlike him, I came to believe the reason science wasn't separate from politics was that nothing was separate from politics. Not science. Not art. Not love. In this way, I was like my mother.

So, that first class with Dr. Bekhterev was held in the fall of 1921, two or three years into my studies. The lecture hall, shaped like an arena, seated about fifty students. The wooden desks perched on steps cut of an ever larger semicircle, so that sitting in the front row felt like being on stage, and sitting in the back row felt like joining the orbit of one of the outermost planets. When the clock shuddered past nine o'clock, a student below me turned back to whisper that Dr. Bekhterev was always late. That student's name was Alexandr Lev Luria. That was how he introduced himself, with all three names. His accent told me he was from Leningrad, though back then we called it Petrograd. Later, we became friends.

Luria was right. Bekhterev was almost an hour late

for that first class, but not a single student left the room. I would have left if they had, but they didn't. He arrived carrying a bundle of manuscripts and an overcoat. He was in his early sixties and had the shape and heft of a butcher: broad shoulders, thick gut. From his neck up, he was all hair. His beard, moustache, nose hairs, eyebrows, and the hair on his head sprouted out of him as if from an unremitting spool of thin, pepper-coloured wire. I imagined someone brushing up against him might come away with small cuts and scrapes.

When I try to describe the force with which Dr. Bekhterev entered my life I feel certain I will fail. I was practically a child then: too young, for example, to know anything about the reputations of my professors. From where I sat, on the outer ring, in my tenuous orbit, ready to be flung out into the deepest black, I had the vague notion that my professors existed only where I saw them: in the lecture hall, in the lab, in their offices. They'd been born with their specializations, just as they'd been born with their eye colour, fingerprints, and dispositions. They had not studied. No commissar had appointed them, no colleague had denounced them, no experiment had failed, no book had been rejected. They had never been intoxicated by the smell of a woman passing them on a darkening street, nor had they ever experienced rage. They'd never been left off the guest list, nor put on. They had been born professors and would die that way. In short, they were not people.

That year, I had started to lose my eyesight. Nothing cataclysmic. Indeed, the loss occurred so imperceptibly that I hardly noticed it at all. I mention it now because it correlated with the period in which I started to sit closer and closer to the front of the lecture hall, as if being drawn in by a stronger and stronger gravitational pull. Month by month, ring by ring, I approached the front of the room, until one day, I was sitting in the very front row. When Bekhterev spoke, he spat.

I don't remember the name of the course I took with him, nor even what the university thought we were studying. The discipline was yet to be named, meaning it had no rules. Bekhterev explained the novelty of the discipline metaphorically, that is, by way of the telescope.

We know nothing! he said.

Bekhterev used the word *neuropsychology* and compared the field to that of seventeenth-century astronomy when Kepler's observations of the universe, which had been made with the naked eye, led to a revolution in our understanding of the solar system and our place in it.

When he lectured, Bekhterev paced back and forth. Kepler had deduced from what little he could observe (his eyesight had been severely damaged by a case of childhood smallpox) that the solar system was heliocentric, thus contradicting centuries of astronomy that placed the earth at the centre. A man with blunted sight, said Bekhterev, looking at us with a fierce intensity, think on that.

We are, said Bekhterev, at that very same threshold. Kepler had no telescope to speak of. We have no telescope. He had reason and imagination. We have reason and imagination. To date, about the brain, we know nothing.

The way he talked about what *we* were doing had its effect: his pursuits became mine.

During Bekhterev's lifetime, we started to think we knew something, but now, I'm not so sure. A little bit more than nothing is still, essentially, nothing. The mathematicians would disagree. They would say that the difference between nothing and a little bit more than nothing was like that between night and day. But I am not a mathematician.

Science was a raised skirt or a missing button, concluded Bekhterev in one of his lectures. You always hope for a nipple, but even its suggestion will hold your attention for a very long time.

It became legendary among Bekhterev's colleagues that after his first year of marriage his wife banished him from their bedroom because he didn't sleep. If his office at the university was any indication, his home must have been a landscape of paper. I imagined him falling asleep reading manuscripts. In the morning, on waking, he'd only have to dig around in his sheets for a pencil before starting to work again. Every lab assignment he ever handed back to me looked as if it had been to war.

Bekhterev never linked our studies with revolution, never drew comparisons, even, to the questions we, his students, were asking ourselves about what it meant to be a comrade, what it meant to be in love, what it meant to touch another and be touched, and what it meant to go out into the street and scream until you had no voice. He'd never been a thirteen-year-old girl living atop an illegal printing press, wishing that she could print pamphlets, too. No. In his class, we talked only about the brain. But he believed in the leap. The leap from one idea to another, from one neuron to another, from one stage of development to another. I could go from his class to a rally and see the same fundamental logic at work. Bekhterev talked about evolutionary leaps; Leontiev talked about societal leaps. They were the same. They were about risk taking and experimenting and moving forward. One thing, then its opposite, then the fight between the two, then a kind of combustion, and then something new. In this way, my commitments to science gradually became political. In neuropsychology, it wasn't even that we were free to make mistakes; it was that we were called upon to make them.

Mistakes were inevitable in the political world, too. In science, the most ambitious took their time, waiting, they said, getting ready for a really big failure, which meant they were doing something totally new. It's not an exaggeration to say neuropsychology seduced me. I remember the ache in my hand at the end of each lecture, how it suffered from trying to keep up.

While the link between the Revolution and the science was mostly meant metaphorically, in the oral exams the link was explicit: I studied for my first exam for weeks, but it wasn't until the night before that my roommate — her name was Rima and she became one of my best friends — told me I'd been studying the wrong thing.

Dummy, she said, shaking her head as she looked over my notes.

My desk was covered in diagrams I'd copied and recopied and copied again. When I closed my eyes, anatomical diagrams floated before me as visions. The new words slipped into my speech, replacing my everyday vocabulary with the specialized lexicon of the new science: sulci and gyri and neural pathways. It had been weeks since I had slept a full night without a pressing question waking me before dawn. I'd flip on the lights and scour my notes for an answer. This was what I thought it meant to be an *aspirantura*. I was aspiring. This was what it looked like. The bags under my eyes were proof of how much it mattered to me.

Which meant I almost cried when she told me I'd made a mistake.

They know you are good; that's why you're sitting the exam, she said.

Then what? I asked.

It's about you, she said.

The examiners had been sent over from the nearby Marxist-Leninist Institute. Two old guys and a young one, all sitting behind a long wooden table, all of them wearing wire-rimmed glasses. From the rumpled look of them, they'd been sitting there for hours. Behind them was a blackboard, wiped clean. I sat in front of them. Because it was something all the students did in those days, I'd eaten extra sugar in the days before the exam. My palms were sticky with what I imagined was sweet, sugary sweat.

The youngest examiner began. His face was pockmarked, though he was handsome. He asked a few easy questions about brain anatomy and the nervous system, but I saw the way his eyes went glassy when I responded. Rima had been right. The exam wasn't about science. We were waiting for what really mattered.

The political exam.

You may be aware, said the older one, that some have started to recognize that certain advantages might accrue to those who profess allegiance to the goals of the Bolshevik party, whether it be in terms of career or political advancement or even housing. We're not accusing you of this—we're not in the business of accusations, by any means. You should think of this examination as an opportunity to refresh not only your scientific knowledge but your political theory, particularly as we move forward into the demands of revolutionary life. What our society needs is true comrades, people who are not aligned with the bourgeoisie, here or elsewhere.

No one likes an opportunist, I said.

Precisely, he said.

So, said the young one.

Their questions, new to me then, were standard. They wanted to know about my family: how my mother had been a card-carrier and had abandoned us to devote herself to the cause, and how, out of grief, my father had left me just as soon as I was of age. Officially my caregiver became my uncle, but I never lived with him. Not that I said this. I wasn't much of a political creature, but I had learned enough to know that sometimes a vague suggestion—the word *caregiver* for example—could create the image of my uncle's participation in my life even if I mightn't have recognized him on the street had our paths crossed by chance. One of the examiners wrote something down. Perhaps the word *grief* had been too much. I wiped my sugary hands against my lap, pushing hard into my legs.

The uncle who got you into school here?

Yes, I said. My uncle's connections must have been very good: none of this was pressed.

They wanted to know what I knew about the West, about capitalism. Things I knew about capitalism and the West, the two being one and the same, were that they relied upon exploitation. They were colonizers; their societies were marred by slavery and poverty, by lineups for the most basic services, by people living on the street. I knew slavery hadn't ended, no matter what the officials said. The reports from the Pullman porters were clear: slavery was everywhere. I knew about the income gap and the basic idea, the rich get richer and the poor get poorer and Christianity justifies the disparity.

How's that? the young one asked.

As an opiate, sure, but more than that. It casts the whole system as a moral one, I said. Rich capitalists still want to believe they are good. Christianity helps, but Christianity can be bought. And that thing they believe: pulling up your boots. They explain poverty by laziness and laziness as a sin. Capitalists confuse the choice to buy with the freedom to think—they only have the former.

Right, they said. And the Tzar?

He enslaved the press. He punished political discontent and political protest. Shooting ranges, and absolute power. Literature was censored. But Marxist thought burst through the lines of the censored literature.

What about Engels? they asked.

Socialism is a science and it must be pursued as such. It must be studied.

I passed.

What I'd said was what I believed, but somehow being tested on my beliefs made them come out strange, foreign, as if they were a second language and not something I'd been born into. I was so young—barely twenty years old— when I had that first exam. In truth, I was the perfect age for such a thing: the thoughts we have then are the purest ideologies we'll ever hold, even if the ideology is to question everything, which mine wasn't. Not exactly. The way I thought about things, when I did think about them, was that everything was a science; questioning was thought. Socialism was a science. Historical materialism explained the mystical religions at the time of kings and queens and the rise of Protestantism under capitalism. The dialectic was what would free the West from capitalism. Dialectical thinking meant first you discovered an atom, then you asked that atom a question: how small are you? The atom said, I am this small, no smaller, and you said, Come on…, and it replied, Okay, smaller than that. It is A meets opposition in B, and they combust and become C (and C was better than either A or B ever were). I was living at the start of the new age in the city that was at the centre of it all. We'd left behind the mystical age and finally begun the inquiry into what really governed everything: our material conditions, our material bodies.

But the examiners didn't speak science.

It was spring when I saw Sasha again. I'd wanted to find
him myself, but I realized only after he'd dropped me off
that first night I didn't know where he lived or studied. He
was one of those people who preferred asking questions
to answering them, a characteristic that was rare in those
days. When I saw him next, he was waiting for me out front
of my residence. I don't know how many nights he sat on
the bench like that, waiting. When I saw him, I laughed out
loud because he looked so much the part of an art student
in his fedora and an ill-fitting overcoat. He'd gotten an
idea into his head, he said, and hadn't let go of it all winter
long. The idea was me.

He wanted us to go back to Osorgin's. I hadn't returned
since the explosion. Winter and my schoolwork reduced my
radius. I felt nervous, but I couldn't tell if it was the thought
of returning to the bookstore or the idea of Sasha himself
that created the feeling, so I said sure. We didn't speak on
the tram ride in. He was different than the men I'd known
before. They'd all been students, studying science, like me,
or politics, like Rima. I'd met Nikolai in the Pioneers, Pavel
at school, Pyotr at a rally, but all of them seemed like boys
in comparison to Sasha. They drank competitively with
their friends, they kissed with over-big, over-wet tongues.
How did Sasha kiss? I wondered.

The tram stopped and we got out. At a cigarette stand,
Sasha asked for Gitanes. The cigarette girl looked at him,
taken aback, and offered him a different brand, which he
refused. We walked on.

No one sells French cigarettes, I said.

She does, he said, just not tonight.

She didn't look like she does, I said.

He pulled out a near-empty pack of Gitanes and offered
me one.

The Gitanes smoked cleaner than other cigarettes I'd tried, like the difference between brandy and cognac I said to myself, as if I knew.

From the level of the street, we looked down at the entrance to Osorgin's. The front window had been blown out and left that way for months. In the blackened interior we spied charred and sodden books and I wondered what it meant, or if it meant anything at all. The green lamp was broken, its glass mingled with other debris from the tobacconist's. Where had the Osorgins gone? I walked down a few of the steps to peer through the broken window. Lying against the chalkboard wall, under remnants of the last image that Osorgin had sketched, I made out the shape of a body, the slow rise and fall of its back as it slept. Sasha and I looked at each other, trying to read one another's reaction, trying to know if what the other's face said meant it was better to go in to investigate or better to leave well enough alone. The figure shifted under our gaze.

Should we go? I whispered to Sasha. He nodded yes.

On the wall that week, Osorgin had sketched this image:

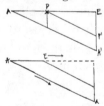

It is Husserl's conception of time, memory, and the pressure the past puts upon our present. Had Osorgin anticipated the explosion? I wondered. Had the bomb—we later found out it was a bomb—been intended for the bookshop, or was it, as others said, intended for the synagogue down the street? The diagram seemed to capture every question I had about what had happened to the Osorgins, what was happening to Sasha and me that night, and what all of it would mean for the future we had, just then, started to hope for. In the diagram, a line moves from *A* to E thus capturing an idea we have about time—that it is linear. Husserl is telling us something, saying, hang on a second, time isn't so linear after all. It gets *punctuated* from beneath the surface as *P* surges up: *P* is a sound from the past, like that of an explosion (or sound's absence, the silence of the million-strong crowd gathered before the poet Mayakovsky), or a scent (like the lime trees that once lined the streets in Moscow), or an impression as vague as summer's timeless heat. The scent of lime wafts by and suddenly we've forgotten what season we're in, what year. Yet we keep thinking of time as progressive, forward moving. The future is a line that stretches out ahead of us, captured in the diagram by the arrow that follows the *E*. The arrow is anticipation, what we project for our future, our imaginations moving forward at more or less the same rate as our memories move back until suddenly, again unbidden, the movement is broken by a memory, say, of a loved one, and then we exist for a moment in no time and no place. The timelessness and placelessness of a scent or a sound: it exploded my heart just to think of it.

That night, Sasha took my hand again, and again we walked away, slowly this time.

The exams taught me one thing and one thing only: everything I needed to know I'd learned from that blackboard in the bookstore, from the clandestine meetings at the hand of my mother, from the pamphlets and speeches, from the all-night conversations in a bar. I'd learned it from hearing Kollontai and Mayakovsky lose their voices reciting poems to thousands of people, from the way a woman could sell Gitanes one night and not the next, from the timelessness of a first kiss.

—⁄—

Over the course of the next three years, Sasha and I would fall in love. The way we came to know each other was so intimate that I spent those years adapting to feeling I had been cracked wide open, feeling another person in the world knew me better than I knew myself. When we would look back on our encounter at Osorgin's, we'd say on that night we found each other, and so our lives were divided into the period before, when we were looking, and the period after, when we had been found.

In January 1924, Lenin would die. That same year I would marry Sasha, and I would start working for Bekhterev at the Institut Mozga, an institute he referred to in private as the Pantheon of Brains. My life seemed to have found its right shape. Then, suddenly, both Sasha and Bekhterev would be gone, and I would need to find them. This story is about that. I call it a story, but it's not fictional. Everything I have written here is true.

1927

On October 27, 1927, the Institut Mozga opened to the public for the first time. We chose that date so that the opening could coincide with the tenth anniversary of the Revolution, and therefore with the parades, the arrival of fellow travellers from around the world, and the general euphoria *some* of us felt at how far we had come. The institute fulfilled Bekhterev's lifelong vision of a pantheon like the one in Paris but, in his words, ours would be better because our brains were elite and our aim was to enlighten. The Parisians had been indiscriminate, displaying the brains of criminals and degenerates with the same care they bestowed on their men of science. We were different. They had put together their collection so easily by way of theft, since no one had asked the permission of the criminals and degenerates, whereas our collection was the result of careful solicitation — letters to the living geniuses, letters to their bereaved. Bekhterev had been slowly collecting this way for years, but it took Lenin's death and the politburo's desire to have his brain on display for the institute to get the political support it needed. Crass as it is to say, Lenin's death had come at a good time for Bekhterev. Lenin's brain allowed Bekhterev's scientific enterprise to align with the revolutionary, and so the institute was born.

Nevertheless, it had taken over two years for any significant research to be done on Lenin's brain, this because the politburo had determined the brain had to be sent out of the country, to the laboratory of a certain Dr. Oskar Vogt, whose techniques were considered the best in the

Communist world. The institute was, by virtue of Vogt's involvement, a joint German-Russian venture, a collaboration that had allowed us access to research, technical advances, and equipment that would otherwise have remained beyond our grasp. Vogt's deadline for any initial results had always been October 1927 because of the anniversary, so there we were, ready to open the doors for the first time to a public that wanted to know how Lenin's brain could explain Lenin's genius. We wanted to know, too. Ten years after the Revolution, Lenin's genius would be revealed once again. Our expectations were high.

Aligning our scientific aims with the revolutionary aims was facilitated by the language of Marx, who saw history as the result of material conditions just as scientists looked to the physical (rather than the metaphysical) for explanations. We said we were looking for the material substrate of genius. *Genius* was a term loosely defined back then, there being no particular test nor any clear physical characteristic that could be discovered post-mortem. In the absence of clear measurables, our only evidence was a lifetime of achievements. Let me try to clarify. In the two years since the institute's establishment we had not yet succeeded in correlating the physical attributes of a certain brain with the excellence displayed in an individual's life. That there must be some link between the physical and the mental, between the folds of the cerebral cortex and the intellectual range of capability it exhibited, was hardly an original hypothesis. Our aim was to prove not only that there was a link but also *how* that link might work. We wanted to *see* genius, not just believe in it. Where, precisely, did music and poetry come from? What about military strategy, plans for space travel, or visions of a life unending? How could a brain's physical attributes explain the order of one mind and the chaos of another?

The People's Commissar for Health, Nikolai Semashko, praised our efforts, saying the institute's work would result in the victory of materialism in an area where metaphysics and dualism were still strong. No god, no mystical order, and certainly not the stuff of dreams could explain how one person delivered perfect speeches while another strained to tell a house guest where he'd hidden a key. All our talents, all our traits, all our truths: they were physical, they were material. For Semashko and for others, what made our research so important wasn't merely that it could explain why the titans of our past had been so powerful. No, our work promised an even greater though more illusory end: the project of remaking man. Change the physical and you change the mind. Change the mind and you change the world.

By then, Sasha had developed a hypothesis about Bekhterev and the institute that meant we'd agreed he should stay at home. His hypothesis was that the institute wasn't doing research; my hypothesis was that Sasha didn't know anything about research. Three years into our marriage this much had become clear: I believed that physical and economic truths lay behind the different fates of people and countries, whereas Sasha believed in the beauty of ideas you couldn't quite pin down, in feelings so powerful they dodged precise description. For me, words captured the essence of things; for Sasha words caught only the most fleeting impressions. Before we married, this difference might have been what made us so compelling to each other, but three years on, its charms were wearing off.

⟶⟵

The morning of the opening was cold and the wind scraped against my cheeks, suggesting an early winter. Walking up the hill towards the building, I looked at it as if for the first time. There was nothing else like it in Moscow. A visiting scholar from Yaroslavl once told me it was the spitting image of that city's Orthodox cathedral.

Strange, he'd said, for a scientific institute to look so... religious.

The original architect came from Yaroslavl, I told him, and he hung himself in the attic.

Yes, he'd responded, I heard.

Over the years, I'd stopped seeing the idiosyncrasies of its design. The turrets and archways, the hand-carved wooden doors, even the red, gold, and azure fleurs-de-lys of the interior, it all disappeared in the haze of the everyday. Besides, it was what happened *inside* that was truly strange.

—⊁—

While Vogt had been hard at work on Lenin's brain in his Das Neurologische Zentralstation, we'd been perfecting our methods for comparing the brains we did have, which involved microtoming certain sections so a cellular study could be undertaken, and leaving other sections whole so a macroscopic examination could also take place. The process was painstaking and still inconclusive. Our hope was that Vogt's analysis would establish irrefutable correlations. In this way, brain analysis could finally become explanatory as opposed to merely descriptive. This hope meant I was just like everyone else that night: desperate to know what he had discovered.

The rumours about Vogt had been good and not good. Good: he was a Communist. Not good: he'd been thrown out of the German university system for "unprofessional conduct."' On the good side: even before Lenin died, as he was suffering the result of his 1923 stroke, he had wanted Vogt among his medical team. On the bad: everyone, including Bekhterev, *especially* Bekhterev, hated him. Bekhterev hadn't said this exactly, but by then I knew him well enough to identify a deep animosity in the way he crossed his arms and bit his lip at any mention of Vogt. For my part, Vogt's expulsion from the university suggested he thought like a revolutionary.

If Vogt were successful, his work would bring our institute to the forefront of all the other scientific institutes across the union, all of which aimed to advance the revolutionary science. Collectively, they would transform our people from backward peasants into efficient workers whose lifespans would be extended, whose energies would never wane, whose collective intellectual capacities would make a triumph of the Soviet system.

It was late afternoon when I made my way to the front entrance of the institute and stood, huddled against the open door, looking out onto Bolshaya Yakimanka. The boulevard had calmed for the night. A taxi idled by the bakery across the way. Denuded, lonely trees lined the street, their naked branches reaching up like supplicant hands. The setting sun snuck under the clouds and hovered a moment above the shops. Its golden light shone directly into my eyes, so I had to squint and look away. The institute's brick exterior glowed bright red and then dulled as the sun descended behind the shops. A car door slammed and the taxi pulled away.

I propped the first door open, then returned through the second set of doors to where it was darker and warmer. Sergei, our custodian, was sitting at the front desk, talking in a low voice with Anushka, one of our technicians. (I liked to think of her as one of "our" technicians because of the way it suggested a hierarchy, but the truth was I was one of our technicians, too). They both looked up as I entered. Sergei winked at me, then resumed the conversation.

At a bar once I'd seen him feign a drunken stumble in order to collapse, hands forward, onto Anushka's chest, and I'd seen her let him. She was only a few years younger than me, but in that time the entire university system had changed. No more lectures, and the exams were taken in teams. Everything was designed to encourage collaboration as opposed to competition. It sounded good in theory. Sergei, on the other hand, was ten years older, a puffy thirty-something, prematurely aged by drinking, and one of those activist-types who, when he was younger, had espoused all the typical values—anti-church, anti-owner-ship, free marriage, easy divorce—right up until his lover announced she wanted an abortion and he refused out-right. Now they were married with two children between them, though I guessed he'd fathered others. I walked slowly past them, past the portraits—mostly scientists, save Lenin—and into the grand salon.

It was empty. The glowing chandelier warmed the salon's ivory walls and gold-tipped mouldings. Underneath the chandelier, the brains were arranged in a perfect semicircle. I went to find Bekhterev, just to have something to do. During the day, the podium had been set and the seats had been cleaned, but now the lights were dimmed and the excitement would be about watching and listening, not doing. I crossed the salon between the exhibit and the wall of mirrors, which disguised doors to the laboratory, back offices, and kitchen. There, too, the lights had been dimmed, but I heard voices arguing in the offices, one of which was Bekhterev's. I zigzagged between the lab tables without turning on the light.

Forget it, said Sarkisov, just as I appeared at the door. Sarkisov was probably just a few years older than me, but he'd trained under Vogt, using the German equipment and Vogt's techniques, so that, despite his young age, he had returned to Moscow as our superior. He had other tricks up his sleeve, alliances only he knew about, debts owed, blow jobs given, as Sasha would have put it. Bekhterev and Vogt were standing at opposite sides of the room, with Sarkisov between them, as if he were trying to bring them to agreement or prevent them from coming to blows. Sarkisov's presence was awkward for Bekhterev because on paper, Sarkisov was everyone's superior, but by reputation no scientist in the country got close to Bekhterev. Everywhere in the country, the newly established power structures butted up against the traditional hierarchies in just this way. Vogt, looking smug, nodded at me, then sat down in a chair, crossing one leg over the other before daintily pulling down on the pant leg that had risen to reveal his hairless leg. He lit a cigar. Bekhterev faced the two men with his arms crossed, leaning heavily against the wall. He stood up straight when he saw me.

The doors are open, I said.

Vogt and Sarkisov started to speak German, which meant the conversation was over, since Bekhterev didn't speak German. He nodded at them and left. I followed him out. I'd interrupted something, but Bekhterev said nothing and I didn't ask. Their voices and then their laughter trailed after us as we walked back through the dark laboratory and into the grand salon that seemed, with its ivory light and its promise of order, a different world altogether.

Having closed the mirrored door, Bekhterev and I stood for a moment, looking at the room. The room demanded a certain sobriety, a reverence, even. Bekhterev put his hands in his pockets and pulled his shoulders back.

It looks good, he said.

Yes, I said.

I could see he was upset, but there was a limit to our closeness, and that was it: I couldn't ask what was wrong.

We stood quietly in the dark, as if not quite ready to set the evening in motion. The room's periphery was dark because the room's only source of light was the chandelier at the centre, whose glow got caught up in the liquid of the displays, so that they, too, emanated a golden glow. Standing against the doors as we were, I realized that from this angle the exhibits lost their singularity and became elements of a collective formation that resembled the ancient ruins of Stonehenge, images of which I'd marvelled at as a child. Suspended in formaldehyde, all the brains appeared to float in their glass displays. Because the clear liquid was viscous, the brains did not rotate once placed inside, meaning there was a distinct front and back to the exhibit, a feeling that was exacerbated by the way the light faded, and so we were, in fact, looking at the shadowed side of everything.

The stillness of the room created a sense of awe.

That is, until, to our surprise, a lone figure moved from one of the plinths to the other, the way museum patrons do between paintings, with a slow, thoughtful step. The figure disappeared again behind the exhibit of Rubinstein's brain.

Each case sat on a plinth, and each plinth was labelled with the name of the brain's owner and a description, detailing its distinctive characteristics. Certain plinths had shelves that held documents or objects illustrative of the owner's life: musical scores for Borodin and Rubinstein, poems for the writers, decrees and speeches for the politicians. Even if my contribution had been more of the exhibiting than the analysis, I still had the sense that the alignment between the musical scores and the thickness of the folds were obvious, as if the folds were etched with notes or the frontal lobe with decrees.

Bekhterev and I listened to the sound of a drawer

opening. Some of the drawers contained photographs, and, in the case of brains whose key aspects were more visible on a cellular rather than a structural level, microphotographs of pertinent histological sections. Lenin's brain, housed at the top of the semicircle, had been damaged by a shooting or by his strokes or by something else—we weren't sure just what had been the cause—and so it needed to be displayed on a specific angle to hide the dead, black tissue. The other brains were displayed on the same angle—the right frontal lobe protruding—so that the choice appeared aesthetic. What very few knew, but many should have suspected, was that the display cases held only models.

We heard the drawer slide shut and the figure drifted on to Borodin.

Luria! called Bekhterev. With a sudden gestalt-like shift, the drifting figure became Alexandr Luria. He slipped between the plinths and walked over to us, squinting as his eyes adjusted to the dark. It had been years since we'd seen each other, yet he seemed the same. Same wire-rimmed glasses, same coal-black eyebrows, like an angry God had gashed his face with them, same jagged teeth too big for his mouth, same skinny body more wiry than that of a ballet dancer. Physically unattractive but so brilliant it didn't matter. Since completing our studies we'd gone in different directions, mine ever aligned with Bekhterev's, and his dedicated to his own research and further study.

Seeing him again that evening reminded me of our last encounter. We were still both students then, both working with Bekhterev in what I imagined was the same sort of relationship, both protégés. Luria had taken me aside, though, and said there were rumours that my relationship with Bekhterev went beyond the professional. I'd known from his tone that he was asking me to clarify, but I refused on principle, knowing no man would ever be asked to do such a thing. The memory of that question and my refusal to provide a clear answer made me blush, as we do, looking back on the errors we made when we were young. I excused myself to attend to the others whose voices I could hear from the entrance.

As I was walking away, I heard Luria ask Bekhterev if he would introduce the exhibit.

In the entrance, I stationed myself close enough to the door so I could feel the cold air when it opened and closed. My greetings and instructions became a kind of litany that, in its repetition, allowed me to think. We had invited scientists, party members, and newspaper reporters. Some had brought their wives.

I surveyed the gathering crowd as an outsider might, curious about why they had come and what the evening would mean to them. The journalists who wrote for *Meditsinksi Rabotnik, Der Tagesspiegel, Neue Zürcher Zeitung*, the *New York Times*, and *Pravda* spoke varying degrees of Russian, ranging from the requisite *spasiba* to complete nuanced sentences and accomplished swearing, the truest test of literacy. Those who spoke well demonstrated it for those who spoke poorly, so that when they gathered around Sergei they were communicating not with him but with each other, establishing a linguistic pecking order they thought also mirrored their authorial rank. I'd seen this before. Capitalism breeds such manners. The foreign journalists always arrived together. They moved around the city in packs, staying in the same hotels, having sex with the same circle of women, and forming singular, neat opinions for export to their countries.

I'd met one of the journalists several years before in the lineup to see Lenin's body in the dark winter of 1924. That was the winter we remembered for its strikes and famines and peasant revolts. It was also the year I'd married Sasha, against the wishes of both our families, and the year I'd started to work for Bekhterev, against the wishes of Sasha.

—⧸—

In the very faces of the lineup that winter's day, I saw an entire world mourning. I remembered a peasant and his two young sons who had walked all the way from their farm near the western steppe, having left home just as soon as they heard the news. Diplomats from France. Whole orphanages. Groups of workers. Residents in communal apartments had come as a group, bringing their petty arguments with them. Reporters from the United States, Great Britain, France, Denmark, Switzerland. Nurses. Young Pioneers. Priests. People from the Caucasus. Secretaries' unions. Teachers. At one point a girl my very same age sat down on the cobblestones and started to weep. A part of me wanted so much to embrace her, but I was at a loss as to how I could. Then an older woman walked up to her, knelt down, and put her hand gently on the weeping girl's crossed arms. Their eyes met and soon after they were holding each other, though they had been strangers just minutes before.

All that day, the line had advanced slowly. Though the boulevards were wide by the university, once we rounded the northeastern corner of the Kremlin walls, the streets narrowed. At points, the noise seemed too much. The Pioneers had begun to sing songs and, because by that point we'd all started attending schools with the same curriculums, the same songs, and the same traditions, the words escaped our mouths without a single thought. Many from the crowd joined in. At one point, we began a folk song, the title of which I forget, but I remember the words *And the Red Sea seethes* and how our voices were suddenly doubled when another crowd that was as large and as diverse, joined in for the next lyric. That was how we realized there was not one line, but two. Our line came from the southern part of the city, theirs came from the east. The lines merged at the intersection of Nikitskaya and Rewoljuzzi.

All that day, I had been looking for my mother. If she were anywhere in Moscow, she would be here, I thought. Strange settings make familiar faces unrecognizable. That was why, when I saw Dimitri waving at me from the other line, I didn't, at first, wave back. I puzzled for a moment, and then knew I knew him, so I waved. And then I knew him as Dimitri, and so I smiled. Dimitri was Sasha's friend, not mine.

I had been wondering what my mother might look like; almost a decade had passed since I'd seen her. By the time she left, I'd reached my full height, though not my full figure. I was taller than her then but had no breasts to speak of, nor hips. She, on the other hand, was petite, yet full-figured. I only knew this because at night we bathed together and I took in her body, wondering in what ways we might, one day, be the same. Her clothes masked the soft curves of her breasts and hips.

Dimitri's line snaked out of view and I forgot about him.

My strongest memories of my mother were of the walks we'd taken on nights when my father attended the English Gentlemen's Club, when the streets became ours, our boots clopping against the cobblestones taking us down alleys, through small doorways and down dark steps to rooms guarded by men who recognized us and pinched my cheeks, ushering us in to smoky halls where people spoke in unison at a fever pitch. After the recitations and the speeches, the formality of the gatherings were abandoned and the adults would greet each other fervently. As they made plans whose details always escaped me, I would feel myself disappear. The less I understood, the more I resented being there. Eventually I would beg for us to leave, if only to have the opportunity to have my mother to myself again. The goodbyes went on forever. Finally, we'd leave, and then we'd be out in the streets again and they were ours. As we walked, my mother would explain something of the plans that had been made. By being included, I would be filled again with idealism, as though a new future were just around the corner. The spell was broken at the sight of our home, which was larger than most. We entered the cozy candle-lit halls with embarrassment, though none of this was ever said aloud, only communicated in the changing way my mother's hand gripped mine, then slackened, and then, at the entrance to our home, let go altogether, so I went in first, as if alone. The way we lived — our wealth — had always bothered my mother, though its comforts were hers as well. Those evenings were the result of a hard-won truce between my parents, the stipulations of which were obeyed at home and which included no pontification, no pamphleting, no proselytizing — on either side. The silence that resulted was anything but peaceful. Perhaps my parents called it a truce, but really it was a war put on hold. She would be old by now, if she's alive at all.

When it got dark on Nikitskaya, I stopped looking for her. The sun sets so early in January; we were in darkness by four o'clock. The crowd had stopped singing. The conversations around me turned intimate, exclusive. Our eyes adjusted to the dusk, and when the oil lamps were lit, they seemed brighter, almost, than the sun. We were walking in the middle of the street, passing in and out of the orbs of light.

The noise seemed louder in the dark, but I know this was just because we could see less. What snow there had been on the ground had been cleared away by the thousands of feet filing through the streets. What remained were slick patches of ice and gravel. Despite this, children were being pulled in wooden sleds over the gritty surface. On snow, the sound of a sled in tow is peaceful, lulling. On ice and grit, it is a vexing sound. A mausoleum was under twenty-four-hour construction; dynamite was being used to loosen the frozen ground. The explosions reverberated across Red Square and into the city streets.

Tatiana! someone called out.

I turned to where the voice had originated, but the lights had made silhouettes of everyone. I saw two heads moving towards me, the outline of a familiar ushanka.

You came! I said when I saw Sasha's grinning face, his cheeks flushed with cold. He kissed me and put his hand in my pocket so that he could find mine, and Dimitri stood there with him, smiling at us in a stupid kind of way, so I knew I looked happy.

You left your spot, I said to Dimitri.

You're closer, he said.

When we got to the boulevard in front of the House of Unions, the line bled into a crowd. All around us, there was the shifting black of the moving crowd and the singularity of the place we were moving towards, the bright entrance and the pitchy silhouette of the guard who granted access to the mourners. We moved together, us three, inseparable. Soon enough, a new pattern was imposed upon the crowd, and we were directed into lines that traversed the boulevard in single-file loops like film that had sprung from its canister.

Sasha stood behind me. Dimitri stood behind him.

I thought you weren't going to come, I whispered to Sasha.

I know you thought that, he whispered back. His fingers

were working hard at the seam of my coat pocket. Every time we stood like this, he dexterously tried to force the seam apart, but still the thread held tight.

The rhythm of our waiting changed. We moved steadily in order to keep warm; if we could not step forward, we rocked from side to side. We cupped our hands and blew into them. *Wshoooooooo.* The folk songs rumbled low and melancholic. When the wind whipped up or a sled passed by, I couldn't hear the songs at all.

Will you come inside? I asked Sasha.

I wasn't going to, he said.

But you just got here.

No, he corrected me. I just found you, but I've been looking for you for hours.

I hated to ask him to do something he didn't want to, hated to ask him to do something for me, hated to need him.

Please? I whispered.

Okay, he said.

Outside the House of Unions everything was sound and activity and movement. When we stepped inside it was suddenly so quiet I felt as if I must have gone deaf. The plush red carpet at our feet, damp at the entrance, but then increasingly dry. The light so white we couldn't at first see. And the smell, like a forest. Boughs and wreaths of pine hung from every column we passed. The columns reached up high to shoulder the clean, vaulted ceiling. In the subsequent room was Lenin's bier.

At each column, guards in khaki uniforms directed us further down the corridor, as if we might otherwise lose ourselves. I went in first. Sasha followed me. Dimitri followed him.

Through the door, it was like the darkness inside a wardrobe on a bright day. I reached back for Sasha's hand, but he was out of step with me and just beyond any subtle reach. I kept moving.

Walking towards a corpse makes you enormously conscious of time. What is the feeling of that time? It must be something like hope, not hope itself but its relative. It's a wish that the thing one needs to feel and consider and share will surface at the precise moment one comes to stand in front of the dead body. As much as possible, the hope is for an alignment of the fullness of your feeling with the appearance—for one last time—of that person's face. This is even truer if you've never stood so close to that person before. I was afraid that when I saw him I might feel nothing, even though what I truly felt was everything. This was a problem I had, my feelings always out of step; too early sometimes, but usually too late.

If others cried, I did not hear them.

When it was my turn to stand before the bier what I felt wasn't grief or sadness, not exactly, or not the way I thought grief or sadness ought to feel, but just the most gaping emptiness, a feeling so familiar with abandonment that even feeling itself was gone.

Sasha had stepped past me, so now Dimitri was there.

Lenin looked less dead than any dead person I had ever seen. Peaceful. He lay under a glass coffin, which was so clean it was as if it were not there at all. A red woollen blanket covered the lower half of his body. Both arms were bent at the elbow, his hands—one in a fist, the other palm-down—lay across his belly.

I wiped my tears away from under my eyes and tried to see Sasha, but he had gone on ahead, too quickly. Dimitri's hand on my shoulder reminded me what Sasha wasn't.

Behind me, I heard a young voice ask, Can he breathe in there?

No, said an older woman, he doesn't need to anymore.

I stepped forward so that Dimitri's hand dropped away. I could feel him looking at me, but I didn't look back.

The slight change in perspective made his death real. I was looking back at a dead man now. I had moved from one era into another as one does from childhood into adulthood, imperceptibly in the moment, but sudden on reflection.

This, I thought, this very moment, is mourning.

Dimitri stood there a minute longer, then walked on as well.

The three of us streamed out of the building past the throngs of people still waiting to go in. I looked at how the light of the entrance cast their faces in deep contrasts like masks from ancient theatres that reduced the complexity of all human experience to the purified, the singular. An expressionless woman was the stoic, the teary peasant was the mourner.

What was the expression on Sasha's face? Was it pity? Was it confusion? He was staring at me with his soft eyes; but what he was feeling was for me and what I was feeling was for our country, and those were not the same. Having Sasha there had made me more sad, not less. More alone, not less. Where could we go from there? I wondered, but then the question drifted away like the morning mist once the sun has risen.

———✦———

In the red entrance hall of the institute that evening, the front door swung shut. It was for the best that Sasha hadn't come, I thought. I'd anticipated the night of the opening for so long, thinking it would replicate the energy of that night three years ago when it seemed as if the whole world had gathered to mourn. Now, instead, we would gather to learn. More and more people poured into the entrance, but none were peasants. I watched the women on the arms of their men. Their faces were flushed from the cold. They wore trim dresses and had their hair cut in bobs. The men wore tunics. A few women wore garish lipstick. The coat racks disappeared beneath the coats. The institute had never been so full, nor so loud. Women's voices rang out. The men laughed and joked. Some paused to see the portraits, creating the kind of bottleneck you would expect at any good event. Triads gossiped and looked everyone else up and down. A young girl tried to go up the stairs, but I called out to her and placed a cordon between the balustrades after that. How could Bekhterev's remarks address a crowd such as this? What small thing might the foreigners, the women, the politicians be able to grasp? Eventually, the crowd gathered in the grand salon.

Sergei assumed my place at the entrance, and I walked down the hall.

In the grand salon, the plinths towered over the people, some of whom had already taken their seats. So many people had come! I hadn't noticed the arrival of Tsiolkovsky, the conjurer of the birdlike flying machine and other fantastical devices, but he had emerged from his hermetic life just for this. He had attached himself to Dr. Segalin, who was, in those days, making a name for himself by studying what he called the *pathology of genius*. I hadn't thought about it like that before, how genius was like any other abnormality, a problem because it signalled you were different, but that was what Segalin said, that genius caused certain vulnerabilities. And there was Alexandr Bogdanov, the activist turned writer turned scientist. In those men you could see how art and science were the same thing. Some scientists were as untethered as any artist I'd ever met.

On the other hand, there was Luria. He sat with them, but he was nothing like them. Even as a student, he had been so orderly, so aware of the correct path, knowing which professors to get on his side, what specialties to acquire, and it was this, as much as any purely scientific talent, that had made his advancement so predictable. If Luria was composed, Bogdanov, Tsiolkovsky, and Segalin all had something mad about them. Segalin, especially, seemed to move around the room like a wasp at a late summer dinner. His laugh was loud and unapologetic, out of proportion to the otherwise tame conversations of the rest of the crowd. Everything about Segalin drew you in, then pushed you away.

Dr. Vogt went to stand at the podium, clearing his throat. He wore a dark grey, three-piece suit, his glasses hung on a chain around his neck. Something about him made me tense. The group quieted, taking their seats. Some sat in chairs in front of the podium, others stood beside the exhibits, forming a perimeter. I was surprised to see Bekhterev make his way behind the chairs to where I was standing.

Welcome, Comrades, to the opening of the Institut Mozga, said Vogt.

Despite his small stature and his almost comical foreignness, his voice dominated the room. He was a man accustomed to attention. When he spoke, he leaned on the podium so that its pedestal cocked forward. He looked athletic, as if speaking in public demanded so little of him that he needed something else, some small or big object to manipulate while he spoke.

Whereas bourgeois education is based on abstract knowledge and sedentary book learning without any connection to practical experience, he said, our pedagogy fuses together scholarship, praxis, and the most advanced forms of production in order to provide new forms of embodied knowledge and thought.

The reporters, scientists, and wives nodded and whispered back and forth.

We have microtomed ten thousand slices of Lenin's brain, said Dr. Vogt, every tenth of which has been treated with an indigo stain and studied using methodologies developed by Drs. Bets, Rossolimo, Bekhterev—and here he nodded in Bekhterev's direction, causing a few heads to turn to look back at us. Our research, he went on, has led to seminal victories concerning the material substrate of Lenin's genius.

I couldn't tell if Vogt was being honest, since I'd never heard of anyone being able to cut any brain, no matter how large, into ten thousand slices, or if he was telling the truth and that was how far the science in Germany had advanced. I felt Bekhterev tense up beside me, and I knew that Bekhterev's problem with Vogt was that he served the state, not the science. Basically, he was lying.

Standing behind the last row of chairs as I was, I could observe all the reactions all at once. Segalin reacted to the announcement by laughing his hyena laugh, but Luria nudged him and he quieted. The journalists translated for each other. Some people stared off into the dark recesses of the room, trying to make out the detail in the mouldings—the angels, the bare-breasted women, historical figures like Pushkin that had been carved into the walls themselves.

Vogt went on, saying that unlike the subjective whims of individual psychological assessment, cytoarchitectonics was superior because it was metrical and, therefore, objective. The mental substrate of Lenin's genius had already been proven in incontrovertible terms: in layer three of the cortex and in many cortical regions deep in this layer were pyramidal cells of a size and number we'd never before seen.

I stood to the right of Bekhterev, whose arms were tightly crossed over his thick chest, and as I heard the announcements about the discoveries in the third layer of the cerebral cortex of pyramidal cells of a size never before observed and in a number never before observed, all I could see was the way the fat flesh of Bekhterev's right elbow bulged in the unforgiving folds of his navy wool tunic that was too small and too hot for a man of his temperament.

Aren't you going to say anything? I whispered to Bekhterev.

No, he said gruffly.

Because of their metrical character, Dr. Vogt said, brain architectonics has an advantage over methods like individual psychology, which is based primarily on subjective assessments. Since architectonics can ascertain the size of the cortical regions involved in certain mental capabilities, in cubic centimetres, and their relative share of the total available cortex, in percentage, it provides objective criteria for evaluating, though only post-mortem, the individual characteristics of a brain.

Why not? I whispered.

It wasn't his night, he said. He'd speak when it actually mattered, in front of a scientific community, not a group with such superficial interest.

The podium was still rocking back and forth. Vogt was fidgeting, like an athlete, yes, but now he seemed nervous.

As such, our findings with regard to V.I. Lenin are at once conclusive, in that there can be no disputing the measurements thus far obtained, and introductory, as without a doubt there is so much more to be discovered.

Those who spoke Russian recognized the conclusive tone and clapped.

Spasiba, danke, merci, thank you, and now, enjoy! he said overtop the initial applause, which had cued the others, so that the whole room was politely tapping their hands together in uneven recognition of what, exactly, the institute had accomplished.

If the lecture said very little, for the reporters and the Party members it was enough to make them experts. They stood before the specimens again. Armed with *cortex, architectonics, pyramidal cells*, they misidentified with confidence. The drawers slid open and shut. I wished they would ask questions of me but knew they wouldn't see me as an expert, being a woman and an assistant. In theory, the role of women had changed with the Revolution, but that was only in theory. Instead of speaking to anyone directly, I drifted through, overhearing snippets of conversation, some about the exhibit, but most moved on to other topics quickly enough. The journalists were in a tête-à-tête about whether or not to go to *another* party, as if this had been one. Bogdanov was surrounded by a small group and seemed to be giving tips on how to rob a bank: step one, act as if it were yours already. Segalin was egging him on, laughing his too-loud laugh. Vogt was surveying the room, his arm resting casually on the podium as if it were a bar and he a regular.

I made my way to the other side of the room, ending up between the Borodin specimen and Lenin's. From there, I could see the crowd, then the row of musician specimens, and then the crowd again, reflected in the mirrors. The first crowd was lit up by the chandelier. Their faces radiated warmth and happiness. They chatted convivially. Behind them, the liquid around the specimens glowed. Behind the specimens, reflected in the mirrors, I saw the other side of the crowd: they were dark silhouettes and moved like puppets on invisible strings.

When Vogt left the room, this signalled the end of the evening, and the crowd began to filter back out the way they'd come. I drifted after them, as far as the front entrance, then I unhooked the cordon I'd set up to block off the stairs, and went up so I could sit out of sight, watching the end of the evening from there.

After everyone had left and we'd closed the institute for the evening, Bekhterev, Luria, and I stopped in at a nearby alehouse. Bekhterev should have been with the senior scientists and professors, but as the last of us were gathering our coats and discussing where we should go, he had muttered under his breath something about the pretensions of his colleagues and then stated with a forced elation that he would close the evening by catching up with his former students. Speaking about Luria and me in such a way set us apart from anyone else our age, marking us as permanently his, as opposed to Vogt's or Sarkisov's.

In the alehouse, we ordered the only thing on offer—a carafe of vodka and a plate of herring topped with red onions. I found us a spot in a corner as far away from the bar and the stage as possible, so that we would still be able hear each other talk once the place filled up. It was early in the night, and the waiters were drifting between the empty tables or talking amongst themselves. On stage, a few men were pulling chairs out of the wings in preparation for the evening show. From their suits and white shoes and from the number and arrangement of the chairs, I guessed they played jazz. Two other men unfurled a red banner and hung it behind the chairs. At first, the one on the right lifted his side too high, then the one on the left did, and so the thing lolled back and forth as the two of them barked at each other about who was to blame. Eventually, a waitress stepped in and silently commanded them by waving her left hand up a little and up a little more until finally the banner was even. Then she continued through the room, clinking three glasses down on our table as she passed, not even saying a word.

So, said Luria, are you pleased?

Luria had sat with his back to the bar, which had the effect of focusing our attention on him because even if we were distracted by the events behind him, we still looked in his general direction. It was odd, really, that our paths hadn't crossed more.

With the opening? asked Bekhterev, who had also been looking over Luria's shoulder, watching the activity on stage.

Yes, said Luria, amused at the idea that he'd be asking about anything else. Were you pleased with the opening?

I thought it went very well, I offered.

The vodka and herring arrived.

Luria poured the first round. The table tilted when Bekhterev leaned forward to reach for his glass, causing the liquid to spill over the rims. He ran his finger through the clear puddle and licked it clean.

To the fruit of your labours, Luria said, raising his glass. The toast was a traditional one and pleasantly archaic. We cheered and emptied our glasses.

I looked from the stage to the bar. The jazz players were hovering there now, waiting for an audience to arrive. For a while we were silent. The alcohol began to warm the back of my head. Bekhterev was folding and refolding a napkin.

Luria poured another round.

Bekhterev stabbed at a piece of herring with a fork and then tilted his head back so he could drop it whole into his mouth. Luria watched. A small bit of oil escaped the corner of Bekhterev's mouth. The droplet caught the light from the stage, making a bright sheen that glistened visibly even as it tried to disappear in his beard. Something about this enfeebled him. Luria handed him a napkin.

Again I was confronted with the unstated limits of our relationship. I felt too young to ask openly how he felt, but I could see a mixture of bitterness and disappointment, which I couldn't address for fear of dismantling his dignity. If there was a way to pretend his feelings didn't exist, I didn't know it. But Luria did.

So tell me, said Luria, why you ordered the specimens the way you did. Why the semicircle, and why not place Lenin at the end?

Not you, too, said Bekhterev, his temper still raw. Everyone is so obsessed with order. Why is that? I think it's because people want to know what to think. If I order these herring will it tell you what to think, too?

This was Bekhterev warming up. He was angry about being brought into conversation, resentful of Luria prodding him, and yet, despite himself, drawn in.

I know it wasn't random, said Luria.

How did Mendeleev order the periodic table, Tatiana? Tell Luria that much, said Bekhterev, looking to me.

It was a guess, said Bekhterev, not letting me answer.

It was more than a guess, said Luria.

A good guess, said Bekhterev, and a few well-placed gaps.

The right gaps, I said.

Exactly!

So there was a logic, said Luria.

In truth, the order had been my doing, not Bekhterev's. This was because the exhibition of the specimens involved some understanding of what the public would want to see, an understanding that Bekhterev thought was impossible for him to access. I don't understand the public, he'd said. The exhibition required someone younger, someone who'd been through the revolutionary schooling, not one who'd taught in it. It was the students who understood the totality of their education and its place in a revolutionary society.

The professors, on the other hand, understood only the smallest piece of what the students were learning, so much so that it could hardly even be said that the professors understood what their students in their own classes learned, since what they taught was the totality of their lives and what the students learned was the fraction of it that would apply to theirs.

So it was me who decided to place Lenin roughly in the middle and me who decided to place his brain on the angle I did and me who decided to let that choice dictate the way the rest of the brains were angled, so that even if we all knew that the reason for the institute was to display Lenin's genius, the exhibit would suggest he was a superman among many.

Explain it to him, said Bekhterev, but again he spoke for me, saying the order was entirely arbitrary, that all order was arbitrary until it's been around for long enough it starts to seem natural. He cited Rubinstein's fifths, and the lines Poincaré had drawn across the globe, making time zones that now seemed irrefutable.

Luria still wasn't satisfied. What he really wanted to know was whether or not the collection was complete. Was our collection like the periodic table in that there were gaps we hoped would one day be filled, or was our collection complete now that Lenin was in it?

I don't know of a single true collector who would ever describe their collection as complete, said Bekhterev. Of course we have empty jars. We have a fair number.

I sat back, looking at the two of them.

We need them, said Bekhterev, because some of the Soviet geniuses are still living.

Luria smiled.

Me, for example, Bekhterev said, with a childlike grin.

I shook my head, relieved that the mood had shifted.

Thinking back on that night, after all these years, I realize that what Luria was really after was some sense of whether or not Bekhterev conceived of the collection as political or scientific. He could have asked directly and if he had, Bekhterev would have put him in his place: the institute was scientific and the only purpose it had was to educate. Yet if the scientific goals could align with the revolutionary, and if the revolutionary made the scientific possible, all the better. Bekhterev was of the generation that had grown up alongside the Revolution, and he was pragmatic about its role in his pursuits. I, on the other hand, was more idealistic about the Revolution, more inclined to believe Marx and Lenin. Perhaps it wasn't possible to be idealistic about people you'd actually known; perhaps Bekhterev's ease with the Revolution had to do with him having been one of Lenin's doctors, with him having had so much contact with the Soviet elite, and this before they were elites at all.

We stared at our drinks, alone in our thoughts, waiting for a new topic to emerge.

I've never been to the Kremlin, I said.

Me neither, said Luria.

Never seen so many chess boards in all my life, said Bekhterev.

So there was no real reason for the order you chose, said Luria.

We had many reasons, Luria. Many. Too many to iterate now, he said, suddenly serious. He was getting bored. Underneath the table, his leg had started to shake.

Each specimen is unique, I said. It's not at all what I expected to find when we started out.

You didn't think they'd be the same? asked Luria.

No, but they were *very* different, I said.

And you could see, just by looking at them, how differ-ent they were? For example, if we took the brains out of their jars, jumbled them up, and then set them out in front of you, you'd be able to identify which was which?

I don't know if *I* could, but someone with more experience could.

Luria had a way of asking questions that unnerved me. With him around, I felt on the verge of being wrong about absolutely everything, my own name, for example. The precision that had led him to pronounce so carefully every syllable in his name had come to this—a predatory approach to knowledge, especially about the mechanics of brain function, and a specialization in language. He studied pedagogy, language, and conflict and soon his dissertation would be submitted.

You could, said Bekhterev to me, his leg quiet again.

Anyway, I said, pushing a piece of herring back and forth on the plate so that it left a wake in the oil, you know all this. And you know we had to be wise about how we displayed the exhibits. We didn't want to suggest anything like a hierarchy, which is why Lenin isn't at the beginning or the end.

Very clever, said Luria, his attention focused on me now. So you *could* tell them apart?

Well, I said slowly. Yes. The weight distinguishes them, for a start, I looked at Bekhterev, who was smiling a little, saying nothing so that I would be forced to.

And we can observe things about the ways the sulci appear, whether they have deep convolutions, a lot of com-plexity—sometimes they're hard to follow, like a jumble of fine thread, and sometimes their twists are easier to fol-low, like thick rope, which can't bend around itself quite so much.

But what do these differences mean? he asked me, his eyes appearing now below and now above the rim of his glasses as he bobbed his head up and down, in sync with his thoughts, which seemed to go first here, then there, then somewhere else, then back again. How do you know the differences aren't arbitrary?

Because they aren't, I thought. Because of comparison.

Well, because of all of the musicians? I said, trying not to sound so unsure. Because they show more development in the left gyrus temporal than we see in the scientists?

Are you asking me? said Luria. How many musicians do you have?

It's early days, said Bekhterev, early days. The physical evidence is coming.

That was the bald truth of the matter, but I wanted to cast the institute in better light, wanted it to have discovered more than it had.

Bekhterev took over then, talking about the scientist's brain versus the musician's versus the poet's. Our used glasses and plates became part of a miniature exhibit.

Luria was watching us like a cat watches a bird, with a dangerous patience. There was something about the exhibit — or the institute or the science or Bekhterev or me, I wasn't sure what — that he didn't quite believe. *There was something that he didn't like.*

One of the musicians had returned to the stage and was running scales on his clarinet.

Where is your husband? asked Luria, tipping the last drops of vodka into my glass. He'd changed his mind, I thought. He wasn't going to pounce, not now.

He's out drinking with his friends, I said. I'd forgotten that Luria had met Sasha until that very instance, and then I suddenly recalled a meal we'd shared some years prior.

To like minds, said Luria, raising his glass again.

To like minds, we echoed.

When *was* that dinner party? I asked them both.

In another lifetime, said Bekhterev in a tone that sounded wistful, nostalgic. When you two were students.

Were we married then? I asked.

Yes, said Luria, but only just.

Funny that you'd remember.

Funny that you wouldn't.

That was the hypnotism argument.

Not an argument per se, said Bekhterev.

I remembered it as an argument. I remembered the small apartment Bekhterev kept, its walls bare, the shelves nearly empty, all signs that his real life was in Petrograd, as we called it then, not in Moscow. I remembered wanting Sasha to see Bekhterev the way I did, as a kind of father, a leader, as key to our future. Sasha had a sort of romantic attachment to being an outsider, but Bekhterev had always said if you want to change something, you had to be willing to belong. He meant you had to become an insider: press from the inside at something's weak points, not from the outside, where it sees you coming. It sounded to me like a kind of philosophy, but later Luria pointed out that it was simple military strategy; flanking, I think he called it. Anyway, it meant to me that Bekhterev was both an outsider and an insider.

Listen, Sasha had said to him that night, I've got a question for you.

Anything! said Bekhterev. Ask me anything! We'll ask each other everything!

I remember feeling that the conversation might go wrong somehow. Sasha had this tendency to make bad first impressions. He came across as opinionated and cocky, supremely confident though nothing could be further from the truth. Introducing him to new people was something I thought about in terms of multiple events, not just one. Sasha needed to mark his territory in the first visit, and then he'd calm down on the second and third. Once people had met him a few times, they loved him. But if it was left to only one meeting, it didn't turn out so well. Luria had looked miserable, as if he were constructing responses to the questions he most feared. Sasha was all seriousness, and Bekhterev, with nothing to fear, thought the whole thing was much fun. That was the Bekhterev I remember most fondly.

Bekhterev went on. You'll explain Rodchenko's overalls, and Luria will tell us about growing up in Kazan, and you, Madame, you will tell us to stop our digressions for one single moment and concentrate, concentrate, concentrate. But we won't, will we? And who will tell us about the dirigible flying over the eastern coast of the United States at this very moment? Did you know that it is dark there and dark here, and so we are, Americans and Russians, experiencing the same night?

Why would it be the same night? asked Luria.

Because the dirigible will block out the sun! It's a man-made eclipse!

I don't believe it, said Luria.

That it could block the sun? I asked.

That they could experience the same sort of black, said Luria. Their cities are too bright, too electric. Everything is bright all day and all night.

Constant light, I said. Like in Petrograd.

It's not natural, said Luria.

Who will ask the first question? asked Bekhterev. Alexandr, sir. You begin!

Well, said Sasha, what do you make of hypnotism?

Why? Something else! I protested.

Bekhterev took his time answering, emptying the carafe into Sasha's glass first, then asking the servant to bring another.

Now this is a healthy topic, said Bekhterev, smiling. Hypnotism can rouse suspicion, desire, hope of healing, fear of the mystical. Well done, Comrade! A perfect thing to discuss!

Sasha flinched at being called comrade. Bekhterev didn't notice, but Luria did.

So? Sasha said.

Well, hypnotism, has, unfortunately, become a derogatory word, Bekhterev said more slowly. The first step, as we well know, is to get our terms straight. Mental suggestion is more appropriate to the procedure we use today.

But does it work? pressed Sasha.

It is a diagnostic and curative tool. It's been known to remedy diseases both physical and mental, diseases that the rest of pharmacopoeia has been ill equipped to address.

But does it cure people? asked Sasha, leaning forward, his elbows on the table.

That's what he's saying, I said to Sasha, willing him to lean back.

That wasn't a real answer, said Sasha to me.

Very good, said Bekhterev. Let's be more precise. Success or failure can be reduced to one single factor, and that single factor is motivation. The patients must be motivated. I know of a case where two hysterical married people were already well improved from the treatments they'd received, but they nagged each other with autosuggestions, and, in consequence, went away uncured.

Even if Sasha knew he made bad impressions—I think he did it on purpose, or at least didn't try very hard to stop himself—this didn't prevent him from forming fully developed opinions of others from the very first meeting. He was always perceptive and, often, even funny. That night, Luria had come away described as a kind of field mole, the kind that mates for life, though in his case the mate might be something more abstract, thought Sasha. Maybe an idea, or a project, but he'd do it until he died.

And Bekhterev? I asked, loving him and his odd ways.

Also as dedicated, said Sasha, but for slightly different reasons. Dedicated, I'd say, because something happened to him once that damaged him, and he doesn't dwell on it, doesn't even think about it, but something about that period of his life has made him totally dedicated to his projects even if their superficial completion lacks something. But—

I know…, I said.

But I don't believe him about hypnotism.

Yes, I think you made that clear, I said, loving him just that little bit less.

—✦—

I didn't think of it as an argument either, said Luria, swirling the fish bones around in the oil, but I'll tell you now that I thought you made a strange couple.

It had been an argument, I thought, but they had seen only its beginning, the drops of rain before the storm. The true argument had happened after Sasha and I left, and it had been about Bekhterev, not about hypnotism.

The saxophone player joined the clarinetist on stage. They made bird calls back and forth, trying to get in tune. The other tables were filling up.

Well, we're not, I said.

Not a couple? he asked, looking up.

Not strange, I said.

I'm just saying, I wondered how you could have met.

Didn't you ever go to Osorgin's bookshop? I asked.

No, said Luria.

That explained quite a bit.

What Sasha hadn't understood was that Bekhterev knew suggestion worked, but it worked unevenly, that is, on *some minds*, not all minds. Bekhterev also knew it wasn't just doctors who knew about the power of suggestion. The Soviets knew as much, if not more. The red banner hanging behind the band, for example. That was suggestion. It worked best if you didn't notice it happening.

Bekhterev poured another round. The clouds of smoke hanging from the ceiling made the atmosphere seem thicker, especially once the lights were dimmed for the show.

Do you play chess, Dr. Bekhterev? asked Luria.

Never had time, he said. Do you?

I've never even learned to castle, said Luria.

That's the most fascinating move, I said.

This is what they tell me, said Luria.

It only happens once in the game.

Both Bekhterev and Luria were watching me. I set out our three glasses on the table and named them castle, king, castle.

It only happens once and when it does, these two, I pointed at the king and the castle, change places, making it two moves in one.

I picked up the pieces and passed them over each other in a neat arc.

Seems like a good deal, said Luria.

Ah, but who is the king of the Americans? said Bekhterev, now lost, or at least, somewhere else. I'd had their attention, but it didn't last.

The Duke, I said, which was how I'd heard Rima refer to him.

Jazz is their single triumph, said Bekhterev.

I'm surprised neither of you play, I said.

I'm surprised you do, said Luria.

Luria stood to go to the men's room. While he was gone, Bekhterev left. The room was now so full that people lined the walls.

I sat there with our coats and bags and listened to the music that sounded strangely like two things at once: a parade and a funeral march.

Luria and I left the bar together.

Want to walk a bit? he asked.

October is a nice time for walking. The leaves had fallen, littering the streets, and the sound of them shuffling beneath our feet made me feel like we had company, though we were alone. Remnants of the anniversary celebrations were everywhere — tired red flags hung from balconies, the streets glittered with candy wrappers and broken glass, and wrapped around street poles and gathered in the nooks of doors were heaps of crumpled up flyers. It had been years since I'd spent any time with Luria, but walking through the streets that night we talked about anything and everything, as though we'd always been close friends, or at least should have been. I can't remember if we'd been walking for ten minutes or an hour when Luria admitted that something had bothered him about the opening.

I know, I said. I could tell.

He glanced at me with a small smile. He was pleased. Pleased that he'd been noticed, even if it also meant, in a way, that he'd been caught.

Did you see Bogdanov there? asked Luria.

Why?

We'd come to the Kitay-gorod. The vendors were all hanging about, drinking and talking after their day. It was illegal to sell things on the streets, so they pretended they weren't vendors when the police were in view and pestered everyone when they weren't. They whispered their offerings as we passed. It was the same everywhere, which lent all street transactions the feeling of criminality, something quite comical since what they were selling were onions, hand tools, or suits. That they whispered indicated something that didn't occur to be then but does now: they whispered because they could tell who were police and who weren't. Now, there's no telling.

Luria didn't like him being at the opening.

Where else would he possibly be? I asked. His institute is in the building, too.

Luria hadn't realized this. Luria didn't understand that Bogdanov cast a spell on everyone he met, so I tried to explain.

There was something incredible about Bogdanov. Everyone wanted him around. He seemed to glow. Not in a spiritual way, not exactly, but as if he were his own source of power, as if electricity flowed through him in the way everyone used to be afraid of. His mind raced with the most exquisite thoughts. Get close to him once, and he'd change your thinking on the working man's connection to vitalism; get close to him again, and he'd tell you how to rob a bank. Then he'd explain the politics of the plot—robbing a bank was not stealing, it was expropriation: liberate the funds so that they can finally go out and do some real good in the world! As I spoke, I got caught up in the thrill of him.

I told Luria I just wanted to hand Bogdanov a gun and say shoot! Get rid of anything that will hold us back, and I imagined he'd do it and no one who would regret it would still be standing.

But you know, said Luria in his measured way, there was a time when, if you'd done that, it would have been Lenin who would have been shot.

Lenin *was* shot, I said, practically yelling, and anyway, that's not what I mean!

I'd had too much to drink.

What held us back was half-way thinking, the tendency to want change that wouldn't actually change anything at all. The angle I'd chosen for displaying Lenin's brain and then replicated for all the others might have had something to do with the gunshot. We didn't know why, exactly, the black had taken over that part of Lenin's brain, but the gunshot might have been to blame.

I mean, said Luria, Lenin would have died if you'd given Bogdanov a gun. Bogdanov's friend wasn't such a good shot.

This was supposed to be a black mark for Bogdanov, the fact that he'd turned against Lenin, but it wasn't for me. Lenin couldn't have been killed in that moment, even if Bogdanov had been the gunman. What had happened was the Social Revolutionaries had lost and the Bolsheviks had won, and not everyone agreed about which one was better. But it was Lenin who was considered a genius, not Bogdanov, and it was Lenin we'd remember. Disagreement was a good thing. It meant we were alive. It meant we were thinking.

I'm not sure about you, said Luria.

This was the difference between science in the universities and science in the institutes. In the institutes our mandate was to do something big. Marx had been clear: philosophers have only explained the world, but the point was to change it. That was what we would do. We would change the world. Science was a fortress; scientists were an army. We were fighting the good fight. Science was lighting the world on fire.

—⊀—

After we parted, I walked along Pirogovskaya and thought of Bekhterev, of the pall that had clung to him throughout the night, and of the institute and how well it ought to have fulfilled everything he had hoped for. I thought of what Luria had said and of Rima, of all the nights she and I had stumbled down that very street, and it seemed almost possible that I could run into the two of us, drunk, on our way into the city, and that if I did, neither of us would be surprised to see time intersecting like that. I'd see my earlier self, my young drunk self who wanted to catch up to Rima, who wanted to stop in the park, who wanted to vomit, who wanted to go home. I wished I could see Rima, but it was too late; her husband, Yuri, would be angry, and Sasha would be expecting me.

In the park near our home, I saw the familiar figures in their usual spots. The three huddled together under the chestnut tree were kids, probably between the ages of ten and twelve. The kids were scrawny, so they looked younger than they were, but they were mean, which made them look older. They scared me. They would light a fire later and try to hide it by doing it in a metal cylinder, rolled over from somewhere, but it wouldn't work.

A few benches away, a man I knew as Tobias was smoking a cigarette. He greeted me with a nod, but I needed to get home and he could tell. He was one of those who hadn't transitioned well; he'd lost everything, whatever that was, and never found a way to get anything back. Sasha and I had met him some years previous on a hot summer's night, when the whole city seemed to gather around whatever water it could find. Tobias was already living on the streets back then, and so he bathed in water fountains whenever he got a chance. He'd impressed us because he'd developed a dignified method of going about it. He'd strip down to his underwear, folding his clothes neatly on the fountain edge, and then wade in, scrupulously avoiding the area of the fountain where the children played because, in his estimation, no parent would want their kid mingling with the likes of him. He carried a small cake of soap with him wherever he went, and on that summer night, after he'd bathed, he sat with us to talk. Back then, he was still relatively healthy. Dirtier than the students and workers who hung around the park during the day, but he ate and didn't smoke so much. He drank, sure, but it wasn't killing him.

When I got home, I stood beneath the window to the apartment Sasha and I had moved into just after we married. On the day we were supposed to pick up our key from the concierge, we'd stood right there, looking at each other, both afraid, but laughing, as though the realness of our decisions had suddenly hit us. We were as surprised as we were delighted. All housing was allocated by the state, but the fact of it being allocated to us as a couple gave it a special allure—it was the first thing that was ours. It was small, just two rooms, but we had a balcony to ourselves, and it was out there that we sat on nights that were warm enough, smoking cigarettes and sharing our days. The lights were off now, but I knew he wouldn't be sleeping, not soundly at least. A part of him would be awake, waiting for me.

The building's concierge only stayed awake until eleven at night, after which he'd lock the building with the only existing keys. The first year we were there, we'd rush home for our curfew, always getting back just as the lock was being turned. Then we got comfortable and started to push the limit, always assuming the concierge would be there, that he liked us, that we were special enough and young enough and charming enough for him to wait. Then one night we were locked out. We stood there bickering—me blaming Sasha, Sasha blaming me—until we saw one of our neighbours come home, casually knock on a ground-level window, wait a few minutes for it to open, and then climb his way in. After that, we made sure one of us got home before eleven, so as to let the other in later. At the beginning, it had usually been me letting Sasha in, but now our roles had reversed.

Sash, I whisper-yelled. Sasha!

The wind had kicked up and his name was swept away on the gusts, indistinguishable from the sound of rustling leaves. I found a small pebble and tossed it upwards. I watched it dance across our window, and then the light came on.

He would let me in via the window to the first-floor communal kitchen. That there were communal kitchens on every floor might sound like a lot, but they served the whole floor, meaning twelve apartments and however many people — legal or otherwise — were housed therein. The first-floor kitchen was always filthy, the insides of the window thick with cooking oil and fat. Only Mr. Cycan, who lived beside the kitchen, ever cleaned the windows. But he'd been ill, so they were covered with a semi-permanent smear that blurred whatever was happening inside.

I waited in the cold, blowing warm air onto my fingers, trying to imagine Sasha's movements, the precise moment when he would leave our apartment, close the door soundlessly behind him, amble down the two sets of stairs, and make his way to the kitchen.

The kitchen light came on and I saw a dark shape move behind the window. Then the latch was released and Sasha's sleepy face appeared.

Hello my darling, I whispered.

The legs of a chair came through the window, guided by Sasha's hidden hands.

I took the chair from him, stood on it, and climbed in. Once I'd made it inside, Sasha reached outside to pull the chair through the window, and then we guided it back through together to make sure it wouldn't bang against the window frame. He was wearing only shorts and wool socks, and in his silent efficiency—he was almost never efficient—I could see that he'd been worried. We replaced the chair and Sasha padded out of the kitchen and down the hall, his shoulders pulled back, as if he were in the military, though they never would have accepted him even if he'd tried. I knew I should not laugh, but a snicker escaped my lips and he turned, quickly, as if about to say, So you think it's funny, do you? But when he turned, he looked down at his feet, the socks slipping away from his toes like dogs' tongues on a hot day. He turned back and kept going, but I'd seen him smile.

Maybe Luria was right, I thought, as I followed Sasha down the hall, maybe we *were* a strange couple, but that smile, that smile had always made me feel like we belonged together. Sasha ambled up the stairs but I lagged behind because my body suddenly seemed to weigh thousands of kilos, and every step demanded all my strength. It was as though the warmth of our building and proximity to our bed had given me permission to feel the deep tiredness that had been building in me for weeks. Inside our apartment, Sasha took off my hat, scarf, coat, then sweater, dress, underthings. I closed my eyes and felt him kiss my neck, my collarbone, the side of my breast, and then pull my nightclothes onto my body as if I were a child. This, too, had become part of our nightly routine. Only when we were in bed and on the verge of sinking into sleep did he ask how it went, and I said very well, and he whispered that he was so glad.

Sasha was a few years older than me, but when we met, we were both studying, so we seemed about the same age. We both were poor, but he was poorer. I received food rations; he had to work. I had my own room; he shared a room with another student. We didn't talk about it, but I knew then that he was poorer because historically he had been richer. The art students got access to studios, though, and those small nooks and corners became their sanctuaries. Sasha's was in an old warehouse that had been divided and subdivided so many times that going inside it was like entering a maze. Ever since going there the first time, that warren of rooms had been embedded in my psyche. It is a place I still return to in my dreams. To this day, I often find myself wandering in and out of the rooms, perceiving the spaces from strange angles—through a window I could never have accessed from the outside—or from above, as though I were an informer, vigilantly waiting for any kind of infraction, whispered or performed. The hastily built spaces had paper-thin walls, so we could hear even the slightest murmur in the studio next door. As I fell asleep that night, it was into that labyrinthian building that I fell.

—/—

The first time he took me there was late spring of 1921. We had been to the theatre for the first time, and I remember feeling extravagant. The theatre was once free but in those years of NEP, it was suddenly expensive, even for students. I had worn one of my mother's dresses because it seemed to me that going to the theatre was as much a performance for us as it was for the actors on stage. We could barely afford the tickets. I don't remember the name of the play, but the set design made such an impression on me that I can see it now, as if I'd last seen it yesterday and not many years ago. When the curtain lifted to reveal something that looked like the inner workings of a clock mixed with the assembly line, I grinned at Sasha, thrilled at the idea that the Revolution had so transformed society that even the theatre reflected it. Against the theatre's crumbling opulence, with its curved balconies and its not-so-plush red velvet seats, the sharp mechanical geometries that played out on stage looked to me like the future.

Yet I've forgotten what happened in the play itself, perhaps because its fictional drama was upstaged by the real drama that took place in the house. Despite our officially classless society, a new social stratum had appeared. Almost as soon as we took our seats, a tangy sweet sunshine smell wafted throughout the theatre, making our mouths water with want. Heads everywhere turned to look. Up in the balconies, some NEP men were eating clementines and our mouths yearned for something as sweet, as juicy, as fresh. The NEP men and NEP women were the special class that emerged in those years. They were newly rich and their tastes were for anything extravagant, anything that glittered or sang or infused the air with desire. Sasha said they had no style; I thought they had no values. The NEP men and NEP women didn't care what we thought. They had furs and nylon stockings. They had clementines. I looked at Sasha as if to say, I hate them, but what he understood from my expression was, I want one.

In the intermission, Sasha disappeared for a few minutes. He slipped away, saying he'd be back in a minute, but it took more than a minute for me to make my way out of the theatre and across the salon towards the stairs that circled down to the milling crowds. I leaned on the balcony railing and watched the people below, the way they tipped their wine glasses to their mouths, the way the glasses captured the glowing light of the room, the way the room was burgundy and gold, the colours of fire, and the deep blacks of a burned log after the fire had gone out. A bell rang to tell us the show would soon resume. This crowd knew how long they had, there was no rush I didn't know how long. I straightened up and tried to find

Sasha. After some minutes, the bell rang again. People were starting to return to their seats. I wondered if Sasha was sick. Had he gone to the bathroom? I wouldn't ask; our relationship was still too new then, and I was too shy.

Then, at the third bell, I looked down the stairs and saw Sasha, taking the steps two at a time. He paused at the landing and looked up at me, grinning, then back down to the lobby where a man and a woman seemed to have lost something. I shook my head because I knew he'd done something he shouldn't. He kissed me on the neck when he was beside me again. It wasn't until the show had resumed that an explanation emerged: he pulled two clementines out of his pocket and handed one to me. Even if he was poor in those days, he wasn't afraid to say he wanted more, and when luxury appeared, like the clementine that night, he ate it as if he always had such things—no slowing down, not for anything. I savoured each segment and didn't eat the last one until the curtain closed. It was both the sweetest thing I had ever put in my mouth, and, for a split second, the most bitter, because I was sure I'd never taste a clementine again.

We left the crowds after the show and walked up Tverskaya beneath the deep blue sky that is so particular to late spring. Normally, Tverskaya is bustling no matter what time of day. Even at night, carriages and taxis troll the street, their drivers pestering those on the sidewalks for money or amusement or both. But on that night, it was quiet. All the city boulevards were strung with lights, which made night walking especially wonderful. Our faces slipped in and out of the warm orbs of light that emanated from each little globe. The trees bore all the signs of late spring, budding or already ostentatiously in leaf. The air was succulent and so fresh I wanted to drink it. The stores had closed early on account of a holiday, but some of the storefronts were still lit. We passed fur shops and bakeries and many remont shops whose signs were nothing more than an image of whatever they repaired: watches, suitcases, boots, and so on. We walked past the windows of Moscow's most expensive stores and turned onto the side street that was home to his studio. Sasha and I seemed to walk at the same pace. Maybe this was because we were about the same height, or maybe it was because of the peculiar way every step he took implied a pause. Like he was waiting, mid-step, for me; waiting so that when our feet met the ground they would do so at precisely the same moment. It was a bit like dancing. With each pause I felt my insides jump, as if I couldn't breathe. Maybe it was the dress, I thought. My mother had been smaller at the waist than me, so her dress held me too tightly there, but then, at the bust, too loosely. When Sasha and I got to his studio, I had to slow down, taking every single step. At any other time, I would skip steps because I liked leaping. Sasha took the steps at my pace, but every time after that we would race, and I would win.

He shared his studio with three other students. The room was dark, so I couldn't quite make out the dimensions of the space, but the echo of it told me the room was large. When Sasha turned on a few small lamps in his corner, the other corners snagged some light, too, and revealed their own distinct shapes and textures. Rusting machinery sulked in one corner, mounds of fabric in another, and the third was a jumble of paper, more archive than studio space. Sasha's was a mix: piles of books—open and closed, dog-eared and bookmarked—and various jars of pens, pencils, and brushes, though with the brushes he was evidently more careful. All of the bristles faced upwards, and every last brush was clean. He had one blank canvas on an easel, a small cot pushed up against the room's only window, and a small desk upon which sat a hotplate, a kettle, and two teacups without saucers. Outside, the night sky was indigo.

I'm sorry I don't have any chairs, he said.

I don't mind, I said, and sat down on the cot.

Where are your paintings?

They're in a show.

Why didn't you tell me?

Shy, I guess, but I was going to, he said. I was going to tell you about it tonight.

He set out the teacups, filling them halfway with vodka. Then he fetched something from behind the hotplate, hiding it behind his back impishly as he came closer to present me with two pieces of marzipan.

Take one, he said.

At one point, we heard voices in the hallway, and then someone went into a studio across the hall.

Who is it? I whispered.

Jack, whispered Sasha. You met him.

I remember.

He sleeps in his studio.

He sat next to me so we almost touched, and by being so quiet and so close, knowing we shouldn't be loud, it was like we were in the theatre again.

What is his real name?

Sasha didn't know what Jack's real name was. No one did, not even his professors. The two of them had been best friends since their second year at art school. In his first year, Jack had read every Jack London novel ever written, and by the end of that year Jack was his name. If he could have, Jack would have told people he had been raised by wolves. He was brusque, sharp, and solitary, but not loyal, not like a real wolf. He didn't think of the pack. Jack, I would soon realize, loved Sasha as if he were an extension of himself. When Jack looked at Sasha, he saw what he wanted to be. If anyone had been raised by wolves, it was Sasha, not Jack. I didn't like Jack because I didn't like fake wolves. I didn't like fake anything.

That night was the first time Sasha and I slept together. We lay on his cot, his inspiration cot, he called it, because he lay there whenever he couldn't figure out what to do next. A painter can't remove a brush stroke, he said. So he would lie down and close his eyes until some feeling, a niggling thing, would say it was time, and then he'd get up and tackle the painting again. What else did he do while he was lying there? I asked, but he just smiled and kissed me, his lips still boozy and sweet. The cot was like one they might've had in the army — metal piping made up the frame and a cross-hatch of coiled wires supported the discoloured mattress. It whined with our weight. If we wanted to lie on our sides, there could be no space between us, which meant we couldn't look at each other. With me on top or him on top, we could see each other's mouths, open and wanting. When we moved against each other, there was the sweet risk that we might fall. At points, I had the sure impression that when my hand touched his chest, it somehow melted into him, as if I'd been inside him for a moment. We kept a playful balance because we were young and our bodies were taut and strong and quick. When I straddled him and he sat up a little so that I could pull off his sweater, I pulled too hard and the cot gave up, collapsing to the floor. Then we really could do anything and Sasha said, If we're going to fuck things up, we might as well fuck everything up, and so we fucked all night and came away the next morning with cuts and scratches from where the springs had come unhinged.

From that night on, we started spending all of our time

together. Falling in love with him seemed like the easiest thing that had ever happened to me. Love had been a total mystery before — something that happened to other, luckier people. When we fell in love, it suddenly seemed like the most natural, inevitable, universal experience in the world. It had to be happening to everyone, every day.

Sasha seemed to understand me like no one else ever had. It wasn't anything I've ever tried to articulate and certainly not a thing I could explain to someone who hadn't seen us together, because it was a feeling, a complicity, an understanding of each other that preceded who we became. We'd sit in his studio, or lie under a tree, both of us reading or trying to, and he'd say, My love, and I'd look up at him and he'd have nothing more to add. Then I'd keep working, but smiling, too. He'd say, Your hair is five of my favourite colours, and I knew from that that he loved me because my hair is just black. He'd notice things about me that I'd never known: that I walk with my head down, watching the street, that when I read, I say some of the words out loud, that I laugh to myself. What? he'd ask. What did you read? And I would tell him some small, simplified thing: the structure of the atom is like the planets, all the little pieces orbit around the nucleus, as if around the sun. Beautiful, he would say. And then I could think of it that way, as an aesthetic object, and not as I had, as a scientific fact.

It was that tendency of his, to see beauty everywhere, that might have made me love him initially, or perhaps it was his sensitivity, which made him so unlike anyone I'd ever met. Not like my parents, or Rima, not like my classmates, or Bekhterev. When he talked, he told stories. Sometimes they made me laugh, and sometimes they made me cry; always they made me know a world I'd never known before. Where I had studied science, he had studied art. I had only ever had one close friend, he had had so many. I spoke in facts; he spoke in wonder. I grew up in the city; he on the farm.

One day when he was still a boy, a cat on the farm gave birth to a litter of kittens. Sasha spent the whole afternoon with them, watching them move blindly to the nipple and then curl away into deep sleep, and then back to the nipple to suckle again. When his father found out about the kittens, he took Sasha for a walk out to the fields. His father said nothing, but when they were at the outer edge of their land, he handed his son a shovel.

Dig the deepest hole you know how, he said, and walked back towards the family home.

Sasha was only seven at the time; the hole he dug was less than half a metre deep. He was worried his father would be angry with him for being slow, weak, so he didn't stop digging until his father returned.

This will do, his father said approvingly, and Sasha felt relieved.

His father had returned with a satchel in hand.

Sasha heard a tiny mew.

His father opened up the satchel and poured the kittens into the hole. Sasha looked down at their furry helpless bodies, saw the confusion in their eyes, and then the image blurred as tears welled in his.

Now cover them up with that dirt, his father said. Sasha willed his tears not to fall.

That was Pyotr, the man who left for war and never returned, and though I had never met him, I hated him.

When we decided to get married, we did it because we couldn't imagine our lives without each other, and we did it with the family we'd chosen, not the families we'd been born into—only Rima and Jack had witnessed the cere-mony—and it hadn't been the ceremony that mattered to either of us. What mattered was what he'd said to me before, when it was just the two of us riding the tram on the way to the commissioner's office. An old couple were sitting in silence opposite us, and the man looked terribly ill. He started coughing a dry, raspy cough. The woman reached into her bag and pulled out a candy and unwrapped it for him. His hand trembled badly as he reached for it. That's how long I want to know you, said Sasha, and I said, Me, too.

—⧸—

When I woke the morning after the opening, I was alone. Before we lived together, I'd fall asleep thinking about Sasha and wake up thinking about him. Every part of my body fantasized about what he'd do if he were there, as if the space around my body was thick with the memory of how his hand could slip past my waist and crawl up between my arms to intertwine with my hands and, like that, envelop me. Now that we'd become permanent to each other, waking up alone seemed like the most luxurious thing in the world. It seemed to me that the luxury of this must be universally felt. The bed, normally annexed by the body of another, is, on such a morning, a vast expanse that is all yours. You may stretch out any which way. The blankets are yours alone. Your lover is seen, from this angle, in his very best light, which is the light of theory, abstraction, or reminiscence. So it was that morning, I woke up alone for the first time in months, maybe years, the sun already soaring towards noon, and me with nothing to do but take in our apartment as I almost never did, in the light of day.

I had no commitments, so my time would be like the bed, luxuriously open from start to finish. Yet as I lay there contemplating my freedom, an unexpected feeling arose.

The solitude, which, days before, I might have said I craved more than anything, now felt lonely, and my freedom weighed upon me; I felt pressured to do something thrilling and wonderful with the day, not squander it, not have nothing to say for myself upon returning to work. And so, because whatever excitement I'd had in my life had always involved her, I decided to see Rima.

—�["/"]—

My first love, in some ways, was Rima. Our friendship wasn't sexual, but in every other way, becoming friends with her had been like falling in love. We'd admired each other from afar, and once we met, we plunged immediately into a world of intimacy that excluded everyone else. We talked about ideas more than anything, and everything Rima thought inspired me, because it seemed so instantaneously right and, also, just ahead of me.

At night, after we'd finished with our studies, Rima and I would read pamphlets to each other and remind ourselves that we didn't need anyone, not even each other. We said to ourselves that all we needed was the idea, and by the idea we would mean history. History was progressing and we were a part of it. Circumstances beyond us buoyed us up, and it was up to us to ride the wave. Loyalty, said the pamphlets, was weaker than Unity. Unity was shared belief. Loyalty was shared feeling. Belief was more important than feeling. Thinking that way helped us get over the constant, low-level hunger, helped us say that being hungry made life feel taut somehow, as though we were living right on the edge. We didn't know anything about how the world worked, but we were constantly trying to behave as if we did. Whereas before the Revolution people had been looking for something to believe in, now we'd found it. Nothing was easy, but we were too young to really think of deprivation as hard. We were making a new world. Tomorrow was going to be better. Living on food rations, having cold dirty water dribble from our taps, well, we were young enough to think of privation as a test. Proving to ourselves that we could survive it—without complaint!—was a way of saying we deserved the future. At least, that's how I saw it. Eventually, years later, Sasha would say to me that being hungry didn't make us better people, and I would respond, saying, Yes, yes it did.

In those years, I could push against the city and it would push back. The cats in the alleys screamed all night long. Rima was powerful. In some ways, Sasha was her opposite because his power wasn't performative; he could sit back and watch, a quiet king.

I went down the hall to call her, huddling myself in the small nook for the phone, because I'd gone in my nightdress on the assumption that our neighbours were working. The phone's distance from our apartment was normally an advantage since it meant we didn't hear the phone ring, nor did we hear the conversations that took place on the phone or around the phone as people fought about whose turn it was to use it. Just as I was hanging up, I saw Sasha coming up the stairs, a bag in hand.

Hello, sleepy, he said, his hand slipping under my dress and between my legs. How is my sleeper?

I smiled and scooted out of his reach.

He'd been to the store and come back to eat with me, and to hear more about the opening. In the kitchen, we lit the samovar to make a pot of tea, and when that was done, we brought the tea, the jam, the bread he'd been in line for since before dawn, and the smallest glob of butter to our apartment. We sat at our table, revelling in the luxury of fresh bread, the sun in our apartment and time together in the middle of the day, all of it feeling stolen, as precious as the clementines we'd suckled that night at the theatre so long ago.

Our conversation turned to the night before, and suddenly I was aware of competing desires within myself. Sasha's disdain for the institute was, by then, already so great that I despaired at the thought of admitting to him how little seemed to have been discovered by that ridiculous man from Germany. Yet that was the truth and rather than admit it to Sasha, I wanted to lie. Lying, however, would build a wall between us that I would then have to maintain. Telling the truth, on the other hand, would make me vulnerable, would make the institute vulnerable. As I looked at Sasha, I could see he was ready to accept that some great advance had been made, and so I began, slowly, with a description of the pyramidal cells, their great size, their great number. Sasha encouraged me, widening his eyes, looking impressed, and I felt a part of me soften, and that softening only served to highlight the resentment that had built up in me ever since he'd first voiced his suspicions about the work we did. But now he was listening closely. I went on, describing the ten thousand slices of Lenin's brain and the indigo stains, all of it amounting to an objective appraisal of genius, an appraisal that would be incontrovertible because it would be measurable in centimetres, percentages, and so on.

I got up from the table and moved to the couch, saying come over here, and Sasha followed, the two of us sitting at opposite ends, facing each other.

But is it obvious, he asked, that a centimetre more or less of this, or a percentage more or less of that means anything? How does this Vogt know that those centimetres mean more smarts and not something else, like a better capacity to detect tones in music or distinguish between flavours of horseradish, or even something else, like a tendency to good or to evil?

Well, Lenin wasn't a musician, I said.

But that isn't an answer, he said, and I knew he was right. I could feel a hollow right at the centre of the idea, a hollowness which was really a gap between one side of the thinking, about the measurements, and the other side of the thinking, about genius. Genius exceeded measurements, yes, but was also identifiable, recognizable, and unmistakably there in the life, work, and thoughts of certain individuals. So I described it that way, saying that we were crossing a chasm, building a bridge, but that like any bridge it had to be built in steps, and the steps were made of accumulated knowledge on one side and accumulated knowledge on the other, and one day, the two would meet in the middle. In this way, I invited Sasha into our vulnerability, into our great question about what final piece would connect one side to the other.

Sasha was quiet for a moment, taking this in. Then he said, with some admiration, that the project was tremendously ambitious, more ambitious than he'd realized, and I asked how so. And he said that the chasm we were trying to cross was the very thing that divides life from death. One side of the bridge depended on life and the other side depended on death. Wouldn't life have to reach into the world of death and death into the realm of life in order for the chasm to be breached?

And so he turned the conversation beautiful, as was his custom, and I followed him there into that world of philosophical questions, because although I believed in objective truths, in the idea of something being knowable, in this instance, and with Sasha who felt his way to things rather than thought his way to things, centimetres would never mean much. I crawled over to his end of the couch and opened his arms up to make space for me, him smiling and allowing his body to follow my orders, and I nestled in, pulling first one arm and then another around me, like a blanket, and said maybe one day the gap between death and life wouldn't seem so far after all. One day, he said, one day.

—⊬—

By early afternoon, Sasha had gone to work, and I had made it to Rima's and had convinced her to see, for the third time, the only film either of us had ever seen, *Bed and Sofa*. The cinema was in the city centre, right next to the café that served Moscow's best meringues. We got there in time for the afternoon screening, just as the sky was starting to darken. In the theatre, we found our past selves. The storyline when we were eighteen had been about the mysteries of falling in love. At twenty-one, when Rima was training to be a nurse and I was training to be a lab technician, it was about predicting the future. And on that afternoon in 1927, it was about the trials of communal living. After Rima and Yuri married, they moved into one of the buildings that housed party members, because Yuri was one. Sasha and I lived at a lower standard, though my scientific work granted us the right to a semi-regular food basket and some extra space. All the same, for all of us, life in the communal apartments was defined by one's relations with one's neighbours, and in every block, it seemed, there were the cheats, the liars, the tattlers. As we sat in the near-empty theatre, the two of us together again, reliving our earlier lives, I had suddenly had enough.

Let's leave, I whispered to Rima, during the iconic fortune-telling scene. Rima looked at me, the whites of her eyes bright and flickering.

Now? she asked.

Yes! I said, almost frantic with my desire to escape.

Okay, she said, away we go!

And so we stood, grabbed our bags and ran out, as if pursued, and in this way caught the last light of the day, such that possibility still seemed to reign.

When Rima and I got out onto the street, we made a rule, which was, Say yes to everything, and we proceeded that way for the evening, following her suggestions then mine, then eliciting suggestions from people we met on the street. She said yes to licking a pole. I said yes to a vodka. She said yes to a vodka. I said yes to reading the front page of *Pravda* aloud on a street corner. She said yes to asking a couple we saw whether or not they truly loved each other. I said yes to a vodka and then another. She said yes to a vodka and then another. I said yes to walking slowly along the river until I caught up with a man we'd seen, then slipping my hand into his as if I were his lover, and then walking that way for twenty seconds. (He played along.) She said yes to lying down in a park and telling me a story about a constellation. (She chose Cassiopeia, and the story made me cry.) I said yes to kissing her. She said yes to telling no one about it. I said yes, it was time to go home.

And so my day off ended the same way as the night before, with me walking home along Pirogovskaya sober enough to walk but drunk enough to be dreamy. I walked through the park, stepping on every leaf I could find so that I could make that crackly, autumnal sound, then saw Tobias again and sat with him to smoke one last cigarette. We talked a bit, though his conversation was hard to follow. Every morning he saw the newspaper boys, and by evening he had internalized the news so deeply that the news pieces were about him or about those closest to him. By then I'd gotten used to the way the stories transformed, so

I could listen to him as though he were a radio on the fritz, some of the story coming through as static and some of it clear as a bell. On that night, books written by his father had fallen into the category of ideologically harmful literature and been banned from the union's libraries. I took this in and wondered if we'd miss his father's contributions. After we finished our cigarettes, I crossed the street to our apartment building and whispered, Sasha! Sasha!

The wind gusted through the trees louder than I could whisper, and so I found a pebble and tossed it up.

It would have been disappointing to have come to the other side of the opening the way we did—with all the attention focused on Vogt and the German part of our German-Russian alliance—if the next big thing hadn't been on the horizon. As it was, the opening ended and all of our energy turned to preparations for the first All-Union Congress of Neurologists and Psychiatrists. It was slated for December, and it was there that Bekhterev would present his version of the institute's findings. As far as he was concerned, it was all that mattered, given that it was for an audience of scientists and specialists and not a spectacle put on to please the politburo, the reporters, and the pseudo-intellectuals. So we let the *Pravda* reporters come back to take a photograph of Vogt at a desk they called *his* and didn't get worked up when *Der Spiegel* named him the lead scientist. When the *New York Times* ran a short piece on Bekhterev, I served tea, a quiet insider. I felt caught between wanting to rise above the whims of the reporters, as Bekhterev had, and a persistent desire to have my own photograph taken, my own name jotted down.

But that wasn't how we talked. About *mine* or *his*.

One thing all the reporters got wrong had to do with the building: they wrote about our institute as if it were the only thing happening there. They didn't know about Bogdanov's Institute of Blood Transfusion. Our institute had a public presence and occupied the grand rooms at the front. Bogdanov's institute was tucked away in the back, hidden, but it wasn't small.

By December 1927, the institute of Blood Transfusion had a ten-bed clinic, a laboratory for blood typing, and its own operating room. At first I didn't know how to talk to Bogdanov because he seemed more legend than person — fearless bank robber, free thinker, revolutionary writer — and I didn't know how to place him because he'd once been an enemy of the state and was now considered a friend. Meanwhile, I was just me. But the more I knew about his research, the more I realized I had something he wanted. I had youth.

Just tell him some of your ideas, said Sasha.

But I didn't really have ideas *per se*. I just wanted to be involved. The ideas would come later.

Well, then talk to him, said Sasha. Say you're interested in what he's doing.

I'd done this before, with Bekhterev, but that was easier because I was his student and he already knew something of me. He knew my work, which he called *meticulous*. Bekhterev wasn't like the university professors because he was in the realm of scientists that existed above all that. He didn't need to know all about my politics, and I didn't need to know his. All he had been worried about was having a competent Moscow team that he could trust; some of *his* students to balance out *Vogt's*.

In the end, Bogdanov addressed me first. We were in the kitchen, which was the only space the two institutes shared, and we were waiting for the kettle to boil.

What do you do here? he asked.

We hadn't actually settled on a specific title for me and I was nervous, so I said a title I'd heard Sasha use that seemed fitting for the way I helped the institute make science public.

I'm a curator.

Don't you work here?

Well, I'm a lab technician, too. I meant I was a curator here.

I like that, he said, a curator-technician.

I liked it, too.

I'm a writer-scientist, he said.

It was always so endearing when someone like Bogdanov introduced himself, as if he weren't already known by everyone. Yet there was being known and knowing someone, and those two things were different; the first seemed to block entry to the second. I knew he was a writer, I knew he had been a revolutionary and had broken with the Bolsheviks, and I knew that he'd somehow come to his institute in what I assumed was something like how we'd come to our institute, but as I pondered it more I realized that I didn't quite know how even that had happened. Somehow, knowing the barest outline of a thing was almost worse than knowing nothing. If you knew the barest outline, you knew the answers to the questions that were easiest to formulate: when did you start work here? Where were you born? What is your name? Awful, almost bureaucratic questions, but without those questions as a bridge, the deeper questions seemed out of bounds. This was worse if you'd happened to have forgotten a basic answer, like a person's name. Asking again would declare that we were strangers, just as we were becoming friends. Not that I'd forgotten his name.

As I was tangling myself up in thoughts of what I could or could not ask, he plunged in, asking how I got into this business, by which he meant science, and somehow I found myself telling him about my father, about the dignity he'd had and the way he'd made science seem like the most noble thing one could study.

You miss him, he observed.

Yes.

And your mother?

I'd admired her, but she was an angry woman.

They saw things differently.

Very differently.

Bogdanov said he knew a thing about shifting allegiances. What he'd discovered since his break with Lenin and his abandonment of active political commitments was nothing less than the secret to human rejuvenation. From the early 1920s on, he had been meeting with a few close friends he called his brothers in blood exchanges. He called these meetings gatherings of the organization of physiological collectivism. They met at a friend's apartment, and initially, the group was a study group, nothing more. Bogdanov had a hunch that blood exchanges—the comradely exchange of life, he called it—would increase an organism's vitality. He dreamed of direct, simultaneous, and mutual transfusion of blood between two individuals of the same species. Several apparatuses would be needed, so that the individuals' corresponding veins could be linked. Young blood would infuse the aging with vitality; old blood would share experience by way of its advanced immune system. For years, his inquiry was purely theoretical.

He leaned back against the sink. I'd taken a seat at the table. It had become common for some people to talk about themselves as if they'd been reborn with the Revolution—they'd say, I'm forty-five years old, but I've only been alive for ten—but Bogdanov was interested in rebirth for real.

By 1925 he had successfully completed five blood exchanges, all involving himself. The first attempt had taken place just two weeks after Lenin died. The exchange was meant to occur between Bogdanov and a student of his — a twenty-year-old male.

My companion — that was the student — and I had hoped to exchange 330 cubic millilitres of blood, but something failed. I got the 330 cubic millilitres, but he got nothing.

He must have been so depleted, I said, feeling faint myself as I thought about losing all that blood. The kettle was about to boil.

He was strong. If it had been the reverse, mind you, that might have been dangerous.

So a blood transfusion but not a blood exchange.

Exactly. A week later, we tried again. Again, transfusion instead of exchange. Bogdanov shrugged, a gesture that seemed to say that this was the way things worked sometimes, nothing to be done about it. Three months later, they tried it all again. It worked. The student received five hundred cubic millilitres; Bogdanov received seven hundred. In the months following, Bogdanov's health, which had been ailing, improved. Dramatically. Then his wife joined in. By the end of that year, everyone agreed: Bogdanov and his wife looked younger if not by ten, then by seven or five years. Increased muscle tone! Expanded lung capacity!

I stood up to face him, trying to evaluate his age without appearing to try to evaluate his age. I guessed late forties, then took the kettle off the stove to make the tea.

I'm fifty-four, he said, smiling at the surprise I failed to hide.

How he'd come to have keys to the Igumnov mansion had to do with something that happened in late 1925, when one of the top Soviet leaders had fallen seriously ill. His name was Leonid Krasin, and he was suffering from anemia. Krasin and Bogdanov were old friends—that bank robbery I'd heard Bogdanov talking about at the opening? He'd robbed it with Krasin. And Lenin. That was before they fell out.

Prior to 1925, then, all of Bogdanov's investigations into blood exchanges had been kept quiet.

If I know one thing, said Bogdanov, it's how to run a clandestine operation.

He gave me a wink.

So when Krasin fell ill, he turned to Bogdanov for help.

Please, said Krasin.

We didn't want anyone to know what we were up to. This was experimental medicine. No one likes experiments.

I gave him a look.

People think they like experimentation, but they don't; they only like successful experimentation. We were prepared for failure.

Bogdanov told Krasin to go to London or Paris or even Berlin because that was where the science of blood was best.

But Krasin was insistent; he knew he wouldn't survive the trip. Bogdanov thought it over. He consulted his transfusion bible, as he called it, and decided he could do it. Krasin was fading. They found a donor who was a match and harvested seven hundred to eight hundred cubic millilitres from him. Krasin's health improved dramatically. It was a miracle. Krasin went on vacation and that December, Bogdanov was summoned to the Kremlin.

As it turned out, Krasin's illness and his miraculous recovery put Bogdanov in the spotlight. This was because over at the Kremlin, an epidemic had hit: heart attacks, ulcers, and nervous disorders. The Soviet elite were burning out. They were dying young. The Party doctors called it revolutionary exhaustion. It was worse than tuberculosis. I'd read about it in *Pravda* and heard about it on the radio.

Stalin said, We are suffering an epidemic.

Trotsky said, Our leading workers must have individual physicians responsible for their health. Not another preventable death!

An army of professionals were brought in to care for the array of strange illnesses that had so suddenly cropped up. The effort was another kind of grief. Beneath the health passports and the individual physicians, the sleeping institutes and the green spaces, what they were thinking was this: if we had taken better care, wouldn't Lenin still be alive? If they didn't deal with the health crisis now, the Revolution would crumble not because of external opposition, but because of a few persistent fevers and too many strange cancers. All these ailments were signs of a broader sickness: the revolutionary effort was flagging. A country's history flows like a river whose path — the bends, the narrows, the rapids, and the stretches of calm — is one of the great constants, unchanging even when everything else does. Floods or landslides might violently and momentarily disrupt its route, but, over time, a return to the old path is practically inevitable. That the country wanted to return to the old ways revealed itself in workers' protests, industrial sabotage, and Trotsky's incessant criticism. Disloyal comrades had exhausted the Soviet elite, making them reckless, making them sick. Revolutionaries always think that the beginning is what matters, that momentum will build following the revolutionary moment, but it isn't so. The Soviet elite were embarrassed by the critics, the terrorists, and the wreckers. No, they were more than embarrassed. Those people, the people the Revolution had fought for, were threatening to wreck it from within. They were the cancers; they were the parasites. Dealing with the fevers and the ulcers was a temporary solution, but a larger solution would need to address the root causes.

As for Bogdanov, he wasn't interested in the river; that is, he didn't give a shit if the country went back to the violent old ways of the Tzar or moved on to the violent new ways of the new leadership. He just wanted a place to continue his research.

All this to say that when Bogdanov left the Kremlin, he had been made Director of the Institute of Blood Transfusion. It helped that he'd been Lenin's main opponent before Lenin led the Party, because the tides were shifting: Lenin was becoming the past and Stalin was becoming the future. Bogdanov had disagreed with Lenin on the question of the lumpenproletariat. He'd wanted to create an intellectual nucleus of workers and wanted them to receive the education they would need for them to be informed and active leaders rather than just ignorant workers. But, according to Bogdanov, Lenin preferred to leave them in their ignorance.

Why would you say that? I asked, pouring us both a cup of tea.

Because Lenin never really believed in the people. All that talk, said Bogdanov, but he was an elitist to the end.

In March 1926 he got keys to the mansion, and started to set up shop. He began by hiring his brothers in blood exchanges.

This was how the world changed, I thought. People took risks.

Maybe if you ever need someone for your experiments, I said, my heart beating a little faster, you could ask me.

Maybe, he said, taking a sip of tea. Maybe.

He settled his cup on his saucer, topped up his tea, and then headed off down the hall. Visit us when you'd like, he said over his shoulder. I started to think of our two institutes as complementary. Bogdanov was keeping our heroes alive, and we were studying them once they were dead. How appropriate, then, that the two institutes would share a building.

—/—

As for our Institute, once we'd gotten past the opening—that is, once we made the awkward transition from the private workings of research to the public display of discovery—the need to attend to both the public and private aspects of the institute forced us all into different duties. Visiting hours were irregular because we didn't always have enough workers to place someone at the front. On most days, we averaged not more than fifteen or twenty visitors, unless a school group or worker's club brought the numbers up.

On those days, Sergei shepherded the worker's clubs around the semicircle of exhibits, entertaining them with anecdotes from the figure's life, always placing emphasis on the political heroism of each. Anushka took care of the school groups, carefully pointing out visible attributes of the brains that even children could identify. She provided the children with pencils and paper so that they could draw on the floor beneath the exhibits. Over time, we acquired a collection of plastic letters that we could pull out when they arrived. This way, the children could remove their boots and have them labelled according to the letter that began their name, as they were accustomed to at school. Children always left things behind, though. Chewed-up pencils, dirt, fingerprints. Afterwards, Sergei would dust the exhibits, buff their metal bases, and wipe all the glass, in a never-ending effort to remove their marks. The point of the space was that it be clean, scientific, and timeless, but every visitor, no matter how old, sullied it. Anushka wanted every child who visited the institute to be inspired. Zhanna, on the rare occasions when she interacted with the children, only wanted them to behave. Children, stop! Children, sit still! she'd yell at them in a shrill voice reserved just for them.

The wall of mirrors created a physical divide between the two sides of the institute. Approaching that wall, I often caught myself off guard. I could see the mirrors from everywhere in the room, and they gave the impression that the room was larger, that there were more exhibits on display, twice as many. But the mirrors lay in the dark, which meant even though they perfectly mirrored the exhibits, they did so from an unfamiliar side, the dark side. When one walked across the grand salon, then, one walked from the warm light of the chandelier past the glowing light of the exhibits towards the pools of dark that lay behind them. One needed to walk through the dark to get to the mirrors, and so, whenever one did, one became silhouetted against the brightness of the background, which was the foreground. I sometimes got caught off guard by my silhouette, by its indistinct shape, the prototypical shape of a woman, any woman, not me.

Though there were many lessons to learn by comparing the structure of a musician's brain with a scientist's, I never once saw a visitor view the brains in anything other than the order specified.

Except for Sasha, who never did anything in the order specified.

Sasha said that the beauty of the institute's collection was its repetition. Back then, he rarely came to visit, and then only when he knew everyone else would be gone. He didn't believe in what we were doing, but he didn't want to fight about it with anyone but me. It's so hypocritical, he'd say. It's scientific, I'd say. Where is the science? he'd ask, and I'd walk away because I'd already explained it a thousand times. Sometimes I thought it would just take time.

That, as with people, Sasha needed to hate the place for a while, piss on it in a way, and then he'd come around and see it the way I saw it, which was basically how Bekhterev saw it: as one of the remaining places one could, in the modern world, come to sit in the presence of genius. What Bekhterev meant wasn't only that the institute was providing something important but also that the universities no longer were. Group examinations? Bekhterev had asked derisively, after hearing about the education reforms. On this point I was wrong about Sasha. He didn't believe in geniuses, he said, or at least, if such a thing as genius did exist, these guys weren't examples of it. But he did believe in transcendence and suggested that maybe genius was simply our word for that.

Anushka often brought the children's drawings back into the kitchen. She would tack them to the wall above the sink — it was the only one without cabinets — and they would stay there until the wet seeped into them, making the images rot away into indistinct shadows and not constructivist-like recordings of the architectonics of the brain.

When the general public started to visit more and more regularly, I worked in the back. Much of what Bekhterev had collected over the years would be put on display one day, but in the meantime, it had to be stored in the back rooms. Organizing it was solitary work, but I was happy, deeply involved in the details required by the paperwork and the care of preparing the glass jars for their specimens. I loved the wavy thick vapour of the chemicals I used for cleaning, how they shimmered as if in a haze of heat. I loved the way the catalogue accumulated, specimen by specimen, line by line.

Each item required its own jar and its own kind of display. The bones of the wrist, for example, needed a small platform and tiny pins. Sometimes glue. The bones themselves needed to be prepared with a lacquer. Once I had placed the platform in the jar, I would use tweezers to arrange the bones, which, with glue already on them, had to be placed quickly in order for them to fuse together. On the jar I would write the type of bones, *human wrist*, the name and age of the donor, *Victor Oshanko, age forty-three*, his profession, *baker, thief*, the date of the donation, *November 1927*, and, written in red ink, a catalogue number. Then, in the book, the corresponding information.

Later I had a typewriter equipped with a specialized ribbon, the top half was black and the bottom half was red, for this task. Sometimes I dyed the specimens with indigo dyes we imported from Berlin. Once, in the laboratory, the tiniest drop escaped the dropper. I cleaned it up without removing my wedding ring. Later, when my finger was itching, I removed the band to find a deep purple circle around my ring finger, as if I'd been permanently bruised in just that spot. I always removed my ring after that. Throughout November and December, I spent my days this way.

All that time, I was wishing I were older. It was on my mind that if I'd been born just a few years earlier, I would have been a real revolutionary instead of someone who came around after the fact. Bekhterev was at his desk, hunched over a book, pencil in hand. I had brought him a cup of tea.

When I appeared in the doorway, he laid his hand across his book and put down his pencil.

Were you there in 1917? I asked.

I'd been asking Bekhterev about his life for weeks then, and now it seemed like the conversation we were having never ended, just paused for a while. Sasha always said that the people he liked best were the old guys who'd seen everything, and I was starting to see what he meant. Sometimes you could see the young man in the eyes of the old.

Bekhterev smiled, Where?

In Leningrad.

Yes to 1917, and yes to 1905.

What was it like? I asked.

I saw a moment of impatience flash across his face, and then he flipped the book over so he wouldn't lose his place.

I set his tea on his desk and sat down.

It was war, he said. And on both fronts, at least in 1917 it was like that. And we'd just had Nikolai. And I'd taken over at the ministry. So there were many demands.

But did you believe in the Revolution?

Yes, he said, bringing the cup closer. Of course I did. Of course I do.

But did you believe in the materialist idea of history? Have you read Marx and do you agree that a proletariat revolution was inevitable?

What is the title of my last book, Tatiana?

I had to think about it for a moment. It was called *Something, Something, and Marxism* but I couldn't remember the somethings.

What I am sure of, he said carefully, is that there is such a thing as a conditioned reflex, and that there is such a thing as mental disorder, and that this new materialism adds to, rather than obliterates, our other modes of inquiry, so that now, in addition to hypnosis and psychology, we have neurological surgery and the possibility of intervening in the material substrate of our consciousness. And yes, perhaps this is best understood as a sort of materialism.

Yes, I thought, the institute was part of the new history.

He turned back to his book then and resumed reading

as if nothing had come between the page he'd finished and the next. It absorbed him entirely, so that I could look at him and never risk him noticing my gaze.

I might participate in one of Bogdanov's transfusions.

That got his attention.

Absolutely not.

Why not?

Because, said Bekhterev, standing up, what Bogdanov does is not science.

Bogdanov wasn't a scientist, according to Bekhterev. But he was a scientist according to *someone*. The People's Commissar for Health thought he was a scientist because Stalin thought he was a scientist. And Stalin took it from Krasin.

It's not science, said Bekhterev again, as if reading my thoughts.

—/—

Luria often passed by mid-afternoon. He always said he was looking for Bekhterev. Inevitably, he found only me. Bekhterev spent afternoons at the hospital, but Luria didn't know, and I didn't tell him. By mid-afternoon, I always wanted a break, so I would walk with him out into the city on one errand or another. Bekhterev was hoping to increase the collection and so, on one of those days, I decided to get us some stationery for the letters we would write to the families of those recently deceased.

The first afternoon Luria came by, I'd thought to turn him away, but then found myself suggesting we walk. I was curious. Curious about him, but also curious about why he made me feel so sick inside; excited but also like I might vomit at any moment. He talked so fast.

What he was trying to get to, he told me, was an understanding of people's motivations. What brings people to love, to hate, to involve themselves in activities in the street, or to hide away behind books or in the darkness of theatres.

Do you ever surprise yourself? he asked me.

Asking him to walk with me on a Tuesday afternoon in early November 1927 was a moment I surprised myself, but I didn't say that.

There was the time Rima and I met Marko, I said, trailing off.

Luria stopped me, saying he wanted to know who Rima was, how long had we known each other, and why were we friends. I had to think about it, really think about it, because no one had ever asked me such questions before.

I guess because whenever I'm with Rima, I can meet someone like Marko.

Okay, so, Marko then. Who was he?

Ultimately, no one, I guess, but that night he was someone, because he was the first bad person I'd ever met. It was early in the summer; the sun had just set. Rima and I had been sitting by the riverbank all afternoon, and I think we were starting to get bored. Marko seemed to appear out of nowhere. You know those trees down there, how their branches hang so low?

Luria nodded.

Anyway, he told us he'd just gotten out of prison, and I think because he told us, unsolicited, just like that, we trusted him and we asked how long he'd been in. Five years, he said, and Rima asked, What were you in prison for? and he said, Scrapping, and Rima said, Must have been some kind of scrap, and he said, Yeah. We stayed out with him until dawn, drinking and walking and telling stories, and when the sun rose, he left, just like that.

I didn't tell Luria that I let Marko kiss me, nor that Rima did, too.

What surprised you about this? asked Luria.

I thought we were more careful than that. We were only eighteen. He could have been dangerous.

Were you wrong about Marko? asked Luria. Was he dangerous?

Yes, but not to us.

So you were right about him, and you were curious.

Yes, I said, pleased because it explained the *fact* of both the evening and the kiss.

We made our way to the stationer's after that. The cost of paper had gone up, which meant I had to resort to the poorest quality. I argued with the lady over the price, but she wouldn't budge, and so I only bought a small package of twenty-five sheets. I could have bought more but didn't think she deserved it.

November progressed in this way. My mornings were taken up with cataloguing the human specimens, my afternoons with errands outside of the institute, after which I would return to help Bekhterev prepare for the talks at Congress. It was on those errands, often in the company of Luria, that I noticed how daily life was becoming more difficult. Everything took more time than it had. Buying bread could mean being in line for hours. Beating the system meant getting up earlier and earlier, but there was no way to beat the system, not really, since everyone else got up earlier, too. All the same, I saw it as a brave and visionary time.

—⊬—

Despite Bekhterev's dismissal of it, Bogdanov's institute looked like real science to me.

It must have been early December when I found myself wandering down the hall towards the blood institute. It was early enough in the morning that I'd come to work when the sun was just making its way back into the world and the institute seemed empty.

I knocked on their door and when no one answered, I walked in. All was silent as I made my way down the hall to the waiting room, then into another corridor and then to the other side where I found the ten-bed room, and lying on top of one of the beds in the middle of the room was Bogdanov, dressed in a hospital gown, his eyes closed so peacefully he looked as if he were dead. The gown made him look especially vulnerable, but then he had a certain vulnerability about him always, something that suggested innocence, or hope, which is a kind of innocence.

The upper section of his bed had been slightly raised. All the colour had drained from his face. Even his skin looked tired.

I should have left, but I wanted to look at him, to be alone with him. I shut the door gently behind me and approached him. At the click of the latch, his eyes slowly opened. His pupils were the biggest and blackest I'd ever seen on anyone, but they slowly contracted.

Hello to the curator-technician, he said, his speech slowed. Time was ticking by at a different rate for him than it was for me.

Hello, I said.

If you'd been here just an hour earlier, he said, you would have caught us making love.

Excuse me?

He smiled and said, I mean we just had our tenth successful transfusion. Oleg is asleep in the back room, but I like the light from here, don't you?

The room had a small window that faced south. The sun had come up, its pink lighting up the frost on the window, the top of which was starting to melt away.

How much blood? I asked.

Eight hundred cubic millilitres. It's about one-seventh of my total volume. Our most yet.

I looked around the room for evidence of the exchange, but everything had been cleaned. On a counter by the door lay a series of freshly washed tubes, scalpels, and metal trays. I turned back to face Bogdanov.

Aren't you tired? I mean, you must be.

This is the hump, he said. The body reacts this way as it tries to incorporate the new blood.

He lifted his arm ever so slightly so I could see the bandages.

The top one is where the blood came in. The bottom is where it went out. He shut his eyes in a blink that went on too long.

Should I leave? I asked.

Oh no, no. Stay and keep me company.

How long will it take to recover?

About a week or two. Then you'll see. You'll see how rejuvenating it is. How good for the mind.

He was tired but lucid.

You following Frenkel? he asked.

Sorry?

Do you have time to read? You should make time. You have to know something about freedom, said Bogdanov. Frenkel talks a lot about freedom. When do you feel most free?

When I am alone?

Think of it this way, he said. You are your most free with people. That is when real exchange happens. That is when you can be emancipated from yourself. Why hold on to yourself? Why stay stuck in the trap of your own consciousness when you could escape yourself like electrons do, skipping from you to him to you to her to you to him? Frenkel said molecules, atoms, and electrons are microscopic inhabitants of the animate universe. Atoms experience a collectivist freedom. Like land plots that pass from one owner to another, Tatiana. Or, in the end, that have no owners at all. Electrons pass from one atom to the next in a chain. This one, then that one, then the next. Forever. It's so beautiful, don't you think? That's freedom. Collective excitations he calls it.

He closed his eyes again. I wondered about that, about what it would feel like to think I was my most free with people. Bogdanov described freedom as action and exchange, but acting and exchanging was when I felt my *least* free.

His head dipped to one side. I looked towards the window, looked for the light he liked so much, but the sun had clouded over.

I don't know why he talks like that, said a voice from behind me.

I turned, and there was his wife, standing in the doorway.

Like what?

About freedom as if it had something to do with atoms. It's some kind of psychological trick he's playing on himself. Trying to get himself to forget that he's seen the inside of Lubyanka.

She stepped into the room and leaned against the counter, appraising me. You didn't know that, did you?

I guess it was clear from my face that I didn't.

For two months. It terrified him. He almost died in there. They knew he was innocent, but bureaucracy, you know — it's terrible even there. I think they forgot about him. He got so stressed he had a heart attack. If it weren't for these transfusions, I think he'd be dead.

I didn't know, I said. What did they accuse him of?

I guess they'd have called it treason or apostasy. It was because his philosophical writings had garnered some attention, especially from an opposition group called Workers' Truth. You know of them?

No, I said.

He didn't either, she said, pushing herself away from the counter to approach me.

I'm Nataliaa, she said. Nataliaa Bogdanovna Korsak.

He took your name? I whispered.

She smiled. Yes.

That the two of them were getting younger as they aged showed up not just in their heart rates and skin tone. They *thought* young, too. Youth explained the difference between how Bekhterev and Bogdanov ran their institutes. Even if they shared the building, their approaches couldn't have been more different.

—⁄—

As we got closer and closer to Congress, Bekhterev and I started staying at the institute much later. I was photographing sections of slides that Bekhterev would use in his talk. He'd say, What can you get me that shows the occipital fold, and I would go through our files and look in the drawers of the exhibits until I found the perfect image, or I'd find the right specimen and take its photograph. On one of those evenings, when we had stayed too late to be productive but were too energized to go to sleep, we went out for a drink. He walked quickly, so that even though we had no set destination, he was always just ahead of me, no matter how hard I tried to catch up. Blackbirds flying overhead signalled our proximity to the river.

When the wind began to gust and the birds disappeared into the darkening sky, we stopped in a bar. It was late, and the room was near empty. We sat at a table from which we could see the river. Perhaps it was the walking or perhaps I had mentioned Berlin by way of Dr. Vogt's findings, but one thing or another led to Bekhterev recalling a time he walked through the streets of that city. It was before the cities were overrun with cars, as they are now, he said. He was walking with a woman, a mathematician named Sofia K— and her friend, a man whose position had become suddenly precarious in Germany, as he was French and the war had broken out. The story unfolded with remarkable precision. I had the feeling that Bekhterev had allowed me into the hidden recesses of his mind so that I might see all of its working parts and some of its hidden hopes, too.

The Frenchman had once been the director of the International Bureau of Weights and Measures and had thus been a key figure at Breteuil on 28 September 1889 for the deposition of the metre and the kilogram — referred to thereafter as the international prototypes M and K—in a secret vault that concluded an underground network of rooms. The series of rooms was strung like a chain of pearls beneath the surface of the earth, each room lay deeper than the one previous, each door locked with a key unlike the last, so that access to the deepest room at the end of the series required not one key, but seven. It was there, in the final room, that the vaults and the Universal Comparator (which had been used to cut the metre to a previously unimagined precision) were to be found. What had led to this achievement was the critical capacity of a single man, a chemist named Monsieur André Dumas, who had determined that the revolutionary metre, conceived of at the height of the Jacobins' Reign of Terror, was neither strong enough nor sufficiently invariable to serve as the prototype for the world's measures. Further to that, the revolutionary metre was based upon a fantastical ratio that imagined the length of the metre to be the equivalent of one ten-millionth of the distance between Paris and the North Pole or one ten-millionth of a quarter of the earth's circumference—Bekhterev couldn't remember which—but in any case it was a measurement that we could not deign to approximate in 1889, a century after its creation, nor even now, in this modern age. His eyes glistened, and I could not tell if they watered from sentimentality or the weariness of age, or both.

Monsieur André Dumas proclaimed that the modern metre escaped the romanticism of the revolutionary metre; it was, he said, *neutral, decimal, international.* According to the Frenchman's description, the international prototypes M and K were ceremoniously laid upon beds of red velvet after which the metres were sheathed in protective tubes and the kilograms nestled under three glass bell jars, each slightly larger than the one before. With the layering of the bell jars, the gleam of light they reflected got ever brighter, and by the third jar, the dark figure of the kilogram beneath them was lost as though it were, already, a relic of a lost age of certainty. This was the last the Frenchman saw of the original international prototypes.

After that they were encased in large brass cylinders, and nobody has seen them since. The Frenchman did say the originals were buried alongside six witnesses, six identical international prototypes, and it was against these witnesses that a further thirty standard bars were measured, one bar being produced for each of the international delegates in attendance. Once the international prototypes had been laid in their vault, the Frenchman was handed the two keys needed to lock the brass cylinders, then a third to bolt the inner basement door, and then a fourth, fifth, sixth, and seventh for locks on the subsequent doors, each of which was handed to him in a separate sealed envelope and which, upon its use, was taken by a deputy to be dispersed among three of them—the Frenchman himself, as Director of the International Weights and

Measures, and two other men, the General Guard of the National Archives and the President of the International Committee, thus ensuring those rooms would never again be opened but in the presence of all three.

Remarkably, said Bekhterev, the very same technology used to cut the metre to a precision never before imaginable is now used by neurologists to microtome the brain. That night in Berlin, he said, was darker than any I've since experienced, due to the blackout blinds mandated in wartime, but as in Moscow in that very moment, nothing could be done to prevent the river from reflecting the stars.

What a truly sad story, I said.

Why? said Bekhterev.

But I couldn't say why, exactly. I sat there, looking out at the black river and the even blacker city, and could not shake the feeling that the weights and measures hadn't been protected; they had been buried alive. My mind's eye stepped down into those secret vaults and opened each subsequent room and left each door behind me open so that something of the surface — sounds, breezes — could penetrate those hidden chambers in a way akin to rescue.

It seemed to me then, as it does now, that Bekhterev knew something he could not tell me. What else could explain his lamentable emphasis on that lost age of certainty? Perhaps I am reading too deeply — loss has a tendency to colour things, as we know — but it occurs to me now that Bekhterev wanted me to know just how much we stood to lose. Perhaps he wanted me to know that there was something I needed to protect, to store, as it were, in a hidden repository where no single soul held every single key. But what was it that needed my protection? Bekhterev, for all his wisdom and brilliance, was not a political creature, so he could not have foreseen what would happen to him, for if he could have, surely he would have tried to prevent it.

Sasha was like me in that, upon finishing his studies, he'd started working for one of his professors. By the end of 1927, he'd been working for Rodchenko for over three years at his studio in the centre of the city; only they didn't call it a studio, they called it a workshop. Rodchenko was one of the first artists hired on to teach at the art school that had been founded by Lenin in 1920. Sasha had studied there, almost since the start. If he'd had a choice, he would have gone to the traditional school, but as it no longer existed, it was Lenin's school or nothing.

I'd heard about the school and Rodchenko even before I met Sasha because of Osorgin's. Rodchenko was one of the artists who'd appeared on the blackboard. His line drawings were roughly replicated there, along with his philosophy: *Both in painting and in any construction in general, line is the first and last thing. Line is the path of advancement, it is movement, collision, it is facetation, conjunction, combination.* Rodchenko used the term *architectonics* to describe his approach to form, and I liked that because it was a word Bekhterev used, too. The architectonics of the brain, the architectonics of art — once again, art and science were one. When I first met Sasha and his friends, I had an idea that I would belong because of that word, but Rodchenko wasn't popular. His counterpoint in my world wasn't Bekhterev, but Bogdanov. Unpopular, but hand-picked by the Kremlin.

At Osorgin's, books had gotten pulled off the shelves and held up as evidence that Rodchenko's work was destructive, the speaker shaking the book on high, quoting a memorized passage, and then throwing it down on the table, as if the idea were a weight whose import had to be heard in the way it thudded, book on table. The revolutionary aesthetic rejected the old idea of art for art's sake and replaced it with the idea of art as production. This was Lenin's *actual* idea—that art should be useful as opposed to beautifully, defiantly useless.

Sasha thought everything about the school was absurd. Absurd that a politician would dictate to artists, absurd that art would be subject to a controlling idea, absurd that the controlling idea would reject all the old masters and all the old media. But he'd had no choice, and he wasn't alone. For most of the years that he studied there, the majority of the students continued in the pre-revolutionary arts, which meant they were painters and sculptors, and the most exquisite thing was still the human form and how it eluded all attempts to represent it.

Only those studying under Rodchenko joined the Metalwork Factory, and they came to be known as the MetFak cadre. For a long time, the MetFak cadre was the object of ridicule for all the rest, since Rodchenko's dream of the artist-craftsman or the artist-constructor had little obvious practicality for anyone in the arts, or not. At MetFak, the students produced revolutionary products rather than *objets d'art*. By 1922 Rodchenko had declared that painting was dead. This was a war cry. Art for art's sake was a bourgeois preoccupation, he said. When Sasha and his friends talked about Rodchenko, they made fun of his aviator outfits and his portraits of his mother. Mama, mama! they'd said. Nevertheless, for all their criticism, every last one of them worked for him. MetFak provided jobs, and with that, the MetFak cadre stopped being ridiculed. Colouring, Sasha had called it. So that was where our similarity ended:

although we both worked for our former professors, Sasha hated his.

When I first fell in love with Sasha, I'd imagined that our coming together would bring our separate worlds together, too. Instead, Sasha asked his brusque questions of my professors and I hung back with his friends, always watching, rarely daring to say anything at all. Sasha's friends talked about art: the sublime, the lines, the depth of the black acrylics they'd gotten imported from France, and so on. Because I had nothing to say about colour — black was just black to me — I couldn't participate in these conversations. But I observed them intently.

If they weren't talking about art, they were talking about "the game." At parties, Sasha, Jack, and Elisa, a friend of theirs I despised, would pile on top of one another — three of them, sitting on one single armchair! — and they'd watch everyone else at the party to decide who played and who didn't. When they were playing the game, they adopted a singular look of disdain, looking everyone else up and down. In the summer, Elisa wore dresses that did not fit and no undergarments. When she leaned forward, which she did often, you could see the little points of her breasts trying to hide themselves in the cloth of her gaping dress. In winter, she wore stockings. I still don't know how she got them. She had long black hair and hardly ever spoke. When she did speak, it wasn't to me. I thought all the men were in love with her. She was that kind of beautiful.

Sasha said I didn't play the game. He said that was why he loved me. He and Jack did play the game, and, it seemed, so did every other person they wanted to fuck. He never explained it to me, but I figured it out. It was about desire. It was about being able to enter a room and make everyone there want you. It was about believing you could do that. Believing they (whoever *they* were) wanted you. And then it was about how they couldn't have you, no matter how hard they tried.

I play the game, I said.

No you don't, said Jack.

—✳—

As 1927 wound down, I continued my work at the institute, while Sasha was at the workshop. Jack called us the proto-typical Soviet couple, which made us laugh. Winter was in its first stage, which was more absence than presence: bare trees, clean streets, a cold that seemed more like a lack of warmth than the thing it would become, a cold that could give you frostbite or freeze you to death. Winter never felt real to me until it became something: snow piled up high and icicles so heavy and sharp that they threatened anyone who stood below.

Sasha had been working on a new piece he wanted me to see. Having left school, he no longer had his own studio, and though a friend had let him keep some stuff at the old studio, it was just a place we went socially now, not somewhere he could work. These days he stayed late at his job, and when the workday was over, he'd start drawing again.

On this night, I'd come by after work. I'd come to the workshop before, but it was only recently that he'd started painting again, and he was showing it to me for the first time.

It's just a sketch, he was saying to me as we walked down the hall towards the end of the workshop.

I'm not proud of it, I mean it's not finished, so don't think of it in your critical way, because it's not ready for that but I thought you might like to see the process because all art begins somewhere — even if this won't actually be art — every idea begins with a sketch, you know? I mean I'm not looking for criticism or anything, so don't be critical.

He looked over his shoulder at me, holding the door open.

I didn't know I had a critical way.

The workshop had everything any other workspace would have, except that each object—the chair, the table, the hanging light, the vase of flowers—was supposed to be both useful and a piece of art. Here a chair was a lined, triangle thing. Instead of four legs, a triangular prism supported the seat, and instead of a simple wooden seat and back, both were made of metal and painted with a thick black line running through the centre, something which made it look two dimensional even as it was obviously a three-dimensional object sitting right before me. Every shape was something even I could draw. Triangles, cylinders, squares. The human figure was reduced to geometry too, even in the photographs that hung on the walls.

This is Rodchenko's? I asked, referring to a photograph of an older woman, her face cast in deep shadow, but Sasha had gone ahead.

Are you coming? he called from the other side of the workshop, peering out from behind a bunch of wood boards stacked against each other. Hanging from nails were what looked like carpenter's tools, cut-outs of circles, squares, and triangles of varying sizes.

This place is kind of—

I followed him behind the stack of wood, around the corner to where there was a small workspace I recognized as his. He wasn't methodical like I was. Not orderly. I would have placed all of my pens in one place, and at the end of the day would have squared up my papers, bookmarked my books. But his materials all lay on top of each other—books opened and placed like flattened tents, one on top of the other, pens and pencils everywhere.

Sterile? said Sasha. He clicked on a light and twisted its

head so that its bright beam circled out over his desk, then onto the floor, until it found its resting place on a large canvas on an easel. Beside the easel was his jar of brushes, as clean and dry as always, so that the bristles wouldn't split apart.

Amazing, I said, taking the whole scene in—the cramped workspace, the disordered desk, the ordered brushes, the smell of wood, oil, and dust, the feeling that the whole workshop was a labyrinth and we were hidden away at one dead end.

Huh, he said, surprised.

It's called *Stream*, he said, taking out a stool for me to sit on and gesturing for me to sit while he talked. Or maybe *The Race*, I don't know, I mean I haven't decided, because the title can come last, or it can come first, it really depends on your approach—on one's approach—and so I haven't really decided on my approach; I mean I haven't decided whether to name it first or name it later, but probably it will be later—

I'm sorry, I said, sitting down to focus on him. I'm paying attention now.

Okay, he said.

Most of the canvas was blacked in, as Sasha described it, except for a figure of a young boy standing before what appeared to be either a dark box or a dark hole; I couldn't tell whether the points of the shape came towards me or receded.

Why *Stream*? I asked.

Or *The Race*, or something I haven't thought of yet; actually, I don't really like either of those.

What is the boy looking at? I asked.

I don't know yet, he said. I'm waiting for him to tell me.

I know that might sound weird. But I haven't finished his face, so I don't know how he feels about it.

I looked more closely at the child's face. I don't think he wants to get too close to whatever the thing is or maybe he wishes he could get closer, but knows he won't.

Sasha let out a contented, quick, Hmm.

It's nice here, I said turning to look up at him, being here with you, in your space.

Yeah, he said.

I looked over to his desk again and noticed two small cups.

Have you shown it to anyone else? I asked.

Not really, he said. Just Jack.

I nodded, jealous but not saying it.

It's him, said Sasha. I needed a model.

I looked at the boy again and there was Jack.

It *is* Jack, I said. And it impressively, convincingly, was, but it was a Jack I didn't know so well. It was the Jack that Sasha knew.

You're next, he said, which filled me with a warm and good feeling that I couldn't quite name. I don't know if he really meant it or not because I didn't ask.

Sasha swivelled the light away from the painting — its bright orb retracing the path from easel back to the desk — and clicked it off.

We walked back past the slats of wood and out into the workshop he thought of as so sterile. First editions of the posters they made were tacked all over the walls. Bold, primary colours, with a strong emphasis on red, white, and black. All of the lettering was crisp and strong, and I wondered how Sasha could produce posters so bold in his little nook of workspace.

We do the posters out here, he said. They need a lot of space.

I hadn't met any of the other people Sasha worked with, because he never saw them socially. On this night, we were back drinking in Sasha's old studio, a place we'd spent so much time it felt like a second home.

Jack had brought a bottle of spiced vodka. Unlike the others, he had managed to keep his studio down the hall, but as far as I could tell, making and bottling moonshine was all he did in there. He was stingy in every way but this: he kept his friends drunk. Those were the dry years when we couldn't buy alcohol except in restaurants and couldn't buy vodka anywhere. I think Jack knew his moonshine got him invited. That was why he was so petulant about it, like he resented the moonshine for guaranteeing his friendships because he knew nothing else would. When he showed up somewhere things were always awkward at first, because he took his time bringing it out. We couldn't ask and he'd take his time, testing us to see if we would. That night, we'd borrowed chairs and crates from the other studios, so everyone had a place to sit. At first there were only four of us: Sasha and I, Elisa and Jack, but it was early; more were bound to arrive.

Elisa sat alone on Sasha's old cot, picking balls of lint off her sweater and placing them in a small mountain.

I sat on a crate that was low to the ground so everyone seemed a little taller than me. Sasha didn't sit. Jack watched him as he lit a cigarette and exhaled into the night.

Jack lit a cigarette, too, but then rested it low on the shelf where I watched it smoke itself out.

Elisa pulled a compact and a tube of lipstick out of her satchel. Their metal containers snapping open made the sound of femininity. She bared her teeth for a second, looking in the mirror for food, then began with the methodical application of colour.

Abruptly, Jack sat down next to her, making the springs complain under their combined weight.

She knew how to predict him, though, and held the lipstick away from herself while he settled. The mirror from the compact caught the light from the lampshade and reflected an oval flash on the ceiling. I wondered if the cot would collapse. Thinking that it might made me smile.

Elisa had finished the top lip and started in on the bottom.

Do me! said Jack to Elisa.

The ash on his cigarette curled like a long fingernail, almost touching the bottom of the saucer. A draft had kept it alight.

In a second, she said distractedly, the compact now hiding the lower half of her face. Why don't you pour us all a drink if you've nothing to do?

Sasha watched Jack for a moment, appraising him, then took a bottle from Jack's bag, opened it, filled our glasses, and, with his in hand, sauntered away to look out the window. As in all things, Elisa and Sasha were the exceptions — they could ask Jack for anything.

Jack shoved himself back against the wall, leaving his legs hanging over the edge.

He'd made her mess up. She dug her pinky finger into the errant line, trying to erase it, but the pigment was stubborn. Somehow she managed to fix it, maybe because she was a painter and they knew how to make strange things look normal.

Now that Jack was sprawled across the whole cot, it was if he were performing some sort of feat — cot-covering — as if it were a display of strength or courage or something. His cigarette had smoked itself out. He picked up the butt and walked it over to the ashtray and, on recrossing the room, picked up the bottle Sasha had put down.

I chose one of the glasses — it was the only one without

a chip in the rim—and walked over to Sasha. I pressed my body into his, wrapped my free arm around his waist. He kissed my forehead, then took a drag and exhaled into the black.

Read us some of your poetry, Jack, beseeched Elisa. I looked over at them. I couldn't tell if she was being sarcastic.

You've heard it all before, he said quietly, looking at Elisa only, as if they were alone.

Tatiana's never heard it, said Sasha, walking us back from the window.

To friends, said Elisa. We emptied our glasses.

Jack surveyed me for a moment. Why don't you wear lipstick? he asked me, as if the question were penetrating.

I thought you might have written some new poems, Elisa said, licking her lips for the last few drops of alcohol.

Well, I haven't, he said to her. Let's play cards.

He'd forgotten about me. He downed his drink and poured another glass for himself, downed it, and then filled all of our glasses, before filling his again. He got up to get another cigarette from Sasha and the two of them stood together, smoking, like real men.

Elisa found the cards by the boxes of tea while I pulled a crate in front of the cot. She sat down to sort the cards by suit to see if any were missing.

Elisa offered to do a reading of the cards, and in this way indicated that she'd decided to be kind.

The modern deck comes from the tarot card deck, or they have the same root deck. The hearts are the same suit as the cups, the diamonds are the coins, the spades. Then she stopped sorting the cards. What were the spades, Jack?

Oh, I don't know, Lis, he said, exhaling a big puff of smoke.

Swords, said Sasha.

I looked at him, surprised.

She used to read for us all the time, he said to me.

But the future didn't look like this, did it? said Jack.

Elisa ignored him, shuffling the piles back together.

We were all relieved when Dimitri showed up. The addition of a fifth body disrupted the awful symmetry of two men and two women.

That was when Elisa said that the bookstore owner, Osorgin, had disappeared.

What about his wife? I asked.

Have *you* been there? she asked me, incredulously.

That's how we met, said Sasha.

Yes, she said, getting past the shock of my belonging. Her, too. Yuly, Boris, everyone. They sent them to Leningrad. Then they put them on a boat, along with thousands of others, and off it went.

Dimitri pulled up a crate next to the one I'd been sitting on and poured himself a drink. I watched the way his hand cradled and tipped the bottle, heard the slight clink when the bottle chanced against the glass. Who else had been on that boat, I wondered.

Who were the other thousands? Dimitri asked.

People like us, said Jack.

What are we like? I asked.

You're not like us, said Jack, giving me a hard look.

Elisa smiled to herself, then looked at Dimitri, and made a display of saying, Jaaaack, in a slow, admonishing tone. She had gathered up the cards and was spreading out the whole deck into a large fan. I was watching her hands again. I was looking down because looking down hid my eyes, hid the tears that threatened there, hid my incomprehension of exactly what had happened to the Osorgins.

But who were they? said Dimitri.

It had been years since I'd seen Dimitri, but still his presence calmed me.

From behind the fan, Elisa said, They were on a list. Religious scholars, philosophers, scientists. Enemies of the state.

Enemies of Lenin, corrected Jack.

Same thing, said Sasha.

Dimitri wanted to know where the boat had gone, and Elisa said that for a long time no one knew, but that lately news had trickled in that suggested they'd been sent to Germany. The boat had landed in Rostock, and most everyone had gone on to Berlin after that.

I wondered if my father might have been on that very boat or one like it, years before. No doubt, if he wasn't, he would have liked to have been. Dimitri asked how Elisa knew. Had she, for example, read about it in the newspapers?

Don't be naive, said Jack, looking at Dimitri first, then at me.

Jack's hair was the colour of dirt, I thought.

Elisa presented the fan of cards to Dimitri, who knew what to do. He pulled a card and announced it to the group of us: king of diamonds.

That's you, she said to him.

I got my sweater and went out into the hallway, just as one of the current studio-mates arrived with his friends. The marble steps continued upwards to another floor. I climbed up to the landing so I could sit there and think in the dark. I couldn't believe the Osorgins were gone. It was one thing to know I hadn't seen them, but quite another to know I'd never see them again. I always assumed they'd re-open. I thought of all the books I'd read in that little shop and of the wall and of Rachel, and even though I'd never liked her I didn't want them gone. That they were gone meant that time had passed and I hadn't even noticed. Jack had called us naive. Time at the studio always seem to pass steadily in this way, measured out by the steady rhythm of Jack's recriminations and Elisa's knowing commands. Sasha didn't suffer their moods, but he knew that I did. You're strong, he said, which was his way of saying he expected me to either fight my own battles, or opt out, which I preferred. I felt foolish, then, at how slowly I'd put it all together—the abundance of mystical texts in that store, their religious commitments, which I'd paid little attention to, the closing of churches in those years and the destruction of their building. *Had* they been enemies of the state?

From my spot on the landing, I heard the door open and watched as Jack walked past the foot of the stairs. I thought about the word *naive*. I could dismiss it as merely another of Jack's rash statements or I could take it seriously, separating the accusation from the accuser. I sucked myself back into the shadows of the landing, tucked my feet beneath my skirt. His shirt was rumpled and he walked in a slow, exhausted manner. His shoulders rolled forward as if protecting his concave chest. If I really were naive, I could strive to know more, or I could accept the limitations—one might say protections—of the world I inhabited. He continued down the hall. I heard him drop his keys, then pick them up, argue them into a lock, and then open his studio door, letting it slam shut behind him. The hall was quiet again, so I readjusted my legs and undid the top buttons on my boots. I pulled my cigarettes out of my skirt pocket. If someone saw me, I would seem like a person who wanted to smoke alone. The party spilled out into the hallway; I heard Elisa's voice and then Dimitri's.

Let's go, King of Swords, she said.

They walked in front of the steps and Dimitri looked up at me, a warm smile on his face. They went downstairs.

Even after all the years I'd known these people, I still didn't understand them. Couldn't believe, for example, that they were together.

I lit a cigarette.

Sasha came out and stood at the foot of the stairs with his hands on his hips for a minute before he squinted up into the dark and saw me.

Jack came out of his studio and yelled at Sasha, Why did you invite that asshole?

Sasha had already taken a step up towards me, but he stepped back down to face Jack. Sasha's back was to me now, and Jack, holding a new bottle, was facing him, which meant he also faced me. I tried to shift even further back into the shadows.

Come on, Jack, take it easy, said Sasha.

You know he's with her, said Jack. The look on his face was almost that of the young boy in the painting.

Stop worrying about it, said Sasha. They've left, anyway.

But why'd you invite him?

He was coming to pick her up, that's it.

He's useful to you, said Jack.

You're drunk, said Sasha.

He'll help you move up. I'm just a drag.

Right now you are, said Sasha.

Jack looked down the hallway, towards his studio, then back at Sasha, which was when he let out a sob, collapsing in the hallway, letting the bottle slip, though Sasha caught it. I could hear the sharp intake of his breath and felt badly for witnessing a moment which so obviously ought to have been private. Sasha pulled him up and seemed about to embrace him, when Jack collected himself and got his anger back.

I can't believe you're siding with those faggots.

We're not going to fight, Jack, said Sasha, because we have nothing to fight about. Go on back in there, bring them a drink and pour yourself another.

They were standing almost side by side, looking down towards where a party had gotten underway, Sasha looking at Jack to see whether or not he'd do what he'd been told. Jack straightened up, and Sasha slapped him on the back, as if to send him on his way, but Jack turned back to him and hugged him, whispering something I couldn't hear.

That was the only time I ever saw them come close to arguing, and the only time I ever saw Jack's anger lift to reveal the sadness beneath.

Sasha turned to face me then and took a few of the steps up before turning back to Jack. You'll be fine, he said, and then took the steps two at a time until he was beside me.

Jack raised his eyes up to me, and in their flash I saw that the return to anger was complete. I smirked at him, then immediately wished I hadn't. He walked back along the hall to the studio and cheered loudly as he walked in.

After Elisa reported that the Osorgins and the others had gone missing, Sasha started to get afraid. After that, the game they talked about changed. For a while, I still thought it was about sex, but eventually I realized it must have been something else.

D ecember passed quickly and all of a sudden, Congress was upon us, bringing together 750 participants, 288 neuropathologists, and 475 psychiatrists from all over the country. Such gatherings had happened before, but this was the first of its kind since the Revolution. The truth was we called everything *first* in those years. In the foyer, tables had been set up and covered with pamphlets, treatises, scientific journals, and books. Behind the tables, men adopted a variety of positions: if alone and if they did not have a belly, they leaned over their table and read; if alone and with a big belly, they leaned back in their chairs to give their bellies room; if they were the active types and not alone, they were huddled in vigorous conversation with colleagues; if they were active types and alone, they stood and shouted witticisms across the room to someone they thought they recognized; and if they were women, they were at the one table everyone visited at some point, handing out name tags to all the participants at the Congress, and they were never alone. When I went to pick up my name tag, therefore, there was a moment of interspecies recognition where the eyes of a mousy young academician met mine and hers said, You are one of us, why aren't you on this side of the table? And my eyes said, You are mistaken: I am not one of you.

Within hours, the place smelled like a neglected boys' change room.

As I drifted back out of the foyer and down one of the halls towards the largest lecture hall, I had the clear impression, as one does at events of this sort, that the universe had begun to revolve around the busy hive that was Congress on that day. It was impossible to think otherwise: where else could such a maniacally productive exchange of ideas and knowledge be taking place but in that busy network of stairwells, corridors, rooms, nooks, and lecture halls, all of which swarmed with scientists rushing from one idea to the next. This was an opinion I kept to myself. Bekhterev would have disapproved, thinking me young. Solipsism, pure solipsism, he would have said. Yet I knew something he didn't: where he could see the universe continuing to spin on its course, I could see that the universe continued to spin around him. Now that I think about it, Bekhterev might have approved heartily of this second opinion — whether in reality or merely in appearance, no one gets to be the centre of it all by accident. Bekhterev was no wallflower.

In the back of my mind, however, I was aware of a competing universe across town: the Congress of Pedologists and Psychologists overlapped by a day or so with our own. Indeed, many would participate in both congresses, and though Bekhterev had privately referred to their approach to human personality as a crime, he, too, would give a paper there. You have to know your enemies, he said, though he was wrong about who his enemies really were.

The hall was lined with official pamphlets and posters that had been printed the day before. They outlined the locations, subjects, panellists, and distinguished speakers for each session, but before anything had even started, the posters were already obsolete. Nevertheless, they remained on the walls, remnants of what we'd hoped for just days before, now edited and cross-hatched with *Updates!* and *Important Changes!* that made them into nearly indecipherable yet thrilling palimpsests of the new upon the new upon the new. It was a matter of etiquette that Congress participants ought to choose one session and stick with it for its ninety-minute duration. No matter what field, the brightest always imagine themselves above etiquette and thus, in this case, prided themselves on their ability to slip into and out of two or even three sessions during one ninety-minute session. The hallways evidenced this misbehaviour: lecture doors creeped open and were silently shut as participants prepared to dash from one session to another, always in the direction of whatever seemed most promising. Sessions took place in rooms as grand as a lecture hall and as humble as a bedroom closet. If one of the spaces happened to be free for a session, it would be filled instead with people eating, conducting interviews, or, as the day went on, sleeping.

That morning, I snuck from Astvatsaturov's presentation on linguo-statistical studies of aphasia (where amnesia for nouns was blamed on motor centre disturbances, while amnesia for verbs was due to Wernicke's area lesions) to Pavlov's homage to Claude Bernard, before sitting down to absorb what I could of the technical sessions on the histological methods of Ehrlich and Golgi, the famed discovery of the sensitive terminal apparatus in the electric skate, and the pioneering experiments by Sherrington on muscle spindles and cut nerves. Neurosurgery was then still in its infancy. It was at that first Congress that Pussep bravely admitted that his clinic in Leningrad had produced what could only be called horrendous results. We applauded his honesty; some even got a little teary over it, imagining it might pose a risk for his career. His party credentials were unimpeachable, however, so any notion of risk was an exaggeration.

Over lunch, we caught up on what we missed in other sessions. Of those I remember by name, there was Luria and Anushka, Segalin, Sarkisov, and eventually, though not for long, Bogdanov. I can hardly remember what we ate that day, but I do remember the endless pots of tea. That and the sour cherry jam, which I and others took to eating by the spoonful, as much for the sugary surge as for the flavour we all associated with childhood. This was fitting because we were, all of us, like children — overstimulated and tired, cocksure and ignorant — and it was these qualities in combination that led Segalin to his speech and Bekhterev to his mistake.

Segalin had by then been publishing his journal the *Clinical Archive of Genius and Talent (of Europathology)* for several years. Segalin had always struck me as a man who was too sensitive for his surroundings, as though a sudden gust of cold could kill him. His proposed field of study, aesthetic medicine, was, as I saw it, a cry for help, an expression of the anguish he felt in adapting to the pace and demands of revolutionary society. In every issue of the *Clinical Archive*, Segalin would diagnose a famous person. Dostoyevsky had hysterical epilepsy. Nikolai Tikhonov was a psychopath; Alexandr Blok, an epileptic. Because of Pushkin's irony, Segalin waffled: was he a cycloid who suffered hypomaniacal states or an erotoman with hypertrophied gonads? With others, he was more certain. Gogol was also hypogonadal and schizophrenic; Jesus Christ, paranoic with an asthenic constitution due, perhaps, to his petty bourgeois background.

He didn't see it this way, of course. Sitting on a low table, surrounded by the most accomplished scientists of the union, he seemed to be almost pleading with them to understand the special class of people he called geniuses.

I mean, he said into his hands, that geniuses suffer persecution whenever their creative innovations contradict the tastes and wishes of the powerful. Editors, resellers, agents: these are the exploiters! Geniuses die early, and they die in poverty.

He looked up and reassured himself that we were listening.

He went on: You must see how this poses a serious threat to Soviet society. Geniuses end up clowning, prostituting themselves to the bourgeois demands of pseudo-art and performative acts, without which they would starve. The state must protect them! Without such protection the abuse of wunderkinds will continue!

Tsiolkovsky and Segalin had been colleagues for many years, so it was natural that it was Tsiolkovsky who took a seat at the table next to him, a move that in other circumstances might have seemed aggressive but which had judged Segalin appropriately: he quieted.

Bekhterev had been absent that morning on account of his role on the Medical Advisory Committee to the Kremlin. He had been on the committee ever since Lenin's first stroke, and his being called there that day seemed only further evidence that whatever problems he might have experienced with the Party were behind him.

In the afternoon, Bekhterev was slated to deliver a lecture to the entire Congress, a lecture in which he planned to definitively address the erroneous thinking of the pedologists and psychologists about human personality. But he was late. Late, therefore, for the People's Commissar for Health, Nikolai Semashko, who had been standing awkwardly to the side of the podium, a small box in his hands that was too big for a pocket and, I presumed, too valuable to be placed on a table. When Bekhterev arrived, the microphones were set, and this might have led to his excuses — intended for the few gathered at the front of the room — being captured and amplified throughout the room. He had been visiting, he said, an everyday paranoiac with a withered hand. If it weren't for the microphones, who would have heard him?

I remember the comment now as if it stood out in the moment, as if, when he said it, a chill went up my spine, but it is just as likely that I learned of the comment later, "remembering it" only once its significance became clear. It was widely known that the man with the withered hand was our Georgian, our Patriarch, our Stalin. That our Patriarch feared more than he ought to would also have been well known, especially among the small circle to whom Bekhterev addressed the comment. Less widely known — and completely unknown to me at the time — was the kind of damage such an "everyday paranoiac" could inflict.

Though the sound of Bekhterev's amplified voice served, for the most part, as a signal to the room that his talk was about to begin, it is clear now, in light of what happened afterwards, that some were listening more attentively than others.

I sat between Segalin and Luria in one of the rows towards the front. Luria sat straight backed with one leg crossed daintily over the other. He'd cleaned his glasses and opened his notepad to a fresh page. Segalin leaned forward, his elbows on his knees, as if this were a sporting event. Segalin was old enough to be my father, and yet he seemed to be in a state of constant astonishment or trembling, as if he'd learned nothing during the course of his life that could grant him any kind of security. As for Luria, we were very close in age, yet he seemed older, as if, in contrast to Segalin, he had been born with some sense of how to play along, an intuition perhaps, that had already served to protect him in many ways. For myself, I rarely thought about what it would mean to protect myself.

Semashko had stepped away from the podium to make room for Bekhterev. The room quieted.

In the years to come — indeed, perhaps until my final days — I will think back to that afternoon and to the way Bekhterev addressed us. He spoke to us as comrades, as equals, as fellow seekers, as disciples who would take up his earliest questions and make of them a discipline. We would follow his footsteps, we would continue with bringing the rigour of scientific inquiry to the study of human personality, and in doing so, we would release society from the impoverished thinking that had prevented our understanding not only of the cherished people in our midst, but also of every aspect of our existence, from the smallest particles known to man to our very conception of God. He trusted us. We must correct our thinking, he told us. Reject analogy. Throw off metaphysics completely.

In its extremes, he said, you will easily join me in identifying the problem. The Greek philosopher Protagoras taught us that man is the measure of everything. At first glance, he said, looking around the room, this seems a just statement. Until, he paused, until we ask ourselves against which touchstone such a measure could be made. Therein lies the problem. Protagoras did not imagine man with a measuring device in hand. He imagined man, himself, as the measure. This anthropocentric attitude has invaded science from philosophy, such that writers like Wundt and Espinas ascribe even complex manifestations of conscious activities such as patriotism, sense of duty, sense of property, aesthetics, love, and so on to the lowliest creatures, to ants, bees, termites, spiders, and others. Other scientifically minded individuals have cited the feeling of penitence in a Spanish mule that has been punished for disobedience — its coronal and bells given to another mule; and, conversely, a feeling of pride in the rams and bulls that wear bells and other ornaments given them as leaders of the herd.

A few in the audience laughed.

Outrageous as those examples may seem, do not imagine yourselves immune to this error in subtler, seemingly innocuous ways. Human thought tends to pursue a subjective direction in all questions related to the study of man, but in addition, as the examples above demonstrate, the tendency to think that what I know of myself — that I desire food, sex, drink, that I feel sadness and fear death — must apply not only to my fellow man but also to any other entity on earth that moves. Primitive peoples endow everything with a soul. But are we so much better?

Bekhterev swayed as he spoke. Something about him seemed so free, so young, though by then he had already celebrated his seventieth birthday.

Think of General Wolseley, he went on, who lamented that the main facts of the Battle of Waterloo, despite having been witnessed by hundreds, remain largely unknown. The English General found it distressing that we could know who were the victors and the vanquished, but beyond the main events of the battle there is only mystery. Subjective testimony — what one man saw, what another felt — is distressingly unreliable. On the other hand, objective data — the number of men wounded, killed, or taken prisoner; the amount of ammunition used by what number of guns; how and whither the vanquished withdrew — all of these calculations will give a full and objective account of the battle, such as can never be given by the subjective testimony of eyewitnesses. It is clear that, on the basis of narration alone, we shall miss the truth.

In his conclusion, Bekhterev became wistful.

We can, he said, looking out to us all as if wanting to speak directly to each and every one of us, only lament the wasted genius of those who devote their energy to the subjective methods. From the Pythagoreans and Platonists all the way through to Descartes, Hegel, and even Bergson, these thinkers have indulged in exploring one's own mind or soul to discover universal laws and solutions to the great secrets of life. Today this approach can only generate feelings of sorrow and compassion — the latter because of talent squandered in the pursuit of chimeras, and the former because of all the time and work so pitifully wasted. The human mind is fundamentally incapable of answering metaphysical questions that address the origin of life and movement, the nature of matter, and the appearance of consciousness. When the human intellect turns its gaze inward, it loses itself in the turn.

It was this point that would be so roundly refuted by our colleagues at the Congress of Pedologists and Psychologists, and it was this point that, for a moment, made me feel utterly lost. Pushed to its limit, his dismissal of analogical thinking meant accepting not only that atoms do not have souls, nor do mules feel pride, nor do plants "reach" for the sun, but also that there was no God and Sasha was a complete stranger. At the end of his speech, Semashko stood again beside Bekhterev to confer upon him the title of Honoured Scientist. It was the absolute peak of Bekhterev's career and, for everyone gathered in that room, a moment that was thick with history and promise.

That night, Bekhterev took his wife to the theatre. From what I have learned since, his wife insisted they go, despite Bekhterev's reluctance. The tickets had been a gift, left with the organizers of the Congress that afternoon by a man no one recognized. I myself had brought them to the apartment where the Bekhterevs were staying and have, ever since, regretted my diligence. *Swan Lake.* I remember thinking that Sasha and I should see the same show once we returned from the country. The tickets were meant as congratulations.

—⊘—

Actually, I'd brought the tickets over to Bekhterev with Luria because when the organizers went looking for Bekhterev, they'd found us talking. When they asked me to take the tickets to Bekhterev, Luria asked if he could join me. He'd given a talk that afternoon that I'd missed, so as we walked he filled me in. All his work was about two kinds of people—twins and criminals—and what he studied in both was how they spoke. What he'd discovered was that criminals always give themselves up, but most people aren't paying close enough attention to see it.

How? I asked.

They sweat, twitch, cross and uncross their legs.

Maybe they're just nervous.

Of course they're nervous, he said, laughing.

I mean, I'd be nervous even if I didn't do anything wrong.

That's an important distinction, said Luria. But we're using words to figure out the difference between good nervous and evil nervous.

Who's the "we"?

He never answered questions he didn't like.

We ask them to associate words. Like Freud does, but without the dreams. And we time how long it takes them to associate neutral words versus trigger words. When someone is guilty, said Luria, their response times become erratic. Everyone has a signature response time. You do. I do. So when a normal person gets over the initial discomfort of this kind of questioning, they settle into a pattern. Some even enjoy themselves. They enjoy the surprise of themselves, of what they come up with. Not everyone, of course, but even a generally nervous person will still settle into a pattern. If they sweat, they sweat the same amount throughout the session. But a criminal is different. They don't trust themselves to say what they ought to. They want to respond quickly, because they think speed suggests a kind of naturalism, a comfort, but they can't do it all the time.

Can you give me an example? I asked.

There was a man who'd murdered his wife. She'd been found, bleeding out in the hallway of their apartment. He tried to blame a neighbour. When we met up with him, even the top of his bald head was sweating. He kept swiping it with a kerchief, but it didn't help. We gave him all sorts of prompts. Words like *kind, cut, bread, neighbour, wife*. Anything that related to the crime took him longer to respond to, and usually involved an echo. Echolalia, it's called. It's symptomatic in liars. Wife, wife, wife, he'd say and then focus and try to start again. He'd tell us we were barking up the wrong tree. He'd say we were asking in vain. He'd say he didn't do it. *Kind* took him 6.1 seconds — a kind husband, a kind one, he'd say. When we gave him *love*, he said nothing.

I thought of that man, a murderer, who had no answer for love.

We had walked all the way down to the river and along the walkway towards the east. A couple were standing on top of the wall, the man's back to us. The woman threw a rock so hard and so far I thought she must be aiming for the other side. The man laughed at her.

Close, he said.

She turned around to throw a rock at him but saw us and didn't.

We walked past.

Why did you tell me about the criminals? I asked. Why not the twins?

Because you like criminals, he said. You told me that already.

I suppose I had.

But that's normal, he said. Most people like criminals.

What he was talking about was a version of the lie detection machine he'd developed many years before. He was a man who was interested in liars, I thought, but then maybe that was the same thing as being a woman with an interest in criminals: we're all interested.

When we turned onto the street of Bekhterev's Moscow apartment, I asked Luria why he'd wanted to join me.

I have some lessons to teach you, he said. Life lessons.

Life lessons? I scoffed. We're the same age!

Some people learn faster than others, he said.

You're ridiculous, I said.

Bekhterev still kept a servant, so it was she who answered the door when I knocked and to her that I gave the tickets.

Luria continued as we walked away, saying that everyone likes criminals, and most everybody likes life lessons, too.

You want to get better, don't you? he asked.

What I wanted was to avoid his questions, so I asked him what he thought of Segalin's studies, happy with myself because I'd learned a life lesson from him that I'd been able to use against him.

There are two questions there, said Luria. No, three. Your first question is, what do I think of Segalin? The second is, what do I think about his project: can we diagnose someone based upon the stories they tell? And third, if we can, what do I make of his results?

Okay, so all of those, I said.

Three questions. One answer. Segalin is crazy, he said.

But you diagnose people by their stories, I said.

No, he said. I diagnose them by their words.

Does this make you a good liar or a bad liar?

I don't lie, he said.

So then I can trust you, I said.

Not the same thing, he said.

Is this one of your life lessons? I asked.

You could say that, he said.

Months later, when I repeated back to him what he'd said about Segalin, he looked at me as if I were the one who was nuts: Crazy? he said. I meant crazy-smart.

What he meant was, he didn't want to be pinned down.

I just don't know if all geniuses suffer pathologies like that, I said.

Maybe they hide it.

Bekhterev seems fine, I said.

Maybe he hides it, said Luria.

Maybe he just isn't a genius.

Maybe...

I was joking.

He tried to recover, tried to make like he knew I'd been joking, but we both knew he didn't.

—/—

I was the last person to leave the institute after Congress. In the institute's kitchen, the frost had already begun to accumulate. In the markets, peasant women would be selling lace that replicated the patterns of frost they saw on their home windows. They called them frost flowers, but I thought they looked more like the leaves of the ferns that grow everywhere in Moscow, their feathery fronds swept up and replicated ad infinitum on panes of glass across the city. The frost diffused all light, so the lab, even though it had natural light, had lost the warmth of the fall. The institute felt so quiet and timeless, as though it were, itself, a protected space, a place that could not wither or erode, a place where everything we believed could stay intact. Like Lenin's embalmed body in Red Square, the institute would not decay and there was no mystery in that, no miracle, no. Science had rescued us from miracles.

Locking the door, it felt like I was sealing the institute off, protecting it from the darkest nights of the year, promising it that it would remain undisturbed until my return.

The day after Congress, Sasha suggested we walk through the markets. The holiday season meant that the city was covered in tinsel and cheap decorations. Christmas roses, postcards, and children's toys were everywhere. The Chinese vendors sold artificial flowers made of paper, sea monsters, and brightly patterned deep-sea fish. The peasants hawked yellow and red glass orbs to hang from the trees. The glass caught the sun's winter light, seeming to draw it into their inner spheres, heating it up and then radiating it back out again as if they were, themselves, sources of light. Just reflections, of course. On every corner, we passed the grandmothers with baskets full of sugar figurines. They never smiled. Rotted teeth, I figured. Everywhere we went, Sasha would say that one, and that one, and that, too, as we walked past posters he had coloured: Into Production! Books! The Streets are our Brushes, The Square our Palettes!

Sasha knew the names of the shops, their owners, and what products they sold. His favourite was owned by Michel, an old family friend. By virtue of his connection to Sasha's family, I was immediately wary around him. Originally from a small town in France, he had come to Russia before the Revolution, married a woman from Moscow, and never left. It was more difficult now to import things from abroad, so the lavender soaps and lilac perfumes he sold cost more than we earned in months. Sasha spoke to him in French. They sang their words. When Sasha began to speak to Michel, I stopped listening and started watching. Michel stood behind a glass counter but was bent forward, his arms outstretched, so that they made a triangle underneath his head. Sasha was on the other side of the counter. His hat was in his hands and he'd unbuttoned his wool coat. His other hand was in the pocket of his coat, but he was gesturing with both hands all the same, so that the pocket of his coat on one side and his hat on the other darted out and then went slack as he talked.

I walked around the shop but felt uneasy. The soaps and perfumes smelled like a place I didn't belong. Rima and I had a word for such things: *poshlost*. When we said that word, we emphasized the harsh consonants, the *p* and the *st*, because they sounded out our judgments so decisively. Michel's shop was full of things created for the sake of being things. There were small boxes full of note cards, vases full of plastic flowers, porcelain statues, and matryoshka dolls, a whole collection of miniature musical instruments — beguiling objects, all of them, each little bourgeois fetish more cloying than the next. When I looked at them, I saw the dust they would summon. These were objects that would sit on a shelf somewhere, telling the women to dust more, clean more, stay at home. This was a side Sasha rarely showed me, a side I had hoped he wanted to leave behind, a side of him that was his mother. I wondered how much a person could change over the course of a lifetime. A lot? Not at all?

There was a small part of me that desired these beautiful things. Wasn't it true that art and science and politics belonged together? Wasn't it true that a thing of beauty was also, then, a work of art? I saw a pair of silk gloves so fine they caught the light in pools of white and silver. When I pressed my finger on each of the fine, perfect buttons, the pools of silver-white shifted, like bright mercury. The stitching was so delicate. These were things brought over from a separate world. I thought of the time and attention it had taken to make them. I inclined my head to see the pools of light flow back and forth. Surely a thing like this could be an exception. Not for me, perhaps, not for me or my friends, but for somebody, some *other* person. The gloves could be art.

I heard Sasha laughing, again, and looked through a glittering Christmas display in the direction of the counter. Sasha and Michel had been watching me.

—✕—

Sasha and I left for the dacha the next day. He called his mother from the station in Moscow to say we were coming. She said something to him that he disagreed with but when he got off the phone he said that everything was fine. The train rolled slowly out of the station and picked up speed as we neared the edge of the city, the scene out our window changing from cement walls to the final clusters of buildings to snow-dusted trees and trees and trees. Sometimes we'd cross a river and get a view of the landscape as whole—an endless, snow-covered forest interrupted only by the occasional red-roofed dacha—and just as quickly we'd be swallowed back into the darkness of the forest. Before too long, we couldn't see much at all because the sun had set and the moon had yet to rise. Inside, the train was crammed full of people escaping the city for the holidays.

I'd only met Sasha's mother once, and it was three years previous, the summer after we were married. Both of us were working by then, but we were as poor as ever.

According to him, on that day, she had come in from her dacha in the countryside, leaving behind an exquisitely clear river and a cloudless sky, with the single purpose of meeting me. From the minute we met—Sasha and I had come from his studio, she had just gotten a lift from the station—I knew that this wasn't true.

She had chosen a restaurant on Nikitskaya. From the street, I looked up at the balcony and its patrons. Nikitskaya still had lime trees, and some of their leaves rubbed up against the balcony railing, so I wondered if the air up there smelled of citrus. The evening light calmed my nerves.

Sasha, she said, clasping his face, kissing him. She was tall and thin and wore her pale hair piled in a bun atop her head. When she looked at me, her eyes were so light, like wisteria, that I wanted to look away. She limply put her hands on my arms and kissed my cheeks without actually touching my skin, as if she were French, but she wasn't. Her translucent skin made her look fragile, but I don't think she was.

We'll sit inside, she said, because I can't stand another minute in the streets. I trailed up the steps behind the two of them. Mrs. Pavlovna's arm hung on Sasha's back like a bird's outstretched wing.

We took a table in a quiet corner of the restaurant. Sasha and I sat with our backs to the wall, on one side, Mrs. Pavlovna on the other. Sasha's hand found its way to my thigh. The more she stared at him, the younger she looked. The same was true for him. Sasha pulled his hand away, crossed his arms on the table and leaned toward her.

How are you, Mama? he said softly.

Oh, fine, she said, looking at me momentarily before looking back at him. The same.

Do you need help? asked Sasha.

She pulled her napkin out of her glass, shook it loose, and laid it neatly on her lap.

Of course not, she said. We manage.

I wasn't sure who the "we" referred to. Remarrying would have been out of the question.

The waiter came by to fill our glasses and paused until Mrs. Pavlovna waved him away.

Natasha sends her regards. She's absolutely desperate for you to visit. You really should come soon, she said, looking at me again, as if forcing herself to remember I was there. Both of you.

The waiter returned with warm wet towels so that we could wipe the city from our hands. She ordered for us.

The high ceilings, the neatly buttoned waiters, and the polite hum all said the place was fucking expensive. If I thought about it that way, as fucking expensive, as another fucking example of fucking *byt* bullshit, I could tell myself that I didn't belong.

Mrs. Pavlovna's face tensed each time the terrace door opened, as if the city itself galled her.

I fought the urge to change my order.

The truth was that my father had frequented restaurants like these, and so, as a result, had I. One way I'd come to understand the differences between my mother and father had come to me on Osorgin's wall. Freud's concept of the narcissism of minor differences wherein the darkest forms of hatred emerge between groups who are not diametrically opposed — my parents were both left-leaning intellectuals — but between groups whose differences are as small as a splinter in one's toe, and as painful.

And how is your art? said Mrs. Pavlovna.

Pointless, said Sasha, with a kind of laugh.

He'd never said anything like that to me, so I turned to face him.

Mrs. Pavlovna looked at me, as if I might understand, but I didn't.

What a preposterous thing to say, she said.

Your posters are everywhere, I said. How can you say they're useless?

Oh, but those aren't art, said Sasha. She's talking about my paintings. I knew he made this distinction, but it surprised me all the same to see how little value he placed in the posters which were, even then, displayed all over the city.

His paintings are very beautiful, such dark expressionism, she said, explaining him to me.

I bit my lip, refusing to compete with her over him.

Sasha placed his napkin on his lap. I followed suit.

But what are these posters? she asked him.

I do colouring, he explained, for some of the artist-engineer types. Colouring in their thick black images of trucks and galoshes and trains and cigarettes and cosmetics.

Oh, said his mother. Well, that is useful, isn't it? she asked. But it wasn't a question. She brushed her hand across her cheek as if wiping away a crumb, though really she was trying to erase the confusion that had clouded her face with the mention of the artist-engineers. They were a type for Sasha and me because they were ubiquitous: men and women whose careers had begun in the arts but had transformed into something more practical, not engineers exactly—their designs could hardly be trusted to withstand a person's shifting weight nor the pressure of wind and snow—but another post-revolutionary class with which we were familiar and which told people like Mrs. Pavlovna that the world was no longer theirs.

Our meals arrived: three identical plates of roasted goose sliced up on a bed of sour apples with a side of golubtsy. I picked up the cold towel and put it on the waiter's tray.

Divine! said Mrs. Pavlovna, clapping her hands together like a child.

We ate in silence for some minutes, all in the same manner. We caught a small piece of the tender meat and one single slice of sour apple on our forks, and then slid it into our well-bred mouths, our lips unchapped, our palates attentive to the apt pairing of sweet and sour on our tongues. I hadn't eaten food so rich in years. If Sasha found it hard to digest, it didn't show.

After tea and petit fours, Sasha said he couldn't walk me home because he wanted to take his mother to her lodgings.

My stomach started to hurt when I watched them walk away, her arm linked in his. Without thinking why, I turned up the street, toward Rima's. I wanted to smoke a cigarette and talk. I knew Yuri would be out because he was always out, working or running a meeting, whatever. He'd been a member of the Party since before the Party existed.

—⁄—

I lay down on the floor as soon as I was inside her apartment.

The night was hot and humid; nothing moved. On the table beside the balcony, the fabric covering the phonograph had been pulled aside.

What were you listening to? I asked.

Rima's arms draped over the balcony railing, moving only when she brought the cigarette to her mouth for a long, slow drag.

Irving, she sang, exhaling slowly.

From my position on the floor, I admired her.

What's she like?

Rich, I said.

That's still possible?

Come on.

Where does she live?

Near Sokol'niki.

So, she hasn't been through collectivization yet. *Lishensty* class, said Rima, which was apt.

Sasha's mother still had all her money, but she'd lost the right to vote. She could vote with her dollars, I thought, and I could vote with my vote. Eventually, her dollars would run out.

In the ceiling of Rima's apartment, a small crack had appeared in the upper right corner. It had gotten so hot and humid that, lying there looking up, I could almost believe that I was at the bottom of a pool and the strange play of light and that crooked line were happening where water met air.

The pure thing, I said.

Didn't you already know that? she asked from far away.

I suppose.

I saw Rima reposition her body so that she was still leaning against the railing, but facing me at the same time, looking down at me at the bottom of the pool.

Was she awful?

I took a deep breath and imagined myself surfacing, She was like a weary little doll. She barely looked at me, didn't ask a single question about me.

I rolled over and pulled myself up so that I could step out into the night air, where there might be some semblance of a breeze. I leaned onto the railing like Rima, taking a few drags of her cigarette, then threw it down into the courtyard. The bright ember split apart on landing, then dulled.

I wonder if Sasha's father ever hit her, I said.

Did he hit Sasha? asked Rima, looking at me.

I don't know, I said.

—✕—

A man Sasha knew was waiting for us at the station to transport us to the family home. Sasha raced ahead of me when he saw him, and then remembered me and came back to carry our suitcase, hurrying me along. We got into the back of a car, which made so much noise it was impossible to talk, but Sasha was talking anyway, yelling excitedly back and forth with the man as he caught Sasha up on the lives of people he no longer saw.

The moon had appeared on the horizon and was almost full, so its light spread ominously across expansive white fields, which were periodically delineated from other fields by a lonely line of trees. As a child, I had visited country homes before, but it had been years since I had left the city. The vastness of the landscape terrified me a little, making me feel exposed and spied upon rather than safely anonymous, which was how I felt in the city. I couldn't decide if it was just me or if it was true that it was colder in the country than in the city. I looked at Sasha then and saw that he was happy out here, more peaceful somehow.

Everyone in Sasha's family, except his mother, had left for Europe. His father, Pyotr, was long gone — a blessing for everyone — and his siblings, an older brother and sister, were in Berlin and Paris, both with ideas of returning that would never be realized. Only the mother remained. Sasha had been raised by his grandmother and a nanny, Natasha, who was an Old Believer. Even after the children had grown, Natasha had stayed on. The two women seemed to cohabit without speaking. Natasha was younger than his mother by a decade or so, and stronger, too. If the house was warm it was because Natasha had stoked the stove; they ate if Natasha cooked. It was Natasha who greeted us at the door.

Come in, come in, she said. She stepped aside to let us pass, then closed the door quickly, saying, No point heating the whole country.

Natasha was round and robust, her cheeks flushed as if her body contained its own source of heat. Looking around, I could see that although the house had once been beautiful, it was starting to fall apart.

We put down our bags and walked down the hall to the sitting room where Sasha's mother was waiting, hands crossed on her lap.

Her eyes softened when she saw Sasha. She didn't look at me. I wondered if she regretted the decision, or fact, of not having raised him. Sasha walked in and pulled her up to hug him.

I stood, for a moment at the edge of the room, awaiting some sign that I was wanted. Only Natasha noticed my discomfort.

Come to see the tree, she said.

It hadn't occurred to me that they would have a tree. I followed Natasha down the corridor to a room with a fireplace and a tree scantily decorated with tinsel and trinkets as old as Sasha. Christmas trees hadn't officially been forbidden yet, and anyway, everything comes later to the country.

It's beautiful, I said.

Mrs. Pavlovna didn't think you would like it, but how couldn't you?

It's beautiful, I said again, reminded of Luria's liars and their tendency to repeat themselves.

You'll be sleeping in here, she said, gesturing to a bed in the corner.

With Sasha?

Of course.

⎯⎯/⎯⎯

Over dinner, Sasha's mother seemed to warm to me. She'd heard of my father, she said, through a friend who went to the English Gentlemen's Club.

I suppose my friend might even have met you, as a girl.

Maybe, I said, but I only went there once or twice.

Yes, you would have stayed with your mother.

Yes, I said, without expanding, in the hopes that she would summon her own image of what those times might have been like for me, and that the image she created would soothe her.

For the first time, she inquired about my work. And how is your museum? she asked.

It's not quite a museum, I said, more of a scientific institute, really.

Well, said Mrs. Pavlovna, folding her napkin and placing it by her plate, Nikolai spoke highly of your father.

I saw Sasha smile from across the table, so I knew that at least one barrier had been overcome.

There was a girl in town, said Sasha as we lay next to each other that night, a strange girl who always had gold dust underneath her index finger. She was one of those people who is born an outcast and stays that way her whole life.

The fire was still roaring, but we'd covered ourselves with blankets all the same.

Why was she an outcast? I asked.

I don't know, he said, pulling the blankets up under his chin. Her family was poor, but that wasn't it.

Where did she get the gold, if she was so poor?

This was a mystery for a very long time, he said. She never had gold anywhere else. No gold rings or earrings. No necklaces. Nothing except the gold crescent under her fingernail that should have been dirt, but because it was gold it made her into a strange kind of beauty. The first people to notice were the local merchants who saw her hands when she came to their stores to buy flour or sugar.

Outside, the wind had kicked up.

Her teachers didn't notice? I asked.

She didn't go to school, he said. Well, she did go to the school, but she didn't attend classes. She arrived in time for our morning break and we'd find her perched high in the trees, waiting for us. I only saw the gold once, and it was because I caught her hanging from a branch, about to drop to the ground. Mostly she kept her hands in her pockets. Anya Solovyeva.

Did you talk to her? I asked.

There must have been a chink in the chimney because sudden gusts of wind outside made the fire spark.

No, but a friend did, that's how we found out why she was doing it.

Doing what? I asked. Where was she getting the gold?

Eventually, the priests at the local church noticed that the corners of their icons were being chipped away. Devotion icons, the ones that sit at the entrance to the church beside the font, were the most affected, but so, too, were the ones in the sanctuary. Some had only been scraped away at the bottom left corner, but others—those hung at a more accessible height—had had every last flake of gold removed from a part of the image, usually the hands, though sometimes the baby Jesus would have lost his lustre, too. It took a long time for anyone to notice, and even once they did, no one suspected the girl, though the height of the scratchings should have been a clue.

When was this? Was her family Bolshevik? Is that why they were outcasts?

Oh, it was too early for that business, said Sasha, though the story's been changed over the years, I think, and people probably do tell it that way now.

Her family could have been Communist, I said, sitting up.

Sure, said Sasha. But they weren't.

If she wasn't rejecting the church, why was she doing it?

It turned out that she was seeking enlightenment.

I laughed and settled back down under the covers.

Sasha rolled over to face me and took my hand. He closed all of my fingers to the palm except for the index, which he took into his mouth, wetting it, so that it was cold when he took it out.

She was ingesting the gold, he said. Ingesting it because a visitor to our town had told her that it would bring her to a vibratory plane, a place that would allow her access to a universal psyche. Or so some said. Others said she wanted access to the streets of heaven, which were paved with gold, and she felt that if she had enough gold in her system, she'd be guaranteed access.

Would you ever try such a thing? I asked.

Yellow gold wouldn't work, he said. She didn't know that it's only white gold powder that works.

You're joking! I said.

You'd do it, he said.

No I wouldn't.

Just think of it as a kind of hypnotism, he said.

Hypnotism is a medical practice, I said.

So you say, he said.

———⊁———

When I woke up, Sasha was gone, and I heard voices in the kitchen. I pulled on my wool socks and padded down the hall, past the white room with the framed photographs whose glass caught such a glare from outside that they seemed like windows themselves. I moved quietly, but it wasn't on purpose that I came almost to the doorway without having been noticed.

Sasha's mother was talking about me. I heard her say that she didn't understand why he'd married such a cold woman, a woman who didn't want children, who wasn't a proper wife. She asked him what she had done wrong. Sasha sighed and tut-tutted, saying little. Was this Sasha's way of rejecting his upbringing, she wondered.

But you like her, said Sasha.

I might, she said. But I'm afraid. I'm afraid of you both, afraid that you'll denounce me!

Oh, mother. You won't be denounced! You don't believe in anything. No one will denounce you.

It's happened to the neighbours, she said. They lost everything. It was their daughter, they say.

I could hear the strain in her voice, I could hear the increasing pitch, the way fears build on fears, and I didn't want it going any further so a took a few steps back down the hallway, then cleared my throat as if I'd just woken.

Christmas Eve night, when Natasha and Mrs. Pavlovna had already gone to sleep, Sasha and I stayed up. Sasha had spent the day chopping wood, and like a child who knows no limits, he piled the fire so high with wood that it sparked and flamed in a joyful waste. He pulled the sofa close to the fire and spread blankets and pillows on the wooden floor. We had sex and then, after, pulled the blankets up over our bodies and, on a small marble board, played an unskilled game of chess. Neither of us was good, but he was better. When he had taken all my knights, he pulled a slender box out from behind one of the pillows on the sofa.

Are you trying to bribe me? I asked.

Wait until you open the box before you say that, he said.

But Sasha, I said, I didn't get you a present.

Then you'll have to play well enough to make me think I'm winning, he said.

He moved the chessboard aside. The pieces wobbled when they were set down, but the game remained intact.

The box was from the store on Tverskaya. I'd never liked receiving gifts. The expectation was too great. Someone else had thought of something that they thought you might like. They had spent money on that thing. They had wrapped it up, lovingly, lovingly, cloyingly, lovingly. While they wrapped it they thought: this item symbolizes my love. They thought: this item symbolizes recognition. The gift meant: this is how I see you. But then it was never knowing nor recognition, and yet you could never say how much it wasn't because when you were given a gift, my father had said, you must always say thank you. You must always appreciate the thing. My mother would have said, throw the thing away, you don't *need* things. I didn't want to pretend. And now Sasha had bought me something from a store that had beautiful boxes, a store his mother would have liked, and so I felt unknown, as if he'd suddenly forgotten how to pronounce my name.

The slender white ribbon tied around the box came undone easily.

Sasha was watching me with the awful, hopeful happiness of a gift-giver.

I peeled back one layer of silly tissue, and then two more.

I wanted him to enjoy this, even if I couldn't.

At the core of all the layers, though, was a very small paper plane. Its paper was from an old pamphlet, the black and red block letters were letters no more, now they made abstract patterns on the wings and fuselage. I lifted it up to look closely, and there noticed a pilot and a co-pilot, their heads poking out of the plane's body. In another life they had been silk buttons, but now they were Sasha and me flying a plane!

Where did you get these? I asked.

I knew you loved-hated those gloves, he said. I thought the buttons might be the part you loved.

Did you steal them?

I won't be going back there, if that's what you're wondering.

Sasha's face was soft with happiness, but also with satisfaction, because he'd done the right thing.

I hadn't expected something so wonderful from a box like that.

So we're co-pilots, he said.

He wrapped himself around me then, as I flew the two of us around to the backdrop of a raging fire.

I'm not a cold person, am I? I asked.

Never, he said. And then, with a gentle smile, Mostly never.

He said he was going to leave the two of us flying the plane for a while, but eventually I'd find us somewhere else and in that place we'd be permanent.

I liked that idea very much.

—⁄—

Later that night, Sasha suggested we go for a walk in the snow.

I guess I looked concerned because Sasha laughed at me, saying, City girl, city girl.

Behind their home, there was more open space than I'd ever seen in my life. The moon was full and bright. Only the smallest wisps of clouds drifted across the sky. We walked without speaking so the only sound was the crunch of snow as we headed towards the hill. Every few steps I'd think I had seen something shift just beyond the range of my vision, and I would pause to look more closely, trying to discern the real threats from the imagined.

There's nothing out here, said Sasha, don't worry.

I'd try not worrying for a few steps, but then I'd see some low-to-the-ground eyes lit up behind a tree, and I'd know some small black thing was watching us.

At the top of the hill, the wind came furiously, but we stayed there for a while, looking out across the valley to the other houses, some still lit with warm fires, others asleep for the night. I hunched down, my knees bent up against my chest, so that I could hug them and rock back and forth on my feet. I wondered if the fears I felt were the fears of all country people and whether those who lived continuously amongst the threat of the imagined and the real were people like Sasha, who had learned to yell back. When my feelings of unease returned, which they did, in waves, I tried to attribute them to the landscape and to overheard conversations, but there was more to them than that.

You know who your Anya reminds me of? I said, looking up at Sasha.

Who? he asked.

Bogdanov, I said. We laughed at the thought of it, Bogdanov as a small weird girl, sneaking into churches, ingesting gold, and seeking higher consciousness. And it *was* funny, but true, too.

Sasha went off to the tree line to pee. A thin slip of cloud drifted in front of the moon, making it look, I thought, like a circle with a line dividing the upper half from the lower.

When he came back, he was smiling. He said that when he was a kid he used to come up here to yell. Sometimes he was with friends, sometimes he was alone.

What did you yell? I asked.

Moon! he yelled, hands high and reaching for the moon. Moon! You are cut through and through by a sword-fish! Moon! That swordfish is getting you! That swordfish will eat you whole! Moon! It's over!

Moon! I yelled, mimicking Sasha as ferociously as I could. Moon, you are finished!

Moon! We will eat you whole!

⸺⸺

The days in the country bled into each other, marked only by walks out on the fields, and occasionally into town, where I'd see the tree that little Anya had sat in with her gold-dust fingernail, her loopy higher plane. I'd pass by the town's station, too, where sometimes I'd see a train sitting, waiting for its passengers, and I would wish I could get on it, to go wherever it was going, no matter where that was.

One morning, we received a call at the house from the station master, who said there was a telegram waiting for me, that it had been there for some days. The same man who'd come to pick us up when we arrived took us in because a telegram seemed to require a faster response than we could muster by walking. Once we got back to the dacha, I opened it:

Dr. Vladimir Bekhterev died of unknown causes on 24 December in Moscow stop

I read the words but didn't understand their meaning.

Sasha! I said. What does this say?

He took the paper from me. He read the lines twice and then looked at me.

It means that he is dead, he said.

But I don't understand, I said. He gave a talk just days ago at Congress! What will happen to the institute? What will happen to his family?

My voice didn't sound like my own. It came from somewhere else. It was trying to be reasonable, but there was an unfamiliar tone to it, a kind of distortion that came from deep inside me.

Sasha lifted me up out of the chair I'd collapsed into and held me. I was shaking.

You will be okay, he said. He took a step back and looked at me, his grey-blue eyes promising me just that. I didn't believe him, felt my eyes fill up with tears and saw his, out of sympathy, do the same.

You didn't even like Bekhterev, I said, pulling my fist across my eyes, trying to get rid of the tears.

But I love you, he said.

He sat me on our bed and wrapped me in blankets. I pulled my knees up to my chest. He went away for a few minutes. I heard his mother down the hall cry out in a shrill voice and then the murmuring sounds of Sasha and Natasha trying to calm her down. When he came back to the room, he set a small table in front of me and two glasses of vodka on top. He pulled on a sweater, as if he were getting ready for a long period of stillness. Then he sat next to me and it was only then, with the warmth of his body beside me, that I realized I'd been sobbing the whole time.

We have to go back to the city, I said.

We'll leave tomorrow.

Today, I said.

The trip back into the city had been quiet, as our mood had shifted, and the train had been empty since no one who had left the city wanted to go back before the new year. Practically every year since we'd met, Sasha and I had celebrated New Year's Eve with Sasha's friends at the studios. We'd planned to miss it that year, but then the news made the ritual of it seem suddenly important to us both.

Standing in the hall outside the studio, we could hear the sound of clinking dishes and the radio on low. I was about to go in, but Sasha stopped me. Would you rather see Rima tonight? he asked. Or be with your friends rather than with mine? Do you want to go home? Whatever you want. Just say.

No way, I said.

Rima would want to know everything. She would want to dissect all the things that happened, she would want to *talk*. At least for that night, I wanted to forget it had happened at all. Sasha knew what I meant.

Let's get drunk then, he said.

I thought there would be more people there — the combined friends of all the studio-mates, as there had been all the previous years — but when we walked in, the only person in the studio was Jack, and the space wasn't even his.

Where is everyone? asked Sasha, looking around.

I pulled my watch from my pocket. That was why. It wasn't even seven.

Even though everyone had finished school by then, the studios were still a place we congregated, Sasha, Jack, and the others having moved into this very particular age group where they were admired by the current students for the fact of being older without any expectation (though this was coming) that they would have been, in some way, successful. Everyone was hoping to be the next Malevich, and if that wasn't possible, they wanted to *know* the next Malevich. Sasha's work in Rodchenko's studio made him one of the students who had been moderately successful almost immediately upon graduation, even if he and most of the people he worked with wished they could be doing their own thing.

You're so early! said Jack. He was standing at the back wall beneath the window where he had been moving glasses and glass receptacles (jars, mostly) from a drying rack to a tray on top of some crates. He moved the last one over and then came over to hug us.

We didn't think you were coming.

Yeah, you know. Change of plans, said Sasha.

Mothers, right? said Jack, looking quickly at me and then back at Sasha.

Something like that, said Sasha.

—⁄—

Sasha's painting of the boy had stayed with me, and I looked again for the boy in Jack's twenty-eight-year-old face but couldn't find him. What I did see was that Jack was happy, happier than I'd ever seen him.

I looked around the studio. The section that used to be Sasha's had been taken over by a really smart kid named Tova. Most of his art involved taxidermy—amateur taxidermy, Sasha had clarified—and most of the taxidermied creatures were birds, mice, rats, or, on the rare occasion that he found something bigger, cats. It involved chance, Tova had once explained, and one of its goals was preservation without nostalgia. His professors had called it morbid politics, but they said it with admiration. He was almost spiritual about the practice, always entering a trance-like state when he talked about the various steps he took to preserve a body in its final resting state.

Want some soup? asked Jack.

Jack had been alone for weeks. All he'd done was read. More Jack London? I asked.

No.

Look at him, said Sasha. Can't you tell he's been reading Akhmatova?

Because he's not acting like a wolf? I asked.

Because he's being so moony, said Sasha.

What do you mean? asked Jack.

The soup, said Sasha.

A man can make soup, said Jack.

Nope, said Sasha.

I'm with Jack, I said, tentatively aligning myself with him.

I wandered over to Tova's section. Sasha's old bed was still there, its frame having been repaired. I couldn't imagine Tova getting much use out of it, but then it was hard to say: he attracted the strangest people.

A large table sat in the centre of the room now, and Jack and Sasha were sitting at it, talking about a woman Jack had met.

A real lady of the night, said Jack. She was fucking old, I mean *old*, I mean her tits hung down past her waist, and she'd done something to her two front teeth, so that she could whistle through the gap. Came back here and hung about for a few days, cooking on the hotplate, telling me her stories. He looked at us and shrugged, Everyone's been away, and all.

Sasha laughed, and then whispered over his shoulder at me, Don't believe him.

It's true! said Jack.

She had a son, said Jack. And she knew a thing about flavour, I can tell you that much. And I liked her. I mean now she's gone and I wish you'd met her.

Did she teach you to make soup? I asked.

Among other things, said Jack.

You should read Kollontai, I said. She'll straighten you out on your ladies of the night.

Sounds dangerous, he said.

Eventually Elisa and Dimitri and a few others I didn't know showed up, but the group stayed small, just a few of us passing the evening, waiting for the new year to sound, waiting for something new to start. There would be bells and fireworks. That Jack was generally happier could have explained why he was gentler towards me, but Sasha must have said something to the rest of them, because they were kind, too. Jack had made his best vodka yet. It tasted like sweet summer air, like sky blue and cloud drifty, and when I swallowed a gulp, I only wanted more.

I went out to the central staircase to have a cigarette by myself. Someone had tacked thick canvas over the one window in the studio, making its air hot and thick with smoke, but out in the hall, a draft let in the clear winter air.

A couple of the younger students were out there. I stood in the doorway for a moment, watching them the way you watch people just a little younger than yourself, thinking, did I look like that? behave like that? There was a girl with short cropped hair, red lips, and a silky dress that looked like a nightgown, a skinny guy with a full mop of curly hair, and a third, pudgy tag-along. They were taking turns aiming bottle caps at a bottle they'd set up towards the landing. When a cap made contact they'd whoop and holler. In between throws, they were talking about someone they seemed to have met recently, trying to situate him, drawing conclusions about his politics and his aesthetics based on the books he was reading and a few comments he'd made in class. When they'd thrown all the caps they had, I walked past them towards the landing.

—⊬—

Jack was already sitting there.

Tell me one of your stories, I said, sitting down next to him.

He took a drag of his cigarette.

A true story, I said, lighting a cigarette of my own.

He thought about it for a second. Do you want a story about twins or about a woman and a chicken?

Twins.

Okay, he said, gathering the story together. So I met this woman, a lady of the night.

That lady of the night? I asked.

Well, yeah, he said. You know she had that gap in her teeth.

I nodded.

Well, she had a twin sister, and both had a rare disorder that meant they passed out at the sight of blood. When they were around twenty, one of them had started having terrible seizures in the night.

Which one? I asked. Her, or her sister?

Her sister, he said. They lived in the same building, in rooms that faced each other across a courtyard. They didn't have a phone, but once the seizures started, they rigged up a system that connected their windows using a rope with a heavy wooden block hanging from either end. Pulling on their wooden block would cause the wooden block on the other end to knock against the other's window. Early one morning my lady woke up to the knocking block. She went to her window and looked across the courtyard. All she could see was the shape of her sister hidden behind the curtains and her arms flailing. Come over, the curtain yelled, and bring someone with you. Her voice was garbled, as if she'd be drinking.

My lady asked her sister if she was bleeding, and her twin answered yes, a lot, that she had broken the mirror by her bed and cut her hand. So my lady twin went running over to help, and as soon as she walked in and saw the blood, she passed out, chipping her two front teeth in the process. The teeth cut into her lip, so she started bleeding profusely and her sister, hearing the fall and the cry that went along with it, knew she couldn't look. She closed her eyes and made her way to the window where she started pulling on the rope again, banging and banging on her sister's window, in the hopes that someone else would notice. Finally a neighbour did, so when she knew someone was coming, she could finally help her sister. When the neighbour showed up and found both of them lying on the floor, passed out and bleeding, it looked as if they'd had a terrible fight. The neighbour called the police, and it took a lot of explaining for the police to believe that neither was at fault.

Funny, I said.

She likes her teeth like that. Chipped like a vampire.

A vampire who hates blood, I said.

Hadn't even thought of that, he said, nodding at me, like I wasn't so bad after all. Or maybe it was just I who felt that way about him.

Really? I said. That was a true story?

True enough, he said.

I don't like true enough.

No? Isn't true enough sometimes better for everyone than true?

My boss died, I said.

I know, Jack said. I'm sorry.

—⁄—

When the hour got close to midnight, we gathered around my pocket watch and counted down as its little hands ticked towards twelve. At midnight, we shouted from the top of our lungs that it was 1928, and soon after that we tired. The six of us melted down into a warm little puddle in the middle of the studio, wrapped up in whatever blankets we could find, each of us carrying our own patch of weariness into the new year. When before I'd felt alienated at the sight of Sasha piled into a ball with Elisa and Jack, now I felt included, like I understood what that kind of touch meant, the way it was safe and not safe, but safe overall, and the way it satisfied an ongoing need to touch and be touched. No, not even that — the way it stoked that need, like we were being fed, and every touch made us hunger all the more. Even if I still wasn't sure about Jack, I could rest my head on his stomach and feel like at least in this way, this physical way, I could appreciate the flatness of his stomach, the slow rise and fall of his breathing, and I didn't have to love him for this to feel good. Sasha had closed his eyes, and Elisa was tracing letters along his arm.

A, he said.

Then Jack would describe a couple leaning towards each other, a woman in between, her mouth sucking the man off.

Elisa would say they were disgusting, but she found it funny too, this way of remembering the erotic alphabet, the new politics of sex.

Outside the streets were loud with car horns and people partying, but inside we were our own little puddle of bodies, breathing together, our gazes lazy and drifting from the hazy ceiling to the taxidermied creatures to the flickering of the candles as they got caught and twirled in the drafts. Every once in a while I'd think of Bekhterev and the emptiness would threaten to pour in, threaten to make my whole body a container for loss. Then I'd move closer to Sasha, and his touch was consolation, not just comfort, and then another body would slide against mine and I'd be back to the group and the taste of the summer sky.

—⁄—

Sometime after one in the morning, we were about to go to sleep when the door flung open and a gigantic man came in, yelling, Where's Tova!

He went into the city, said Sasha, sitting up. He went out with Oleg.

But the guy had come with ten other friends, and they knew two things: one, Oleg had a phonograph none of us knew about, and two, Oleg made vodka and kept it in the studio. (One thing we knew: Jack's vodka was gone.) The music got turned up and the glasses were filled and there was no question of sleeping then. One of the new arrivals tried to have a conversation with Elisa. She didn't seem to be aware that they were having a conversation. The guy wanted everyone to know that he'd met the Mexican artist.

Diga someone, he said, not knowing how to pronounce Diego Rivera but knowing, nevertheless, that he was famous.

The city had been full of fellow travellers from the West for months now. They'd all come for the anniversary and many had stayed on. I wanted to know about the Mexican artist, but I also wanted to *already* know, so I didn't ask.

Now Jack was telling the chicken story. I'd never seen him animated this way. The students who had been out in the hall and part of a different party had followed the new arrivals in, and were now sitting on the counter by the sink. They looked proud of themselves — they'd infiltrated an older, more refined group, if only for the night.

Jack had been in an accident. He'd gotten on a tram without paying and was spotted, almost immediately, by a policeman. So he jumped off just as a woman was about to get on, and they'd collided, landing in a puddle, while the tram pulled away. The problem was, she'd been carrying a chicken in her bag and the chicken had jumped out. It started squawking and running around in all directions. He didn't want the chicken to escape, so he had grabbed it and wrenched its neck like his mother showed him once, and the chicken died. When he put it down on the ground, it kept running around for a bit. He realized when he looked at the girl that she was hurt, and she laid into him yelling bloody murder. But even as she was yelling at him and he was hating her for it because it wasn't his fault — you can never see anything out those windows anyway, they're so goddamn filthy! — he could see this intensity in her eyes. She was staring at him with total clarity, and suddenly they were kissing, right there in the middle of the street. And then he was taking her home with him, back to his room and they spent the whole day together and then the whole night and only the following day, when she woke up screaming, did they realize that her arm had broken in the fall, and then he'd taken her to the hospital.

Elisa and Sasha were watching Jack, too, but they were different than the rest of his audience: they knew which parts were true. I was wondering if it was the chicken lady who had made him happy, up until the moment that

Elisa glided away from Sasha towards Jack. That was the change—the way she slipped into his arms told me that what had happened between them was new, but also, probably, permanent.

At some point, someone suggested a drinking game: enter the dragon. This is how it went. Everyone began the game sitting at the table. Elisa was the game leader, because everyone knew she couldn't hold her alcohol. Everyone put a few kopeks into the pot. Oleg's vodka filled our glasses. One of Tova's rats was also drinking.

Elisa yelled, Enter the dragon! and we obeyed, drinking and then ducking under the table until she said the dragon was gone. Falling out of one's chair signalled elimination. I gave up early, positioning myself under the table to watch how green the faces got as they hid from the dragon. When they resurfaced to pitch in another kopek, the coins bounced on the table just above my head. Jack was next to be eliminated, so the two of us sat beside each other, a good level of drunk, by which I mean functioning.

He hates to lose, Jack whispered, pointing to Sasha's legs. I knew Sasha would drink until he couldn't function anymore.

Enter the dragon, Elisa called out again, and everyone was under the table, breathing fast, in and out, a sluice of breath so saturated with alcohol that it alone could get you drunk. The dragon was gone, and everyone was back up, but not all at once, and the rules changed to whoever was last to sit upright back at the table was out. There was a momentary debate about what constituted *upright*. More and more of us gathered under the table. It was a hot, sweaty world under there, people folded up into one another as knees and elbows multiplied. Suddenly the heat got too much. I crawled out from under the table and realized that the only ones still up top were Sasha and Elisa, the two of them passed out with their heads resting on their folded up arms. I unfolded Sasha and said it was time for bed.

We pulled the mattress from Sasha's old cot into an empty studio across the hall. These studios had no windows, so the heat made them absurdly hot. We stripped down to go to sleep. The party across the hall kept going, but the sound was muted, and we were bone tired. Maybe we'd slept for an hour when Sasha got up to pee, leaving the door open behind him. I sensed someone in the doorway too quickly after Sasha had left and opened my eyes to see that the figure in the doorway wasn't Sasha, but the pudgy student, just standing there, staring.

Hey, I said, propping myself up to look at him. The pudgy student was very drunk. Could barely talk, it seemed. Sasha came back to bed, both of us naked, but the guy just stood there, staring.

Aren't you guys going to have sex or something? he asked.

No, Comrade. We're sleeping now, said Sasha, using the word *comrade* because the student wasn't a friend.

Come on. Just kiss her! he said to Sasha. She's exquisite!

It was funny, having him stand there like that, the party going on and he, like a lost dog, looking for something exciting, but in the wrong place.

Yeah, not tonight, we're just going to sleep, said Sasha.

I mean, we're here, he said. When are we ever going to be here again? He said it as if fate had presented us with a miraculous gift, and all we needed to do was to take full advantage of it.

I think we forgot he was there and laid back down, we were that tired. The student pulled our door shut, and I could tell from the sound of the studio door being opened and the rush of music and laughter that poured out that he'd gone back to the party.

Eventually, the music quieted and we fell into a really deep sleep, something you don't notice or remember unless it's interrupted, which it was, sometime later, when the student opened the door again and waited for us to notice him, standing there in his socks, underwear, and a tunic.

I just need a bed. I just thought I'd crawl in with you guys. There's nowhere else to sleep.

Whatever, we said.

He had been kind of cute just standing there. But then he was on my side with his hands, just gently first, wanting to find their way around my waist, which was okay.

And I said, Sure but we're just going to sleep, okay.

He mumbled, Yeah, yeah, I just want to sleep, I'm so tired, but then his hands groped their way to between my legs. I yelled out and Sasha hopped between us and said in a sleepy but stern way that all we wanted to do was sleep.

He agreed wholeheartedly, saying, Yeah, no problem. Really, I just want to sleep, too.

A few moments passed and I drifted off, until Sasha suddenly jerked into me, away from the guy, and that was the end of him. The poor thing basically didn't care where his hands landed, whether on female parts or male; he just wanted *something* that night, *anything*.

So that was the first day of 1928; Sasha and I having to fight off a guy who looked like a bear and wanted sex so bad he'd try to get it from anywhere.

—⁄—

When we walked home the next morning, the city felt as if it were a place I'd never been. I can't say for sure if Sasha felt the same way, but as we walked he smoked one cigarette after the other, pausing on street corners to light the next one from the previous, so I knew he was nervous and I worried he'd make himself sick. We'd barely slept. Somehow, the city had shifted just enough to make us dizzy. As if the streets and buildings and parks had been lifted up off their grid and then given a sharp kick before being laid back down, so that they were now ever so slightly askew—north not so north anymore.

Give it a few days, I said to myself as I walked just ahead of Sasha, trying to stay out of his haze. I wanted to tell him I'd never go back to the dacha again. I wanted to say I didn't care if his mother hated me. I wanted to say that the family unit was bullshit and that she could go fuck herself. When we got to the park and I saw the mean group of kids and Tobias huddling with a woman I'd never seen, I wanted to kick them all in the shins because something had to hurt real bad and it might as well be them, since they were accustomed to hurting and might as well hurt some more. But I walked past, and so did Sasha. If Tobias saw me, he didn't show it. The truth was that what had changed was Moscow itself, and the change was because Bekhterev was gone, and we both knew it.

1928

When I returned to the institute on that first Monday after the break, I knew from the fresh blanket of snow between the gate and the back entrance that I would be alone. The lock had frozen over and at first resisted my key.

Inside, I looked around the kitchen for signs that anyone had been there, but there were none. The light filtering into the kitchen was diffuse and grey, made so by the layers of frost that had accumulated on the windows while the heat had been off. The frost always came in delicately at first, in fine, fern-like formations, but in our absence, it had thickened into a solid sheet, effectively cutting the institute off from the outside world. This small change was enough to make the whole institute feel abandoned, yet it had been hardly more than a week since Congress had closed.

I pulled on my slippers and lit the stove. While the kettle started up, I drifted down the hall to the lab. A lamp had been left on in Bekhterev's office. Its pale light reflected off the shiny surfaces of the lab tables and followed me around, just as the sun's last rays strike out across a surface of water, following the walker on the shore. I wove in and out of the tables, in and out of the light, passing the glass cabinets, but not seeing inside them, as I saw only myself.

In the doorway of his office I lingered for a moment, but it was inevitable that I would go in and sit down, as I always had, in the chair facing his desk, and, in doing so, begin to adapt to his being gone. His death seemed to have slowed time down, fucked with it somehow. It seemed simultaneously possible that it had been years since I'd last sat there but also that I'd sat there minutes ago, that Bekhterev had died years ago, or had left on a train bound for Leningrad just that morning. I had no words for how I felt. I wasn't numb exactly, but nothing raced inside me, no feeling I could name, nothing as clear as fear, or sadness.

Maybe he had left the light on because he'd planned to return.

His desk was as it had always been: beside the lamp, there was a cup full of pencils, a ragged pile of papers, and, towards the outer edge of the light's beam, a mortified hand floating in a glass jar. On the other side of the desk, a small framed photo faced Bekhterev's chair, an image that had always existed in my imagination, since I'd never sat where he did, never crossed to his side of the desk. I'd always assumed it was a family portrait. It had been so real to me that I'd even conceived of how they had posed: Bekhterev standing behind his wife, his hand on her shoulder, and she, with the youngest baby in her arms, flanked on either side by the older siblings, two boys and a girl. And behind this image of domesticity, Bekhterev, staring straight into the camera, stiff and unyielding, a patriarch, an old man.

Just then, I heard a door close. A slight draft grazed the back of my neck between the edge of my hair and the collar of my dress. I'd imagined the closing door, I thought. Again the ghost-like draft, but I didn't believe in ghosts.

It seemed to me that there might be a good way to do this, to adapt to his being gone, and that it might begin with my making it more real. I went to the other side of the desk. Being where I normally wouldn't have been might be a place to start. *Being* different would make me *think* differently.

It turned out the framed photograph was not an image of his family at all, just the same portrait of Lenin that could be found everywhere, a portrait so ubiquitous it was invisible. I felt some small disappointment not to have known that this was what he'd looked at every day. It galled me to discover something about him now that he was gone, as though I were betraying him rather than just wishing he would come back. I'd actually never really been close to anyone who had died. If my parents were dead I didn't officially know, which kept them alive, in a way. I'd known Bekhterev was old, but he'd always seemed invincible to me. His death seemed to come out of a cruel nowhere. I didn't know what to do with the fact of it. Yes, death was inevitable, but Bekhterev had been exceptional in all cases, so why not this one? What was I supposed to do with the sadness of it? With the emptiness?

What is there to be done? That was Lenin. *Get going.* That was Bekhterev.

—⧸—

It was towards the end of that first week that I started to understand how the institute would change. Initially, even once everyone had returned from the holiday, no one spoke of Bekhterev. Our silence on the matter seemed to prevent all other conversation. Anushka was the type to talk about such things; Zhanna would do anything to avoid it. The one time Anush said she couldn't understand how he'd died, whispered it, really, into her teacup, when we were all sitting in the kitchen, Zhanna stated loudly that he was old, and then, strangely, segued into a discussion about a painting they'd both liked and then on to a history of that painter who she said had an unbelievable capacity for capturing the sad eyes of horses. The painter was born in Samara she said, and in that way, she led the conversation south, then east and away.

In part, we were able to go on in his absence because we were so accustomed to it. It wasn't so different, after all, from him being in Leningrad with his family, or away at a conference. I tried not to think about it too much, tried to keep busy. Bekhterev had always been the person who pushed us, and so even when he was away, he was there, in an expectation or a deadline. Now, with his death, the danger was that we would not only be quiet, but aimless, too.

Sarkisov saw to it that we wouldn't stay aimless.

Late one afternoon, I found myself walking towards the doors at the end of the laboratory that led to the grand salon. I thought I was alone. At the doors, I exhaled, then pulled them open.

The exhibits were silhouettes, their dark, floating shapes backlit by the pale grey murkiness that seeped in from the entrance hall. The grand salon was as we had left it, and yet it was not the same. I stood still to let my eyes adjust, waiting for something, a movement maybe, or some kind of sign. Not even the dust in the air shifted. The light was so grey it barely deserved to be called light.

I took a chair from the side of the wall and set it beneath the chandelier, facing Lenin's brain. The chair scraped against the floor when I sat, the sound echoing for but a moment. Then the room fell, again, into silence.

I remembered the work that had been done on Lenin's brain, how the autopsy report had described some parts as showing a pronounced collapse of the cerebral surface, and then elsewhere, two adjacent spots of collapse, and then elsewhere, additional signs of decay. The amateurs described him as having water on the brain, and I wondered about the links between water and melancholy, melancholy and collapse.

Sitting there, I had the feeling of a question in me. The feeling that, if I sat still for long enough, a clear question might form, and then I'd be closer to an answer. Yes, I was waiting for a thing to happen. The chair creaked ever so slightly as I shifted. It seemed absurd and a little dramatic to be sitting alone in the room like that, thinking about melancholy and collapse, but life was different without Bekhterev. I felt unhinged. I leaned back in my chair, looked up at the chandelier, at the scraps of light shivering there, trapped in the prisms.

And then I was aware that I was not alone. I had the feeling of having been caught.

The chandelier clicked on; its filaments jumped to life. I stood up.

Sarkisov walked slowly around the other side of the exhibits, picking up a chair from the opposite wall, dragging it behind him, slowly, as though it were made of lead and he were exceptionally tired. The chair caught on an uneven square in the parquet flooring and righted itself with a small jump. All of this happened in a regular amount of time, that is to say, quite quickly, yet I noticed every small thing about the way he was moving, the sweep of the chair, its arc as he swung it around him, and how he sat down and motioned for me to sit squarely in front of him, so close our knees were almost touching.

I was still beneath the chandelier, but now its lights were glowing and I felt very much on display.

It must be difficult for you, he said, to be here without Dr. Bekhterev. He leaned forward, as if looking for a sign. All this time, the two of you together, teacher and student, he trailed off, waiting for me to respond.

I realized that I'd never particularly looked at him, never noticed the deep creases that cut down his cheeks, nor the wrinkles across his forehead—none of these lines the result of joy.

Yes, I said, looking down at my hands, wondering if he was being kind to me or if the knot in my gut was some sort of instinctual response to a legitimate threat. The institute would be different now. The edges of the room receded and the corners on the exhibits sharpened. Like any other worker, I would need to prove myself. Like any other worker, I could fail. All this was communicated to me across the silence Sarkisov and I shared.

He was an important mentor to you, a kind of father figure. I know he was very fond of you. He went on, Did you know he thought you were very gifted?

I looked down at my lap, almost happy with this news but wary nevertheless. He was asserting himself, explaining that he'd seen my special status under Bekhterev — and that now it was gone.

It is a shame that he fell ill so suddenly, he said, leaning back, crossing his arms over his chest.

Because everything he said was not declarative — not a statement of fact, but investigative, a probe into me and my capacity to work without Bekhterev— I knew not to react. Yet inside, I was imagining myself at the deathbed, at the moment of sickness, at the moment of passing. I'd not been able to imagine it before because Bekhterev was unassailable. When he moved to St. Petersburg from the countryside at the age of sixteen, he had suffered what he called a mental derangement. He'd told me about it in the context of something else, but all I'd ever thought about it was the strength he'd shown: an unwillingness to succumb to pressure — even when it came from within. He'd diagnosed himself with severe neurasthenia and healed himself within a period of twenty-eight days. Despite that strength, ever since he'd told me about the incident, I'd watched for its recurrence, worried that I was wrong, aware that everyone was vulnerable in some way or to something. I'd gotten old enough to know that.

And to have died, despite all the medical attention he received, Sarkisov went on.

Oh? I asked, looking at him.

He looked up at the chandelier. The warm light had softened the lines on his face, making him appear younger.

I looked up as well and noticed that one of the lights in the chandelier had burned out. Perhaps it had never worked to begin with.

He sat up straight and said categorically, I was there, of course. As was Prozorov, Professor Blagovolin and, on the request of the Health Commissioner, a close colleague of Bekhterev's, Professor Ilyin was called.

I knew some of those men.

We didn't leave until we were certain he would pull through. It was a great shock, then, to hear that he had died the next day. Sarkisov coughed into his hand and said, But we move forward.

Yes, I said.

He stood up and moved behind his chair. Again, I noticed his height. Holding on to the chair back, he said, I have a special task for you — a way that you can recognize the special contribution that Dr. Bekhterev made.

Anything at all, I said. I'll do anything.

I thought so, he said, clapping his hands loudly and then rubbing them together, producing a sound that was chalky, as though they were both exceptionally dry and exceptionally soft.

He began, then, to question me about my experience at the institute. To what degree had I worked on the exhibits? Had I prepared the specimens? Despite the fact that I hadn't, did I feel as though I had acquired enough knowledge to prepare a good specimen? If not, did I know who to ask? Would Anushka be of help? What about Zhanna? Did I know, for example, about the particularities of the microtome that Dr. Vogt had left with us, and had I familiarized myself with the locations for purchasing a new blade and was I, as it were, on good terms with Dr. Vogt, and could I not, perhaps, be in touch with him directly with any questions I might have about the microtoming of our newest acquisition. This was how I found out, or it would be more precise to say that this was how I realized — and it made me sick, I'll admit it, though only briefly — that we would be displaying Dr. Bekhterev's brain; I had at once the feeling that this was as it ought to be, and yet it was terrible, terrible, terrible.

When the corners of my eyes itched with the first threat of tears, I coughed and made a display of sniffing so that there might be some other reason for any emerging redness in my eyes. There was no question of sentimentality with Sarkisov. Was I, he asked, familiar with Dr. Bekhterev's biography? Might I feel equipped to write up a sort of *memorandus*, and would I know people with whom I could speak in order to gather further information about his life, his commitments, his activities, *such as they were*. He said this in a tone I couldn't quite put my finger on. Perhaps I might be able to ascertain whether or not he was a true Communist, perhaps I might find out if he had ever attended the rallies, the meetings, the speeches, and, if he hadn't — and here Sarkisov raised his eyebrows pointedly — I might find out *why*.

Hadn't he written books on materialism? I wondered.

All this information would permit of a larger goal, said Sarkisov, one which would become clear, but only in due time. Of course, a report would be required, a report that could condense the *memorandus*: we would condense it, he said, emphasizing the *we*, and all of this must be finished quickly and efficiently because our public will expect to see Dr. Bekhterev's wishes fulfilled, and soon.

I looked disoriented, I suppose, because he clarified that Bekhterev had willed his brain to the institute, a statement that seemed to be Sarkisov's final attempt, a conclusive effort, to upset me. And again, I willed myself to remain blank. I felt ill-equipped for the task, felt that I owed that much to Bekhterev, but hoped also that Sarkisov had chosen me for a reason, seeing in me some innate skill I didn't know I had.

Good, then, he said, and left me sitting there with my hands knotted up in my lap, as if they been tightly holding onto something, though there was nothing.

—✶—

That night I met Sasha at Max's, a small bar near his old studio. On the phone, I'd left a message telling him to meet me, telling him we'd be celebrating because if I was going to move on, it would be like that—in celebration. I was no longer an assistant; I was in charge. Before too long, I thought, it would be my photograph that would be taken.

Nothing about Max's had changed over the years except that when we'd first gone there, the ban on alcohol meant we'd had to fill our glasses under the table. Now we could order drinks directly. The place didn't have more than five tables, but it was packed. Smoke clouded the room. When I first got in, I couldn't see Sasha anywhere, and then I found him, hidden in the back at a corner table. The barmaid he liked so much was there talking to him, standing between him and the door so he didn't see me when I entered. When he did, he straightened up and she slipped away, taking a glass with her. The ashtray overflowed with his smashed-up cigarettes.

I was about to take off my coat when Sasha stood and said, Let's go.

I imagined telling him the good news, describing the assignment from Sarkisov as a kind of promotion. A recognition and a challenge. I thought that Sasha and I would order cognac, or maybe go home, and how maybe somewhere in the apartment he'd hidden a bottle of something, saved it for a special occasion. We'd bring it out and set out our two good glasses and pull on our warm socks and smoke cigarettes and laugh and feel like things would get better. Feel like we had felt when we were younger.

But when we left the bar, he walked ahead of me, and too fast for me to keep up. In the conversation we were going to have, I was going to ask him about his day. How was your work? I would have asked, and Sasha would have told a funny story. The more I thought about what I wanted to have happen and then put it up next to the dark image of his figure hurrying ahead of me, the sadder I got.

When he lifted up his arm to hail a taxi, then stepped out onto the street before it had properly slowed, and in doing so, almost got himself run over, I knew that something was quite wrong. We couldn't afford taxis.

What's the big news? he asked, once we were both inside.

I told the driver where we were going. Do you have money for this? I asked Sasha, reaching across his body to look in his pockets for change.

What are we celebrating? he asked, stretching out the words, making them taut and strange, because he was feeling sarcastic and didn't want to celebrate at all.

His pockets were empty and we had only made it halfway home.

We need money for this, I said, and told the driver to stop. I gave him all I had, but it wasn't enough and he cursed at me as he drove away.

Sasha's arm draped across my shoulder, transferring all of his weight onto me. From the level of the street, up over the worn curb, and clean across the whole sidewalk, lay a continuous sheet of ice. If I'd ducked out from under his arms, he'd have fallen.

So what's going on? I asked.

Nothing, he said.

I let go. A nearby lamppost took hold of him and held him up.

All that week, Sasha seemed to be home earlier than me, something which didn't solidify into anything strange, until he told me that he'd lost his job.

On this night, Sasha was sitting on our couch when I walked in. I'd been at the institute far too late, completing a preparation that Anushka had started but had gotten too tired to finish. Ever since the conversation with Sarkisov in the grand salon, I'd felt more and more responsible for what happened at the institute, for what would happen to it now that Bekhterev was gone. I'd made myself a tea down the hall in the kitchen before continuing to our apartment.

He'd been reading, which was something he'd decided to do more of lately, but he put the book down and got up when I came in. Beside him there was a collection of teacups stacked precariously, one on top of the other on the ledge of the balcony door, a spoon sticking up out of the top one. The air smelled stale.

How are you? I asked, handing him my tea so I could take off my boots.

Thinking, he said, blowing on the tea to cool it down for me.

When my boots were off, Sasha handed it back.

Do you ever think about the Osorgins? he asked. I mean, wonder where they are? Or what really happened?

Sasha was nostalgic for something that had never happened—the conversations he'd wished we could have had at their place, with them or without them, in the bookshop or afterwards at the bar down the street. That place gave him ideas, he said, in a way that hardly anything else did. This was why he was reading again, trying to get it back.

Whenever he got like this, thinking about the past all the time, he got an aura about him that enveloped me, pulled me in.

I always used to feel, he said, as if the messages on the blackboard had been written specifically with me in mind.

Whoever does not wish to sink into the wretchedness of the finite is constrained in the most profound sense to struggle with the infinite. That was Kierkegaard. That was Sasha.

I had thought about them that night on the landing, when Elisa first told us about their disappearance but since then, hardly at all.

Of course I think about them, I lied. But they got sent to Berlin, didn't Elisa say that?

She said Finland.

Elisa hadn't said anywhere, but he didn't seem to remember.

I set the tea down on top of the bookshelf and opened a jar of jam, smelling it to make sure it wasn't off before delivering two spoonfuls into my cup: extra sweet because I was so tired.

Anyway they *would* have gone on to Berlin, I said to Sasha. That's what everyone does. They would have found a life there.

I guess, said Sasha.

I walked over to him and opened the balcony door a crack.

Does it smell in here? asked Sasha.

Like a boy's bedroom, I said, but he looked hurt so I added, Have you been here all day? I bent down to kiss him, but he was distracted.

They've probably set up a new bookstore in Berlin, I said. It's probably got the same name. Maybe they hired Schopenhauer.

He's dead, said Sasha.

I set my tea down and stretched my arms back behind my head. The thing with winter was that its aches stayed with you even when you went inside. I was depleted, and Sasha was depleting me further. I could tend to his existential concerns for only so long.

I lost my job, said Sasha.

If I thought I felt tired before, it was nothing compared to the draining dismay I felt inside me then, thinking of how we'd have to struggle now, how being the youngest boy in a rich family meant he'd always be that child, thinking that someone, somewhere, ought to provide for him, and how now he thought it would be me. I'd always tried not to think of him as a type, but it was becoming harder to resist the idea that our types were so different that no amount of love could bridge the gap.

Schopenhauer's dead? I asked.

Did you hear what I said? said Sasha.

I sat down next to him.

He'd had an argument with someone at work and had, as a result, been transferred from the studios on the second floor to working in the gallery on the first. The argument had been so bad that Sasha had been told to stay at home until the gallery needed him. He hadn't been fired but he'd put it that way—worse than it was—so that I could get angry and then be relieved that it wasn't as bad as it seemed.

I'll start next week. They have a big install coming up, he said in an optimistic tone, but I still felt so tired inside.

What did you do? I asked.

That's nice, Tatiana.

Well there must have been something, I said.

A difference of opinion, said Sasha.

The clock ticked. The two spoonfuls of jam had been a mistake. As the tea cooled, the mixture tasted more and more like cough syrup. At what point did a difference of opinion become a difference of values? And at what point did an ideological difference mean working with a friend was more like working with an enemy? Had he become someone's enemy?

He wasn't happy with the transfer but he was powerless to do anything about it. The state provided everything except choice, but choice seemed to be what Sasha wanted most.

What hurt was that Sasha had started to like his work in the studio. Not the work itself—he could never enjoy the aesthetic— but he liked the people. He liked having lunch with them, and going to Max's at the end of the week.

You'll still see the people, I said. You'll just be downstairs.

I stood and added my teacup to his collection. I grabbed a cigarette from my bag and went back to the balcony door, pulling it open a little farther to let the smoke out and more fresh air in.

I used to make art, Tatiana. Now all I'll be doing is hanging it.

This was the real problem. It wasn't that he'd liked working with Rodchenko, nor colouring, nor any of that. No job would ever be a good job because he'd never wanted to have to have a job at all. He'd wanted to be a painter, but nobody wanted that kind of painting now, and this meant he felt that no one wanted him.

I thought these years were good for artists, I said, lighting my cigarette. I'd heard someone say that.

No, said Sasha, these years are good for illustrators, not artists. Illustrators don't have original ideas, but artists do.

I wanted to ask what original thoughts he'd had lately, but, for the sake of marital peace, refrained. I knew him, though, and I knew that even if the new job wasn't perfect, he'd make it work because although he was a rich kid at heart, he knew how to work things out. People had different ways of adjusting to change. Some people were re-signed; other people complained. And some extraordinary individuals were able to turn a bad situation into a good one. That's what Sasha had done with the colouring job. He was a guy who knew how to buy contraband cigarettes from a girl in a public square in the middle of Moscow. He knew how to find clementines. He would figure this out, too.

It's not that I want fame, he said. It's that I'm not myself here. I can't *be* myself.

You'll find a way, I said. And anyway, why can't you *be* a part of something bigger than you? Why do you always have to be yourself? Why is it all about you?

Don't make it like that, he said. I'm not being selfish, I just want to feel like I'm more than just part of a machine. That's how we're treated here, like we're nothing more than cogs in a wheel. Why don't you hate the timekeepers as much as I do? he asked.

I tried to find it in me to hate the idea that someone might be trying to make us more productive, but I didn't hate it. I *wanted* to be more productive. I *wanted* to be more everything. Not only that, the timekeepers were a fixture in factories only—no one was really tracking the time it took Sasha to draw a line nor me to catalogue a figure. He only hated them on principle and he wanted me to hate them, too.

He was still talking, saying, Don't pretend you don't understand what I mean, when I know you do. You don't work as hard as you do because of some damn timekeeper, you do it because of you. You used to do it for Bekhterev, maybe you still do.

I took the last drag of my cigarette and then leaned out the door to throw it off the balcony. Sometimes Sasha's attachment to the past was beautiful, and sometimes he would get so caught up in how things used to be, or could have been, that he seemed to be drowning, and pulling me down with him.

I'm sure the Osorgins are fine, and I'm glad you have a new job, I said, coming fully back inside.

—⁄—

At the institute, the silence persisted for the first few months of 1928, so that work sounded like the shuffling of papers, the pouring of tea, the clinking of glass jars meeting each other in the sink. Drawers, cabinets, and catalogue trays slid open and closed. The typewriter cartridge shunted back to the beginning with a familiar ding.

The word about Bekhterev's death seemed to have spread, though I don't know what would have been said, exactly; only that in the fall we'd been poised to be a central public institution, and by winter, we seemed to have been completely forgotten. For those first months, no one came to visit, not even Luria, whose company I had come to look forward to more than I liked to admit. He was the one person who I could have talked to about missing Bekhterev, so without him I felt like I lacked even the words that would have helped me understand how I felt.

The isolation and silence that fell over us were the first signs that the mood had changed, but something else had, too. Before, we'd been in pursuit of something—an idea, a vision—and now there was the faintest feeling that we were being pursued. I started to see what Sasha meant by the tyranny of the timekeepers, because that was what Zhanna seemed to have become, an observer of our work, even if she was also meant to be part of our team. I realized that Sarkisov must have had personal conversations with each of us, tasking everyone with slightly altered responsibilities that put us on edge, at odds with each other in a way we hadn't been before. He was our quiet puppet master. I tried to believe what I'd said to Sasha — that I appreciated the idea of someone keeping us on task, that all incitements to productivity were the same, no matter where they came from — but then Zhanna would glance my way, and I'd hate her a little for whatever murky accusation she was communicating with that glance. The atmosphere of appraisal infected us all like a disease. Just as I imagined Zhanna was evaluating my use of time, I started appraising the others, wondering what motivated them, what special role Sarkisov might have given them. It was a lonely way to be.

Instead of sharing how daunted I was by my new responsibilities surrounding the Bekhterev exhibit, I sought sympathy for how much remained to do from the cataloguing I'd begun in the fall. That work had the command of Bekhterev behind it, which meant it was an acceptable reason for delay.

So, I spent January and February absorbed with the specimens we would never display publicly. In the fall I had finished the human specimens — the baker's wrist, the hand of the thief — but now I was cataloguing the creatures. I emptied the top shelves of their dry specimens — their weightlessness was all that united them — and began to marshal them into factions, uniting the winged creatures, the whole skeletons of rodents, the partial skeletons of larger mammals.

When I finished with the dry specimens, I moved on to the wet specimens, which were, I am not shy to admit, of a grosser, less ephemeral nature. I took Bekhterev's specimen of the mortified hand from his desk and added it to the human collection, and for more than a moment and on more than one occasion, I found myself drift off into a reverie in which I found myself atop the mountain, standing with Sasha, screaming at the moon. There were tapeworms and leeches.

The process continued for weeks, until I came to the final set of specimens, from the ocean, which represented for me a mythical world of non-beings because they didn't breathe or smell, and — for those that came from the deepest depths — did not see.

Eventually, I could stand back and look at the cabinets full of exquisite, strange specimens and feel satisfied with their display. The preparations lined the glass shelves, casting their shadows on the specimens beneath them, which cast their own shadows on those beneath them, so that the bottom row was all darkness and dust. Some specimens prefer the dark. They degrade in the light.

There was only one moment that interrupted this ordering process, and that was when I came across a perfectly prepared dry specimen of a human heart. I'd missed it, somehow, in the fall. I held it up and marvelled at the perfectly shaped ventricles and veins and folds of tissue, all intact, nothing torn. Everything about it was so wonderful, except that the label was not in my hand, nor in my red ink, and all it said was *no data attached*, which meant that the specimen had no scientific value at all. Whose heart had it been, I asked. But no one knew. If Bekhterev had been alive, I thought, he would have admired the perfection of the specimen in the same way I did. But he was gone.

—⊬—

Please, said Sasha on one of the nights before he'd started work again, tell me about order. I don't understand, he said, why one thing comes after the other. Did you choose Mendeleev over Rubinstein?

I protested: Why all these questions to answers you already know?

Between Sasha and me, a cool distance persisted. I wasn't ready yet to let him in.

But I don't know, Tatiana.

But you do, I said. I've told you before.

No, he said, I thought I knew, but sometimes these things get turned around and I want to hear it all again. I don't think the way you do, but I want to.

He leaned back into the couch then, his legs crossed at the ankle, his arms crossed over his chest, waiting. Then he reached out to me, saying, Come back, and he pulled me towards him. Tell me what makes one specimen go on a top shelf and one on the bottom.

I sat next to him, allowing our sides to touch, signalling that I might allow him back in after all.

As for the question, I didn't quite know, except that the order imposed on the specimens, our private collection, and the order imposed on the brains, the public collection, was different. The first listened to science. The second listened to the politburo's ideas of science. I thought he wanted a more precise answer, but the only thing that came to mind was the red pen and the red typewriter ribbon. No, now that wasn't true either. There was a logic to how the private collection was ordered: by species, by habitat, and additional considerations such as the specimen's susceptibility to light. I started with those. Sasha wanted more detail, more. Not only about what governed the display cases, but also about which ones touched me.

Touched me? I said.

I mean, he said, do you love any of them more than others?

There was the heart, but also the sea urchin with its thousands of spikes and its wine-red colour that had faded over the years, the dust that had gathered on it having been so hard to remove and, in places, impossible without risking breaking off another of its spindly reaches. But these things were private to me and not scientific.

I thought that what Sasha wanted was a scientific perspective as opposed to my own perspective, and so I said, No, it's not like that; we don't get *moved* by things.

Nothing at all? he asked.

No. Nothing.

Not even the brains?

Well, yes, I said, there is something thrilling about the blacked-out section of Lenin's brain, the way the blackness registers on the slides and the way the black seems to become substantial when the slides lay atop one another. He nodded then, and I could practically see him creating a mental image of the slides laid atop each other, black upon black upon black, until the empty, watered-out, collapsed, melancholic part of Lenin's brain became as wondrous to him as it was for me. I understood his questions differently then, saw that what he was after wasn't so much the logic of our collections as it was the logic of me. Then I wished that I'd told him about the heart, but I couldn't go back so said nothing more. While I spoke, he looked at me with such attention that a certain heat accumulated in me, making my nose and upper lip sweat. I felt nervous and electric to be listened to in such a way, and had to laugh because I was reacting as though I hardly knew Sasha, as though I were exposing myself to him for the first time all over again. What an extraordinary curiosity he had. Even after all those years together, even after we had disappointed and hurt each other, he could turn a page, make me feel unique and new all over again. And this even though there was no other person on the face of the planet who knew me better than he did.

Every last detail, he said, more.

It took months for it to happen, but finally, just as we'd started to get truly tired of winter, Luria came round. Maybe it was late February, or maybe we'd made it into March. That was him, the man I saw through the window, the one wearing the dark overcoat and hat, the man picking his way through the knee-deep snow from the gate to the door, trying to make his steps fit into ours. I hadn't seen him since Congress, and realized as I watched him approach that I'd missed him. Once inside, he collapsed into the chair closest to the door. He kept his hat and coat on, pulled his pipe from his coat, asked for matches. I wanted to hug him, to kiss his cheeks, but he was too stiff for that, and maybe I was too.

Where have you been? I asked.

He sat down and lit his pipe saying, Can I have some tea? and then, after a moment, I've been thinking.

Once I'd made tea, he put down his pipe and stood to remove his layers. He wore a rumpled grey suit, a red silk scarf, and the same wire-rimmed glasses he'd been wearing for over ten years. He could have been dapper, but everything about him that day seemed damp and worn. Exhaustion pooled under his eyes, his hair seemed to have suddenly greyed, and whereas months ago his wiry body had seemed taut and athletic, now it just seemed frail.

About what? I asked.

He looked up at me and said, You look exhausted.

Oh? I said.

Horrid season.

His coat and boots were dripping onto the floor.

Take your boots off, I said.

I'm not staying.

You're staying for tea.

For warmth, we settled in the kitchen. I sat across the

table from him with my knees pulled up to my chest, the tea too hot to drink. I waited while Luria stirred jam into his tea, losing himself in the small whirlpool he created in his cup. Then he looked up at me.

Did you ever hear about the Beilis trial? he asked.

No, I don't think so, I said.

He held the spoon's handle lightly between thumb and forefinger, so that the bowl of the spoon wavered up and down.

About that Kiev boy who was murdered? he prodded, watching the spoon. *Murdered*, I thought. The word seemed out of place. I knew the way Luria thought; I knew this was preliminary work he was doing, laying a trail for me to follow so that we could arrive at the same conclusions by way of the evidence, but I felt impatient and wished he'd take the straight path, just come out with it.

The blood libel case, I said.

I remembered it as the newspapers my father took away from me, as conversations that quieted whenever my mother took me into a café on a late afternoon, as the gossip we shared in the coatroom at school when I was still a child.

I remember the basics, I guess. I was only twelve or thirteen.

Same age as the boy then, said Luria.

Yes, I said, recalling our childhood speculations about what had happened. Not everyone's parents were as protective as mine.

So you don't remember anything, said Luria.

Sure I do, I said. I remember that the boy's body was discovered in a cave, that there was something strange about the wounds, and that the Black Hundreds were involved. I don't remember just how. I remember a gang of thieves, but maybe that was just kids talking.

It sounds like they got it right, said Luria.

You're bringing this up for a reason, I said.

Bekhterev testified at the trial, said Luria.

I remembered. This was what it was like getting older, suddenly all these disparate pieces of life—the forbidden newspapers, the hushed conversations, the darkened cave, and the fear that marked those few months when all I really wanted was to have my parents leave me alone—all those pieces now suddenly became a part of today, part of my adult life, which is to say part of my real life and not the netherworld of childhood.

Luria paused and then asked, Doesn't it seem strange to you that there was no funeral?

For the boy? I asked.

Tatiana, he said, his tone both condescending and exasperated. For Bekhterev.

He'd finally come to the point of his visit. He didn't care about the boy in the cave. The boy in the cave was a tool for Luria, a bridge of sorts.

What kind of strange? I asked.

What kind of strange? The only kind, suspicious strange, he said. He leaned forward ever so slightly.

What I'm trying to figure out, Tatiana, is what exactly happened to Bekhterev. Ever remember him missing a class, missing a lab, missing *anything* in all the years you worked with him? No. Of course you don't. Because he didn't. Dr. Bekhterev *never* got sick. *Never* missed anything. He was like a tank or something; he could eat anything, drink anything, never sleep, *not* eat, and still he'd be seeing patients at eight in the morning and working into the night and we'd only complain because we couldn't keep up. How does a man like that die of stomach flu?

I thought of the strange illness from which Bekhterev had cured himself at such a young age, and then about the night we'd walked along the river, and how he'd seemed so weary and nostalgic, as old men sometimes are when they know that death is nigh. I'd been telling myself that Bekhterev was vulnerable in a way that few understood, and that I'd understood his vulnerability better than most because we'd worked together for so long, because I'd seen his moods, seen the weariness in his eyes as he'd looked back on himself as a younger man, exploring Berlin by night. Geniuses had particular vulnerabilities. I'd come to see that.

Luria was still talking: *I* could die of stomach flu. *Sasha* could die of stomach flu. You're a woman, so you couldn't. And Bekhterev was the kind who couldn't either. But he did. So what happened?

It seemed as if Luria was doing the work that Sarkisov had asked of me.

He went on: So, the trial. The murdered boy was named Andrei and his murder wasn't even the worst part of the story. His playmates found him dead in a cave near a brick factory in 1911. His body had been mutilated.

How? I asked, waiting with my arms looped around my knees. I could see that he hadn't talked this through with anyone yet.

Luria repositioned himself as though he were giving an academic lecture: his chair pushed back from the table, his knees apart, his hands moving like birds caught in a too-small cage, though perhaps that wasn't quite right. Maybe birds, when they feel caught, just stay still. Maybe *I* was the caught bird. When he set his pipe down on the table, it fell to one side and some burned tobacco spilled out. He didn't notice.

The murdered boy had been found in a cave near a brick factory in 1911. His body had been mutilated and abandoned.

Now the circumstances of the murder and subsequent trial started coming back to me. The trial had involved secret Jewish rituals, but my memory of it was that of a child's: grotesque and overburdened with a moral weight I had never thoroughly examined. It was a kind of fairy tale for me where evil was pure, where blood was black and congealed and hidden away in the secret chamber to which one ought never have a key.

Luria described the wounds to the head: it had been perforated as a result of a rhomboid-shaped metal tool. Thirteen holes exactly. Made by a probe, perhaps, something one might find at a shoe-maker's or in a factory, something meant for cutting leather, the investigators thought. No one knew why thirteen holes. The body was nearly bloodless, but he hadn't bled out there, in the cave, so that was one of the questions at the trial. What had happened to all that blood? Some said that a total of five cups of blood could have been taken from it. *Taken* was the word they used at first, but later they used the word *harvested*. The blood had been harvested, they said. Initially, the police accused some local thieves, a woman named Vera and her associates. The boy knew about their undertakings, so, in order to protect themselves, the thieves killed him.

So, it was Vera's trial? I asked.

No. No, it wasn't. It should have been her trial, but it wasn't, and that's why the whole affair was so fucked up. And that's why Bekhterev was a kind of hero, but maybe not the Soviet kind.

On second thought, I realized then that Luria was doing the work Sarkisov hoped I *wouldn't* do. Luria wasn't investigating whether Bekhterev had contributed to the revolutionary effort, but rather whether the revolutionary state had contributed to Bekhterev's death.

Luria took his pipe up again, and nervously tapped

some new tobacco into it, and I understood that the length of time he took to complete this mundane activity was equal to the degree to which what would follow had upset him and might upset me.

No, no, definitely not the Soviet kind, he said, as if to himself.

It was just then that a sound from the laboratory startled us. I tried to stand up, but my legs had been curled up against me for so long by then that millions of pins pricked into them and forced me to sit back down.

Luria's dark, tired eyes flashed up at me.

It was Sarkisov who appeared in the doorway, standing so erect his head almost touched the frame. Why do you have to be so tall? I thought. He smiled in a way that seemed to damage his face, as though it were poorly suited for the expression.

Luria shuffled his legs under the table.

Morning, said Sarkisov.

And to you, I said, all of us nodding at one another in a polite way, the formality of it suggesting something was wrong.

Alex, he said to Luria, which struck me as oddly familiar.

Luria nodded, then looked down at his watch.

Who wasn't a Soviet hero? asked Sarkisov.

Luria was already standing, saying that he needed to leave immediately, that he hadn't realized the time, time flew so quickly these days, it just snuck up on you. He was late.

Oh? said Sarkisov.

Luria pulled his coat over his shoulders. He put his hat on before his scarf, so when he tried to wrap the scarf the hat fell into the puddle his boots had left. He cursed and apologized and was gone.

Sarkisov and I stood at the door, watching him fumble with his belongings as he negotiated with the ice and snow.

Such a nervous man, said Sarkisov.

Yes, I said. I could feel him looking at me, but I trained my eyes outside, watching Luria a moment longer before stepping back into the kitchen to take up my tea.

He followed me in, saying he'd been contacted by the "higher-ups," who wanted to know when the exhibit would be ready.

It's been months, said Sarkisov, we ought to have something to show by now.

The namelessness of those higher-ups signalled that a shift had occurred not just in our institute, where the change could be attributed to grief, but beyond it, where the change would more be precisely attributed to Stalin, whose whims were beginning to be acted upon as though they were the commands of a god, which they were. There was no particular scientific imperative that said the exhibit should be up sooner rather than later, and Bekhterev would have wanted us to produce a perfect exhibit for him, one that was meticulous and enlightening. But Stalin wanted the display done quickly, and like all gods, Stalin inspired awe, obedience, and fear. Stories would circulate of a particular kindness displayed by our Stalin, and they would be relayed as illustrations of a warmth and humanity whose expansiveness matched his great strength. Within that paradigm, when Stalin forgave a wrongdoer, it was described as a miracle.

When I managed to leave later that afternoon, I saw from the imprint of a body in the snow, that Luria had slipped and fallen on his way down the path.

In his writings on suggestion, Bekhterev had explained the directive function, saying that disobedience was unlikely in cases where fear had been effectively instilled. Fear was suggestive. Fear suggested that the deadline Sarkisov proposed — Labour Day, which would be upon us in less than two months — was not negotiable. Meanwhile, Luria's question dug itself into me the way a tick insinuates itself into the skin. Why *hadn't* there been a funeral?

Outside, winter stretched on.

As March progressed, the days lengthened perceptibly, so that even if the cold was as bitter as ever, the sun blazed off the snow for more of the day, glittering the upper edges of the frost leaves on a window here and there. Occasionally the frost leaves would melt completely, unveiling a glorious patch of blue sky for a moment that was always too fleeting. Then the sun would be gone, and the window would freeze over again. It was around then — when Sasha regained his footing and Luria's questions meant I was starting to lose mine — that I saw Bogdanov again, for the first time since the blood exchange. By then, the exhibit deadline was looming. Every day that I put it off meant a sleepless night and 3:00 a.m. resolutions — I'm tempted to call them deals I made with God, even if by day I didn't believe in God — to begin the following morning.

By the middle of the month, Sasha said, Enough, just get started already. I didn't eat that morning. Many years ago, I had instructed Sasha not to speak to me in such moments. Over the years, he'd learned to stay quiet. That he'd broken with our tradition told me I was being impossible.

Fine, I said, enjoying the feeling of him taking charge.

So it was that on the morning I saw Bogdanov again, I was sleep deprived, anxious, and determined to get started. He strode into the lab with his shoulders back, walking as though he were twenty. I'd been prepared to be impressed, but in the context of that silent place and my own desperation, his recovery seemed gauche — an affront to Bekhterev and those of us who were grieving.

Anushka came over to take a look at him. She was probably in her thirties by then, but youthful, too. Sergei had even said she'd posed for the erotic alphabet, but everyone wanted to know someone who'd posed for it, Sergei more than anyone.

Did the other guy age as much as you got younger? she asked.

What? he asked, as though he'd not been waiting for a statement of the sort. No, no, of course not!

Anushka smiled, then glanced at the clock.

But he'll have better immunity because of me, and other things besides, said Bogdanov, as she walked back to her station. Maybe it was gauche that he was doing so well, but it was cheering, too.

What's on the docket today? I asked.

Writing, said Bogdanov. Ignoramuses everywhere.

In a past life, he'd written fiction, but now it was the scientific literature that kept him busy. Before meeting Bogdanov, I would have said the fictional world and the scientific were totally separate, but now I knew they were the same, that one could test out ideas for the other. His *Red Star* had featured male-female blood exchanges on Mars, resulting in a future on the red planet where gender had been obliterated. His was a future of absolute equality. I hadn't read the book, but I'd heard Jack and Elisa making fun of it one night at the studio. They could make fun all they liked, but at least Bogdanov had a vision. *Some* of it was going to work out.

Who's an ignoramus? asked Anush from her station.

Zavadovsky, he said, projecting his voice for all to hear. He's a biologist lecturing a physician, but he has no idea what has been done on the question of blood transfusions in medicine.

Lecturing you, I presume, I said, surprising even myself at my audacity. On the few occasions that we'd talked, there always came a moment in the conversation when I would say something I'd regret immediately, and he'd always surprise me by not being offended, for enjoying a gentle teasing, as if it indicated friendship rather than preventing it. Bogdanov was grinning gleefully at me.

He's an opportunist. Your age, he said, but not so smart.

I tried to hide my smile.

So, he said, quietly now, shall we figure out what blood type you are?

Even if he impressed me, by then, I wasn't so sure.

When Bogdanov left us, I pushed a stool against the bench and climbed up so that I could reach the top shelf. *Get going.* Despite my weeks of cleaning, the box that housed the tub with Bekhterev's brain in it had remained stowed behind a row of bottles. They were clear and brown, full and empty, labelled *use gloves* and not, dated and not. I parted them as though dividing the seas, clearing a path for the box. The first strange thing about the box was the address of origin: there was none, even though originating and destination addresses were by then required by law. The box hadn't been delivered by any official body, just dropped off, as one might drop off a house key or a note of thanks.

I opened the box to reveal the tub. When I pulled it out, the liquid inside began to slosh to and fro. *Bekhterev* was scrawled across its side, which seemed at once absurd, but also reassuring that a label had been put to it to say that this brain was certainly his, and not like the heart whose origin would never be known. Removing the lid, I stared at the brain floating in the swirling preserving solution. It was the epitome, it seemed, of an alienated object. It was human; it was not. When I finally lifted it from the liquid, the weight of it shocked me, and I dropped it back into the fluid which splashed up against the sides of the bucket in a noxious wave. Across the lab, Anush shifted at her station to peer over at me.

In the moments after death, when the blood still fills our veins and arteries, our organs and tissues hold on to their living colours. It is only once two small incisions are made in the heart, and it is pumped full first of saline solution and then of fixative, that their hues begin to fade. The deep burgundy of the liver washes away. The heart, the stomach, the intestines, all of varying shades in life, fade. The fleshy pink of the brain pales. It was this lack of colour that allowed me to continue. Life has colour and death has none. *Keep going.*

I picked the brain up again. Because it had been fixed in formalin, the tissue had hardened to the point that each of the sulci had the feel and consistency of hard rubber or cold wax. The various white-grey folds of the brain glistened in the harsh light of the overhead lamp. I turned it over, feeling its weight first in my left hand and then in my right. Whoever had removed it had been very careful: only low on the temporal lobe did I find any damage. That the cut was smooth told me that the damage had happened in the very moment of extraction, when the brain was unfixed, that is, when its tissues were soft, gelatinous, and easily scarred. Had something frightened the person who removed the brain?

I was thinking about this when Sarkisov appeared, as if out of nowhere.

I thought you might need some help getting started, he said. His urgency clashed with the contemplative pace I was trying to establish for myself.

He took the brain from me then and laid it on the table top. He opened the drawers and fumbled around for a minute, looking for something. Out came a knife. He positioned it neatly between the two hemispheres, then cut straight through. The two sides rolled apart like two halves of a cabbage. I heard myself gasp and looked up at the windows. Over at her station, Anushka dropped a glass. Shit, I heard her say, under her breath.

The windows let in a dull, foggy light.

Sarkisov was speaking quickly, explaining things I already damn well knew. All of our large specimens had come from other labs. German labs. Socialist labs. Labs so well equipped they could microtome an elephant's brain if they wanted. We weren't so fortunate, which meant our specimens had to be divided before being sliced. Yet, in exchange for the problem of needing to divide a brain into its hemispheres, we could count ourselves lucky because our modest little microtome rewarded us with a perfectly plane slice, something other models, such as the Cambridge Rocker, couldn't manage. I was nodding as he spoke, aiming for the blankest expression I could muster, which wasn't so hard, since shock has that very effect. Slices needed to be plane he was telling me, not convex; the equipment needed to be kept clean and organized; microtomes were only as good as their blade. I know, I heard myself whisper. It was winter, commented Sarkisov, in what seemed an aside, so keep the blade warm. I know.

When he walked away, Anush looked over and mouthed, You okay? And I couldn't say.

Keep going.

I didn't let myself feel anything then, except the urgency Sarkisov had impressed upon me. I found the manuals we had on microscopy and thumbed through them, looking for the protocols I'd need to create the block, prepare the fixative, and mix the dye. The manuals were basically recipe books; they had no advice for my own rapidly beating heart. I continued.

By that afternoon, I was ready to prepare the block. I began by soaking it in cedar-wood oil, which served to dehydrate the brain completely. I knew it was done when the brain sank to the bottom of the tank. Then I placed it in a paraffin-filled mould. Each step was a palliative, in a way, because with every step the brain looked more and more like every other specimen I had ever worked with, and less and less like an organ that had once been pumped full of blood and words and memories and the most original thoughts in the world.

I'm coming with you, said Sasha the next day.

I told myself he needed the company, but I was as desperate, probably more so. The gallery opening had been pushed back and his questions about the Osorgins had returned, mushrooming into questions about everyone. He worried about old friends he hadn't seen for ages, was resentful of me because I could keep working even under conditions that ought to have broken my heart. It *is* hard for me I'd said, and he'd conceded, saying I know, I know. His questions about the Osorgins had led to questions about Bekhterev, and his questions about Bekhterev aligned with Luria's questions about Bekhterev, which had insidiously become mine, too. *Why hadn't there been a funeral?* My heart sped up when I thought about it.

Work is how I make it make sense, I declared, to myself or to Sasha, I wasn't sure.

That morning we rode in on the tram together. It rumbled toward the city centre, moving between white patches of light at the intersections and the dark shadows cast by the buildings. Even on the tram it was so cold I could see my breath. Neither of us found a seat, so we hung on to whatever pole or seat back we could find, swinging erratically when the driver braked too suddenly or took a corner too fast. I felt sick to my stomach and irritated with the smallest thing—even the children licking their dirty kopeks and pressing them into the tram's still frozen windows disgusted me as I thought about the spit circles their peepholes would leave on the windows for months afterwards, even once the ice had melted. The tram emptied as we neared the Kremlin and then veered right to cross the bridge. On the other side was the institute.

Though we'd come in together, I insisted Sasha go to the library for a few hours before coming to the institute, so that his coming by would seem more adult and less like he were a sick child I couldn't leave at home alone.

We parted ways at the corner.

That afternoon, he joined me.

—⁄—

For the rest of that week, we sat side by side in a room on the second floor of the institute, repeating the same series of movements. We kept the room warm as per Sarkisov's instructions. A cold draft could lead to a poor cut. Time became hard to measure, as though we were swimming in time, pushing up against time, resisting time, expanding time, telling time we didn't believe in its measurements anymore. The room was small and warmer than the rest of the building, so on what could have been weeks into the project, but on what was probably only our second or third day, we took to stripping down to our first layer of underclothes, leaving everything else in a pile at the door. It wasn't sensual exactly, but it was a new kind of intimacy.

Mechanically speaking, the microtome resembled a

sewing machine. Executing a cut meant that the right hand brought down the rotating handle as a tailor would bring a sewing needle down to nudge it into the cloth, but here, it was the specimen that was lowered onto a blade edge and then through it, so that every section that fluttered up once the cut was done was a thickness of precisely eighty micrometres. We were silent mostly, side by side at the table, one sitting, the other standing, the first one lowering the block over the edge of the blade, the second one holding the paintbrush, ready to lift up the cut section. At the bottom of every cycle, the microtome landed with a kind of *chunk* sound. If I was lowering the block, this was Sasha's cue to dampen the paintbrush and then brush it against the glass to take up the papery section and any stray pieces of wax. On the tray beside, he would lay the section out on a sheet of white paper. No one disturbed us; even the slightest gust of air caused, say, by the opening of the door, could have caused all the sections to go flying. I found myself able to relax for the first time that winter and realized that it was Sarkisov's capacity to appear without warning that had put me on edge. In that room, no one could disturb us.

Sometimes one of us would break the silence, remembering a story one or the other had wanted to tell, and like that, I started to see how the years had changed us both. When he was younger, he'd wanted to be a baker, then later, someone who worked in a fruit shop or a bookstore. What he'd wanted was regular customers — the kind of people who would need him every day and whose needs he could predictably satisfy. But his mother insisted on an education. Their compromise was art school.

When we'd first met, we found each other foreign, compelling, and we called that love. But now, sitting in that hot room in our underwear, not talking for hours on end, I saw that my definition of love had changed. Sasha turned out to be a perfect assistant: nervous and careful.

When we tired, we would swap tasks and after we'd collected enough sections, we would turn to mounting them on slides. The sheer size of the sections made the task especially cumbersome. Paraffin sections almost always wrinkle or fold when cutting, but one advantage of the paraffin was its tendency to expand when warmed. For each section, I would drop the smallest amount of albumen fixative on the middle of a slide, spread it around with the tip of my finger to make the thinnest layer possible. Sasha would pipette the tiniest drops of water on the slide, and then we'd lay out the section as evenly as possible. More water afterwards and then I would hold the slide over the copper heating plate to warm, but not melt, the paraffin. The remaining steps required less care. Once dried, the sections would be de-paraffined using the xylene that we had at the beginning, though we ran out and had to rely on benzine at the end. I'd heard that a similar effect can be achieved using gasoline, but then there's the potential for fire. When Sasha took in the threat of fire, his eyes lit up, and in that second he was the boy-man I'd met in a bookstore, ready to run out into the night and to take me with him. Some parts of our character are more or less permanent.

On the Friday of that week, the gallery called Sasha to tell him that he would be starting on Sunday. By then, we were getting really good at the work, which also meant we got a little distracted. Sasha stopped needing to be so alert to the mechanics of the thing and started to look more carefully at the slices themselves as they relaxed onto the slides.

In the manual, what we were doing was supposed to look like this:

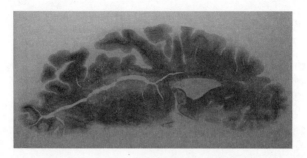

But what we got, when we held up a slide against the backdrop of a window thick with melting snow, was this:

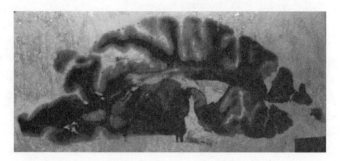

I mention the watery melting snow because it's visible in the image. That's Sasha's handwriting, there, on the note along the bottom. The photograph we took of the slide is shoddy, but not that shoddy. We didn't include the brain stem on the slide. We were using the manual as a guide, and the authors hadn't included the brain stem either. As I mentioned, in Bekhterev's case, the brain stem was the only sign of damage, the only sign that whoever had removed the brain had slipped.

But then Sasha noticed something I hadn't seen before. There was a strange degradation in some of the tissues that didn't appear elsewhere in the brain. Looking closely at one of the slices, he described the edge as *jagged*.

What does this mean? he asked me.

But I didn't know if a jagged edge was normal or not, or if a jagged edge was not normal, what kind of not normal it was.

But you'll try to find out, said Sasha.

Of course, I said, but I was lying. The only person I could have asked about the jagged edge was the one whose edge had become so jagged.

—✝—

The next step was staining the slices.

To this day, no one quite understands the mysterious workings of the Golgi stain, which is, perhaps, unsurprising, given the mystical qualities of silver nitrate, with which the staining process begins. Once called *lunar caustic* because the ancient alchemists associated silver's strange properties with the moon, silver nitrate is both miraculously antiseptic — diluted drops in a newborn's eyes can prevent an infant from contracting disease — and imbued with the capacity to permanently blacken the skin. Over time, minute quantities of the substance can accumulate in the organs, creating in the population of a whole town who drink from the same source, say, a skin tone that is unmistakably blue-grey. Alternatively, a splash of more concentrated silver nitrate can immediately, and permanently, render the skin black. That such a substance could unlock the yet unknown workings of the neuron is, perhaps, also unsurprising.

Once a slide has been prepared with the silver nitrate, a chromate is added, and after some minutes, though sometimes over a period of hours, an unpredictable number of neurons transform from their indistinct grey to China-ink black, and suddenly their arms and legs snake out like the receivers and messengers they are, and the whole structure of the spindly little neuron is revealed.

We got to see it happen. Sasha said it was as if the neurons were trying, right there before our very eyes, to find something else like them, another neuron, with which they could communicate. This rarely happened. I mean, it rarely happened that the synapse between one neuron and another would be revealed. It was more typical for one neuron to be dyed black and all of its neighbours to stay grey.

No one knows why, I said.

How random, said Sasha. And, in any case, they were not communicating with one another. They were dead.

But still, they were beautiful. Sasha would draw them, and somehow these drawings would bring us back to a feeling that something we were doing was right, and something we were doing would lead to a knowledge that was new and elegant.

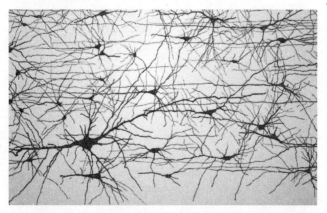

When I looked at the drawings later—some of them had been left in the room and others of them turned up elsewhere—their aspect seemed to change right before my eyes. They stopped looking beautiful and started to look, instead, like the shaky sketches of a cowed man. The spindles looked not like the hopeful upward reach of slender arms, but rather like the legs of spiders all tangled up.

Once Sasha had left, I started to obsess over the jagged edges he had noticed. They looked like putrification. Like heat blisters. Like disease. Now that the brain had been microtomed, I could examine the edges of the cells under the microscope and see that they were bloated and puffy, as if they'd been injected with something or tricked into superhydrating themselves, but beyond that I didn't know what this meant, nor, as I said, if it meant anything at all.

I completed the microtoming in just a few days, though without Sasha there to keep me company, time passed much more slowly. While the process had initially been fascinating and challenging, alone it was merely exhausting. I started to obsess about my technique, certain that the results of my labour were bound to be scrutinized by generations of scientists to come. Of course the opposite turned out to be true: no one would look carefully at these because they would be hidden away like every other trace of Bekhterev.

Under the pressure to be exacting, sooner or later my hands would rebel. I would will my right hand to pull the rotating handle slowly and continuously toward me, and it would refuse, jerking sharply. The resulting haggard slices charted my emotional state much as the polygraph diagrams the sweats and rapid heartbeat of a liar.

I tried to overcome the mental and physical exhaustion, but eventually a sample would fall to the floor or into the muck between the samples, and I would know it was time to stop. Sometimes I didn't even notice the thing fallen. Sometimes nothing fell. But my mind had drifted so far away that it was my thoughts that disturbed me, not my errors. Luria and I had never talked again about that murdered boy. I hadn't cared about him, or his family. I'd only cared about Bekhterev. But what *had* happened to the boy in the end, then? Had the thieves tried to imply a ritual murder? Had they been that clever? Was Vera that clever? Then I'd look up and see what a mess I'd made.

At the end of every day, I always turned off every light but one. The remaining light would shine over top one of the display cases, and I would stand in front of them. At that time of day, I could forget that what we displayed were models and not the brains themselves. When Lenin's brain was first extracted, it had been squishy, like dense black bread that had been soaked in water. Kozhevnikov's had been more solid, the consistency of cooked squash. By the time they were analyzed, microtomed, or sectioned they were all hard, like beets. When I stood in front of the displays like that, late at night, the defining characteristics resounded in my head like words from a foreign language: the sulci of the third category, a complicated convoluted aspect, the gyrus temporalis. Like a kind of proverb, I repeated to myself, Our research would result in the victory of materialism in the area where metaphysics and dualism were still strong. I rarely thought of the specimens as men and women who had lived lives, because I had not known them. The only woman's brain we had, as it turned out, was that of Sofia K—the mathematician who had befriended a Frenchman who had buried the international prototypes M and K, which had never been seen again.

When Luria didn't come back to see me, I decided I had to go to him. From the outside, the neurology building at the university was white and clean. Inside, it was filthy. Beyond the initial set of double doors, two guards sat smoking. One was sitting on top of the desk, the other behind it. Hundreds of empty coat hangers hung from three long iron rods that spanned the foyer behind them. Only two coats were hung there. The guard who had been sitting on top of the desk stuck his cigarette in his mouth and took my jacket, hanging it by the others, so that now there were three.

Is no one here? I asked the guards.

Just you and Professor Luria, said the one behind the desk.

And the lab technicians, said the other.

Oh, and the doctors' assistants, said the first.

But they don't leave their coats with us, clarified the second.

The one sitting on the desk indicated the general direction I was to walk. Over there and up the stairs, you'll find him.

The halls, by their echo and by the lighting, which was oddly greenish and lost intensity as I moved towards the back of the building, seemed like caves or tunnels bound for the centre of the earth. Signs tacked to the walls had arrows pointing in the direction of auditoriums, offices, and laboratories.

Luria's office was at the end of the hall on the third floor.

So was it Vera's trial? I asked Luria from the doorway.

God, Tatiana. What are you doing here? Can't you say hello?

He'd been standing there, staring out the small window behind his desk.

Shouldn't you shut the door if you're going to have your back to it like that?

Out that window, all he could see was another wing of the university, its grey walls and its dark windows, a few old pigeons, and the leaves and litter that escaped the cleaners' reach.

He turned to face his desk, as if he were about to sit, but then he squinted his eyes at me and said all right, so I knew he'd tell me the rest of the story, just not there.

We walked shoulder to shoulder down the green hall to the stairwell, toward where the windows let in dismal squares of light. As we were walking, he told me about the building. Despite its orderly exterior, he said the interior was a mess.

I can see that, I said.

I don't mean dirty, though it is that, too, he said. I mean that no one knows, exactly, how many rooms there are in this building. Down there, he said, pointing to a dark corridor, is what appears to be a broom closet. But at the back of the closet is a door, and if you open it, you'll find an empty auditorium that no one can use because there's no other entrance, and anyway most people don't know about it. The lecture hall is small, though fully functional. At one time, it did get used, but that was years ago, when it had a proper entrance. When the university was expanded and it got closed in by accident, no one wanted to take responsibility for the mistake and then the medical staff were turning over so quickly — change was so constant in those first years after the Revolution — that before long, those who had given or attended a lecture there were no longer around to tell of it and it was basically forgotten. Too many architects, summarized Luria, looking at me, and none of them talking to each other.

We'd come to the end of the hall and descended the stairs in silence. I wondered how many other rooms in the building had been locked away and forgotten forever.

At the bottom of the stairs, in a voice so quiet he didn't seem to be speaking to me any more, Luria muttered, All of them dead by now, every last one.

At the entrance, the security guards gave me my coat and asked, Leaving so quickly? They didn't say anything to Luria. He had never had much to say to people he didn't know.

We walked on the side of the street that was still getting the last rays of sunlight. For a moment the street was bathed in red and gold, but then the sun dipped behind a building, and the sidewalk was cast back into the monochrome of late winter. The drop in temperature got right into my bones. We walked down to the river. I thought we'd stop at the benches where we might have found some protection from the wind, but Luria took me by the elbow, pulling me towards the bridge. As we crossed the bridge, we could see the sun again, catching it just before it would sink behind the farthest reaches of the city where the rivers meet.

No, he said, stopping. No, it wasn't her trial, but it should have been.

We were at the peak of the bridge. The winds were fierce, so it was as though all his words raced past me and then disappeared into the night. Even someone walking right by us had no chance of overhearing him, though he had begun to yell. My cheeks burned with cold.

The authorities had dismissed the evidence the police gathered and went looking for an alternate explanation, asking any locals who would talk if they had any evidence as to the fate of the boy. One day they happened upon two key witnesses: a lamplighter who said he'd seen a man with a black beard speaking with the boy and a Catholic priest who professed to be an expert on local Jewish practices, including ritual murder. The lamplighter's evidence led the authorities to Mendel Beilis—it didn't matter to anyone that he was a non-practising Jew—and the Catholic priest's evidence aligned the thirteen wounds on the boy's right temple with a mystical text, the *Zohar*, that "required" ritual murders to be executed using twelve plus one stab wounds and that the victim's mouth be closed.

Why was a Catholic priest called in as the expert on Jewish rituals? I asked.

Exactly, he said.

A further witness, a local member of the Decadents or Symbolists—they alternated from one name to the other—had testified that the shape and distribution of the wounds revealed a code of letters and that each letter stood for a word, and the words taken together formed a magical sentence that identified the boy as a sacrificial victim to God.

The prosecutors argued, on the strength of all of their research, that Beilis had committed an act of magic in accordance with secret Jewish rituals from which he could expect to gain power, and through the inscription of each of the letters, the release of God's emanations. Another witness was brought to the stand, this time a poet-philosopher who explained that the blood, which would have been harvested from the boy's body, was necessary to Jewish spiritual practices in the way that vowels are necessary to the living, breathing language. Without blood, the ritual has no power. Without vowels, the Hebrew consonants are but bones on a page. And without mysticism, transrational poetry has no meaning.

That's absolutely mad! I yelled.

Of course it is! he exclaimed, then leaned in and said, but the whole charade had a purpose.

Which was? I asked, but I already had a sense because the word Luria had used — *charade* — was the same word people were just starting to use to describe the trial of some engineers brought in from the Ukraine to face prosecution in Moscow. The prominence of the trial had made judge and jury of the whole city.

The Tzar had lost control of the region and needed an enemy. Those witnesses were a farce. The priest had a criminal record, the lamplighter had been pressured by the prosecutors, and the philosopher was more interested in aesthetics than in justice — he'd even written about it.

I looked out over Moscow then, taking in the near-black sky, the cold bright halos that had formed above the lights on Hunter's Row, the red of the Kremlin walls spot lit, and then below me, the black river and the occasional ripple. I can't say why, but I thought of the girl with the gold under her fingernail, saw her small frame crouched beneath a tree, her finger in her mouth, and thought of what it might feel like to slowly poison oneself, how the hallucinations would have blurred with reality, how there must have been some comfort in the idea that she had conjured the surreal rather than passively witnessing its arrival.

It was the Black Hundreds; maybe you've heard of them, said Luria. They target Jews, and they were at the height of their power in those years.

I turned to look at Luria. I hadn't known that he was Jewish, but then I realized I had. He stood up to face me and pulled his scarf tighter around his neck.

There was another reason, too. The Tzar was worried about the Revolution, which was, by then, a legitimate concern.

What did it have to do with Bekhterev? I asked.

He conducted a psychiatric examination of Mendel Beilis that established his innocence and led to his release. Beilis, by that point, had been in jail for two years for a crime he hadn't committed. His release made the state look bad.

I took a deep breath. The cold of the bridge's railing pressed into my side.

The story doesn't end there, said Luria. Bekhterev was, then, the president of the Psychoneurological Institute, but immediately following the trial, the Minister of Public Education informed him that his appointment could not be renewed, and that same day, he was fired from the Military Medical Academy and the Geneva Medical Institute.

So he was punished for it, I said.

And for years, said Luria. It was only recently that he seemed to be coming out of it.

We walked on in silence then, crossing the remainder of the bridge, and for several blocks farther. We passed the Kremlin. In the history lessons we'd had as young Pioneers, we'd heard all about the violence of the Tzars, how Peter the Great would string up the bodies of his political enemies outside his palace so that they could rot publicly in a diabolical display of power.

Does Sarkisov know about this? I asked.

I don't know, he said.

Our path took us to Hunter's Row. We heard the music first. The kiosks were bright orange, green, and blue. Roasting meats and hot steam warmed the air. Luria held me at my elbow to keep me close.

It will happen again.

What's that? I asked.

Bekhterev wasn't even the first.

Our voices rose to compete with a man playing a balalaika. A woman I took to be his wife was leaning out the window, yelling at him to stop, yelling at him to come home.

The first what?

The kids hold their own trials. On playgrounds, they denounce each other. Kids with parents in the Party rule everything. Children denounce their teachers. You need to be careful at work, Tatiana, be careful with your words.

Looking back on it and all the life lessons Luria had said he wanted to teach me, I realize there was only ever one lesson he wanted me to learn, and it was that one—be careful with what I say.

This is your last chance! yelled the wife.

The music stopped. A balalaika can sound like every single feeling in the world and then thud like an ordinary box of wood when it's set down. I couldn't tell if Luria was right. Had Bekhterev said too much? Were today's children so clever, so much wilier than I had been?

At the intersection near the obelisk, we parted, barely saying goodbye. As I walked home, I thought about what Bekhterev might have said on the night that he suddenly turned so ill. I began to wonder how he might have explained to himself the sudden diarrhea, the weakness, the vomiting and fever that plagued him that whole night, and how might he have interpreted the faces of those men who attended to him, men who, I now realize, would have been unknown faces, unknown doctors to our country's most well-known doctor.

This is when the new feeling started, though at the time I wouldn't have described it as such. It wasn't fear exactly, but fear's beginning: a stranger seen once too often.

The work at the gallery finally got underway, and whatever melancholy had taken hold of Sasha in the first few months of the year drifted away, as I'd known it would. Yet, as though we were trapped in a closed system whereby darkness must always counteract the light, just as Sasha re-emerged, I began to feel myself being pulled under. I tried to ignore the feeling, but every once in a while my chest would feel so tight that I couldn't get a breath. The feeling would pass, sometimes quickly, and sometimes more slowly, but it always did go away.

That Sasha seemed to have found his footing again gave me some comfort. There was a part of him that wanted to save art and a part of him that wanted to abandon it completely. It was the first part of him that started to like the position at the new gallery. Being there had brought him back into the conversation he had missed. He didn't know his old friend Dimitri had been hired at the same time as him, but the fact that he had changed the job completely. They'd moved in different circles when they were at art school, but Dimitri had been like Sasha: suspicious of Lenin's attempts to influence art.

Politicians don't know shit about art, Dimitri said to Sasha, speaking the language of Sasha's heart.

Dimitri had his hands in everything, Sasha thought. Dimitri this, Dimitri that. Dimitri, Dimitri, Dimitri. The hermitage was being gutted, said Dimitri, and Sasha was infuriated.

Just last week, two Raphaels were sold to an American

millionaire, Sasha relayed to me, one night after he'd just started.

Don't we need the money? I said.

They're Raphaels!

The first thing he planned to do at the gallery was turn up the heat. The cold was ruining the paintings. That he had plans made everything better.

Sasha and I seemed to have resolved our differences, reuniting after those first weeks of winter when we'd felt so far apart. We stayed up late talking and had sex before falling asleep. Sometimes I would wake in the middle of the night, breathless and afraid, but then I would curl myself around Sasha's warm body and, like that, fall back asleep.

If I couldn't fall asleep, I'd lie in bed staring at the ceiling, listening to the building at night. The walls were so thin it was almost possible to hear conversations in the neighbouring apartments, and if the hallway doors had been left open, the sound of the kitchen—the clatter of late-night cooking—rattled down to me. Sometimes Sasha could feel my restlessness and he'd seem to call out, from the depth of his own exhaustion, saying, What's wrong? Why aren't you sleeping? And I'd come close to him, whispering in the dark, that I didn't know, that I was okay.

But I did know. I was plagued by all that I'd learned from Luria and worried about the institute and the exhibit, about what I'd been asked to do. What kind of report could I write, what kind of honest could I be? How could I keep going when I'd lost all sense of direction? I wanted Sasha's momentum to be mine.

Even if Sasha didn't initially see the value of his work, it cheered me to see him find his way because it suggested that I would, too. His hands roughened up, got calloused. He swapped stories with his friends about the art they were hanging and complained about the curator, and all this made him more rugged, more durable, as if he'd finally grown up.

—/—

Although Dimitri was an old friend, it wasn't until he and Sasha worked together at the gallery that they got close. Their first install was so straightforward, they had been able to do it on their own: a collection of paintings, all of them reasonably sized. The curator, who Sasha never said much about, had walked them around the gallery saying that the show was standard—the paintings would be hung at eye level, a standard distance apart, nothing fancy. After the install was over, they had all the time in the world. While the show was up they were more like security guards than art handlers. They floated through the gallery when it was open, talking to the occasional visitor, then took long breaks to smoke and drink in the loading dock, where they could watch the weather without having to be in it.

When that show ended and they were getting ready for the next install, a new guy was hired. In contrast to Dimitri, Sasha thought Lukas was only okay. He was young, officious, slow speaking. He'd come over from Spain, and planned to go back. Like Dimitri, Lukas had worked in the gallery associated with the art school, so he was an expert in things Sasha had never had to think about: walls, hardware, forklifts, and the kinds of pulley systems they'd need for big shows. Old walls in Moscow had three layers to them: stone, then a layer of wood or wire, and then a layer of plaster to finish. Plaster doesn't stick to stone, Lukas had explained. The softer layer gives the nails a place to go.

He'll be useful, Sasha said, since I don't know shit about that stuff.

Lukas's father was a party member back in Spain, where the war was with the anarchists not the capitalists.

Everything about Lukas was foreign to Sasha, but especially the fact that Lukas admired his own father.

These people who never depart from their parents' views of things: are they stupid or just really lucky? What's home life like if you never disagree with your parents? mused Sasha.

You didn't disagree with your parents, I said.

Sure I did, he said, chucking me under the chin. How do you think I married you?

More often than not, the loading dock conversation involved the future of art. Dimitri was into an idea that Sasha wanted to think about more carefully. Because they'd come from the same place — same art school, same medium, same resistance to change — what Dimitri had to say about art's future mattered to Sasha. That, and Dimitri was older. Dimitri was interested in what it might mean for art to reach the end of representation altogether. Rodchenko, according to Dimitri, hadn't pushed things far enough. Dimitri agreed that art shouldn't be decoration; art for art's sake was over. But it shouldn't even be representative.

At the gallery, Sasha started to get what he'd been missing from his time at Osorgins'. A conversation that mattered to him had started up again.

At home, Sasha's brushes had been taken out of their boxes, the tubes of paint and jars of oil reunited, as if readying themselves.

It was around that time that M—, the pianist, moved out of the room down the hall. It wasn't unusual in those days for people to disappear suddenly, and that's how it was with M—. One day he was there, the next day he wasn't. In his youth, M— had studied at the Moscow Imperial

Conservatory and had often bragged of his friendship with Nikolai Rubinstein, something Sasha and I knew was impossible, given that Rubinstein had died of tuberculosis in Paris some decades before M— was even born. We entertained the lie, though, because it was like entering another person's fantasy and it was harmless and we could do it together. Later, it turned out that although Nikolai *Rubinstein* hadn't taken much interest in M—, Nikolai *Bernstein,* the neurophysiologist, had. All of this surfaced the way all communal knowledge did in those days: in snippets overheard or rumours shared in the hall or in the kitchen as one waited for a pot to be cleaned or the hot plate to be freed up.

Everything ends in neurology these days, said Sasha.

Ask our neighbours yourself, I said, but I knew he wouldn't. He avoided contact with them as much as I did, maybe more.

They'll be explaining the blue sky according to neurology soon enough, he said.

He was smoking at the balcony again, the first cigarette of the day.

So tell me, he said.

Bernstein had studied athletes at first, but later turned to virtuoso pianists. The mystery of parallel octaves was that piano instructors at the conservatory didn't know how to teach the technique. Students who tried to learn by the instruction *take it slow, then speed it up,* suffered tremendous muscle pain in their backs, arms, and hands. Bernstein solved the mystery by attaching small light bulbs to the performer's arms and then recording their performance on a moving celluloid film. M— had been one of those performers.

It sounds like an art piece, said Sasha, exhaling.

I smiled at the thought, and at how often our conversations went this way, with me explaining an experiment and Sasha calling it art.

They discovered that the movement required of parallel octaves simply cannot be achieved at slow speeds. The momentum forces a vibration that permits the hand to lead the arm and not the other way around.

Yeah, said Sasha, I remember a piece like that. A film. Didn't we see it together?

I didn't remember.

With a gymnast and light bulbs? I think it was Pudovkin. Or maybe it was a documentary of those same experiments?

I knew I should know who Pudovkin was. Sometimes Sasha accused me of living in a bubble, and when he mentioned names like Pudovkin I knew he was right. I knew of him, but if I'd been required to guess what he did, I wouldn't have guessed filmmaker.

So it couldn't be taught, said Sasha, butting the cigarette out.

Exactly.

Until it could.

He shut the balcony door.

No, I said. They couldn't teach it. It had to come from within.

But they could teach a way to let it come from within, he argued.

M—'s room stayed empty for months, which was strange, given the housing crisis that had overtaken the city by then. Normally a room wouldn't stay empty for a day. That's why we assumed M— was coming back.

Did you notice that he only ever played Liszt? asked Sasha. I hadn't. I knew as much about musicians as I did about filmmakers.

M— didn't come back, though. I wished so hard that he would, kept looking for him in the kitchen, strained to hear his playing. That was why, when a new man moved in, I had the feeling that I'd conjured him because he took up the piano and played all the same songs.

Do you hear that? I asked Sasha.

The *Valses oubliées*, said Sasha.

Liszt, right? I asked.

Sasha leaned his head to one side and nodded absently. It was summer by then, and the noise of the city competed with the noise of the building. We toyed with the idea that M— was back, but then M— had been a good pianist and the new guy wasn't. He repeated the same section over and over, so the pieces came out like thwarted thoughts, incomplete and disconnected. Ideas too isolated to ever mean anything.

Now, when I hear the *Valses oubliées*, I expect to hear it the way I heard it then. Deformed and disjointed, with great leaps. If, by chance, I happen upon the pieces performed as they were intended, I hear the notes in a strange way such that some phrases are layered and thick with memory and others sound so thin to me, as if they don't belong at all.

By the end of April 1928, I was close to finishing the exhibit. It was the *memorandus* that loomed and the damn report I would have to distill from it, a report that would cast me as the arbiter of who or what Bekhterev had been. Everything! I wanted to say. I was as hesitant to complete the work as I had been to start it, afraid of what it would or wouldn't mean and, more than that, of the chasm that would appear in my life once the work was done. The struggle to make sense of a man who had been more enigma than I'd known consumed me. I felt as if I still knew so little, and I kept hoping for something more to say, a missing fact or hidden narrative that could protect us both — preserve his vision, prolong mine. I wanted there to be a way to write the truth of him as I'd known him, but writing's relationship to objective truth seemed to be unravelling the more I tried to do it. Against all my years of training, against everything I'd learned from Bekhterev himself about the knowable material world, in the spring of 1928, as the river's layers of ice broke up and washed downstream, as every remnant of winter seemed to melt away on a single day, as the city became water, I had to ask myself what I truly knew.

I was upstairs going through Bekhterev's notes one afternoon when I heard someone on the stairs and looked up to see Bogdanov standing in the doorway. The way he stood there so politely told me he knew I'd become shy of him. He was there to say they could test my blood type. The way he put it suggested it was then or never, though the timeline I would have preferred would have been more along the lines of *not yet*. He sensed my hesitation and gave me room to breathe, asking how my work was going, if I'd made the progress I'd hoped. I heard myself tell him that I'd come across something strange, a puzzling characteristic of Bekhterev's brain cells, and that the mystery of it was bothering me. He took this as an invitation, coming closer and so, in part because I thought it couldn't hurt to have a second opinion and in part because I wanted to direct his attention away from me and onto something else, I led Bogdanov in to see the slides, showing him the peculiar jaggedness that marked the cells of Bekhterev's brain. I mused that they seemed to be distended somehow.

He said, Yes, yes, they are just that. Hypersaturated, one might say.

Yes, I said, but why?

I don't know.

And I heard Bekhterev's voice just then, saying that what Bogdanov did was not real science, and then Bogdanov asked again whether or not I wanted to have my blood tested. I wanted to blurt out my absolute refusal, but instead I said I wasn't so sure anymore.

Why? he asked, looking wounded. The answer wasn't only Bekhterev's dismissal of Bogdanov's work, though that was part of it; it was also that the idea itself had always been about Bekhterev, designed, really to elicit his reaction, his concern, a feeling that he was more like a father to me than my boss. What point was there to it now? But I didn't say any of this and instead followed Bogdanov down the stairs, through the kitchen, and into his institute. I berated myself for being so juvenile, but then which was the juvenile part—my desire to elicit Bekhterev's concern or my present fear? As we walked through the waiting room and into the place where I had once found Bogdanov, I concluded that the test couldn't hurt, and who else was left for me to trust anyway, who else but this maniac and his pseudo-science?

He'd been telling me about his wife, having forgotten that we had met all those months ago, telling me that she was a nurse, which I knew. And then suddenly I was seated and she had persuaded me to unfold my arm for her, exposing that soft blue network of veins at the fleshy fold of my inner elbow. The alcohol she swabbed across my skin tingled. Bogdanov stood to the left of the chair, she to the right. He wanted to distract me, so he told me about a character he'd met in prison, hoping to make me laugh, though it frightened me instead.

You're all right, he said as the blood was sucked from inside me. I felt that the loss of blood created a vacuum in me, an empty space that would collapse in on itself should nothing come to replace it. A part of me was being taken, and I would never get it back. The room swam with great patches of black and purple, and Bogdanov nudged me, saying take this, eat it, words so liturgical in nature I couldn't refuse them, though had I been clear-headed I would have rejected the words and the candy and everything else besides. As the sugar melted on my tongue, I revived.

How many types are there? I asked Bogdanov's wife.

Five, she said, confidently.

———✝———

The next day, I resolved to bring the *memorandus* to some sort of resolution. I would get clear on Bekhterev's politics, as though such a thing were possible with a man as complex and intractable as him. I returned to the piles of paper Bekhterev had left behind, and a diary I hadn't been able to bring myself to look at. The diary was small with a soft black leather cover and gold-leaved pages so thin they could have been transparent if held up to the light. I sat for a moment feeling the cold of the black leather. Then it was time, and I opened it up, flipping through casually at first. I noticed right away that it bore witness to the frantic quality of Bekhterev's time in Moscow and the relative quiet of his time in Leningrad. His travel plans were noted in the following fashion:

M—P
P—Y
Y—P
P—M

Y meant Yaroslavl. *S* meant Samara. *P* was Petrograd, though sporadically he would cross out the *P* and replace it with *L*, as if suddenly remembering it was Leningrad. Soon enough he'd forget and revert to the *P*. He never went anywhere else.

In his wife's hand there were dinner plans; in his hand, there were conferences; in hers, the dates when they would be at the dacha, these written in a weighty dark script as if saying they were incontrovertible. In his hand, appointments at the military school; in hers, a list of things to bring back from Moscow, toys usually. In her hand, the chapter by chapter deadlines for the book he'd been writing when he died; in his, the final deadline from the publisher, which wasn't until the following year, meaning a manuscript was somewhere, though who knew where. Nothing in the diary surprised me. In fact, I was comforted: the life Bekhterev had itemized corresponded to the one I had witnessed. That is, until I registered a name that recurred, a name written in light pencil, as if after the fact, the name of a psychologist, about whom Bekhterev had spoken once, and had written disparagingly.

His problem with psychology was that it believed in consciousness above all else. He called it a subjective science, and this was a criticism. *Consciousness is regarded as the fundamental and inalienable stamp of the psychic activity not only of oneself, but also of others.* That psychology relied upon the so-called introspective method as fundamental in the investigation of inner or psychic processes made it suspect. Above all, Bekhterev was a materialist, and nothing about the psychological approach could be measured. All this made the biweekly appointment with the psychologist an anomaly. It had occurred on Thursday afternoons, and I thought back through the Thursdays of the year past, but they were indistinguishable from any other weekday afternoon — Bekhterev was usually out, at the hospital I had assumed, incorrectly.

And so, along with the spring melt, and the movement of the river, and the collective sigh of the city returning to life, I went out, above all to meet the psychologist.

My visit would have been entirely without consequence, except for the intrusion of a secretary, and the mention, upon seeing me and knowing my connection to Bekhterev, of Asja. Asja lived most of the time in those days in the sanatorium connected to the building, a place she eventually told me she'd chosen for herself on account of her wildness, though on the registration form she'd described herself as having a case of nerves. The visit to the doctor, it turned out, had been a visit to see Asja.

When I got to her room, I introduced myself as Bekhterev's student, and she said my name immediately, her eyes bright and smiling, and got up to embrace me. That she could be so open and so immediately welcoming surprised me so much that tears sprang to my eyes, and I found myself almost wounded by the warmth with which she'd greeted me. To be hugged so genuinely, to see such happiness in her eyes — all of this was so unlike every other part of my life. She looked to be about ten or fifteen years older than me, but terribly frail, so thin I'd felt her bones collapse when we'd embraced.

She began to chatter immediately, saying she had heard so much about me, that Bekhterev had thought of me as a daughter, and all this on the assumption that I knew as much of her, which I was embarrassed to admit, when finally she paused to take a sip of water, that I didn't.

Who are you? I asked.

She threw back her head in laughter at the absurdity of it, of the lopsidedness of what we knew, and her hair — a coppery shade with streaks of a blond that was almost white — caught the light from the window behind her, the shimmer of it almost like liquid.

I am his first daughter, she said, and I almost choked as I laughed out of bewilderment and wonder.

I surprised myself, not only because my first instinct was to hug her again, but also because that was what I did. And so we held each other, laughing and so strangely happy to be together, and then the feeling shifted and we held on tighter, crying, too, so relieved were we to have found each other and to no longer feel so alone with our grief.

You saw him every week, I said.

Yes, he kept close tabs on me. He was worried about my health.

Are you healthy?

Not very, she said.

Bekhterev had married late, and before that had had only one lover, a woman who'd loved him but had refused to marry him, a mathematician who had never wanted the trap of marital life, not even once she fell pregnant with Asja. He had pursued her, and more than that, he'd loved her and devoted money and time to her, but she'd never allowed him to become a significant or permanent part of her life, not even after the birth of their girl. For Asja, it had meant a cosmopolitan life, because she had spent it in Sweden and Berlin, and when she mentioned Berlin, I had to shake my head at the improbability of it all.

Was your mother Sofia?

Yes, she said, her eyes tearing up ever so slightly.

Fuck, I said.

I guess, she said.

Her mother had died when she was a young child, less than ten, and it was for this reason that Bekhterev had been able to maintain such steady contact. She spoke at length about her mother's research and her time in Sweden, how unhappy it had been, the controversy that had surrounded her mother's appointment to the academy and how quickly the honour was retracted, the disappointment it had caused, disappointment being too soft a word, for her mother had plunged into a depression that had lasted years. Even once the darkest periods seemed to be over, they had recurred at the onset of winter every year, a phenomenon that seemed to have been passed on to Asja, who, at the beginning of December, would find herself similarly transported into a melancholy from which she couldn't escape until solstice had passed and the days had begun, again, to lengthen. Asja spoke so quickly and with such a brightness that it was immediately evident to me that she had inherited not just the melancholy of her parents but also their fierce intelligence, and it struck me again that intelligence might truly be more burden than gift.

I asked her if she'd ever known anything of Bekhterev's political activities, and she answered in riddles, or what sounded like riddles to me. I heard many names I recognized and some I didn't. Some were party members, some were scrappy specialists who had made their way without party connections. He was a good man, she said repeatedly.

We talked so long about the past—hers and mine and what we knew of Bekhterev's—sharing what we knew, marvelling at what we didn't, and then we turned to the one that seemed to be occupying everyone, which was the Shakhty trial, the judge and jury having been recently selected and just as soon thrown out, by then for the third time. We speculated about the severity of the accusations and what the consequences of a guilty verdict would be, concluding that all the men would die because the accusations levied against them included treason. They were wreckers, after all, accused of sabotaging industrial equipment and therefore our industrial future.

Asja was troubled by it, though it wasn't the trial that bothered her as much as the media circus that surrounded it; the way it turned people against each other. They became like wolves, she said, ready to devour each other, rip each other to shreds. Her face drained of colour as she spoke. I imagined a snow-covered field, a group of poorly dressed engineers huddled in a circle, their backs to each other, their arms alternating between clutching their necks to protect themselves from the cold and thrusting out a desperate hand to ward off the pack of wolves that was circling, ever narrower, coming in for the kill. It was pointless the way they tried to defend themselves, and the scene turned bloody as I tried to redirect my attention to Asja and our present circumstances: did she want water perhaps? I heard myself weakly assert that the trial would be just, that even if the trial had become a kind of cockfight for some of the workers, it would be conducted with dignity and justice; only the guilty would be convicted.

I feel afraid, she said.

When the nurse came to say that I had to leave, we hugged fiercely, and I left, walking towards the train station, intending to cut through it because it would be shorter and safer, I thought, by virtue of its public nature. The station was almost totally empty but for the occasional person sleeping on a bench, and a few families who seemed out of place, given the hour. They were clearly waiting for one of the last trains out of the city, and their children were either bundled up and sleeping or running about in circles, their small, singular cries echoing up to the ceilings and back down, piercing the nests of the sleeping birds, who, irritated, flapped their wings and flew across the station to somewhere more peaceful. My steps echoed back at me as I walked. The sound of the space was lonely and timeless. But then, out from nowhere it seemed, three uniformed men turned a corner and approached me swiftly, fanning out into a *V* so that I was suddenly caught, suddenly surrounded.

The middle one struck a friendly but firm tone, saying good evening, miss, and asking to see my papers. What papers, I asked, and they said don't you follow the news, and I said apparently not, regretting my insolence almost immediately. Time to get with the times said the short one, and the officious one said where are you from, and I said don't you hear my accent, and he said not really, and I said Moscow.

The short one said you never know, but I didn't know what he meant.

The third one, who had been silent the whole time, said that this was a warning, but it would be the only one, and I said, but how will you know I've already been warned, and he said, I won't. I'm just saying that the warnings will be happening this week and starting next week, either you'll have your papers in order or you won't. What will they prove? I asked. What you said, he replied, that you're a Muscovite true and true. Everyone else has to leave.

Everyone, he said, gesturing to the near-empty station, suggesting that the process had already begun and that those remaining today wouldn't remain tomorrow.

The next morning, I went early to the library because one of the names Asja had mentioned had floated around in my head as I slept, or didn't sleep, next to Sasha. I realized that I recognized it from a dedication of Bekhterev's, the book he'd written after the Revolution but before Lenin died, the one whose title I could never remember, *On Materialism* or something of the sort. The library was downtown, and on that morning, the newspaper boys were hanging out at the top of the steps, smoking and chatting after having done their morning work. I had spent so many of my hours as a student in one or another library. I'd always been impressed, almost inspired, by the order imposed in some collections and by the complete lack in others (though it was merely that some collections had an order that appealed to me — by subject or last name, say — and others were totally pointless, such those ordered by date of acquisition, which resulted in a history of the Great War sitting alongside a tome about marine animals in the Black Sea, alongside a book which described itself as a meditation and addressed a theological concept such as grace.

Thankfully, the main library was ordered by last name, which made me independent. On the second floor, I found the stacks and proceeded to where Bekhterev's books ought to have been, though try as I might, I couldn't find them anywhere. I asked a librarian who dutifully pulled out the call cards that should have surrounded his name, and she, too, could find only a reference to an Arkady Bekhterev, a distant and unimportant relative. I tried not to react, asking in a mild enough tone if there happened to be any books by the one to whom Bekhterev had dedicated his book, and there were none, a thing which was so improbable as to be impossible, and this was how I saw the way that libraries themselves wrote history and that history was forever being rewritten.

I later heard that in those first days after Congress, when Bekhterev was supposed to speak to the pedologists and psychologists, questions about his sudden death had permeated conversations in the city's bars, hospitals, and universities, but such conversations had come to a halt by the time Sasha and I had returned. As I walked around the city in the week after meeting Asja, one comrade after another admitted that the mood that had surrounded Bekhterev's death was one of "embarrassment." Despite his celebrity, his death had barely been noted in the newspapers. It had been easy for some to assume they'd simply not been invited to his funeral, but those who thought about it knew there hadn't been one. It wasn't long after that that his books had started to disappear from the libraries and bookstores. It embarrassed the librarians to claim they'd misplaced all of his works, but they did so, allowing that embarrassment to stand in for the more pervasive shame of their complicity in this union-wide betrayal. Later, his research contributions started to disappear from reprints of scientific articles. Monographs that drew on his research were also reprinted without mention of his participation or were permanently shelved, which was a different kind of death.

Within a week, my papers were checked again, this time on Arbatskaya, on the corner where I'd grown up, the absurdity of it absurd only to me, because by then I already knew not to make any extraneous commentary with these men — not to say anything for the sake of friendliness — because the more I said, the more various the ways it could be interpreted. All this led, of course, to a new industry developing, an industry around fake papers. But you had to have money for those.

—⚊—

I had missed the Labour Day deadline, but by June the new exhibit was up. It looked like all the rest and just like Bekhterev would have wanted: professional, scientific, informative, and enlightening. Like the other exhibits, in addition to the model of the brain, we had a few original slices and copies of some of his most well-known articles. Excerpts from *Reflexology and Materialism* and *Objective Psychology*. We placed the exhibit where he'd envisioned: at the end of the semicircle. By our logic, this wasn't a high point, but it wasn't a low point either; it was just another gap that had been filled.

I wrote the report that Sarkisov had asked for. In it, I said, There's nothing to report. This was true, especially once I'd erased the faint markings in the diary, eliminating all reference to Asja.

Astonishing how lucky one gets if one works hard enough, said my father. *Plunge in*, said my mother. *Don't be an outsider*, said Bekhterev.

O ver the course of the summer, Stalin became First Secretary, and the trial concluded with either the worst possible outcome or the best possible outcome, depending on who one was, the city having divided itself along those lines—for or against the engineers—though in truth no one would admit to being *for* the engineers since that could easily be understood as being *against* the country, even if one didn't mean it as such. Decisiveness and transparency started to matter more than nuanced thought or creative interpretations, for the latter could too easily be misunderstood and misunderstandings had become dangerous. On the one hand, that summer people were judged with a new moral clarity; on the other, some people were lying.

At the time, no one really understood how drastically our lives had changed, but the tone that was set then would stay with us for decades. News circulated via official and unofficial channels. In the unofficial channels we heard of civilian attacks and a renewed class war—priests targeted, kulaks disenfranchised, the old bourgeois experts coming under assault, all things my father had predicted. The official channels reported on unprecedented growth in our industries, the promise of agricultural yields that would surpass any from recent history, and on the wisdom and charity of our First Secretary whom children were invited to refer to, should they so desire, as Papa Stalin. In increasingly private spaces, and only among those who could be trusted, a new term was coined and adopted which referred to the targeted people: we called them *former* people, and they could be seen moving throughout the city like ghosts—no voice, no future. The wise among them accepted their fate, seeing clearly that the change was irreversible, but many seemed to say, over their shoulders, as they departed, I'm leaving, don't throw dirt at my back as I go! I'd see them from time to time, waiting for a tram to come, a small case at their side, and I'd scrutinize their faces, looking for some sign that they did or did not deserve their exile. But there was none. I never left home without my identification anymore.

The summer was the hottest on record. Forest fires threatened the countryside, demanding extreme caution from anyone who dared to venture beyond the city limits.

—⁄—

Meanwhile, Sasha was happy. His next install was mostly sculpture, and the sculptures were mostly bronze. Heavy, in other words. On Sasha's suggestion, the gallery hired Jack to help because they had less than a week to bring the pieces in from the loading area, up a staircase, and into the gallery space whose sloping ceiling and easily chipped walls exacerbated the delicacy of the operation. The size and weight of the pieces made them both cumbersome and dangerous. They'd arrived with a rumour attached: someone said they'd crushed a man's hand in the previous gallery.

The technicality of the install made Lukas the authority, something Sasha could see, even from the outset, was going to be a problem. Lukas could be charming when he wanted, in his Southern European way, but he was annoyingly self-sufficient, which often left the old trio of Sasha, Dimitri, and Jack on their own, waiting for Lukas to come back.

That was the week that the nurse called me at the institute. It's not serious, she said, but he can't walk, so you'll have to pick him up.

It so happened that the morning the pieces arrived, Lukas had run off to do an errand, leaving the triumvirate to their own devices. The pieces were still sitting in the loading bay in four large crates.

Where're they from? asked Jack.

Sasha walked around one of the crates, looking for some kind of indication. On top of the crate was a requisition sheet.

Leningrad, he said.

Dimitri walked to the end of the loading bay and pulled the large doors shut. They'd learned with the paintings that the cold could affect the art, and that morning the temperature had dropped substantially. Bronze seemed like it should be immune, but what did Dimitri know?

Because of the weight, they would have to rig up a special system for moving the work around. The gantry was a kind of pulley system that could hoist up very heavy pieces and roll them slowly from one side of the room to the other, but only across a single axis. An elegant solution, but it wasn't perfect. Because they couldn't have all the pieces of art lined up along that one axis, they needed to have a way to lower the pieces onto plinths that didn't sit right beneath the pulley. On the first day, they set the system up. A block and tackle would hoist the work and this would be held by a pulley connected to a crane.

On the second day, Lukas wanted them to call the architect. They had to know how much weight each panel could hold. The pieces were so big their weight might damage the structure of the building itself. That much was obvious when they'd seen the forklift almost tip over with every crate it took off the truck. They would have called the architect in if they had found him. But they didn't.

On the third day, with Lukas off doing who knows

what, Jack and Sasha started prying open the crates in the loading bay. A thin knife wedged between the front of the crate and the frame got them started. Once they had that sliver of space, they found a sturdy piece of metal to widen the gap until finally the staples popped out of the frame. The crate's front panel fell off all at once, slamming loudly against the concrete floor. Jack let out a whoop and Sasha felt, he later said, like he had in art school, free. They pulled the crumpled-up newspapers away from the structure, revealing the moody, discoloured bronze. It appeared to be part of a circle.

The architect was dead, reported Lukas when he returned.

That night, I met the four of them at Max's. All the tables were full, the crowd was lively. We were sitting in Sasha's favourite corner. A group of Pioneers had gathered in another. While Sasha, Lukas, Jack, and Dimitri talked about the next step, I watched the Pioneers. They were young, the oldest not more than twenty. One of them was hanging from a pipe that ran parallel to the ceiling. The waitress didn't notice because she had her back to them, flirting with a table of old men. I watched him pull himself up and do one, two, three, and four chin-ups before dropping to the ground. One of the girls watched him, but the other girl was slumped over, holding her head in her hands. The guy did a few more, jumping down from the bar when a cook came out of the back to yell at him, and our waitress turned around to see him land. The slumped-over girl was looking sick. The chin-up guy started singing to her. The waitress could see what was about to happen and kicked them all out. The sick girl puked as soon as they got outside. I knew its colourful spray would be waiting for us when we left.

Dimitri was talking. They'd abandoned logistics and were onto ideas again. Sasha looked like he was thinking about the ideas, Jack was watching Sasha, and Lukas was taking in the whole scene: the artists, the Pioneers, maybe even the way the place was steaming up, everyone removing whatever clothing they could. More and more skin was revealed, Lukas was still taking it all in. When Sasha laughed, Jack laughed. When Sasha leaned forward, so did Jack.

What I want is some way for art to free itself from all of its traditions, Dimitri was saying. An art without paint and canvases. I want a way to overcome the abyss between representation and that which is represented. How can they become one? Art and life, one thing? Art for everyone. No more poems. No novels. Fuck paintings. Just art's very tensions in the day-to-day labours.

Wasn't that Lenin's position, I asked, earning an impressed look from Sasha.

I guess I'm coming around, said Dimitri. Why would we need a gallery for art, when art should be what we have in every single moment of the day? Art and anti-art as the same thing. Does it make sense to you? he asked.

I'll think about it, I said.

Dimitri's interest in what I thought seemed genuine, but then what I had to say never sounded very interesting. There was an earthquake in Yalta, I'd report, or there was a blackout in our neighbourhood last night, or the markets in the Ukraine have no food.

Dimitri would turn to me, appearing to change gears —like a truck racing downhill suddenly navigating a turn. I could see the effort it required. And he made the effort, which was admirable, but he rarely completed the turn. He'd nod in acknowledgement of the turn, and then keep going downhill, forging his own stubborn path.

Not art for consumption, but art as life itself? he'd ask, loosely trying to knit my questions into what he'd been talking about before. He'd try to see how the earthquake, the blackout, the food shortage, could be art.

In a sense, what Sasha was discovering was that being an artist might necessitate not making art.

—⧸—

I made it to the hospital in under an hour, my heart racing and raging, full of love and fear. In what seemed like the farthest reaches of the building, I finally found Sasha sitting in a rolling chair, pathetic and crumpled up between Jack and an old woman who'd fallen asleep, her body curled over to one side. The two of them looked like fugitive workmen, as though they'd put on the appropriate gear — canvas pants, heavy boots, thick sweaters, and the requisite work belts — but then gone to the bar, or back to bed. That they were so clearly unharmed tipped my feelings towards rage. As soon as I entered the room, Jack stood up to leave. I sat where he'd been sitting and immediately regretted it — his spot was warm with his gross, sticky heat, and I had to look up at him to talk. He stood there for a second, his hands shoved so deep into his pockets it was as if they were full of rocks and pulling his shoulders ever forward.

—⧸—

What they should have been doing at Max's that night was figuring out the block and tackle. If even one of them had been in the military they would have known how to tie a proper knot. A thicker knot was not a better knot.

—⧸—

Well, take care, said Jack, standing there, hovering.

A man wearing a dark overcoat sat opposite us, pretending to examine a pamphlet that read *Guard against infection!* in heroic red lettering. A microscope, a needle, a stethoscope, and a tool I didn't recognize emboldened the outer corners of the front and back pages.

Want anything else, asked Jack, before I go?

Jack reached behind me for his jacket. He gave Sasha a look I couldn't quite read and then skulked towards the door.

Sorry, called Sasha when Jack was at the door.

Jack glanced at me briefly, his head bent forward in line with his shoulders.

Well, he said, casting his words in our general direction, listen to the doctor. Rest. Lots of ice and whatever.

The man had lowered the pamphlet completely and was watching us with interest.

Jack took care of me, drawled Sasha.

He's on a lot of medication. The doctors said he can go, said Jack.

Yes, I said to Sasha, I can see that.

Well, Jack said again, and walked out the door.

I turned to Sasha.

Can't we leave? he asked. He looked so pale and pathetic. As I bent to unlock the brake on the chair, I caught a whiff of stale alcohol.

When I'd rolled him through the hospital doors, I said, Let's get you out of this thing, and walked around to pull him up. He peered out to the parking lot in the direction of the taxi stand.

No one's even here yet, he whined.

The sky had turned an unnatural orange and russet, and full of a thick dark cloud that I realized was smoke. I think you'll feel better if you stand up, I said.

I feel fine.

The hills must be on fire, I said, and his gaze followed mine.

Get up, I said. You can stand on one foot just fine.

—⁄—

That morning, they had hoisted up the largest piece, and as they were congratulating themselves on being able to raise it off the ground, it fell, directly onto Sasha's right foot. The piece had crushed several bones, including those in his little toe. It would be months before he would be able to walk on it properly, and he wasn't even to attempt crutches for at least a month.

Upon returning home, Sasha decided that the best thing he could do would be to return to his art.

You're going to be reassigned, I said, exhausted already by the thought of Sasha back at home all day long.

I'll do art until then.

The far corner of our room became his workspace and though he left the windows open all day long, the smell of the oils seeped into every article of clothing and seemed, almost, to soak into every paper and book. I found oily linseed shadows on notebooks and fabrics throughout our room and sometimes down the hall and into the communal kitchen. On dish towels. Smeared in a line across one square pane of our glass-windowed bookshelf. On the cover of Akhmatova's *Anno Domini MCMXXI*. On me.

Yet in that month-long period when he could not walk, I never saw a single painting.

What happened to your painting of Jack? I asked one morning.

I painted over it, he said. It wasn't working.

The paints were mixed. The oil, as I said, was everywhere. But he hid his canvases behind a sheet.

Tell me something about what you're doing.

I can't, he said.

What is the idea?

I don't think I can express it in words, that's why it's art, he said.

Do you believe that? I laughed.

I used to, he said.

He didn't know how to start again. Dimitri had fucked it all up, he said, made painting seem ridiculous. But painting was all that Sasha knew.

—⊬—

Over the course of the summer, I began to wonder with more and more frequency who I was. I seemed to be losing touch with people, or losing touch with my capacity to connect with other people, and the feeling was so pronounced that I soon wasn't sure if I'd ever been able to know anyone or be known by them at all. Rima seemed pregnant all of a sudden, but of course in those days it was hard to notice when the body changed shape, especially when one dressed as Rima did, as most party women did then, in loose-fitting shifts that gave nothing away, until suddenly, they did. Her hands started to hold her belly, tracing it the way pregnant women do. I don't want a screaming child, she told me, but I couldn't tell why she said it, with that tone of regret, when she seemed so happy.

I scrutinized her expression for too long, perhaps, because she teased me, saying, Stop looking at me like that! I'm not an alien! And I pulled back, looked away, and then looked back quickly, laughing, though the feeling—that *I* was an alien, not her—persisted.

So you'll put it in a nursery, I said. Isn't that what they do these days? I wanted to ask her, as I might have if we had been younger, who I was, but we seemed too old for existential questions now. They were a luxury that the child would force us to forego.

In the last week of August, the forests outside Moscow burned to the ground, dark smoke billowing into the city as though it were the end of time. Through the layers of thick cloud whose colours ranged from dark plum to burned orange to a dense and dangerous grey, the sienna sun crossed the sky. Old people died from breathing soot. When I washed at the end of the day, the white basin streamed with blackened water as my face and hands came clean.

And then, Bogdanov died. A boy had come in who was sick with tuberculosis and malaria. All of the blood exchanges had been going so well. Bogdanov had been getting younger. Krasin, his friend, had continued to flourish after his blood transfusion, so it must have seemed obvious that Bogdanov could help the young boy. His parents were present. By then it was so common to see people coming and going for these sorts of transfusions that I don't even remember exactly when this was. The procedure was standard: Bogdanov and the young boy had exchanged about six hundred cubic millilitres.

The boy survived.

Bogdanov was given a state funeral, perhaps on the request of Stalin — one could imagine such a thing — since Bogdanov had been Lenin's sworn enemy and, possibly by implication, a friend of Stalin's, and with the final phase of Bogdanov's work at his institute dedicated to the health of the Soviet elite, the politiburo could claim him as an ally. In the elegy Bukharin gave, he began by acknowledging the rift between Bogdanov and the Party, which he described as *a party of fighters in a harsh and beautiful time* whereas Bogdanov had been an artist of thought — the truest kind of artist, in other words. Bogdanov had thought of the body itself as art, and of the body's organs as both internal, like the liver, and external, like a machine or tool, or, indeed, the blood, which could intercourse from one body to another, linking two bodies in perpetuity. And, in death, Bogdanov had returned to his own fight which had always been a principled one, ever since his earliest days. Bukharin quoted from *Red Star* and made reference to the portents of that book, in which industry eventually destroyed the planet Mars, forcing its inhabitants into an exile, which might also be an extinction. Bukharin described Bogdanov's death at a moment of blood exchange as a death earned in deepest battle, fighting as he was for the idea of the thing, the art. *No effort of thought can gather and organize the parts of a shattered body into a living whole. Philosophy cannot work miracles.* That was Bogdanov.

Bukharin didn't mention that Bogdanov had stayed true to another principle of his, which was that the Revolution should never have happened, that it was a rotten movement, rotten at its core. Rumours circulated that Bogdanov had committed suicide, but by then I'd had it with the rumours. I'd had it with feeling, too, and so refused to grieve his death because, suicide or not, I decided that Bukharin was right about Bogdanov and his battles, and this was one he had chosen.

Looking back, the news of Bogdanov's death did something to Sasha, freezing him in time like Lot's wife, always looking back, or the mythical Orpheus, whose failure to look forward had lost him his true love forever. It took some time for Sasha to be able to walk again, and even longer before he dared go outside. When he did start going outside, he started coming to the institute. At the time, it seemed a positive step, as though he were returning to our world, limping his way into the future. He always told whoever it was that he'd come with the idea of picking me up, so he'd hang around my bench for a while, or sit in the front waiting area, or even hobble around the semicircle of exhibits, lingering (according to Sergei) on the exhibits of the musicians. Sometimes they reported that he had been cheery or in a talkative mood, and at other times he came across as insular and cold. Although he told my colleagues that he was coming to see me, his timing was uncanny: he missed me so regularly I started to wonder if it were intentional.

This was the period I've come to know as Sasha's inner migration. I wondered what he was thinking, but no amount of questioning led anywhere.

What is this, the Spanish Inquisition? he'd ask, rebuffing my questions. Or, even more exasperated: I don't hate this place, Tatiana. I'm not going to bomb the building of the General Committee of the Bolsheviks. I'm not. I like them. Nice guys over there at the General Committee, committed to their work. We agree on a lot of stuff, me and them. We agree. Who wants the filth of commercialism? Not us. Who wants humiliation before the capitalists? Not us. Who wants the good, no, glorious future for our homeland? Us! And who is willing to suffer the pains of the meanwhile life? Us. We want to suffer together. It is the good suffering. The best. Let us suffer! See? We agree. And even if in other places an artist can be free of the black raven that might come after you at daybreak, in those other places, all the artists starve. Look at me, I'm walking again, healed by our miraculous health system, and soon I'll be working again.

He'd learned the right things to say.

Sasha, who had always been so opinionated, stopped arguing with me. Even when we were together, sitting side by side on a park bench or across from one another at the small table in our apartment or curled up against each other all night long, I had the feeling that he had turned his back to me and would never face me again. I wondered what he was doing in that private world of his. I wondered what fantasies he was constructing, what life he was living. Sometimes I would ask, but he wouldn't say. Later, he would accuse me of living in my own little world, and I would think we had fallen out of love.

Now I feel differently. Now I see that what happened to us happened to everyone in a way. People stopped trusting each other. So they'd say he'd left one shore and not yet landed on another.

I started staying later and later at work. At night, when Sergei was shutting the building, I'd hear him approaching my bench. He rapped his knuckles against the lab tables as he walked, the sound echoing throughout the room. Staying late? he'd ask. I always said yes.

On one of those nights, I came home to a pitch-black apartment. In the corner by the window, a radio I didn't know we had was on. A woman was interviewing the leader of the local Pioneers.

Tell me, she said, about your recent activities. The man being interviewed cleared his throat. His voice sounded respectable and strong, but I knew differently because I knew him. He was a skinny man with a thin, wispy beard, a hypocrite. He worked as a cobbler and overcharged for everything and everyone, except card holders. There were so few official card holders by then—even I wasn't one—so he was making a profit *and* claiming to be better than that. I'd seen his apartment once when I still ran errands for the Pioneers. Large, warm, well-lit: it was better than any other apartment I'd been in and obviously the result of well-placed friends. On the radio, he was describing a local initiative to close down the bars.

Again? asked the interviewer, a whine in her voice.

In the dark, a radio sounds like abandonment, I thought. I walked across the room to switch it off.

That was when I noticed Sasha, passed out on top of the bed. The dark of his profile made the rest of the room seem less so. He'd fallen asleep waiting for me. I turned on the bedside light. He didn't stir at the click of the switch. He was lying on his back with his mouth open slack. His breathing was languid, light, and practically soundless. He'd pulled up his shirt before he started and, having exerted himself, passed out straight away. His hand was still draped loosely around his penis. He hadn't even taken off his pants. It was the laziest kind of pleasure. I cleaned him without tenderness, then covered him up. I'd been working, and *this* was what he'd been doing.

You're pathetic, I whispered. I never told him that I'd seen him that way. It would have been like admitting how low I'd sunk, as if, in seeing him like that I'd become pathetic, too. It would have been better if I'd caught him with another woman.

I turned on all of the lights then, and lifted the sheets off Sasha's canvases. Every last one was blank.

I looked at him as I had looked at countless people of his type in the streets: the selfish, spoiled rich who had lived their whole lives eating *madeleines* and *macarons* from France and now wanted pity from those of us who worked. I looked at him and could not find, anywhere in me, pity. He was too velvet-skinned, too delicate. He was drowning and wanted to drown me, too, but I refused to go under.

In the morning, I opened the balcony doors and let the cold wind blow over him. Then I went back into our room and picked up all of his canvases and threw them off the balcony.

What the hell are you doing? he cried, struggling to sit up in bed.

You're not doing anything with them, I said.

When I left, I had the impression that when I locked the door I was locking him away from me, and that eventually I would have to free us both. Whatever art he *was* doing, it didn't involve painting.

I thought of Sasha as being out of date. He was only a few years older, but everything about his upbringing had prepared him for a time that could never exist again. I wondered if our society would be better off without him, or if I would be better.

—⊹—

It finally happened that I ran into Sasha at the institute one afternoon, and so we walked home together, or rather,

I was following him home from the city, scouring the ground as I went. He had healed well enough that he could walk faster than me, especially when he was in a vile mood, which he was that afternoon. So I followed him, looking for shards of glass that I could kick: I'd shunt them hard with the toe of my shoe and not even care how close they got to Sasha, who was walking straight on with his head held high. I was sick of his crap. He entered the apartment first. Even though it was summer and the days were long, our apartment was perpetually dark. Sasha had left a lamp on, its incandescent bulb flickering an orb onto our small table. I thought to blame him for wasting energy but couldn't be bothered. Sasha leaned against the bookshelf and lit a cigarette, not even opening the door to the balcony. I sat down at the table, waiting.

You think you're a special case, he said to me.

I considered my strategy.

You think that you're on the right side, aware that, *sure,* things aren't perfect and *sure,* they could be better, but you're on the right side because you're on the scientific side.

It was true, I did think that. The books he'd been reading lately were mine. I'd vaguely thought it wasn't a good idea but hadn't been able to identify quite why.

But you know better, I said.

There wasn't anything particularly new about what he was saying, except the way that he was saying it: as though he despised me.

He reached into my pocket for my father's pocket watch. I cringed a little because the way he was moving was so aggressive, so not like him. I felt backed into a corner, and I watched him unroll the watch chain in his fingers, looping one end of it around his index finger so that he could unfurl it and dangle it right before my eyes. He brought his other hand level to the watch and, with a slight push, sent it rocking back and forth, back and forth, back and forth, back and forth.

Stop it, I said.

How blind did he make you? he asked.

Who?

Your doctor.

What doctor?

Your hypnotist. Your beloved Bekhterev, he said.

I sighed. As we'd walked home I'd shouted at him that we needed to talk, and eventually he'd slowed enough to walk beside me. By then, we were at the park across the street from our apartment, and it was there, as we walked past the stands of trees and bushes that were homes for the former people, I'd told him what I had learned about Bekhterev, about Asja, and about the circumspect report I'd written. Sasha asked me to be straight with him about what I thought had really happened, and I said I still didn't know enough to say. We crossed the street then and walked quietly into our building, saying nothing until we got into our apartment, where the single light had been left on.

As our door closed behind us, Sasha shook his head at me, saying it was obvious that Bekhterev had been killed. When I asked him why, he said I should start paying more attention to the real world, which I said was rich given how often he left the house. He wanted to know why the jagged edge, and I said I still didn't know.

So what *do* you know, *objectively* speaking? he asked.

I thought about it and admitted that less and less seemed to be objectively true these days. All I knew for certain was that Bekhterev was old, had sometimes been psychologically unhealthy, that he'd had a daughter who seemed similarly compromised about whom he'd never said a word, and that his testimony had released a man named Beilis from jail and imprisoned a woman named Vera.

Sasha didn't give a shit about the trial. What interested him, he said, was the fact that the state had punished Bekhterev, but only temporarily.

How does one become a scientific superstar in this country? he asked, finding his way to a new concern, which was Luria. After that he wound back to the topic of Bekhterev, which was where he was when he stood there, still rocking my father's watch back and forth, back and forth, back and forth.

He didn't make me blind, I said, and hypnotism doesn't work like that.

Sasha lowered himself down and said slowly, Did he make you dumb?

I tried to duck my head away, but there was no away; his body was taking up all the space in the room.

Because you weren't always dumb to the world, he went on, and you're really fucking dumb now. Who made you so dumb?

I tried to snatch the piece from him, but he pulled it up higher, just out of my reach, and then, in a manner that appeared too slow for reality, the watch slipped out of his grasp, hit the table with a hollow clunk, and slid onto the floor where it burst open, exposing the delicate inner cogs and sending the glass sliding across the room.

Sasha's face was all conflict. He hadn't meant to do it, but he was still angry with me or with the world — I didn't know which — so he didn't know what to do with the apology he wanted to say about the watch when he still hadn't proven his point, whatever that was.

I was on the ground, trying to clean up. The watch face, hands, and miniature fasteners had all broken apart, but the mechanics of the thing were still going. The cogs ticked over but without the watch hands, the time didn't change. Sasha came around the table as if to help me but instead he callously trod upon the watch hands. A larger ring had come off, too. It was rent and the watch face itself was smashed, a tiny white bruise swelling across the glass surface.

I was shaking.

I could see the back of Sasha's legs and feet, but didn't look up. He was facing a wall, as though he were a child being punished, but I saw his right foot step back and heard the smash as his fist made contact. If it hadn't been a new wall, the kind we called a listening wall because its poor construction facilitated eavesdropping, if it hadn't been constructed in order to hastily partition apartments, then Sasha might have broken his hand. The wall cracked and splintered at the point of impact. I might have pitied him if I had had any energy left at all. But I didn't. Everything felt impossible then.

He opened our door and slammed it shut behind him. I heard him pull on his shoes and then the slam of the door down the hall.

I don't know how long I was on the floor like that, trying to separate the pieces of the watch from dust and small pebbles, when the neighbour started in again with the *Valses oubliées*. He was a shit piano player.

A few minutes later, I heard footsteps in the hallway that stopped in front of our door.

The door didn't open. No one knocked. I held my breath.

Sasha? whispered a man's voice.

I stood, put the pieces of the clock in my pocket and opened the door. Dimitri. I hadn't seen him for months.

He's stepped out, I said.

No problem, I can wait.

I don't know where he went, Dimitri, I don't think he'll be back for some time.

What's going on here? Are you crying? he asked. He was kind enough to stay in the doorway; other friends of Sasha would have barged right in.

Everything is fine, I said, but even trying to say so upset me.

You need help finding him. I know where he is if he's upset. I'll take you there. Then you can talk.

No, no. I am absolutely fine, a little tired. I'm just about to go to sleep.

Come on, he said, get your coat and leave this mess for later.

I could trust Dimitri. He didn't judge me like the others, and I believed him when he said he was worried and wanted to help. I thought he might be the best part of the day, the part that would make sense, and that being outside, too, would change things. When we walked past our neighbour's door, the music stopped and then restarted, several bars back.

It was warmer outside than it was inside in the way that late summer evenings are.

We always go to the same place, said Dimitri. I come here on my own a lot, you know, to sit and think and watch the sun rise. The dawn teaches you unexpected things, he said, poetically.

Because it was late, we walked down Pirogovskaya in the middle of the street. Dimitri balanced on the street car tracks. We walked to the end of the line, to where the buses turned around and to where there were never any passengers waiting, or at least none that I had ever seen, as the end of the line was right across the street from a monastery, which was, improbably, still in operation.

So where do you go?

Behind the south wall there, he pointed. There's a little garden shed. We sit on the roof. He laughed at me then but didn't say anything, and I didn't know why he was laughing.

What will we drink?

I've got something in my bag.

And Sasha will be here?

That's my guess, he said.

We were beyond the range of the street lamps by then, so I paused to look up at the twilit sky, its blues blackening by the minute. As we walked along the stone wall of the monastery in the damp grass and the unnaturally warm night, my eyes adjusted slowly to the dark. I began to see details in the wall I had missed at first. Lush lines of ivy snaked their way around, up, and over the wall. The irregularity of the stone. When we rounded the corner, a dark mass of moss looked like a continent creeping up the wall with a slowness that looked like stillness, but wasn't.

At the shed, Dimitri jimmied the door and went inside, coming out seconds later with a stool to which he gestured, saying, Go on.

So I stood on the stool, grabbed onto the ridge of the roof, and clambered up. The roof was flat and made of thick wood timbers that had been worn smooth by the weather.

I lay down, my stomach on the roof, my fingers curled over the edge, and looked at Dimitri below.

Are we allowed to be here? I whispered.

Best place for sorting things out, he said, hoisting himself up.

From the roof I could look all around us, taking in the monastery and the cemetery and a great body of water that the light from the rising moon had just lit up, making it seem like a vast mountain lake and not what it was, a small city reservoir. The water's surface rippled as if thousands of the insects we called water boatmen were crossing it all at once. Beyond the reservoir, the rail lines glistened and beyond that, I could make out the dark curve of the river. After the river there was a great, black nothingness that, by day, were the forests and fields beyond the city limits. This was the quietest place in the city.

I'm not sure we should stay for very long, I said, though I remember wishing I could stay forever.

He sat down, took a bottle from his satchel and unscrewed the top. He tipped it to his mouth, and I saw the flickering river of clear liquid flow from one end of the bottle to the other, then back. The liquid caught all the light around us and didn't let go. He lowered the bottle and handed it to me.

He placed a cigarette in his mouth. He lit a match and cupped his hand around the cigarette so his hand and lower face were lit with a deep, soft orange, and then he shook out the match, so that all that was left was the flare of the glowing ember. The fading ember glided down to where he rested his hand on top of his knee.

I took a small sip from the bottle. The liquid skipped past my tongue as if it had no flavour at all or as if my throat were suddenly the place for taste buds, because there, along the back of my throat and then all the way down to my heart, I felt the cool burn of the vodka and then after it was gone, the memory of it finally claimed the tip of my tongue. I felt my cheeks flush, and I set the bottle down between us, propped against his bag.

What happened tonight? asked Dimitri.

I thought of the swinging pocket watch and the way Sasha looked at me so hatefully. I pulled my knees up to my chest and hunched over them, resting my chin on my arms. Like that, I could look out at the water, or press my face to my knees and see only the shadowy folds of my skirt.

Could I have a cigarette? I said.

I didn't want help. Dimitri handed me his cigarettes and took a drink while I removed one.

When I put the cigarette in my mouth, he lit it and his hands glowed orange again.

Before I met Sasha, when I was alone and more vulnerable to the world, my friends and mentors had concerned themselves with whether or not I would marry, with whether or not a smart woman like me could find a complement in the world: in short, with the most personal things of my life. I remembered a time I went shopping for a dress with Rima. We decided—it was unlike us—to go into the fashion district on the other side of the city, near the bridge, where all the shop owners were French. We were the only two in the store. It was one of the more rundown stores, but they had beautiful glass lamps whose oil reflected the double flames and radiated a honeyed light throughout the room. Racks and racks of old dresses made it almost impossible to move and even more impossible to avoid the two saleswomen—a mother and daughter. Rima was cornered by the daughter, and I by the mother.

When I retreated to the dressing room to try on three dresses, the mother stood outside the room, hovering with her hunched back, her cigarette with the dangling ash. I drew the curtain and slowly undid my dress. I slipped it off my shoulders, first one, then the other, stepping out of my own dress and into a dusty dress I could never wear. Before I had even pulled it up to cover me, the old woman threw open the curtains demanding to know how it fit, if I liked it. I was so angry. I could not respond. The woman zipped up the back of the dress and spun me so that I stood, dazed, facing the mirror in the small space.

C'est parfait, said the woman. And then in Russian, You should buy it, it's perfect for you.

I stared at myself, at my meagre breasts barely visible beneath the worn silk.

Look at yourself, said the saleswoman. Look at yourself, she said, and say, I love you, I love you, I love you.

What? I said.

Do it! Say I love you, I love you, I love you.

Leave me alone, I said, pulling the curtain between us and then tearing the dress from my frame. I put on my own dress and rushed from the store. I walked a whole block before I remembered Rima, and then I had to walk back.

I felt Dimitri's hand resting on the top of my back. I butted my cigarette out on the roof, then tossed it down below. He began to press the flat of his thumb into the muscles on either side of my spine, pushing them upwards. I relaxed a little, and let him. I watched the water.

You have to try to understand him. He's an artist. He's not made for ideals alone. He's not like you.

I'm not so idealistic, I said.

Not to hear Sasha speak of it, said Dimitri, which made me sad somehow, to think of how Sasha spoke of me, and also sad to think that in Sasha's mouth, idealistic was a negative thing, but in Dimitri's, it was a positive.

What was different now was that the sky was so dark and the water boatmen were making their way across the ocean towards a new life of adventure and discovery, and the railway tracks were glistening with the promise of foreignness, and beyond that the past was underground, and no one could tell me what dresses to buy. I hated the word *artist*. The way people used it to mean exceptional, when really it was an excuse.

I didn't know he thought that, I said and looked at Dimitri for the first time. Yes, we had spent time together, but never alone, and here I saw that he was a caring man. He had dark, dark eyes that sparkled with the moonlight, and he was patient.

He's always saying it, said Dimitri.

We stared out at the blackness for a while. The dark shapes of birds winged by. In a tree, I saw a strange shape dangling from a branch and realized that a pair of boots had been slung up there. Would they fall when the laces rotted? Would the laces rot?

Do you still love him?

Of course!

A quick answer always means its opposite, he said.

That's ludicrous.

You can love him in a way, but maybe it's not the right kind of love.

I wanted him to say something easier.

Don't take offence, said Dimitri. All loves are not the same.

I straightened my back, and Dimitri's hand slid down to the roof. I took another drink and thought about the shape of the rocks that made up the wall that supported us. My back was cold where Dimitri's hand had been, and I wished he'd put it back.

I don't know why he's so angry, I said. The vodka was having its way with me. Its light was flickering through me, making me warm, making me feel like I was just about to do something, I just didn't know what.

He's angry because the world around him has changed, because he was born into a family that promised wealth and security with a little bit of work, and now he's got to really think about who he is and what he is doing, and he doesn't want to do that. He's angry because you know what you want and he doesn't.

He paused and squinted to watch a single bird fly along the length of the tracks, heading west.

You saw him today, I said.

Yes, he said.

We sat there as if waiting for something, but we'd forgotten about Sasha, even as we talked about him. More birds sailed by. I heard their wings flap against the night air. Beneath them, the cemetery, train tracks, and reservoir started to seem mean and unforgiving. The birds lost their formation. I saw them drop away from one another, losing their way, falling to the ground, one by one, isolated and away from the group, alone and without their natural guides. It was unfair, I thought, the way we created false lakes, like this one, lakes that are stagnant, unmoving, black pits into which the birds might dive and never resurface.

I think it has started to rain, I said.

Dimitri held his hand out to feel for raindrops, but there were none.

I moved to the edge of the roof, my feet dangling down. I looked back at Dimitri.

He slid down beside me, and we looked down at our feet for a bit, the ground below just out of focus.

No one can ever know a person, and no one can ever know the inside of a love, I said.

I know, he said, looking at me. I felt an energy between us, a feeling I wanted to deny. It was the accident of his hand placed close to mine. I leaned towards him and his arms enveloped me and he felt so strong and certain and smelled like pine, and I told myself it was nothing and kept telling myself that, even when he put his hand on my leg and then slid his hand around my inner thigh and pulled it closer to him so my legs were apart, and I lifted my face to his, and he kissed me and I him. His lips were cool and wet. I closed my eyes and thought of Sasha and even felt that maybe this was for us, that I could be with Dimitri and it would be a thing that would make me want Sasha more, like I would reach for him again because, in that moment, I was with Dimitri and wishing for Sasha, and it was the first time in too long that I wanted Sasha and so I said to myself that this was good. Except I hated Sasha. Was that the same as loving him?

Dimitri's leg pushed between mine and his arm looped beneath my back. I pushed myself back up the roof's smooth surface so that Dimitri now hovered over my waist, and it seemed as if his mouth had always known how—with what rhythm and with what pressure and with what speed—to do this. When we kissed again, his mouth was salty and warm and my whole body relaxed as if after a long cold winter it had experienced warmth for the first time. When Dimitri said to me, Sasha mustn't know about this, I said, I doubt he'd care.

He would, said Dimitri.

You don't come here with him, do you? I asked, feeling a welter of emotions that included betrayal, desire, and pride.

No, he said.

We sat up, and I inched my way to the edge of the roof again and looked down.

Dimitri brought his feet underneath him so that he was crouching into a ball. He leaned onto his right hand and kicked off, dropping to the ground. From there, he held the stool for me.

Go down backwards, he said, it's easier.

—⁄—

When I got home, the balcony door was still open, and the curtain was twisted around itself like a piece of thick rope. I crossed the room to close the door, feeling pieces of the watch like grit underfoot. I looked out the window. I wanted company that night. When I went down the hall to the bathroom, it was occupied, so I waited at the door in a familiar way, thinking it might be Sasha. When the man we called Uncle Gregory — not because he was related to us but because he was the age of an uncle and a kind man — opened the door, a ratty towel clutched with one hand around his hips, his steamed-up glasses in the other hand, I looked away.

Later, I swept the floor of our apartment clean, emptying the dustpan into the garbage without ceremony. Then I watched the ceiling for hours, tried to count the patches of peeled paint, tried to burn their irregular forms into my mind. There was a moment when I heard the door at the end of the hall open and shush closed. I propped myself up on my elbows. Footfalls approached our door and there was no time to think of what I most wanted to say or whether or not I ought to feign sleeping.

Next door, the deadbolt retracted.

I lay back down, pretended to myself that I wasn't crying, and when I couldn't pretend anymore, I told myself that I was exhausted. When I stopped, I still couldn't sleep. I watched the play of shadows on the curtains, listened to the building sleep, wondered if people dreamt anymore these days.

In the morning, a metal crate being pulled across the courtyard woke me. I had slept in my clothes.

—

It wasn't as though I didn't see, then, what was happening to our country. I saw the homeless. I saw the corruption. I saw the lines outside Lubyanka. Of course I did; I wasn't blind. But where Sasha saw only the negative, I thought things would get better. We were building something totally new. Of course it was difficult. All great endeavours are difficult. Art, love, science — they all dream big and fight hard before they achieve the grace of being settled. We didn't want to be held back, but it was human nature to want to return to the familiar.

When I was younger, I'd been a regular at Komsomol meetings, but by the summer of 1928, I hardly went anymore. I guess it was in an effort to find my old self that I returned to them, and that was how I started to see Tobias again. When Sasha and I had first met him so long ago that summer's night at the fountain, he was still a man who lived in society — he knew what the parents might think of a man bathing in his underwear, but he also knew that a man had to be clean. The short-term indignity of bathing in a fountain was counterbalanced by the dignity of a refreshed mien. When I found him again in the summer of Sasha's inner migration, Tobias had lost all his dignity. One night he rattled off a story about a boat he'd seen and how it had been bigger than any that had ever, would ever, exist, and how his father was its captain, and that's how I knew he was lying.

I said, Hey, Tobias, you're lying to me, and Tobias said, It's not a lie, it's a story, and if I don't tell you a story, then we'll have to talk about death.

Why, I asked.

Because I'm dying, he said.

We're all dying

I'll be the first to go.

Go on, I said, say more about the boat, and so he continued, saying that the boat was meant to sail to the new world but sunk after collision with an iceberg, and it was the *Titanic* he meant and his father couldn't have been the captain, but I humoured him because I didn't want to talk about death either.

I didn't tell Sasha about things like that anymore. Sasha would think Tobias was suffering, but I knew we had to be brave about the change that was coming and that some people would need to be braver than others. And if they couldn't be brave, well, then we'd be best, in the long run, to be without them. Not that it was easy.

———⟋———

Sasha didn't come home. Alone, I started listening through the walls using the technique my father had taught me so long ago. The hollow clink of the glass against the wall. The heat of my ear pressed to the bottom of the glass. The oceanic sound of my blood swooshing inside my own head. The listening made me feel like I knew the people around me. In the afternoons, I listened to the shit piano player, and later, the opera singer. She sang only arias and only at night. Her husband left for work at 5:00 p.m. every day, and after that she would start singing until 7:00 p.m., when her brother came home. If he came home later, she would sing later, but the later he came the more drunk he'd be, and the later it was, the more horrible it became to listen to what happened once he'd slammed the door. The husband was home by midnight or 1:00 a.m., so things often improved then. When the husband and wife talked, I couldn't distinguish the words. I knew they were talking because the wife's voice, even when it whispered, was like a song, and so her whispers lilted and laughed through the walls. Sometimes, I thought she was crying, but even that was beautiful in its way.

One night, I tired of listening through the walls and decided, instead, to turn on the radio. Instead of the station I'd expected, I heard a slight crackle and then the unmistakable intonation of a voice speaking in French. At first it was one voice and then it was two. From the tone and rhythm of the conversation, I could tell that the voices were listening to each other and that the topic was grave. The woman's voice — it was a woman and a man speaking — was worried. I had heard about people listening to the radio stations from Europe, but I'd never thought to do it myself. Apparently Sasha had. I wondered what the French people were worrying about at this time of night. I fell asleep listening to it, though I couldn't understand a thing.

—⁄—

Sasha stayed away a long dark week, and then, one afternoon, he showed up again at the institute. He'd come in from the back, but had had to walk to the front to find me in the entrance. I could see that it was raining outside from the droplets of water that dotted his hat. A pure happiness washed over me at the sight of him. Relief, I suppose. I wanted to embrace him and forget about everything, but then he was just so cold. He was on his way to Dimitri's.

He wanted me to invite you, he said, loosening his scarf.

Oh? I was sitting behind the desk, which gave our exchange a certain formality. I looked for signs that he knew about Dimitri but there were none. He walked a little closer, but even as he did, the distance between us seemed to grow.

He invited Rima and Yuri, so he thought you'd want to be invited, I guess, or that they'd want you to come. He was telling me he didn't want me there by telling me that they did.

He took the brim of his hat in his hand and shook it over the floor to get rid of the water droplets.

It would be weird if you didn't come, he said.

He looked down and kicked at something I couldn't see. If the desk hadn't been between us, the distance mightn't have felt so great. Maybe without the desk there, I would have been able to slide from my stool and grab his hand.

This place is full of creeps, he said, looking around.

He was jittery. I could see it in his eyes, the way he wanted to run.

I'll be there soon, I said.

Sure, he replied.

By the time he left, it felt less like we were repelled by one another, and more like we were tired of being so tired.

———✠———

Before I could leave, Zhanna rushed up to me, placing her hand on my arm and looking at me with desperation, saying she needed me to stay. She sat me down and quietly explained that some things had gone missing.

What things? I asked.

Small pieces, she said, of almost every exhibit we have.

What she was most worried about were the necrotic tissue from Lenin's brain, the lantern slides that documented it, and multiple slices of Bekhterev's brain. I wanted to ask how long she'd known about the missing items, but her lips were quivering with emotion already. What she was worried about, and what I got worried about, was Sarkisov.

I need this job, she said.

Me, too, I said.

I took my coat off again and together we went through the entire collection, going through the cabinets, the boxes, sliding open and closed the hundreds of drawers that lined the back wall of the lab. They made a wooden *shrrrr* when slid open or closed, and this sounded like some kind of progress for the time being. If the drawer was empty, it was just the *shrrrr, shrrrr.* If the drawer contained something, it was *shrrrr, clunk, shrrrr, clunk,* as the object inside shifted. One of the drawers was looser than the others. Where the other drawers required an initial tug to pull them open, one of the drawers slipped open so quickly that a small glass slide—no more than the length of my thumb—slid to the end of the drawer and skipped out. It would have broken into thousands of pieces had I not caught it, its keen edges pressing into my fingers and palm. Once there, it seemed careless to return it to that faulty drawer, and so I slipped it into the fold of my pocket and forgot about it.

We didn't find anything.

Who would want the leeches? she asked.

I could think of plenty of young boys who would have wanted them. *I* would have wanted them if I were a child.

oing through the collection made me late, and the sky was black with clouds that threatened rain. I went to the dinner directly, not stopping to pick up meringues or pies. Just before I arrived, the downpour began, the big fat drops soaking me in seconds. The buzzer to their apartment didn't work, so when an older woman arrived with a key, I followed her inside. In the lobby, she asked me who I was visiting. When I told her it was Dimitri, she nodded in what I took to be approval. They all lived on the fourth floor, Dimitri alone, Yuri and Rima with Rima's parents and her brother, Kolya. After all that had happened, I needed to see Rima first. My shoes, wet from outside, slapped loudly against the marble stairs for the first few flights but quieted as they dried.

I rang the door to Rima's hallway, hoping that Rima would answer and not one of her neighbours.

I heard a door inside open, then the yapping of her dog, Marksena, and then the shushing sound of Rima's slippers against the tiles in the hall.

Oh! she said, smiling in the genuine way that she did. You're drenched!

I followed her and the dog down the hall and into the apartment. At the door, I stepped out of my shoes and tiptoed over the pools of water and dirt that had gathered in the vestibule and into their main room. The apartment had three sleeping quarters. Koyla's was a closet really, especially for a man of his size, and Rima's parents occupied the third room. Kolya managed a herring plant. He brought herring to dinners, as if this were an act of generosity and not a sign of his pilfering. Rima handed me a new shirt and a towel for my hair, then resumed her position at the hotplate, her left hand on her hip as her right stirred the pot. This was something I'd always admired about her. *She* could get a hotplate while every other idiot (myself included) had to make do with the communal kitchens. She was always the exception.

As I towelled off my hair, I saw that her body was taking on the shape of middle pregnancy. She tired more easily these days, but tried not to show it.

Marksena ran circles around my legs.

Where's Kolya? I asked, removing my shirt.

Right here! he said, appearing in the doorway to his room.

I scrambled to cover myself. Kolya laughed at me saying don't be so shy, but Rima instructed him to give me some privacy, so he turned his back as I slipped the new shirt over my head.

I went to stand next to Rima, so that the two of us stood side by side watching the liquid in the pot swirl and steam. Beside the hotplate, there was a sink so deep a small child could bathe in it. It was not hooked up to any water. Both the hotplate and the sink were illegal, but Yuri had lost the argument over it when they'd moved in together. I tasted the soup, salted it, and turned down the temperature. Rima looked at me and understood that I needed some time with just her.

Watch the soup, will you? she said to Kolya.

Meaning? he asked.

Stir it, dummy. And bring it to Dimitri's with you when you come.

Rima and I walked down the hall, through the doors, and further on to the communal kitchen, where we paused. I lit a cigarette. We stood in the hall, just outside the kitchen doorway, passing the cigarette back and forth, not talking.

I peered into the kitchen and saw that the old woman who had let me into the building was sitting there at the table with a cup of tea and a small notebook. She'd closed her eyes for a second, but looked up when we came in. She nestled her age-spotted hands under her round belly, her slippered feet planted squarely on the floor.

Oh, she said to me. Weren't you visiting someone else?

Dimitri Petrovich, I said, but then wished I'd stayed quiet.

That's the one, she looked at us both for a moment, as if drawing some elaborate conclusion. But you two are friends, too. How nice.

Rima sighed, Yes, Mrs. Bonner. We're friends.

The kitchen was filthy. A single electric bulb hung from the centre of the room, spreading our shadows out over the countertops, into the drawers, into whatever direction we looked. Scratched into the wood of the cupboards were the names of the residents—an attempt at ownership that no one respected.

Haven't seen you for a while, the woman said to Rima.

No, you haven't, said Rima, turning her back to look for the plates in the cupboard. How many are we, Tatiana? she asked over her shoulder.

I watched the old woman fumble her fingers around the notebook and pull it closer to her. Her hand shook slightly, and I thought she would be better off if the book were more substantial; it might weigh down her fluttering hand.

I looked back at Rima: We're bringing these to Dimitri's?

I have no idea. You, me, Sasha, Yuri, Dimitri, Kolya. Who else?

It's odd how rarely we see one another, said the woman.

Is it? said Rima. Let's get eight settings, she said to me, taking several plates from her cupboard, and the remaining ones from someone else's.

The Brodskys are away, then, are they? said the woman.

Rima ignored her. I put the forks and knives into the glasses and fit everything into a basket so that I could carry them all at once.

In the hall, Rima balanced the stack of plates on her hip and leaned against the wall.

Well, you look tired, she said.

It's the institute, I said, setting down the basket.

That's not all, she said.

We're fighting, I guess.

Your lives are too entwined. You need other people around to make it work, she said.

We have you and Yuri, I said. And he has Jack and Dimitri.

Other lovers, she said.

Sasha would never, ever accept that.

Maybe he'll have to, she said.

We said nothing for a few minutes. I thought of Dimitri, but didn't say anything. In one of the apartments a radio turned on. In another, a baby cried. Rima shifted her weight and the plates shifted too, clinking.

The baby's started to kick a little, she said, smiling. I smiled back in a stupid way, because it seemed miraculous, but then it happened every day; a miraculous everyday thing was happening to her.

In those years, it was pretty normal for people to sleep around. Sometimes a couple would live with an additional lover and other times the entanglements were more fleeting. But most people did it, and I had no reason to feel embarrassed or ashamed. In fact, it should almost have been a source of pride, of liberation from old ways, from the traditional. Dimitri and I had had that, but there was no reason for anyone to know about it. Or to talk about it. Or even to hint at it.

When we got to Dimitri's, Sasha and Dimitri were sitting at the end of the table, smoking. On the wooden table there were a few ceramic cups, several plates of onions and herring, and three carafes of vodka. One of the carafes sat between them and was half-empty. Sasha raised his eyebrows at me, then got up to greet Rima. Dimitri sprang out of his seat to take the plates and dishes from us and then returned to hug us with a warmth I wanted to resist but couldn't. If he held onto me longer than he did Rima, no one noticed but me.

Get drinking, Comrades, he said. You're behind!

Rima laughed.

Yuri, Kolya, then Sergei and Anna all arrived one by one. Sergei and Anna were friends of Yuri's so I'd seen them regularly over the years but knew little about them. Mismatched bowls and dishes accumulated in the centre of the wooden table. When we were ready to eat, Rima, Kolya, Sergei, and Anna sat down on a row of crates and chairs of approximately the same height. Sasha and Dimitri lifted the table from either end, pinning them in so that there would be room for the rest of us to sit on the other side. The table stopped where Kolya's stomach began.

No escape now, Dimitri observed.

Rima and I sat on the end, then Yuri beside me, Dimitri beside him and, on the end farthest from me, Sasha. The distance between us could have seemed accidental.

Dimitri filled the ceramic cups for the first toast.

As the meal progressed, I noticed how Sergei looked at Anna every few seconds in a way that made me know he loved her. Either she didn't know, or did but didn't love him back. When she wasn't eating, she leaned back against the wall and crossed her arms over her small frame. Sergei stayed hunched over his bowl. Anna probably thought they were friends. He probably knew they would never be friends, even though he'd keep trying because the way it hurt when he was with her was better than the nothing he felt when he wasn't.

More and more carafes appeared and disappeared. The room started to blur as if a grease-smeared pane of glass had descended between each of us, or perhaps it was just me, me in my very own grease-smeared bell jar, separated from the rest. The room resonated with the ordinary—the clink of cutlery against dishes, Kolya's grunting agreements, Rima's chatter—but *visually* nothing was quite right. I resisted the urge to run my fingers through the air around me. Of course I *knew* there was no jar. But what use is knowing there is no jar when you are plainly trapped inside of one?

Inside the jar, a series of images started overlapping for the first time. There was Luria, saying that there had been no funeral and then there was the jagged edge that Sasha had noted in the brain stem and the unique way that those particular slices had curled, as if they were chemically different than the rest of the brain, which they were, because that is the way the blood-brain barrier works; it is a barrier, a real barrier—blood on one side isn't the same as it is on the other. And then I thought of blood as a vehicle for meaning as it had been proposed in that mystical text by the lamplighter, no, the Decadents, the ones who interpreted the death of the boy just as if they were interpreting an occult text: blood for vowels as opposed to what it really was, blood in exchange for the life of a child, and none of it made any real sense. Then I thought of Bekhterev and of the Health Minister and what he had said about our work, that materialism would triumph, and what Bekhterev always said, which was not to be an outsider, and my father, work hard, but then there was the child who had been buried, and Bekhterev who had been buried, and Bogdanov who had been buried, and Lenin who had not. And I wondered where the refuge was: was our refuge in the mausoleum that people lined up to visit day in and day out, or was our refuge in the deep dark chambers that housed the witnesses to the original M and the original K? And again I thought of that jagged edge and of the relentless movement of the microtome, the solid *chunk* sound it made at the bottom of every cycle, and I just hoped to God, because this was what one does, one resorts to childhood superstitions in such moments. So I said, God, please don't let me remember any of this. I was saying it to myself, but then Rima took the bell jar off my head and I heard myself saying it out loud. And then the room spun a little as I stood up and walked down the hall to the bathroom to vomit, which I did, in the hopes of eliminating something more than just the alcohol, but it didn't work and neither did my prayers, because here I am writing this, which is a sign that even if I'd left behind my childhood superstitions, my adult superstitions wouldn't take their leave so easily.

—✕—

When I came back, the table had been cleared and the door had been opened to let in a cool breeze. The cold felt all right, except that I had been sweating, so my skin took that cold and turned it into goosebumps. Sasha looked over at me, concerned, and I smiled that I was okay, and this exchange was almost the same thing as us getting past all that had come between us. Sergei was speaking for the first time, saying that he wanted to tell a joke. Okay, everyone said. I sat back down at the table and Rima poured me a glass of water. I concentrated on the sharp cold path the water carved out of me.

So three men are sitting in a cell in Lubyanka. Beside me, Yuri's leg tensed up. Rima's face betrayed nothing, but her eyes flashed at me, as if to say, make him stop. Mine flashed back the question, why me? Yuri was a card holder, a man with principles. Sasha called him the automaton. When Yuri walked into a room, he held his head high, his body thick and strong. He wasn't the sort to be nuanced about principles. If someone, like Sasha, had suggested the possibility of nuance, Yuri would have called them weak. I admired him because he was hard. Dimitri stood to close the window.

I know this one, Anna whispered to no one in particular. She was the kind of woman who, when faced with someone political, would feel poorly educated, and when faced with someone who abhorred politics, someone like Sasha for example, she would fidget then, too, like whatever political affiliations she did have were indications of her tiresome nature. She was a suspicious person; more than anything she suspected herself of being a fraud.

I knew the joke and so did Sasha, but Sasha said nothing and neither did I.

Rima stood to clear the plates.

Sergei sensed a problem. It's just a joke, he said.

Go on, said Yuri, wiping his mouth with his handkerchief. Let's hear your joke.

Sasha wanted to know if I would admit knowing the joke; I wanted to know if he would. The room had started to fog up. I kept sipping my water.

Sit, Rima, said Yuri, in a tone that once again cleared the blur from the room.

I'll take those plates and smash them, offered Sergei,

trying to pull his legs out from under the table. He pulled up one knee and then the other but couldn't manoeuvre them to either side without running into Anna or Kolya, and so he pulled them straight up, hiccupping the table and causing the remaining carafes to topple.

Sasha caught the one closest to him and poured the liquid down his throat.

To us! cheered Kolya, grabbing another.

Sergei was standing on his box now, fumbling with his belt.

Do something, said Rima to Yuri.

This is why we need a ban, said Yuri to Rima.

He stood swiftly, placing his kerchief in his pocket and walking neatly around to the other end of the table. He reached over top of Anna, who had cringed all the way into the wall. Sergei was making to step up onto the table, one leg lifted like a dog about to urinate, his belt unbuckled and dangling.

Yuri managed to use Sergei's imbalance in his favour so that in less than a minute, he had been steered over Anna and roughly onto the floor where he crumpled into a heap and started to laugh and then cry. It was all impressively athletic, the way they moved, and moved while talking, and moved in the way they wanted to move.

I heard myself ask if someone might open the window again.

Perfect, said Yuri.

Anna and Kolya still thought Sergei might go on. What's the joke? they asked.

Sergei looked up from the floor and said, So the first asks the second why he has been imprisoned, and he says, Because I criticized Trotsky.

I was getting a chill.

Sasha was waiting for the next part.

Sergei said woefully, And the second one says, But I'm here because I spoke out in favour of Trotsky!

Dimitri hadn't said anything all night, as though he'd been biting his tongue, but then he spoke up. Best to stop there, he said to Sergei.

Sasha had also been quiet but now got offended on Sergei's behalf. Or what? he asked and stood to face Dimitri, which was a ridiculous thing to do, and it embarrassed me.

Sergei was the most passive person in the room, but a part of him was involved in a fight.

This night is over, said Dimitri to Sasha, but also to the room in general. Sasha was still thinking about doing something, but his thinking was getting in the way of him doing anything.

We're leaving, said Yuri, taking Rima by the elbow and ushering her to the door.

Everyone moved ever so slightly, which indicated that the room agreed with Dimitri. Rima moved so she was standing next to me, Sasha shifted toward the door, Anna and Kolya, who had been sitting on their boxes the whole time, collaborated on shunting the table out far enough to give them space to move.

The night *was* over.

Sergei wasn't ready for it to end. You want the punchline or what!?! he yelled from the floor.

Everyone already knows the punchline, said Sasha as he pulled on his shoes. The third guy is Trotsky.

Sasha fished his jacket out of the pile and said to me, almost as an afterthought, I'll wait for you downstairs.

Come on, Rima, said Yuri.

I'll have a cigarette with Tatiana, she said, and then come home.

Dimitri's balcony looked onto the park. Rima pulled the door shut behind us, to separate our world from theirs. Inside, Kolya and Dimitri were discussing what to do with Sergei, who had curled up into a ball on the floor and seemed to have fallen asleep. Anna was clearing the table. Yuri had left.

Rima lit a cigarette and offered me one, but my stomach was so knotted up I couldn't smoke. I wanted her to say something, but she didn't, and I didn't either. We leaned on the balcony like we had so many times before, but something had changed. And so, for the first time with Rima, I didn't know what to say.

The night was black, silver, and green. At first I saw nothing but inky darkness and the random bright glare of a moonlit puddle. Then two little fireflies glowed bright red, then dulled. It was Sasha and Jack. The movement of their arms, the hunch of their backs. Where Jack had come from, I didn't know, but I could recognize the two of them, their silhouettes tensed up and conspiratorial, anywhere. I turned to go back inside but Rima stopped me to see if I was okay.

I wanted to be able to explain the extent to which my entire world was disintegrating all around me, but I had no words.

I'm okay, I said, and went back inside to find my things.

Outside, the rains had cooled the city.

Sash, I called from the entrance.

I saw him look over at me.

Sasha, what's happening? I said.

Shhhh, he hissed.

He and Jack walked over.

Night, Tatiana, said Jack, tossing his cigarette onto the pavement and going inside.

asha and I crossed the courtyard, and I looked back at Dimitri's balcony. All I could see of the inside was the ceiling brightly lit and the rubber plant on the top of a shelf. If they were still talking, I couldn't see them.

Our footsteps echoed between the buildings. Sasha was quiet at first, then asked if I was feeling better. I said yes, and now it was true because I had started thinking again, a good thing because it meant I was better, but bad because thinking always seemed to come between Sasha and me.

All his earlier bravado dissipated so that now he walked as though he had no pride at all. How closely linked pride is with its opposite, I thought. Shame was always just around the corner. Was it shame that Sasha felt? And had I caused it? No. I couldn't be to blame for his failures. It was he who could not let go of the world that had coddled him, first his mother and then his school and then later his work, if it could be called that. Drawing. Colouring. What had he ever contributed? I thought of him and Jack, slouched together at the tables in the dark night, deep in discussion about some trivial thing. And what about Dimitri? What was I to do about him? Did Sasha know or did he sense it? I wouldn't apologize, if he asked me to. If I apologized it would be like saying I wanted a marriage I didn't want. I didn't want to be his. I didn't want to be owned, to be like property.

The whole way home I felt as though I were walking behind Sasha, even though we were side by side. As though he'd turned his shoulder on me, although he hadn't. The truth was that I didn't want to fight anymore, and I did, in some part of me, still want to be his.

When we got home, he said we couldn't go inside.

Why? I asked.

Because I have something to tell you, he said, and I don't want to do it inside.

Because you don't want me to yell?

No.

Because I'll yell out here, too, I said.

He pulled me across Pirogovskaya and into the park. I knew that somewhere in the dark bushes, Tobias was sleeping.

I'm going to leave, said Sasha.

I stopped walking.

We can't stay still, he said, walking ahead.

What kind of leaving? I asked, catching up to him.

I'm leaving the country.

Is that what you were talking to Jack about? Why, Alexandr? We are fine here.

I'm not, he said quietly. Don't you see that? I'm definitely not fine. Why can't you see me? I feel like I am dying here. I'm worthless to this place, worthless to you.

We walked on in silence. It had started to rain, but under the cover of the trees we could stay relatively dry. There were no lights in the park. The only sound was the rustle of the trees and the rhythmic patter of raindrops landing on the canopy of leaves above us. The blacks were carbon, velvet, and oil.

Why? I asked. Why can't you be fine?

My question angered him because it implied he had a choice.

Fuck you, he said, his voice tight. I tried.

Under a tree, I stopped, waiting for him to say something more.

I can't live this way. Don't you see what is happening all around you? If it isn't safe here for people like Bekhterev, it sure as hell isn't safe for people like me.

Very slowly, I said, You're nothing like Bekhterev.

I thought you would say that, he said.

In my head, I mimicked Sasha: *I thought you would say that, I thought you would say that, I thought you would say that.*

A man was walking in our direction. As he approached I saw myself struggling to form an opinion, which was not about the man, though he occasioned it. My thoughts swung as a pendulum does, from one side to the other, between the notion that Sasha was right that Bekhterev had been killed and the idea that Sasha was wrong and something else had caused Bekhterev's death. From the notion that the engineers were criminals to the state was turning violent. From things were missing from our collection and we would be held responsible for the destruction of scientific evidence to our collection wasn't even science, no one would ever care about what was or wasn't missing since science was politics and nothing about our politics had been tarnished. The man was almost upon us, but I still couldn't see his face because what little light there was, was coming from behind him. I could see that he was tall, but also I could see that he was uninterested in us, his frame directed steadily to the left side of the path and we were on the right. Sasha took my hand to get me to move, and soon we passed the man. When we'd been walking for a minute or so, I looked over my shoulder and made out the shape of him receding into the dark.

It's not possible to leave, just like that, I said.

It is possible, said Sasha. Jack knows a way.

Jack.

You could come, he said. He would help you, too.

How kind.

I want you to come with me, he said.

We walked on, past the shadowy trees and whoever was

sleeping there. We didn't talk over our footfalls on gravel. We walked towards the morning, towards the dead grey light that seeped into the park at its end. At the exit, we came to the end of the tramway line. It was like a graveyard of trams. All night they stayed like that, their antennae folded above them in angular misshapes like giant, desiccated insects.

I realized there was so much more I wanted to know about everything. And I knew by looking at him that he wouldn't tell me anything else.

I know what happened between you and Dimitri, said Sasha. And the truth is, I don't mind. I know why you did it, I mean. I know it's important to you that you not be owned by me and that even though I've never acted like I owned you, you needed to prove that you weren't. I understand. And you'll have him once I'm gone. Which is good, because he can help you, too.

When did you find out? I asked.

I knew it years ago, probably long before anything ever happened between you. But I knew, then, that one day he would try, and that one day you would let him.

When we got inside the sun was rising, slow and white. We went to bed and held each other, my hand on his heart, its rapid beat. He rolled over to face me.

When the time is right, will you help me?

Sasha thought he was in danger because he thought the city, no, the state as a whole, was dangerous. But I was still walking along the path, still watching the man approach, unclear whether or not I believed that state violence could be justified on the grounds that it was righteous, which is a way of saying I hadn't yet decided whether or not some violence could, indeed, qualify as righteous. And similarly, because I still believed the Revolution would be good for all, I hadn't decided whether or not that ultimate good was tarnished by the occasional evil along the way. For some, this was a time of moral clarity; for others, moral clarity was a lie.

Yes, I said, I'll help.

O nly a few days later, Luria told me he'd found a car we could take to the country for an afternoon. I agreed to go, vaguely hoping my absence, if only for a day, would jolt Sasha, make him reconsider. Luria picked me up from a corner early Saturday morning before the cicadas had woken to the late-summer heat. We drove out along Tverskaya, past the train station and past the end of the city until we were in dacha country, their red and black roofs poking out of the forest. Parts of the forest were charred, the result of the fires.

They look bad, yelled Luria over the noise of the car, glancing in the direction of the big black patches, but fires are good for forests, as long as they don't go on for too long, or spread too far.

The car made too much noise for me to feel much like responding.

Kids rambled along the side of the road, aimlessly it seemed, though at crossroads they packed together, hawking fruit and brightly coloured sugar animals. I wondered how they'd gotten there as we seemed far from any one village. They yelled out to us as we passed. Farther out, there was a park. A few cars lined the street, so we parked behind the last one and then walked through the entrance, past a former mansion, and along one of the many pathways that led to the river.

The path along the escarpment gave us a good view of the whole park, from the relative quiet of the path down to the clots of picnicking families, and then to the river where a single row of birch trees obscured the water with their winking, silver leaves. Luria tramped ahead. The path, though there hadn't been serious rain for some days, was slippery. I followed in a distracted way, my hands in my pockets, my mind wandering. Hidden in the fold of one of my pockets, my hands found the keen edge of the slide we'd found the other day, when, just then, the heel of my shoe pitched into a muddy puddle and I slipped and fell. Luria turned in time to see my hands thrown up, but I was on the ground in seconds, so by the time he was at my side I was sitting in a pile of mud, the broken slide having cut my hand.

You're bleeding, he said with such intensity that it almost felt like a performance. Caring for someone looked like exclamation, excitement, attentiveness, so he was performing all of those. Or doing his best performance of those.

It isn't serious, I said, and it wasn't.

He was standing above me, holding my hand up to examine it. It's a clean cut, he said, looking around, but what cut it?

I didn't want him to know about the slide, so I said I didn't know, but he persisted, eagle-eyed, spotting the glinting glass. Still holding my hand, he leaned over and picked up the slide, its pieces still glued together by the sample inside.

Where did this come from? he asked, turning it over in his hand. Is it yours? Were you carrying this around with you?

It was a mistake, I said, explaining that I had been moving things around lately and must have gotten distracted.

He dug around in his bag for a moment, pulling out a piece of paper that he folded around the slide. He placed it carefully in his bag, as if suggesting he would be responsible for it from now on, then leaned down to put his hand around my waist, as if that would help.

Up, he said.

I shifted out of his reach and stood up on my own.

We walked down the wooden steps towards the bank. At the shore, I crouched down to let the water run over my hand, cleaning it. I could see that there were more swimmers than I had thought, their bodies cut in half by the river, their heads, torsos, and arms doubled in the distortion mirror of the water's surface. The water was crisp and refreshing. A boy was playing dead, allowing his body to be carried downstream, buoyed up only by the air in his belly. He and his bloated belly floated past, and I turned to where Luria was setting up a blanket.

—⁄—

At a bench in front of us, an old couple was getting ready to go for a swim as well. The husband was almost entirely bald, but in a way that conveyed strength or masculinity, not frailty. The wife flitted around him, stowing their things. The husband pushed himself up and together they walked towards the river, their steps slow and measured. I heard her say something about a drop-off. At first the only sense of feebleness in him was revealed by his shorts, which no longer fit.

When they were in the river, they found their lost agility. He splashed her and romped around. She tried to keep her hair dry by doing breaststroke out of his range, but he lunged towards her and his bulk caused small waves to nip at her chin, and then he swam towards her and, though she tried to escape him, she couldn't, and he got to her and picked her up in his arms, almost lifting her out of the river, he was still that strong.

She said, No, don't! I just had it set!

He pretended to drop her but didn't, and they laughed, though she hit him on the arm like she had been doing her whole life.

—⌐—

On our blanket Luria had made a makeshift platter out of oiled paper, on which he'd placed some cheese, salami, bread, and a wedge of halvah.

Hungry? he asked.

I wasn't, but I flaked off a piece of halvah and let it melt on my tongue.

We sat in silence. I was thinking about the missing specimens, about Sasha's plans. The boy who had been floating down the river walked past us towards some older boys, but as he neared them they turned their backs to him, so he returned to the shore and slid back in.

I was waiting for Luria because I knew he wanted to tell me something, but knew also that he didn't know how.

—⌐—

The wife was the first to come out of the water. Her husband followed her, stepping gingerly through the reeds on the shore. He cursed the silty bottom of the river whose depth was deceptive. She asked if he wanted help and offered her hand. He gruffly refused, though he kept his arms held out, as though he anticipated falling. Careful, she said. He pulled one leg out of the mucky bottom and onto the cement pathway, placing his long arms on either side of the one stabilized knee in readiness for the next step. She stood to his side, her hand hovering over her shoulders, in the posture of helpfulness, but she was watching something else up on the hill. He launched his other leg up, and the force of it threw him out of balance, lurching his bulky body forward. His arms didn't have time to react as he would have liked them to, and so he plunged forward, as if in slow motion, his head leading the way towards the cement.

Watch! yelled someone, and the wife looked down, her husband now on his hands and knees, one hand pushed to his forehead which was bleeding, though not badly. Two men came from behind us and put their hands under his arms to help him to his feet and to the bench, but his wife, it seemed, was embarrassed and stood only to the side, feigning interest in whatever was happening on the hill. Once he was seated and the men had walked away, she joined him on the bench and chastised him before undoing her bag to find a small kerchief. She shook it vigorously, then pressed it to his forehead. His hands, knees, and elbows were covered in gravel, and his feet were still slicked with mud. He wanted to go back to the water to clean off.

No, she said, enough of the river.

But he didn't listen and hoisted himself up. He was in front of me when he did this and so, when he lost his balance again and bent forward to steady himself on the bench, I saw that one of his balls had escaped the confines of his shorts. He balanced himself like that for a few moments and then, like a sea animal poorly equipped for movement on land, he pushed himself back into the river and was content and dominant once more. This was what happened when people got old. Maybe they were the same age as Bekhterev and Bogdanov had been, but somehow, in water, they seemed much younger. I'd always thought Sasha and I would end up like that old couple.

—⁄—

I started packing up the food because I wasn't hungry at all and Luria wasn't eating either, but just as I was about to stand up and head for the car, Luria used his sharp voice.

Sit down, he said.

Another life lesson? I asked in a tone that said I was tired of this. He didn't answer and I could tell he was collecting his thoughts. It occurred to me that maybe he was to blame for our missing specimens, but before I had time to think on that more, he started talking about Bekhterev.

I don't know if you thought it was normal the way he died, he said. You probably thought it was strange, like everyone did, but maybe you also justified it, like everyone else did, by saying to yourself that it was just old age. I don't need to know what you made of it, but you should know what happened. Exactly.

I pulled my jacket around me. Why couldn't it be old age compounded by something else and still have old age be the thing that mattered most? I wasn't blind.

I looked into it, he said.

And?

He must have been poisoned when he was at the theatre.

I remembered delivering the tickets and shook my head, not wanting to be implicated, not wanting Luria's questions and Luria's truths.

He went on, saying that he'd heard from Bekhterev's wife that Bekhterev had been offered cake at the theatre and he'd taken it greedily, since he'd not eaten all day. Since his wife was diabetic, she'd not eaten any of it, thus sparing her life. He was sick that night, attended to by doctors throughout the night; then the next day, according to her, he seemed to be improving. Some new doctors came to attend to him and they stayed with him until he died.

Which ones stayed? I asked.

No one remembers their names, said Luria.

Sarkisov told me their names, I protested, they were well-known.

Luria shook his head saying that everyone knew the names of the doctors who first attended to him, but the second shift, the ones who were there when he died, they were completely unknown.

How did you find all this out? I asked.

I told you I tell the truth, and this is the truth.

The question wasn't whether or not it was true, the question was what do you do once you admit to yourself it is. The tickets, the sudden illness, the nameless doctors: all of these were facts. But, then, what was one to do with facts? What relation did those facts have to one's interpretation of them? In other words, the question was whether to say to oneself that Bekhterev must have done something wrong, otherwise nothing would have happened to him, or to say that Bekhterev was blameless and his murder was arbitrary, that what had happened to him could happen to anyone. It could happen to me.

What Luria was saying was that Bekhterev had been killed.

That he'd been poisoned would have shown up in an autopsy if they'd done one, and even the brain would have provided some clues, if someone experienced had done the microtoming, he said, but obviously you didn't see anything.

I thought of the jagged edge. I hadn't told Luria what role I'd played in creating the Bekhterev exhibit and now didn't seem the time.

Why are you telling me this? I asked.

Because I like stories that come to an end. And you still seemed to be in the middle.

So you thought I needed help?

Yes.

How does knowing this help you? I asked.

It makes me careful, he said.

On the drive back into the city, we were silent. My hand still smarted from the cut I'd given myself, but I pressed the wound into the folds of my dress, because the physical pain felt good. Were Luria and I closer now that he'd told me, or farther apart?

—⁄—

The road on the way back was empty, no evidence remained of the children who had trampled all over the road just hours before. By saying so little, I had let Luria think that he alone had been inquiring into Bekhterev's death. On the drive back in, I stewed over his condescension and considered telling him about Asja, if only to point out that he wasn't the only one to have discovered that there was more to Bekhterev's life than we had previously known.

What would you do, I said to Luria as the city came into view, if I told you that I knew someone has been stealing some of our exhibits?

Has someone been stealing some of the exhibits? he asked.

This is hypothetical, I said.

Have you? he asked. I didn't answer.

Don't make a mistake here, he said finally. I won't lie to you. But I won't lie *for* you either.

He was silent for a while. We both were. I couldn't decide if Luria had told me about Bekhterev because he was afraid or if he had told me because he thought I should be.

Give me one of your life lessons, I said.

Are we friends then? he asked.

Are you afraid of something? I asked.

We'd arrived at the institute.

No, he said as he parked the car, I know how things work.

And you think I don't.

I know you don't, he said, looking at me directly. That's why I like you.

We walked into the institute together. My hand still smarted from the cut, and Luria was still performing care in his awkward way, which was, in fact, *because of its awkwardness*, endearing. We'd gone in the back and so, for the first time, he was the one putting the water on to boil. He lurched when he moved, like every movement was a beat of his heart, or a pulse in his veins. Nothing so smooth and graduated as breath, his movements came in beats. I would never know him, I decided. I realized I knew nothing about his personal life, nothing about where he had come from, apart from the occasional slip into his Leningradian accent, the way he pronounced *milk* with a longer *k* than any Muscovite ever would. I had known him for longer than anyone else in my life then, yet he remained a cipher, and it was probably this that allowed me to think I could trust him.

Down the street, at the government house, a few men were being arrested. So said Anushka. We speculated about what they must have done. They were talking about the men down the street. I was talking about Bekhterev.

Autumn passed in a blur. The leaves turned blazing red and gold one day, and the next day the trees were bare, their fire stolen away by winds I'd barely noticed. The parades came and went with less fanfare than the year previous; the one-year anniversary of the institute's opening went unnoticed by all. At work, we were at a total loss, and yet we made ourselves look busy at all times for fear that our idleness would be reported to whomever our activities were being reported to then. Following his death, Bogdanov's institute had been closed down, the rooms empty for a week, and then a secretary showed up with a typewriter and a bunch of files, and that was that, she sat there typing something for most of October and November. Then, more desks were brought in and more files, and with them, two more secretaries. The noise from that wing of the building was unbearable. The schools and workers' clubs continued in their visits. Our collection of children's drawings grew. I started to wonder if we were waiting for someone else to die.

By Christmas of 1928, Sasha and I were barely speaking. If he'd thought to visit his mother for the holidays, he said nothing of it to me. For all I knew, she'd been to the city and left without a word to me. The year was almost over and Sasha was marking it by pulling all of our books off the shelves, dispersing them into piles on the floor. I heard him pull the latch on every glass window and then heard it rattle when he let it close. By mid-morning, the entire apartment was covered in books.

What are you doing? I asked.

He didn't answer.

I asked again.

No answer.

I walked through the piles of books, knocking them over as I did.

Tell me what the hell you are doing, I said slowly.

Putting books here, he said in a slow singsong voice as he straightened one of the piles I'd knocked over, putting books there.

Here, he sang, and there. Here and there.

That morning, because of the renewed cold, I'd put on my winter coat and slid my hands into the pockets only to find, sewn carefully into the seams he'd always tried to pry apart, the two silk buttons. I didn't have to look at the pockets to know: the two perfect nubs of smoothest silk were unmistakable and their presence made me miss the life we'd lost so suddenly, perhaps the way a swimmer who has plunged too deep suddenly misses air. I missed the Sasha I used to know, the one who would have sewn the buttons into my coat in happy anticipation of how much I'd love discovering them once the seasons changed. That Sasha was gone now, and I had no idea how to get him back. I gave no sign of noticing the buttons, or at least no sign he could see, since the heart sinks imperceptibly and tears can be wiped away. I stood there staring at his back, watching him perform his lonely, angry singsong as he combed through our collection of books, looking for something, I didn't know what.

On Christmas Day, I left the apartment and walked through the city. The streets were empty and I was alone.

—✗—

The books were back in place by the time I returned.

1929

The new year came and went without any celebration, without a visit to the dacha, without much of anything at all. It had barely begun when I came home from the institute one night to find Sasha packing his things. He explained that he would be leaving on the night train and there wasn't much time. This wasn't a surprise. Ever since he'd rearranged the books on the shelf, I'd felt the shift, and of course before that there had been the long, darkening season of small and big arguments, and then the evening at Rima's, where she'd thought I was pregnant but I knew I'd just realized what was wrong with everything and how people like Sasha were to blame.

He'd put a flower in a vase, just a single stem. The flower was yellow. A daisy, I guess it was called. I couldn't imagine where he found it until I could — a restaurant somewhere, perhaps a place he'd gone to with his mother, the flower slipped into his jacket's inner pocket while his mother was settling the bill.

The curtains were drawn. I took off my coat as he snapped the latch on his suitcase shut, a synchronicity that seemed appropriate to the moment.

I'm sorry, he said, turning to face me.

I'd settled on the arm of the chair, perched there, really, which made a spectacle of Sasha.

His suitcase was badly packed. A small piece of cotton had been caught in the latch, but I wasn't his mother.

There's something I need you to do, he said.

It occurred to me that we would never sleep together again, and it resonated as an ache somewhere inside of me — a real sensation inside my body — that I tried to ignore.

He sat down at the table, then stood up again, facing me. He altered the tone of his voice. It went from matter-of-fact to something kinder.

What I most want is for you to come with me. We could start a new life, he said.

I went the other way, from matter-of-fact to angry.

That's the difference between us, I said.

Don't yell, he said.

I'm not yelling, I said, taking a breath.

What is the difference? he asked.

The difference is that you always think life is something that will happen in the future, whereas I think that life is what is happening right now.

I agree with you that we are different, he said, but that isn't the difference.

I slipped off the arm of the chair and onto the seat. He leaned against the table, crossed his arms. For him, the difference between us was that he was transparent and I kept everything hidden, which was funny in a not-good way because it was what I thought of him — *he* hid everything, and *I* was transparent. He said that he had been trying to understand me for years, that it had consumed him, his effort to understand me. But now he knew that there were rooms in me that had no keys, rooms he had tried to unlock, but that now he knew he'd have to give up if he ever wanted to be happy.

I said that he didn't tell me anything anymore and he replied that he couldn't, that he didn't want to anger me or put me in a compromising position, that his silence had been for my benefit.

Just say you'll think about joining me, he said.

I will think about it, I said, and I was serious and not

serious. I thought of travel by boat and what the sea would look like, how it might be the same or different from the rivers I'd known my whole life. I thought about what I'd be leaving behind. We were quiet for a while.

Then I asked him what he needed me to do.

I need you to lie, he said. I need you to lie and say that I am dead.

For a moment I thought to myself, no problem, you've been dead to me for months. But then I heard myself sobbing, saying that I didn't want him to die, that I wanted him to stay.

I can't, he said, stepping towards me as if to hold me and then catching himself in the act, stopping, and retreating to the table. My heart ached.

We'd all heard of soldiers who, on the front during the Great War, thought it'd be better for everyone if they killed each other rather than killing foreigners, because at least that way their absence would free up some land for those who remained. And we'd heard about men who murdered their wives because they'd been nagged one too many times, and about police commissars who agreed that nothing good could come from nagging. We'd heard there was a shortage of coffins to such an extent that coffins could now be rented. *Please Return* was always scrawled on the top. People were dying in greater numbers every single day.

Sasha was going to be the exception. He had found a way to die without dying, and the only thing that was required of me was a small lie. I had to say he was dead. And I had to take someone else's death away from them. He explained the finer details to me, and I said I would do it.

Then he got angry with me again and he asked me if I'd ever loved him. He said, Maybe that was our problem: either you couldn't love me, or you couldn't love anyone.

I got angry back. It could be that, I said, as slowly as I could, containing myself. It could be a problem with me. And then I said, cruelly, Or it could be a problem with you.

I could see from the way his lips pursed together that I had hurt him, but rather than respond, he picked up his suitcase and walked out. I hadn't wanted to be so cruel. There was no problem with him. But I'd left it open. Even if I couldn't figure out why anyone could not love him, he surely could.

When I pulled back the curtain to watch him walk down the street, I imagined the moment when that small piece of cloth stuck in the latch would graze a pile of snow and then how it would stay icy for as long as Sasha was outside, melting the second he went inside, and how he wouldn't notice this change, might not notice the piece of fabric until much later, and I wanted, in that moment, to yell after him and say, Alexandr Lev Pavlovich! You are alive! You are loved! *I* love you!

But I didn't.

———/———

In winter, there were always a few nights when the temperature dropped below minus twenty. There were not enough shelters to sleep all of the city's homeless, and some of them wouldn't have slept in a Soviet shelter even if there had been space. (Tobias, for example.) The cold was killing them. There were mornings that I walked through the park by our house afraid of every mound of snow. Afraid it was a man or a child. Too afraid to look closely to find out. Eventually the snow would melt and the body would be taken to the city morgue. If no family member appeared, the body would be cremated.

Jack knew this, Sasha knew this, and I knew it, too.

I also knew who slept in the park. I knew the shades of

their blankets as they shifted and shivered beneath them. When they talked to me, I couldn't ignore them. This was a weakness. That was why I talked to Tobias in the bar, and it was why I noticed when Tobias looked so close to death, something I had mentioned to Sasha some months before.

The best lies are mostly true. That's how we remember them.

I saw Tobias alive one more time. I was in the grocer's. He came in with a pile of kopeks and wanted to change them for a gold tchervonetz. His eyes were normally a bright crystal blue, but that day they were watery and pale. And he had a cough, a cough that started deep in the smallest parts of the lungs and ravaged up through every breathing part of him until he doubled over and, finally, spit.

Get out of here, said the grocer, stuffing a few paper rubles into his hand.

Several weeks passed and no Tobias.

By early February, the bright yellow of the flower that Sasha had left deepened. The petals became thick and striated, like wood. And then, overnight, the whole flower went to seed. All the petals fell off, and a pile of seeds equipped with hundreds of tiny filaments that could have been caught up in the wind or on the wing of a bird or the underbelly of a dog drifted into a sad pile of potential, settling, instead, into the dust of our desk.

On the morning that the seeds fell, I dressed in black and walked along Pirogovskaya.

I went from hospital to hospital and in each place descended to the morgue with the same question: have you seen my husband?

In each of the hospitals, I was asked to describe him.

A thin man, I said, with white hair. Seemingly homeless, but he came from somewhere, I said. With bright, crystal blue eyes.

Eventually, I found him.

When the mortician removed the white sheet from atop his body, I looked down at that man who had come to the fountain, stinking and lonely—and the room began to swim.

Yes, that is him, though I could no longer see anything through the water that had filled the room. That is Alexandr Lev Pavlovich.

The funeral would take place in the same cemetery Dimitri and I had seen from the roof of the shed on that late summer's night. At the commission, I had read a pamphlet outlining the new procedure. It specified that the cremation ceremony called for *order* in the crematorium and demanded *complete silence, no shouting, no smoking, no spitting on the floor.* I took a taxi from the funeral commission, the urn of a strange man's ashes on my lap.

As we drove through the city, the windows steamed up, so that I couldn't see where we were. Though it was winter still, the morning was unseasonably mild and it was raining. The taxi was draped with boughs of fresh pine because this was his one route—from the funeral commission to the cemetery and back, all day long. From inside, I saw how they flopped with each pothole: each rut launched a synchronized spray of droplets that would land in unison on the windows and then shimmy, silver and grey, down.

The driver wiped the windshield every few minutes with a rag he kept on the dash. When he took a turn too quickly, the rag slid along the dash and out of reach.

I told myself that the funeral would be for Bekhterev and for Tobias, and that for Sasha's loved ones, it would be a way to say goodbye. My life felt more and more absurd.

I didn't think he'd be around forever, said Dimitri, but I didn't think he'd be gone so soon.

I didn't know who of his friends knew what had really happened, but I did know his mother deserved this, or at least that, in theory, *a* mother deserved this, so I supposed she did, too.

When I'd been here last it was late summer and Dimitri and I had only seen the cemetery from the roof of the shed; now it was winter and we were walking amidst the ruins of what might once have been quite grand. Now all the largest and most stately monuments were broken. Some of the broken angels and crosses had been tidied up into little mounds of limestone. Others had sunk into the earth and were slowly taking on the rough dimensions of ancient ruins.

The group of us—Rima, Yuri, Jack, Dimitri, Sasha's mother, and myself—followed the assigned deputy down a smaller path that had once been inlaid with stone. The path was overgrown and icy in the parts that never got sun. At the end of the pathway, the stone wall that enclosed the cemetery had been built into a columbarium. The deputy stopped at the end of the path and his assistants set down the urn.

—⁄—

He pulled a small book from his breast pocket and cradled it with his right hand, while his left removed a slip of paper that marked the required page. The book fell open and stayed that way comfortably, as if it had never been opened to any other page.

Today we honour the contributions made by Comrade Alexandr Lev Pavlovich to our beloved Fatherland, said the deputy.

When it was over, the deputy refolded his paper, which was now so damp it did not crinkle when he slid it into the leather-bound book. *The Soviet Ceremonies*, it was called.

I was the last to leave the grave.

⁓

The rain had turned to snow. The group walked back toward the entrance, forging a wet black path through the thin layer of white that had accumulated while we buried Tobias. I watched the easy silence they shared.

Now the cemetery was empty. Where I had seen the occasional mourner before, now I saw no one.

Quite unexpectedly, the day seemed to be coming to a close. It was still early afternoon, yet the sky hung ominously low.

The group walked past the guards and through the cemetery gates.

I was about to follow them, when I looked behind me and saw that Sasha's mother had hung back, as though she could not cross the threshold and re-enter the ordinary day. I felt sorry for her. She had not cried, and it occurred to me that I had been unkind.

I walked back to stand beside her.

She was watching another family I hadn't noticed.

The men wore crisp black coats and hats; the women held umbrellas. They began to sing a hymn I had heard many years before.

We watched the priest toss the earth into the grave, heard the dull thud.

Mrs. Pavlovna turned to me. I did not recognize the expression on her face, except to say that in place of the blankness I normally saw there, I saw an indisputable ugliness, something mean.

I'm very sorry for your loss, I said.

Don't be silly, she said.

She looked me in the eye.

He's somewhere better now, she said, raising her chin ever so slightly, from which I understood that she knew he was alive.

I looked at the lines that cross-hatched her fine features and wanted to stop thinking, because I knew I would feel something later and wanted to know what to feel immediately, which was when it would matter, rather than later, when it would be too late. I felt my eyes scrutinizing her, hating her. She was taller than me, but thin, wretchedly thin. She'd never wanted her son to love anybody but her.

She reached one hand up to her neck to close the gap in her coat, then pulled herself up straight and said in a slow, haughty way, You were never the same breed.

And then I knew what had happened. Love had had nothing to do with why she had come. She had been playing her assigned role, and she'd done it to spite me. I saw it in her eyes then and grabbed her by her skinny upper arms and shook her with all my might so that she let go of her coat and it flared open. I was hating her with every single part of me, feeling the bones in her arms beneath the wool of her coat, and blaming her for everything that was wrong in my world because anything that had gone wrong had gone wrong because of people like her. I shook and shook and shook her, causing her arms to flail helplessly at her sides and her arms were all I could see because I was looking down or at nothing at all. She let out a cry and pulled away from me, or perhaps I let go. She fell back into the mud and snow. She was a frail woman; she was defeated. I turned to see if anyone had seen me, but the snow had started to fall thicker and the moment was ours alone.

I left her lying there and walked towards the friends I had known for years, but I could not see them and they could not see me. I was shaking. I had a choice. If I veered in the wrong direction I would step onto the road, or perhaps I'd go in the opposite direction and it would be accidental. The wind gusted and I caught sight of them, huddled together. Yuri's arm around Rima who was, by then, *very* pregnant. I felt I didn't deserve them, but also that they mightn't deserve me.

Moon! I thought. You are being sliced through and through by a swordfish!

—⧸—

That was the week I began to see Sasha everywhere. He was always just up ahead, slipping into a bookshop, or out of the corner of my eye, I'd see him across the street in a café, or I'd see only the back of him and I'd follow him wherever he was going, until I got a close enough look to know that I was mistaken, and then that stranger and I would part ways. In all the years that we had lived in the same city, and then in the same room, I'd never accidentally run into him. Once he was gone, it happened all the time.

Just once I got a postcard from him. After that, if he wrote again, or sent anything else, I didn't know about it because he didn't know where I'd gone. But I knew where he'd gone. He'd purchased the postcard in Leningrad. It was a picture of a pocket watch. He'd mailed it from the port in Rostock. I love you, he'd written. This was how to leave, he was saying. Leave on a boat. Go to Berlin.

For months afterwards, I had a recurring dream that my heart was not muscle and blood and flesh but a cave-like bone, inside which I could stand upright and barely touch the roof, and there I could yell out *I* and it would echo back as if I were in a magnificent outdoor amphitheatre. Or, as if I were inside an operating theatre. From all sides I was surrounded. The sharp points of infinitely long needles stabbed me. Some were so sharp that their points were invisible, and these stung the deepest parts of me. Then, I would wake up thinking of Sasha, of how he had, inside him, an ocean.

After Sasha left, I stopped sleeping well at all. The bed was too big and too cold.

When Rima came over the day after the funeral, I wanted to tell her I was too exhausted for visitors but she would have said, When have I ever been a visitor? When I opened the door, she was standing there with her face turned soft, doughy almost, with sympathy. He's not dead! I wanted to yell at her. She held up a loaf of bread and some jam.

Don't worry, she said, handing me the food, we don't have to talk about anything. I was just passing by.

But Rima never just passed by, and she would have lined up for hours for the bread and been given only one loaf, which she was then giving to me.

She bent down to take off her boots, then reconsidered.

I'll make us some tea, she said, and she headed down the hallway towards the kitchen.

I stepped into some slippers and followed her.

I really don't need this, I said quietly, holding the bread and jam out towards her back, and then more loudly, You should really take these home to Yuri.

She looked over her shoulder, puzzling over me. Your friends want to take care of you, she said, stopping so that we were now face to face. She looked me right in the eye. Let them.

I looked away. Over her shoulder, down the hall, to the doors of other apartments where other people lived, people who had also been by, also with small gifts, and the smaller the gift, the worse I felt, because I knew they were giving as much as they possibly could.

Rima continued to the kitchen. I followed.

Look, I said, gesturing to the other food sitting on the shelf that had once belonged to Sasha and me, people have already given me too much. More than I can possibly eat.

She ignored me and lit the samovar.

Maybe feeling bad about the lie would look like mourning, I thought. Didn't shame and mourning look much the same?

Rima sat down at the table, looking up at me.

I know you weren't getting along, she said, but he was your husband; you would mourn him even if you hated everything about him, and you didn't. I know you didn't.

The samovar was warming.

I thought we didn't need to talk about it, I said.

Sure, she said, but I could feel her hurt as if crying was something I was supposed to do—something I was supposed to do *for her.*

The samovar moaned a little, its warm sides creaking into heat.

I sat down at the table. Rima's face was tight now. I'd placed a constraint on our conversation that she was going to try to respect.

I heard voices down the hall. People laughing. They would stop if they came to the kitchen and saw us, because that's how everyone was behaving around me, as if I didn't want to laugh anymore. But they didn't come and the laughter continued, far away.

—⁄—

Rima came by a few more times. I didn't want to lie to her and I couldn't tell the truth, so all the ways we used to talk were ruined. I tried to ask about her life—she was so pregnant by then that she looked as if she were about to burst—but it was as if by taking away my private life from her, she'd had no option but to take hers away from me.

How is the baby? I'd ask.

Good, she'd say.

On one of her last visits, I told her that I missed him, and that was true, but by then it was too late. I'd been silent for so long, and so had she, so there seemed no way back to the place we'd been when we were younger, not even a year before, when we'd been able to lie on the floor listening to the one record she had, over and over, feeling all our big and small feelings in the company of the music and each other in a kind of honesty beyond words. Now all we had left were words, and even those weren't enough.

I hadn't anticipated much of anything about Sasha's departure. Hadn't anticipated the way a lie could separate me from not only the closest people to me, like Rima, but also the barmaid at Max's, who suddenly seemed to want to be friends, as though, in some way, she thought the grief she felt about his loss must resemble mine. Hadn't anticipated that the worst part about the lie wouldn't be the questions about what had happened but about how I might be feeling and whether or not I needed something, anything. The kindness of others made something inside me feel rotten, as if I was actually decaying.

I certainly hadn't anticipated the housing inspector.

As soon as I opened the door, I knew who she was and I knew I'd have to move. That, or I'd have to ask for help. It had taken nearly three months for them to realize I was living alone in an apartment slated for two.

She wore heavy work pants and a heavy work shirt, both grey. A pack of cigarettes in one of the shirt pockets, pens and loose paper in the other. Her hair cropped short and sprouting as if she'd spent most of the morning hanging upside down and this was the first of her right-side-up visits. Something bat-like about her, I suppose. The strain on her eyes, mouth, and face when she spoke, as if she were about to bite or scream.

She'd been sent over from the housing department to measure the room. She smelled so sour. Your husband died? she said, looking at her notes.

No, I said. Yes.

Yes? she said.

You have had some sort of traumatic experience, she said. We know.

No new boyfriend? she asked. A little cat won't do you any good, you know. No extra space allotted for cats. I was allotted five and a half square metres. She handed me one end of the measuring tape.

Hold it against the corner. No cheating. Flush against the corner. And then to herself, No extra space for rats.

Our space was five metres wide, with the bookshelf included, and four metres long.

Too much space for a little nut like you, she said. This is big enough for a family and their cats and rats. And it is better for you to change.

I would be assigned a room in a hotel. A new family would move into our apartment, and they would smoke on our balcony and look at our night sky.

———✦———

Later that day, I went to see Dimitri. In the past months, he, too, had moved. Now he lived in a hotel behind the theatre. He answered the bell immediately. His room was on the second floor, the top floor. I thought I might ask him to help me stay in my apartment.

His room was simple, but big. In my mind, I measured

its size as I walked towards the window. Nine largish steps. Bigger than mine, I thought. He had a window, a single bed, a commode, a tin wash table, and a small desk. On the desk there were three books standing upright as if they were the beginning of a library. Beside the books were two framed portraits, one of Lenin and the other of Stalin, both standard issue, the kind you'd buy in any bazaar, along with two red candles, which Dimitri also had, but had never lit. I knew that sitting in the top drawer of the desk, he had a gun. I knew because Sasha had told me, but I didn't know how Sasha knew. Lined up on the windowsill, in increasing size, was a teacup, a glass, and a single bottle of brandy. He rinsed the glass and cup at the wash table; the faucet squeaked when it was turned. As he organized himself, I looked out the window onto the dark street I had walked up.

Only the small window opens, he said, gesturing to the trap window. Under the transom, there were two windows, both of which had been sealed shut for the winter.

He had changed. Whatever sensitivity he had once possessed had disappeared in the months since I'd last seen him. In its place, he had hardened. I hadn't noticed the change at the funeral, but it was clear in how he held himself in a way that reminded me of Sarkisov. Imperious.

He handed me the teacup half filled with brandy, then leaned back against the wash table. I sat on the chair that went with the desk.

And now you're here, he said, as if he'd already said something else, though he hadn't.

I looked towards his books but couldn't read their titles from where I was because I'd left my glasses in my bag.

Do you miss him? he asked.

Of course, I said, keeping my eyes on the books.

You looking for a book? he said.

No, no, just resting my eyes, I said.

Can you read the spines from there?

No.

His dress was semi-military — the tunic, the belt — as it always had been, but its meaning had changed. In the early twenties, such dress could mean he was aligned with Rodchenko; now it was the unofficial code of party membership. We all play roles, I thought. Always wanting to belong somewhere.

Outside, a horn sounded in the street.

Dimitri put down his drink and walked towards me, pausing halfway. There are hot spots in the floor, he said. Take off your socks.

In my bare feet, I walked across the floor to where he stood. My toes spread out to feel the warmth of the wooden floor.

How does that happen? I asked.

Hidden fires, he said.

I wondered if he knew how it happened but didn't want to tell, or if he didn't know but wanted to give an answer, any answer, anyway.

I stood still and shut my eyes. I hadn't been barefoot for years, it seemed. When was the last time? Perhaps one of those late summer nights when Sasha and I still climbed atop buildings to drink and smoke, and we would find the day's heat trapped in the metal that encased the top of the walls. We'd lie down on the cooling roof and rest our feet against that still-warm metal, our eyes on the darkening sky.

Dimitri misread me. I opened my eyes just as he was about to kiss me, and I ducked away.

He shrugged and stepped back.

I went back to the desk, my feet cold then. I leaned forward to pull my socks back on, wishing I'd not taken them off before.

You came here for something, he said.

I picked up my cup and swirled the brandy around, letting my gaze drift over the desk and an open book. He'd been reading someone's speeches, studying them. In my cup, the brandy settled.

No, I said, not really.

The housing department came today, I said, but I was sure even then that I didn't want his help.

He stepped closer to me. And they want you to move, he said.

I'm not sure, I said.

I drained my cup and set it down in the wash basin.

You don't need to be alone, you know.

But he was wrong, or rather, the kind of not alone I'd have had to be with him would have been lonelier than the kind of alone I'd be without him.

I'm not alone, I said.

Yes, you are.

—⧸—

After I got off the tram, I walked through the park. Where the trees were thickest, the snow didn't always make it to the ground, so the mud paths had frozen into gnarled shapes that resembled the exposed roots of trees. At that time of year, the body has lost all memory of heat. On the way through the park, I heard a struggle coming from the bushes. Instinctively, I turned to look and just as quickly I looked back to the path, but I'd seen a woman lying on her back and a man standing over her, looking back at me. I kept walking.

A few minutes later, a different man intercepted me.

Did you see anything back there? he said.

No, I said. Nothing.

I kept walking. He followed.

It is a mark of stress, or a mark of history, that there are times when to walk alone and to be followed is to be immediately aware of three potentialities: robbery, rape, murder. Fear reduces our capacity to imagine.

For years, the image of that man standing over that woman haunted me.

Before, when Tobias was alive, the park had seemed safe. Now it seemed haunted.

After the funeral, I had returned to the institute within days. Luria found me there one afternoon, after almost everyone else had left for the day, and that was when I realized how my feelings for him had evolved. It was something like I how I felt towards the oak tree that grew at the end of Arbatskaya when I was a child. I'd watched that tree for years. I'd seen it from my window, the way it got full in spring and went bare in winter. How the shape of its thickest branches always made a perfect *Y* frame into which the shoemaker, across the street, would step when he went outside for a smoke. How I'd see the shoemaker only in the winter because in the summer the leaves would hide him, or most of him, so that if it was summer and he was smoking, I'd see a patch of him — his shoes or his elbow — and imagine the rest of his body by how well I knew it in winter. Is it possible to say I loved that tree? I can say that when it was slated to be cut down to make way for the clock tower, I'd spent one night sitting below it, peeling off its gnarled bark, taking in the smell of its age with a kind of tenderness I'd never felt towards even my own mother.

When she'd spotted me sitting there, under the tree, she'd called me moony. Grow up, she'd said.

But still, towards Luria I felt the kind of tenderness one could feel towards a sunset or a pebble you could pocket, towards the arch of a bridge, or even an anatomical structure whose infinite variations never varied so much as to make the thing unrecognizable (think of the sea horse–shaped hippocampus at the centre of the brain). This was the kind of tenderness one feels towards anything that seems permanent and that, thankfully, cannot feel back. Uncomplicated. So it suddenly dawned on me, that afternoon, that in all of Moscow, the only person for whom I could feel that way was Luria because I had never lied to him. That, and I hardly knew him. I knew what he *thought* about. But I didn't *know* him.

His visit that day had a purpose. I could feel it in his stride. The long, strong steps that showed a renewed vitality.

He had begun to study a man he would later refer to only as S—.

I knew his name, but he shall be S— to you.

S— had been introduced to Luria through a friend who had temporarily employed S—, until it became clear that S—'s talents were less suited to newspaper reporting than they were to something, anything, else. Luria's friend was the editor at the *Evening Standard*, a well-loved rag. S— had been hired as a low-level reporter, but early on the editor had noticed something strange. Every morning, when the reporters were assigned their tasks for the day, S— never took notes. The assignments were complicated: the reporters were told the names of sources, addresses, leading questions, and so on. The editor, himself, read the assignments from his own tangle of notes so that he wouldn't lose track. At first he had thought S— was being insolent, but when he returned every night with full reports of the murders, robberies, scientific cures, train wrecks, and alien sightings, the editor had realized there was something unusual about him. He called S— into his office to ask him why he didn't take notes. S— had said he couldn't imagine it, taking notes would be too distracting. The editor asked what he meant. S— had said that seeing the words on the page would prevent him from remembering. He explained that he couldn't see two things at once: he couldn't simultaneously see the objects in his mind *and* see the words on the page. His memory was better than photographic. His mind's eye so powerful it created the images just as soon as the words were uttered. For him, there was no separation between the word and its image, a word *was* an image.

Standing before the exhibits that afternoon, perhaps both Luria and I were asking the same question: what architectonic feature could explain such a skill? The thrill of the question heralded a brighter future. Luria was overjoyed.

He hadn't seen the exhibit on Bekhterev yet, so we walked towards it.

Who did the slicing? he asked.

He didn't hold back when I told him I'd been put in charge. He found it offensive that I'd been involved at all.

Are we alone? he asked.

He's gone, I said, by whom I meant Sarkisov.

You had no experience, he said in quiet exasperation.

What could I do? I asked, feeling reprimanded when what I'd hoped for was praise.

It's not your fault. They wanted you to be inexperienced.

Right, I said. And in that way, in that moment, I became an accomplice to the erasure of Bekhterev and to the erosion of the institute itself.

We stood quietly together for a moment as I realized what I had done.

Do you believe in geniuses? I asked.

There are two types of people who believe in genius, said Luria. Those who hope they are one, and those who want an explanation for why they aren't. The rest of us believe in hard work. He said this angrily, but it was the most hopeful thing I'd heard in years.

Soon after that, he said he needed to leave, so I followed him to the front entrance where he shrugged into his coat. He hadn't said anything about Sasha. I knew he knew, because everyone knew. That he hadn't said anything seemed kind, as though he knew he didn't need to. But then I saw it creep into his eyes. The sudden quiet that took over.

Please don't say anything, I thought. *Please don't make me a liar. Please don't make me have to lie to you. Please.*

Tatiana, he started, taking his hat off.

Don't, I said. It'll make me too sad. Please don't say anything. Please.

All right, he said.

He put his hat back on.

Listen, he said, I'll introduce you to S— if you're curious.

Sure, I said.

—/—

After that, I returned by myself to the grand salon, but I didn't feel alone. It was as if I had walked into the salon behind someone or in front of someone and we had been courteous to each other, allowing the other to go first through the doorway. I knew that I was the only person left in the building. Yet I could feel Sasha standing beside me.

This is a nice church you have here, he said.

Don't, I said.

I've always loved the lives of saints, he said, and I felt him drift towards the musicians' brains. I was never crazy about Borodin, he said. But Rubinstein was a genius. These are good Soviet saints, he said.

They aren't saints, I said.

Sure they are, he said. These are holy relics, he said. We pilgrims come to worship them, he said.

Stop it, I said.

Don't say it's about science, he said.

I told you it was! I said. We have found out about the dominance of the frontal cortex in the minds of analytical thinkers, the predominance of the small sulci—

But how do you know? he asked, interrupting me.

We know because we see it, I said.

But an iceberg lies beneath the surface and is mostly invisible to us as we float upon the oceans of this world, and like the *Titanic*, we risk striking it and sinking to the bottom of the sea with our lovers and our children, draped at long last in the pearls and perishable satins, not to mention the seashells or perhaps the timbers of a poorly navigated lifeboat that was crushed beneath the bow of the sinking ship as it was pulled under along with us. Imagine you and me, he said, lying there at the bottom of the sea, all because we did not see what lay beneath the surface.

But that's it, I protested. We are seeing precisely that, that thing beneath the surface.

No, he said, this sliced-up object is not what is beneath the surface. Where is the blood? Where is the life? What we see here is an iceberg that has melted and that is hardly the same. This, he said, is a place of worship.

Perhaps it is language that is failing us now, I said. In any case, I have never seen the ocean.

—/—

As I stood there, wondering what would become of me and the institute, I remembered the elements of our collection that were missing. It seemed that just as we'd brought the collection to a kind of whole, an outside force had caused it to fragment. Zhanna and I had started paying closer attention. What had emerged was a pattern. Something was missing from virtually every exhibit. This meant two things: first that there was a shadow exhibit that existed somewhere other than at the Institute Mozga, and second, that someone working at the institute likely knew how this had come to be. The consequence of this second aspect was that Zhanna and I started watching everyone else, sure that one of ours was stealing things away, though we couldn't imagine why. Any institution populated with intellectuals will be defined by paranoia, which was why even though Zhanna and I were in on the secret together I also wondered if the missing items weren't, actually, *her* doing, and she, no doubt, wondered the same about me. The shadow institute, wherever it was, started to seem like the shadow country that was forming elsewhere, in places like Berlin, if that was, indeed, where Sasha and people like him had gone.

Over the years, one by one, most of the lights on the chandelier had burned out. That they didn't burn out all at once must be due to some mystery of circuitry. We didn't immediately try to replace the lights, and when we finally did, they were no longer stocked in Moscow, such items considered too bourgeois for Soviet taste. The missing specimens were like those lights—at some point they'd disappeared without us noticing, and now it was impossible to replace them. When the bulbs were finally shipped to us from a supplier in Paris, we had ordered too few to brighten the grey light they cast in the formerly glorious room.

was curious, but it was springtime before I went to Luria's office to meet S——. The day was unusually warm. I remember being embarrassed by the sweat stains beneath my arms, stains I endeavoured to hide, especially from Luria who would notice.

Hello, said the guards, which made me wish I knew another way into the building.

The door to Luria's office was open, spilling natural light into the dark hall. I heard voices as I approached. Luria was at his desk, and S—— was sitting in a chair facing Luria, so his back was to me. Luria looked up, smiled, and motioned for me to come in. S—— turned to look. What struck me first about his appearance was the ashy pallor of his skin, its surface so oily it reflected the light pouring in through the window. His eyes darted up to meet mine in swift, shy acknowledgement.

Luria came to the front of his desk, saying, Tatiana is the one I've been telling you about, the one who runs the Institut Mozga that you like so much.

With an artist husband, said S——.

Luria smiled and looked at me, hoping, I think, that I wouldn't react.

He died, I said.

Oh, said S——.

You've been to the institute? I asked.

Eight times, said S——.

A silence ensued.

Now that I was inside, I noticed how much cooler it was and wished I'd kept my jacket.

Luria motioned for me to sit.

Well then, said Luria, Let's show her what we've got, shall we?

S— treated the question as if it were rhetorical and didn't answer.

Go ahead then, said Luria, prodding him, give us the first list I gave you. It was on a Monday, in this office, over a year ago.

Actually, said S—, the first series was in your apartment. You were sitting at the table and I in the rocking chair... You were wearing a grey suit and you looked at me like this, and then he tilted his head to the left and adopted a quizzical expression.

I had to laugh at the accuracy of his impression and the seriousness with which he undertook it.

Yes, said Luria, smiling. Right you are.

Now then, continued S—, I can see you reading from a list. It began with an accordion, then a hard-boiled egg, then a red flag, five children, a lock of blond hair like that from a child, a man's fingernail...

S— continued, but I don't remember everything he listed. There was something about the way he recited the items — in a kind of drone — that made them totally forgettable. The number eighty-seven rolled off his tongue in the same tone as the bar of soap, the pistol, the old woman, the hard-boiled egg. When he came to the end, it took me a moment to realize he'd stopped.

How do you do it? I asked.

A warmth came into S—'s eyes. He liked the question.

I recognize a word not only by its image but also by a whole complex of feelings that it arouses. A word can taste or smell or have a weight or a texture. Its sound can cause a slight tickling in my left hand, or I might sense something oily slipping through my fingers. When that happens, I simply remember, without effort.

Perhaps you could explain how the process works with numbers, suggested Luria.

Take the number one, said S—. This is a proud, well-built man.

And two? I asked.

Two is a high-spirited woman; three a gloomy person.

What about numbers of several digits? I asked.

Well, he said slowly. You see, seven is a man with a moustache. Eight is a very, very fat woman—a sack within a sack. So the number eighty-seven is a very fat woman and a man twirling his moustache.

Wonderful, I said.

S— grinned.

He was a true archive. A living, breathing collector. When asked how he remembered such lists in the precise order in which they'd been given, he explained that he did it by walking.

I take a mental walk down a street I know very well. Tverskaya used to be a good one, but not now, not with all the changes. But what I do is walk from one place to another. It happens easily, and more often than not, the walk becomes dream-like in a way and the impossible happens: I begin in Moscow and, without realizing it, end in the town in which I grew up, Torskok.

Outside, a cloud must have covered the sun because the light on the window was suddenly dull. A pigeon hopped down to the sill from somewhere above. The sudden darkness seemed to waken S— from a sort of reverie. Luria suggested a cup of tea. S— declined, saying he needed to be home to care for his mother.

In the hall, his steps were soundless, but after a minute or so I heard him exchange hellos with a woman whose singsong voice tripped back to us, magnified.

We followed him just moments later, but the woman was gone.

Outside, the sun warmed me again.

Luria lit his pipe.

The building was at a high point in the city, so it was only natural to drift down to the river, crossing the bridge and going down the hill on the other side to the small park, where a bench was waiting for us.

He's incredible, I said, once we were seated.

Luria crossed his legs and drew two quick puffs from his pipe.

The problem is, he said, exhaling, that he lacks the capacity to interpret. He thinks like a young child, in concrete images that are associative, thematic, almost like poetry; yet whenever I've shown him a poem, he can't get past the surface images. He's so caught up in the surface of words that he can't deal with their intended meanings. Metaphor is completely lost on him.

I lit a cigarette and took a drag. Every so often, a slight breeze nipped up from the river, but still we were warm.

What troubles you about this? I asked.

Isn't it obvious? Nothing means anything to him.

So S— collected a series of objects, situated them in a familiar place, and then could only remember that they existed, without knowing why their existence mattered.

Is he bothered by it? I asked.

Oh, I don't know, said Luria quickly, and then more slowly, It's just that the more time I spend with him, the more I am aware of a profound sadness about him. It's like he is waiting for something, some great thing.

And you think it is meaning that he's waiting for, I said.

Yes.

But, I said, taking another drag, isn't that true of all of us? Aren't we all waiting for meaning?

But he'll never have it, said Luria.

Will we? I asked.

Luria shook his head, still thinking.

And what's worse, he said, is that his immediate images haunt him for hours. You know, the types of images that ought to fade, like the swirl of smoke above my pipe, or the reflections off the river, the way they dance, or even the curve of the bridge, all these things stay with him, indefinitely. His whole mental world is like a junk heap of impressions.

Some children tumbled down the hill into the park and started throwing stones into the river. I tried to imagine what it would be like to hold on, forever, to the image of the perfect splash erupting out of the river just as the rock plunged in, but just like that, the rock, the splash, the image was gone.

—⧸—

At home again that night, I knew that I would have to move, and I knew how it would go. No warning and a family knocks at the door with their bulging suitcases hanging at their sides. I didn't want to have to leave like that, so suddenly.

I started with the books. I would give them away. Books need to circulate.

The bookshelf was our one good piece of furniture. Glass doors to each section protected the books from dust. To open the section, the doors swung up and slid under the upper shelf. All of the sections opened easily except one.

Its door refused to slide all the way back. Holding the door up with one hand, I removed the books one by one with the other. At the back of the shelf, there was a satchel, and inside that a piece of black cloth encased a series of hard objects that clicked against each other as I pulled them out. I lay them on my lap and untied the black cloth.

That fucker! was my first thought.

Everything we had been looking for was there, stacked according to size. The smallest was a standard glass slide three centimetres by eight. The sample was a follicle of hair, its label torn and illegible. There were sea creatures and leeches, sketches of samples, and if there was one colour that could describe them all, it was black. There were four lantern slides: all of them taken of the blackened edge of Lenin's brain. Placed side by side, they comprised four quadrants of black space, creating the eerie impression that the void had, indeed, been captured and given physical dimension in the photographic process. The lantern slides would not degrade. One by one, I held the objects up to the light so that I could admire the workings of disease and decay. Not just that, though. Here were actual slices of Lenin's brain which also showed signs of the same necrosis. With those, I thought about the passageways that would have been filled with blood, and then I put the slides down on the table and, without thinking, took a knife to the gummy labels, which identified the slides as #1301, #1302, #1303, #1304, all from Vladimir Illyich Ulyanov, or Lenin. I pressed the knife through the labels to make them tear and pucker and become unidentifiable to anyone but me.

In the black, red, and white of Rodchenko's style, he'd inked a portrait of Anushka's dog and named her Witness, though in real life her name was Oktober. Akhmatova's book had become his sketchbook; every page had a portrait. Of Bogdanov. Of Anushka. Of Zhanna. Of Sergei. Of Bekhterev. Of me. They were drawn in China ink that had then been wetted so that its black could spill into the shadows of our faces. The dark pools beneath our eyes, the hollows in our cheeks. It was as though he thought no one would remember us without him. As if he thought we'd be forgotten. Or erased.

And the objects had been left in our bookshelf, hidden in a place only I would look and only if I had to. He knew how I hated Chekhov. He knew I'd only ever look there if I were leaving, and perhaps he knew I'd only need to leave if he was considered dead, and so he'd wanted me to find these objects once he was gone, in order to tell me what? I looked again at the images. His drawing of Bekhterev had made him looked handsome, almost young.

There was, in Sasha's small collection, a picture of what the institute was, at its beginning, at its best. In his collection, Sasha was telling me that he knew me and that he knew me better than I knew myself. I hadn't cried when he left, nor at his funeral, nor at any of the times I'd imagined him on the street, walking just ahead of me or lagging just behind, murmuring, arguing, but now I did, because I saw at once what I had lost when I said to him I didn't care if he left and he said to me that he'd tried and failed to know my heart. He hadn't failed. But I let him leave believing he had.

—⧸—

I gathered all the pieces back together and slid them back into the satchel. I hadn't even realized how much had gone missing from the institute. Now it was clear why I'd missed Sasha so many times there. Had this been his art? The thing he'd been working on these past months? The secret thing that had replaced the Osorgins? This was art and anti-art as the very same thing. Art in the everyday.

I dismantled the entire apartment that night, looking for other objects, but found only one: one of the many

slices of the brain stem that we had catalogued so carefully and that I had later realized meant nothing to anyone
but me.

—⁄—

In the morning, I left the house, tucking the satchel into
another, larger bag without knowing where I was going. My
mind was still preoccupied with what the collection might
have meant to Sasha, though that question changed shape
as I walked, morphing into what the collection might mean
to me, and then, more pressingly, what it might mean to
me were I to be found with it in my possession. On every
street corner, it seemed, documents were being checked. It
suddenly felt as though the police were everywhere.

The objects I had thought of as scientific within the
confines of the institute had, in my apartment, become
artworks: mystical and enigmatic. Now, out on the street,
the specimens changed shape again, and I wondered what
this man, a red guard, would say of the black sections of
Lenin's brain, or what this woman, a nurse, would make
of the autopsy report, or what about those children there,
or that line of people who, to judge from the bedraggled
shape of them, had been waiting for hours. The bag itself
seemed to change shape according to the figure I passed,
its contents accusatory or salubrious, things that might
put me in prison or save me once I was there. Everywhere
I walked there were lineups. Lineups for sugar, lineups
for bread, lineups in front of Lubyanka. I walked past
doorsteps and endless stretches of fence, the posts of which
blurred together while I walked.

The pigeons moaned and flapped out of my way. It was
hot. The city had come into bloom. Oh, spring! I kept going and passed another doorstep in which a middle-aged

man was squatted down on his hindquarters, holding a cigarette between his thumb and index finger, his smoke whirling around in the doorstep, and I slowed down, inhaled deeply, looking him in the eyes. I felt his used-up smoke enter my lungs, and then I breathed out and I kept walking. Then there were three women and then a small man, and then a young child stepped in front of me and was yanked back by his mother. I looked up at her and then back to where I'd come from and then forward to where I was going, and the stream of people seemed to go on forever. Men, women — more women than men — some with young children, all of them waiting, and as I continued they bunched ever closer together, and this bunching together seemed to screw their faces up in irritation with each other and with whatever it was they were waiting for, which turned out to be a state store out of whose door I would see a man exit, carrying a single loaf of bread. I kept walking, the bag of specimens still clinking ever so slightly in the cloth satchel I'd looped over my shoulder as it had become heavy and I was tiring. It became muggy.

Up ahead was St. Basil's, and I was still walking, looking now and again for a face I might recognize, looking, I realized, as I had so many times before, for my mother and then for my father, wondering what had happened to them and into what version of aging they had descended. Had she remarried, had she had other children, what? And he, had he left the country behind? Did they live in the shadow country, the exile place? Had either of them had the good fortune to develop laugh lines, or were their faces worn, like the faces I saw all around me now — coming and going, arguing over bread and sugar, walking in silence, eyes cast downwards in exhaustion or something else — worn with lines of worry and puffy with drink? Had they gotten thin?

I kept on, St. Basil's on my left now, its spirals peering out from behind the buildings, their swirls still like candy stripes, the sky above them the light blue of mid-morning, the sun on the verge of raging the way it would at noon and for hours afterwards. I passed more and more lines. Moving past them, as I was, made it seem as if the lines didn't move at all, but surely they did. Now it was Hunter's Row, but most of its stalls were empty, because there was so little to sell. The vendors still hung about, trying to hawk wooden toys, shoe polish, neckties, and lingerie, but what was the point of possessions when all you'd be able to do with them in the end would be to leave them? Missing were the buckets of apples and sugar figurines and the raw meat that used to be laid out and bought so quickly.

Rounding a corner, I came face to face with three policemen. They fanned out as they had in the train station.

The middle one, Papers, please.

I was sweating. I shifted my bag on my shoulder, heard the clink of the slides, saw the way the sound piqued the interest of the man on my left. I said nothing, presenting my papers to the one who had asked. By now this gesture was becoming almost normal. I felt the man on my left looking at me intently, and I turned to look at him, seeing then that he was a junior cadet. And then I had my papers back, and the three of them went on their way, and I walked the rest of the block, only collapsing in tears on a front step once I'd rounded the corner and they were out of sight.

—⧸—

I hadn't planned where I would go, but somehow I found myself standing in front of the neurology building at the university, looking for Luria, hoping I wouldn't find him.

I wanted to be free of these items but also wanted them to be safe. By now, the security guards knew me. They were playing checkers and barely looked up.

Over the past few months, we'd started to hear rumours that the institute was going to close or relocate. Sergei said it was because Our Great Father of the Union was jealous, but others mused that it was simply that we hadn't published enough papers and funding was drying up. All over the city, institutes like ours were closing or being relocated, the state exerting more and more control. Luria had been named Distinguished Scientist, putting him on par with the new class of distinguished writers, musicians, playwrights, and so on. In public, from then on, he had to be referred to with honorifics and a new etiquette. He accepted this change as Bekhterev might have—it was useful but otherwise meaningless. Science still existed in a realm separate from politics, but the Party was trying its best to play judge, even if its assessments were clumsy *either/ors*. Scientists were either praised or banished, sometimes permanently, as we now knew. I didn't know what was happening, only that somewhere, someone in the building was playing dominoes and that something about the sound was trapped and trying to escape.

The sound was *click, click, click* and so was the sound of my bag, with each step, as I walked down the dark halls in the general direction of Luria's office, but not quite. Just as I was about to arrive at his office, I turned, walking instead down a darker hallway towards what appeared to be a broom closet. The sign on the wall read *Northern Corridor*.

As it turned out, I hadn't needed to ask Dimitri outright. And he hadn't meant it when he said I was alone because obviously he had been involved, somehow, in the room to which I was assigned in a hotel right across the street from his. Our rooms were the same size now, though mine was on a higher floor, which, if the room itself had been his choice, had been gentlemanly of him: granting me the privacy height accords. On the first night, I kept my lights off and looked down into what I thought was his room, but his lights stayed off, too, which meant that maybe we were watching each other.

I'd left virtually everything behind. In my new room, every piece of furniture was labelled with a tin tag on which its inventory number and the name of the hotel were written. My room had a similar wash table to the one in Dimitri's room, but this one had three drain holes that could not be plugged. Above that, there was a small mirror into whose corner I tucked Sasha's postcard. I rearranged the furniture, hoping to make it feel like it was mine, but there were so few objects in the room that, in the absence of my books, it felt empty and anonymous. In the hallway, the telephone rang all day long. Occasionally someone answered it, and when they did it was always for the old woman who lived in the room at the hallway's farthest end. Getting her to the phone was an ordeal we all had to go through. The hotel porter stayed in the small room at the entrance. If I arrived past eleven, I couldn't be sure of entrance, he told me.

Can't I have a key? I asked.

No, he said.

My food deliveries stopped once I moved into the hotel. We weren't permitted food in the rooms, so everyone ate together in the cafeteria or else out in the city. The cafeteria was the best bet, because without that, one had to line up for one's own food, and that could take all day. The other residents, those who had been there for years, grumbled that the servings had gotten smaller, there was no sugar for tea, and even the utensils were becoming more and more scarce.

We haven't had knives for months, they said.

Where did they go? I asked.

Stolen. People have taken them to their rooms, they said, and the state won't replace them now.

This was my new life now. I put a fork and spoon in my pocket.

But it was summer, and food still got wasted, or at least the crumbs left behind were sufficient to attract a healthy population of ants. Every day they congregated someplace new. Every morning a young worker would come out and crush a few under her fingers, pushing hard into the surface of whatever corner, leg, or cupboard it was, until she was sure they were dead. Then she'd drag their crushed corpses all over, spreading the word, she explained, about what would happen if anyone else came to visit.

It's the smell of dead ants that they don't like, she said. Gruesome, but true. They won't return. If I get very organized, I'll make a blend of dead ant juice, she told me one morning, and spread it throughout the cafeteria, get an award for most zealous ant killer, become a Stakhanovite and get a new apartment for me and my boyfriend.

How long do the ants stay away? I asked.

It only works for a few hours. After that they all start coming back. They see the dead bodies, but without the smell, the bodies don't seem to mean anything.

I f I could have made the room bright again for one last time, it would have been later that year, when Dr. Vogt returned to Moscow to hold his last press conference. The summer had come and gone, Rima had given birth to a girl, I'd been round to wish them well—despite the estrangement I felt from their life—and had started to settle in my sparse apartment, started to see how the way the city had shifted so suddenly when Bekhterev died could become normal, the way everything does, with time. In the months since Sasha left, I had become accustomed to my life without him, though this is only partially true because he was with me all the time, everywhere I went, a more constant companion in his absence than he'd ever been in his presence. In his absence, I loved him still. Had he stayed, I might not. My solitary life was not so lonely. Only when I forced myself to be with others did I feel the cold sting of friendlessness. Vogt's visit marked two years since the institute had opened. By then, the lights on the chandelier were virtually ornamental. If two or three lit up, we were lucky. Sometimes we took the bulbs out and rattled them around, hoping, somehow, to reconnect the filaments, but mostly we left them as they were. It looked better that way: the bulbs with a grey sheen of dust reminded me of a time when promise was in the air.

Dr. Vogt had arrived on an overnight train and was early to the institute, arriving before me. His trip had been a nightmare. Border guards had confiscated his equipment. Boxes of slides, microcopies of exhibits, indigo dyes, his best paraffin. All of it, gone.

The loss of those precious supplies was a loss to us as well, since it had recently been announced that the agreement with the Germans would be terminated, and this would be Vogt's last visit. He'd been met at the station by Sarkisov, who hadn't had the sense to delay the news. Instead, he'd sat Vogt down to tell him that his position as co-director of the Russian-German Brain Research Institute or the German-Russian Brain Research Institute —i.e., our institute, whatever it was called—had been withdrawn. News from on high was how Sarkisov had put it. It was a Soviet institute now. By the time I arrived, the two of them were seated in one of the back offices, well into the cognac. There was an air of regret about them, as though nostalgia had set in and was there to stay.

On the bright side, Sarkisov was saying to Vogt, you won't have to deal with any more guards.

Maybe I won't go back, Vogt responded. Or haven't you heard about the crisis we're facing?

We had heard, of course. The official presses wanted nothing more than reports like those that were coming out of Germany in those days, and for a change, the unofficial presses were publishing similar stories. Everywhere we looked, news of capitalism's latest crisis was on the front pages with images of the wheelbarrows full of money, the depreciation of it hour by hour. It made our lineups for shampoo and shoes look good.

I lingered in the doorway for some time, feeling like a child watching the adults, until Vogt tottered to his feet and said he wanted to be caught up on the collection.

Start from the top, he instructed me, but I wasn't sure what that meant and had a feeling I'd be following him rather than him following me, no matter where I started. The question of what to say if he asked about the missing specimens—especially the lantern slides of Lenin's brain—was all I could think about as we traipsed around.

Thankfully, Luria arrived just then, which meant that he accompanied the two of us around the space. Luria had come to hear Vogt's findings, which would be announced later that day.

We ushered Vogt into the grand salon to begin, and Vogt stood before the Bekhterev exhibit.

Arrogant old bastard, don't you think, said Vogt to us. Reserving a place for himself amongst the geniuses?

We smiled meekly.

He never made Distinguished Scientist, now did he?

Luria squirmed a little.

The room had been set up as it had been two years previous, with a podium and rows of seats awaiting an audience. Luria asked about Vogt's work since we'd seen him last, which elicited a vague response before Vogt changed the subject.

What about those lantern slides? he asked me.

Did you say they'd been taken to the university? said Luria to me. For cleaning?

Vogt looked at Luria, then at me, but said nothing.

Yes, I said. Vogt waved it off and set off for the lab, so I realized his curiosity was not scientific but egotistic. He was interested in the exhibit only to the extent that he could remind us what part of it had been his. We walked around some more, and then Vogt announced that he'd go back to his hotel to freshen up before the afternoon. Luria also announced that he was leaving.

I caught him just as he was going out the door.

Why did you do that? I asked.

I don't know where those exhibits are, he said. And as far as I know, you don't know either.

He paused and then turned back to me. But I won't do it again, he said. Here's another life lesson you seem to need, Tatiana: don't get involved in other people's mess. You need to know how to spot it, and then you should stay the hell away from it.

Am I that mess? I asked.

That you need to ask should tell you something.

He was such a prick sometimes.

Aren't you staying for the talk? I asked.

No, he said, I'm going home.

It had never even occurred to me to wonder about his home. I think I'd assumed his life was like every other solitary life I knew—like Bekhterev's had been in the end, like mine had become.

I looked at him then heard myself ask, If I had an opportunity to leave, to go study in Berlin like Sarkisov, maybe even with Vogt, would you suggest I go?

No, he said.

—⊹—

Later that afternoon, Vogt spoke to a sparse gathering of reporters. There were no politicians and no scientists beyond those immediately connected with the institute, which is to say, myself, our two technicians, and one or two people I didn't recognize. At most, there were ten people sitting, all of them towards the back rows, as though they, too, had expected more people to arrive to fill out the front rows. Nothing like two years prior.

With the chandelier almost completely burned out, the brain exhibits were the main source of light. The evolution exhibits we'd set up on the back wall hung in the dark.

Our research has led to seminal victories concerning the material substrate of Lenin's genius, Vogt began, gamely speaking past the empty front rows. Unlike the subjective whims of individual psychological assessment, he said, cytoarchitectonics is superior because it is metrical and, therefore, objective. The mental substrate of Lenin's genius has already been proven in incontrovertible terms: in layer three of the cortex and in many cortical regions deep in this layer, I have seen pyramidal cells of a size and number I've never before seen.

I stood at the back, as I had in Vogt's first speech, alone this time.

Pyramidal cells? said Sasha. You'd think it was 1927.

I know, I know, I said.

Since architectonics can ascertain the size of the cortical regions involved in certain mental capabilities, in square centimetres, and their relative share of the total available cortex, in percentage, it provides objective criteria for evaluating, though only *post-mortem*, the individual characteristics of a brain. As such, Vogt said, our findings with regards to V.I. Lenin are at once conclusive, in that there can be no disputing the measurements thus far obtained, and introductory, as it is without doubt that there is much more to be discovered. In conclusion, the anatomical results show Lenin's associative powers made him nothing less than, he leaned towards his meagre audience, a *mental athlete*.

It was a moment Vogt had hoped would be triumphant, but the room was too empty, his announcement too vague. A few people applauded half-heartedly. When scientists resort to metaphor, they are hiding something. Or imagining something. This was an experiment that had failed.

—/—

After I thought everyone had left, I returned to the grand salon to find a woman sitting on a chair immediately in front of the Bekhterev exhibit. I hadn't noticed her earlier.

Seeing her there, I realized that I had seen her at the institute many times in the past months, but tonight was the first time I saw her sitting in a position that resembled, so closely, that of prayer. She didn't notice me, and I didn't make my presence known. She sat like that for several minutes, her head slightly bowed. I imagined her eyes as closed, or at least staring at the floor, which was something like staring at nothing. Then she abruptly raised her head and stood. I walked towards her, about to say something, when she turned to walk towards me. That was when I recognized her as Asja. At first she didn't see me. Her eyes seemed to register me as an obstacle, a moving one, not as a person, not as someone she knew, but then I saw her break free from her reverie. She looked right into my eyes. She came close, whispered my name, and grabbed my hands to take me in.

He would have been so happy with what you did here, she said quietly.

And then she left. I turned to watch her go. *Drifting* was the way to describe her movements. I followed her out the salon, into the front entrance, and out to the street. It was dusk. I held onto the silhouette of her for as long as I could, but then she was gone, black against black.

It was only once she was really gone that I realized she might have been like Sasha, spiriting away small pieces of the exhibit on every visit. I could have been angry, but now I felt relieved to think that small pieces of our work would outlive the institute, which seemed so blatantly destined for obscurity. It had seemed eerie at first, the way she'd stood there, but then I wondered if this wasn't the way to understand what we'd been doing all along. That Vogt's great discoveries had been delivered in metaphor seemed to illustrate that he didn't think the institute was doing science, either. A place of enlightenment, yes, but not so scientific after all.

After Asja had left, I was alone but not alone.

You have never seen a circle, said Sasha.

Yes, I have, I protested, as I closed and locked the front door.

No, he said. You haven't. That girl might have, he said. But you haven't.

He followed me through the institute as I turned off the lights for the night, and out the back door. We crossed the courtyard, crossed Yakimanka, and turned onto Zhitnaya to follow it as it sloped down to the river. The city had become so bright over the years. Blazing, was how I'd heard tourists describe it, and I'd been proud of our electrified city. But now it seemed sad how the light obscured the night sky as we'd once seen it, so black and so full of stars.

This is our cumulative knowledge about circles, Sasha said. One: a circle is a symmetrical shape with no beginning and no end. Two: a circle has a centre. When a circle is rotated through any angle about its centre, its orientation remains the same. Three: a straight line drawn through the centre of a circle divides it into two identical semicircles. We call that line the diameter. The distance from a circle's centre to its periphery never changes. We call that line the radius. Can you think of anything else?

You haven't mentioned chords, I said.

The diameter being a circle's longest chord, he said.

When did you get so mathematical? I asked.

And a tangent is a line that just grazes the circle at one point, practically missing it.

You're going on a bit, I said, and I know you didn't

come here to talk about circles. We were crossing the Ironworkers' bridge by then. The lights at the Kremlin flickered on.

That's true, he said. I came to talk about God.

Go on, I said.

I began by saying you'd never seen a circle, he said.

I haven't forgotten, I said.

You say you have seen a circle, and I say you haven't.

We had come to the bridge's high point.

I say that seeing a true circle is quite impossible.

A different question then, I said. When did you become so philosophical?

Our minds cannot see circles, though we can imagine them quite well. How is this possible? Circles on earth always involve sides. We don't see the sides, or, in the case of a poorly drawn circle, we forgive that circle its sloppy sides and call it a circle anyway. But the real circle is a form that exists only in our minds and is applied, generously, to the lamentable approximations we find here on earth.

Lamentable?

Yes, he said. Lamentable.

Neither Sasha nor Bekhterev believed in perception. I realize this now. Bekhterev thought the real, objective thing existed out there in the world, but we just couldn't *see* it. Our only protection from the way our subjective views deceived us, distorting the world, lay in the certainty of a measure such as M and K. M and K were the only source of true meaning, the only thing we could really know, the only access we had to the other.

Sasha, on the other hand, thought something quite different. Sasha thought we saw a thing in the world and that the way we saw it was better than it actually was. A circle for a line. A multitude of hues in a colour called black. As artists, we could be realistic, and render a thing as it was

—flawed and asymmetrical. Or, we could use our imaginations. See a thing as it was *meant* to be. Dostoyevsky said that when we love someone we must see them as God intended them. This is what it means to love the world. It is to see a circle where a microscope sees only lines.

This is how I see you, Sasha said, but you prefer M and K.

I did prefer M and K, I said, but they are ideals just as much as anything else.

How so? he asked.

They aren't transcendent ideals, like yours, they don't exist in the starry ether, but they're as out of reach as any other perfect thing, hidden as they are, so deep in the earth and behind so many locked doors. They might as well be imagined; maybe they are.

Bekhterev had believed that everything hinged on a micrometer. Progress, such as it is, depends on our increasing capacity to measure. Time has been measured using the sun's rays, the swing of pendulums, barometric compensation, and now we have the quartz clock. But can we truly say that these sundry devices have actually measured the same thing? We want to speak to others, and we want what we say to mean something, but even words betray us. We are caught by the impossibility of communicating the colour blue.

—⁄—

A few days after Sarkisov told Vogt that things were changing —that the days of the Soviet-German or German-Soviet, whatever, partnership was over—he also told me he had another job in mind for me. I thought of the secretary who spent her days banging away on her typewriter in the former blood institute and wanted to tell him to forget it.

A bigger one, he said. Actually, it wasn't my idea.

I don't need a job, I said. I have one.

Well, that's the other thing, said Sarkisov. The institute is shutting down. Relocating. I meant to tell you that first.

I didn't know.

Funds are being reallocated, now that Vogt has finished his research.

What research? I asked. *That* wasn't research.

As I said, we have another position for you.

So then it's not about funds, I said.

Do you want to know what to do next or not?

Let me think about it.

I turned away.

I turned back.

Okay, I want to know.

The institute was going to be relocated to the university. It wouldn't be open to the public anymore. But if I wanted it, a position there could be mine.

What's the position? I asked.

Someone needs to write a history of this place. I suggested you.

This could be *my* S—, I thought. This could be my starting again.

We liked your report, he said.

All right, I said, which wasn't an answer.

—⁄—

Historians and archeologists know this: war, natural disaster, and sudden regime changes are the best thing that can happen when it comes to preservation of the past. A volcano erupts and sends its lava flowing. In its path, everything is captured *exactly* as it was. How else would we ever have known about Pompeii?

Then I left the institute. Across the street a statue was being erected, a monument to Soviet science, or so the workers told me, though they bickered amongst themselves about who, exactly, the commemorated scientist had been. I didn't recognize the name.

I didn't know what I wanted to do, didn't know if I wanted to be one of those who left or one of those who stayed. Everyone was in exile now. Those who stayed behind experienced an inner exile, afraid to speak to one another except in metaphor, suspicious of intimacy, wary of informers. And those who left were exiles, too, idealists who believed the myth of somewhere else: that someplace else would be better, or at the very least, different from here.

—⊬—

Outside, all of Moscow was white. Blank. The snow had started in drifts that morning, softly that is, so that the rail along the bridge was lightly dusted while the walkway had stayed mostly clear. I knew that my position at the institute would make it possible for me to travel and that, once the institute closed and once Vogt left the city, that window would close. The snowflakes seemed to hover in the sky, not falling or rising, just hanging there, fluttering in a suspended, anxious state. Where people had stopped to rest or had trailed their gloved hands along the rail for a while, cupping the snow in their curved palm until it filled up and they saw fit to shovel it over the edge, only there was the blanket of snow disturbed. At the middle of the bridge, I stopped, too, pausing to take in the whole of the white city, and there I recalled that moment years before, when Luria had told me about the boy from Kiev, about the fatal punctures to his head and of the strangely parallel notions of blood and vowels as *the* special elixirs that keep a language, or a body, breathing, alive.

I leaned forward, lifting my hips up ever so slightly higher on the railing and then edging them even higher and higher with the resulting effect that my head and upper body pitched lower and lower on the other side. My own true weight surprised me as I gripped the railings from the other side of the bridge—the wrong side—and felt the exhilarating question of how far I might go.

Beneath me, far beneath me, the river's frozen surface could have been the moon. Patches of grey and black stood out upon an uneven wash of white, and even with my blurred vision, I could see that it was hard and I was looking down, not up, but what difference did it make.

My hands were protected in thick gloves, given to me so long ago I couldn't even remember their origin. The leather's once sticky pile had long since worn smooth. As for the rails, they were not so cold as to be tacky, and so I slipped farther and farther still, and it was a pleasure. The powdery snow fluttered off the grating; down I slipped. Blood rushed into my head in a satisfying way—thick and heavy.

But then, through the grating, I saw a mess of legs and boots approach and felt myself violently yanked back to the other side of the rail—the right side—and all around me the voices, yelling. I saw their mouths open and close; saw them look at each other and at me with eyes full of fear, but I could not understand their words and had none of my own. My head felt as suspended as the flakes of snow. The people seemed to be swirling all around me, and while they spun, they yelled more words that I did not understand. When they stopped spinning, I walked away. Then the snow that had been suspended in the sky, buzzing ever so faintly the way summer's dragonflies do, suddenly started to fall. The yelling stopped, and again the city was silent.

When I got home, I came up to the door and pulled it as I did every other night, but it was locked. I looked at my watch and saw that it had stopped. It had been cold walking home, but now that I had stopped moving, it was colder still. I breathed into my gloves, steaming them up a little with my hot breath. A temporary solution. I thought of how Sasha and I always used to let each other in. And I thought of how, leaving Russia, I would be locked out of the country forever. No one comes back.

—⧸—

When I was finally let inside, I stayed awake all night. I wanted to leave and I wanted to stay. I wanted to write the history of the institute and I wanted to forget it had ever happened, because I didn't know, even after having worked there for years, what exactly we had accomplished. Had the institute been a scientific effort, as Bekhterev had claimed, or had it been a commemorative project, like the statue, where the idea of a Soviet science was nothing more or less than that of a mental athlete, metaphorical and inspirational, sure, but impossible to measure and impossible to prove? I pulled my chair to the window, and like that passed the night staring out at the city, at all of its rooftops and its bright white lights and the spirals of St. Basil's and the room across the way into which Dimitri entered somewhere around midnight. He stripped down to his underthings, turned off the light, and went to sleep. Goodbye, Dimitri. At some point, I stood before my wash table, turning my faucet on and off, just to produce a sound. I wished I'd saved something of the exhibit for myself. Wished I could look through the lantern slides with the backdrop of the bright Moscow night and see the familiar outline of the dead tissue we'd spent so many years hiding, so artfully, in the angle of Lenin's brain. I was waiting for morning, but the night was unrelenting.

Eventually, I lay down on top of my bed. I thought I wouldn't sleep but I must have because I dreamt of Sasha. I dreamt of Berlin's streets, black the way they'd been described to me in Bekhterev's description of the city and smelling of linden flower, though that was how Moscow smelled in springtime, too. I walked through the streets and came, in what seemed a most obvious or natural way, to an apartment building. The front panel was obscured by ivy and I pushed it aside to find his name. Alexandr Pavlovich. I managed my way into the building and knew, somehow, which wing, which floor, which apartment to go to. The *hof* was filled with bikes and overgrown bushes, and the building reached high into the square patch of blue-black sky. The city was so bright that the sky looked painted there — no stars. His door was unlocked because everything in the dream was as it should be, and I got into bed with him, his body in the familiar shape I'd known for so long. He was sleeping on his stomach, his left knee drawn up towards his chest. He didn't wake when I lay down next to him, and now it was my arm slipping around him and up to his chest and it was he who was cradled, not me. I was aware of sleeping. I was aware that this was not quite real, but was. I was aware of the unbelievable possibility that this might become real and also of the absolute hollow I felt at not having Sasha there with me then. I heard myself moan. I pulled my pillow tighter in my arms and fell into a deeper sleep than I had had in years.

In the morning, I awoke heartbroken and determined to find Sasha wherever he was. I arrived at the Foreign Ministry at dawn, expecting a line there as everywhere, but the street was deserted. I stood outside the office in the cold, waiting for it to open, watching the rest of the city waken. Cats that appeared from around a corner seemed not to have *turned* a corner but, rather, to have come from *within* the corner itself. The sun had risen and was casting its long shadows, their long black reaches retreating swiftly, as it rose higher, then disappearing altogether once the fog rolled in.

Get your photo taken, said the man at the ministry who reminded me, faintly, of Trotsky.

On Strastnoy Boulevard I found a photographer who did rush passport photos; I paid him all I could and still he said it would take hours. Leaving his shop, I caught my face in the store window. Hollow cheeks and tired eyes: I was getting old.

—⁄—

Later, when I returned to the passport office with my photo in hand, a woman had gotten into an altercation with Trotsky. I knew her situation. Her train ticket was already purchased for that night, using the last of her money, for some ennobling purpose. Only the passport held her back. That morning, the Trotsky man had been kind, she said. He had recommended the Strastnoy photographer saying that, if need be, he could be made to work *very quickly*. She had returned within the hour.

Trotsky was still working, and the waiting room was now full. As she sat in her chair, she drummed her fingers impatiently on the pile of papers in her lap but knew better than to ask to be seen immediately. When, finally, she did make it up to the window, she presented the small envelope of photographs.

He waved them away, saying, It's too late.

But less than two hours ago, you said it was possible! she cried.

He shook his head at her, as if in resignation. Slowly and deliberately, he responded: Two hours ago it *was* possible, but now it is not. He shuffled some papers from one side of his desk to the other. Now, he said, it is impossible.

But what has changed in the last few hours? she asked.

Then it was possible; now it is not.

But my train leaves tonight, she wailed.

I understand, he said, sighing, as if that concluded the matter.

She looked around the office in the hopes of finding some kind of ally. I looked away. When it was my turn to see him, everything was possible. I had benefitted from coming after her. In order to prove to himself that he was still a good man, a reasonable man, he'd had to demonstrate it with someone, and that someone had been me. Within a matter of minutes, I had my passport and papers in hand and I walked back out into the city.

—⊹—

If I was leaving everything, I wanted someone to know about the exhibits. Not just someone. Luria. I wanted him to know I hadn't taken them. I wanted him to find them. But not right away. S— was easy to find. People like S— like routines.

Always in the same café. Always in the afternoon.

A waitress came over.

Tea with jam, we said.

I felt jealous of the simplicity of him. Luria had thought S— lacked something, but nothing about him suggested lack to me. The tea arrived.

He spooned the jam into his tea and stirred it thoroughly.

The Northern Corridor, I began, on the other side of a broom closet.

He set down the spoon and let his gaze sweep across

the entire café before looking at me directly. Give me a minute, said S—. You must pause between items.

Did you get that? I asked.

Yes.

I looked around the café, too, realizing for the first time that apart from us and the waitress, who was presumably in the back, it was empty.

Four lantern slides, I said, of necrotic tissue.

He looked at me intently and said, Go on.

A wet specimen of the parietal lobe, I said.

What colour? asked S—.

Grey, I said.

Go on.

Sixteen journals published between 1925 and 1928.

S— paused, and I could tell that he was ordering things, placing them on the walk to Torskok. Go on, he said.

An autopsy report.

Go on.

There isn't anything more, I said. Outside, the street brightened suddenly and then dimmed, so I had the feeling that I knew the shape of the clouds overhead — a fast-moving network of thick, grey clouds with white gauzy strands between.

There must be, he said, looking at me intently.

What do you mean? I asked, aware now that whatever was said would be permanent.

I mean that the exhibit had many more specimens than you mentioned.

Luria had been wrong about S—. It wasn't that S— couldn't make meaning out of things, but that he often *didn't* make meaning out of things. But he was interested in the institute. Eight times he had been there.

Outside it got almost black.

S— tipped his hat when he left, the way they did in the country, so I saw he hadn't fully adapted to life in the city, which was probably a good thing.

He didn't close the door.

The waitress crossed the room to shut it.

Grew up on a boat, that one, she said to me.

Once he was gone, I realized that the list would not do what I'd thought. It wouldn't prove that I hadn't taken the exhibits, only that I hadn't taken them *with* me.

I left the café.

Across the street, in a black huddle that, from up high, might plausibly have been described as a swarm, ravens gathered for something official, a fight or a conference. I was used to seeing them lined up on the tops of buildings, but this gathering seemed more ominous, as if they'd come in cawing from all parts of the city, warned perhaps that one of theirs was dead.

On a balcony up above, a woman was smoking. Behind her, someone was singing a cabaret song I'd heard before. I thought of Rima. Something brushed the side of my cheek as I walked and I considered the small insects of summer and how easily we forget them over the winter and wondered what else we forgot so easily.

One thing we always forgot about was the sleigh drivers. In the summer, we never saw them, but in the winter they were everywhere, long rows of them, lined up to cart off the snow. Also, the temperature. Nothing more impossible to recall than the exhausting heat of summer in the dead of winter. I tried to focus my attention, tried to really see the city so that I would be able to remember it, but soon enough I was thinking of Sasha, and then, again, of nothing at all. I tried to remember the summer's heat, and tugged at my scarf as I might in the summer, wanting to allow my skin to breathe, but then the cold rushed in, and I pulled it tight.

All that day I followed the course of the ring road, through the various districts of watchmakers, remont shops, garment districts. The ravens I'd seen earlier seemed to meet me at every turn—here at a public fountain, there in that empty lot, and later again in Pushkinskaya Square. I kept looking overhead to see if I could spot them in their migration, but I never did. In the familiarity of the streets I knew best, I again found myself walking without seeing. Whole blocks would pass, and I would find myself looking for this or that statue, only to realize I must have passed it on a street corner many blocks back. My fingers would close on the new edges of my passport, and I would worry a corner, wanting to make its pages as used and familiar as the streets. When I willed myself to pay attention, I would see the Mongol faces and the stray dogs and cats. There were animals everywhere.

I wished that Sasha would appear, that he could be walking alongside me as he had been so often this past year, but Sasha had never been one to do what I wanted and he didn't then, either.

Up along this part of the ring road, the buildings were farther apart and more generally residential. Construction was taking place for the new metro system, which would dig down deep under the marshy land of Moscow to where the rock hardened, and there they'd begun a vast network of tunnels that would connect people from all over the city, making us rivals with London and Buenos Aires and New York, or so *Pravda* had said, or so Sergei said that *Pravda* said, because I'd stopped reading it by then.

Night had fallen. Outside the Cheka office, a single man stood in the glare of a streetlight with a fixed bayonet at his side. The carbide lights of the cars came on, floating through the city in their own private world. It was hunger, probably, that suddenly turned my feeling of familiarity with the streets to an overwhelming sense of loss. When I neared the station, perhaps it was that feeling of loss that made me walk faster, fearfully, until finally, I boarded a ring-road tram that could whisk me away on that circular path once again. Just one more pass, I thought.

I wasn't ready to leave. From inside the tram I revisited my whole day, and not just once. I passed the gateway to the country, the ravens, and the vendors. Kitay-gorod, and Pushkinskaya, the bright lights and the dark tunnels. I stayed on the tram for what seemed like hours, passing again the ravens and vendors, the statues and everything familiar, until it became meaningless, actually, until I couldn't see it at all, until I started to feel that whatever had been so intoxicating about the city years before was now the very thing that could make me sick.

When the tram approached October station once again, I got off.

—⚊—

I made my way into the station, bought a ticket to Leningrad, and went into the waiting room that had as many potted plants as it did weary travellers, so it looked something like a jungle. I sat amongst them, looking at their tired faces, wondering if they were former people, if they were leaving for good. A man and woman sat side by side, their child sprawled across them, fast asleep. At their feet sat a single suitcase. An old man in the corner was reading a book. Another solitary traveller had covered himself in sweaters and coats, only his shoes identified him as a man. The room smelled like sleep. I pulled out my passport and slid my ticket into its pages. A nervous thrill quivered in me. I was leaving with nothing.

When the train pulled into the station, people roused themselves ever so slightly, turning their eyes to the slats on the departure board, which started to flip. We all watched the slats as they cycled through the numbers, settling finally on the number three, the platform from which we would depart.

Everyone stood up and started to gather their things. The parents gingerly transferred their child into the father's arms, trying not to wake her. She moaned quietly, moving her fists to her eyes. Most of the passengers had the same idea: sleepwalk to the train. I stood with them.

They floated towards the train.

I floated back outside.

I'd tried to leave, but I couldn't, not yet. I wasn't ready for exile, wasn't ready to be a former person, when I'd only just started to feel like myself.

—⧸—

On the tram ride home, a man sat down heavily next to me, and I knew without looking that it was Sasha. I turned to look out the window. When we passed through patches of darkness — under bridges or anywhere without city lights — the window became a mirror.

How is your somewhere else? I asked, looking at our reflections.

I'm right here, he said.

Yes, I said, I suppose you are.

didn't want to be one of those women who handed out name tags, made the soup, had babies named Oktober and dogs named Marx. Staying to write the history was a way to leave my own mark and I did it, writing *Historya Institut Mozga* and publishing it in an abridged format, a white pamphlet of no more than forty pages. It sits before me now. If that slim pamphlet is the official history, this book is its shadow history, and like a shadow at the end of day, it is an elongated version of the original. Over the years, the mansion on Bolshaya Yakimanka changed hands, becoming home to a workers' club first and then what it is now, the home to France's ambassador who, it is said, dreams inexplicable dreams where language is blood and all the world's measures keep falling short, the space of a millimetre being infinitely divisible, after all.

As I wrote, I visited Asja often, and I saw the way time's passage soothed her.

You were once so afraid, I reminded her.

And she said, Yes, yes, I was then, but I'm not now.

Why is that? I asked.

She said that she had realized the fear would follow her wherever she went, that it was dependent on her.

What did you do with it then? Are you saying you were wrong?

No, no, she said. Of course I was right. There are things to fear everywhere. When the Revolution started, the aim was total transformation. The Soviet project would transform our state into a revolutionary heaven, and what we've got instead is something far less transcendent.

A dim heaven, I said.
Yes, just so, she said, but it is ours,

A NOTE ON THE HISTORY

While Tatiana, Sasha, and their close friends are products of my imagination, several characters in *Uncertain Weights and Measures* are historical figures. The Osorgins were among the first round of intellectuals to be persecuted while Lenin was still alive. Along with about two hundred others, they were sent off in 1922 on what was later called the Philosophy Steamer, the history of which I found in Lesley Chamberlain's haunting book *Lenin's Private War: The Voyage of the Philosophy Steamer and the Exile of the Intelligentsia*. The doctors — Dr. Vogt, Dr. Bekhterev, Dr. Bogdanov, and their wives — are all real, as is Dr. Luria, though the trajectory of his academic work — especially his research on S—, whom Luria referred to as *S.*—, has been substantially altered. The deaths of Drs. Bekhterev and Bogdanov are both true to their causes, and while I have maintained the speculation and timing of the former's death, I've altered that of the latter. The personalities, of course, are all my invention (from all accounts, Luria was a kinder man than he appears here) as is the notion that Sofià K— had a daughter named Asja and that her father would be Bekhterev. That the Igumnov mansion housed both Bogdanov's Institute of Blood Transfusion and Bekhterev's Institute Mozga is historical fact, though the dates of occupancy seem to be a point of disagreement among historians, and of course the layout of the building and of the respective institutes is entirely my invention.

The Igumnov mansion stills stands at its location on Bolshaya Yakimanka in Yakimanka district in Moscow and is the present home of the French ambassador to Russia. The images of the brains are taken by the author from collections at the Musée Dupuytren in Paris, with the kind permission of its curator, Patrice Josset.

Some of the speeches are taken from scientific literature. Peter Galison's *Einstein's Clocks and Poincaré's Maps: Empires of Time* provided the material for Bekhterev's reflections on Breteuil. Santiago Ramón y Cajal's *Advice for a Young Investigator*, Nikolai Krementsov's *A Martian Stranded on Earth: Alexander Bogdanov, Blood Transfusions, and Proletarian Science*, Alexandr Luria's *The Nature of Human Conflicts*, and Vladimir Bekhterev's *General Principles of Human Reflexology* were important sources for both characters and setting, and in the case of Bekhterev's speech at Congress, some of it is taken directly from his book on Reflexology.

For general knowledge about scientific thinking of the period and how it played out in the Soviet context, I relied on a variety of books, including Nikolai Krementsov's *Stalinist Science* and A.B. Kozhevnikov's *Stalin's Great Science: The Times and Adventures of Soviet Physicists*. For general knowledge about the period, Sheila Fitzpatrick's *Everyday Stalinism: Ordinary Life in Extraordinary Times*, Svetlana Boym's *Common Places: Mythologies of Everyday Life in Russia*, McKenzie Wark's *Molecular Red: Theory for the Anthropocene*, and various books by Richard Stites were instrumental. Walter Benjamin's *Moscow Diary* provided much visual detail. The Harvard Project on the Soviet Social System, and interviews contained therein, was an incredible resource.

Innumerable academic articles provided me with historical and neurological detail, but two were especially important: Alla A. Vein and Marion L.C. Maat-Schieman's "Famous Russian Brains: Historical Attempts to Understand Intelligence" (2008), and Jochen Richter's "Pantheon of Brains: The Moscow Brain Research Institute 1925-1936." The novel began with my reading Michael Hagner's brief chapter, "Pantheon of Brains," in Bruno Latour and Peter Weibel's *Making Things Public: Atmospheres of Democracy.*

ACKNOWLEDGEMENTS

I've had the support of institutions where I've studied and institutions where I've worked. I am especially grateful to the Creative Writing program at Concordia University where Terry Byrnes, Andre Furlani, and Stephanie Bolster gave serious critical attention to the manuscript at its nascent stages and to Dawson College, which has been as flexible as any employer could. Susan Gillis, in conjunction with the Jeunes Volontaires program and Greg Hollingshead, Daphne Marlatt, and Dick Hebdige at Banff's Writing Studio all encouraged it forward at key points. In Moscow, Anush Mikaelian and her family revealed a city I'd never have encountered on my own. In New York, the members of NeuWrite workshopped several sections about microtoming the brain, and Rebecca Brachman was kind enough to take me into her lab to see a twenty-first-century microtome in action. Molly Atlas at ICM was one of the book's most faithful champions. In Tübingen, Germany, where I ought to have been writing my dissertation full time, I found a kitchen table of friends and a supportive supervisor in Ingrid Hotz-Davies, all of whom helped me go further with the project. Thank you to Jutta Kling, Shawn Huelle, Rebecca Hahn, and Susanne Jung. Elisabeth Stewart read the book for its history. My editor, Bethany Gibson, gave careful and challenging feedback, and the time to respond, and Goose Lane Editions has been wonderful to work with from start to finish.

As for my friends, this book is because of you and so it is dedicated to you. Even after all these years, I am still so awed at the mysterious alchemy that brings us together and binds us through all the vicissitudes: the heartbreaks, the long distances, the change, all the change. It's customary in such passages to identify one person as the bearer of one specific gift, but I feel incapable of singling you out as if you bore only one, when each of you have come into my life bearing more gifts than I could possibly describe. So, to all of you, thank you for your encouragement, your curiosity, your love and your rage, your wisdom, your energy, your wit, and all the ways you care so deeply. We've traded books, shared cigarettes, stayed out all night. We've gone away and we've come back, we've been vulnerable, kind, angry and our most alive: all of this together. At various points, many of you read part or all of this book or talked about it with me or around it, making it deeper and richer, and so much more true. Beyond that, you inspired me with your art, your words and your thought. Brent Arnold, Darren Bifford, Patricia Boushel, Richard Cassidy, Lindsay Cuff, Fiona Foster, Katia Grubisic, Lesley Johnson, Yana Kehrlein, Nika Khanjani, Brian Lander, Jessica Moore, Carlos Oyanedel Salmerón, Stephen Parr, Leila Peacock, Pablo Rodriguez, Johanna Skibsrud, Jonathan Stewart, Megan Switzer, Marko Teodorski: I am so grateful for your presence in my life and in this work. To M.K. Carr, Catherine Cooper, Sarah Faber, Susan Paddon, and Rebecca Silver Slayter: thank you for reflections on the earliest versions of this manuscript. All those thanks plus more to Samara Chadwick, who has heard more iterations of this than maybe anyone, over kitchen tables in Bergamo and Montreal. And to Heather Jessup, who thought I could do this long before I did: thank you for this and for so much more, your friendship means the world to me. To my family, thank you for your ongoing support, and to Mark Mann, my one and only, thank you for seeing me and loving me as you do.